THE BELLS OF HELL

Michael Kurland

This first world edition published 2019
in Great Britain and the USA by
SEVERN HOUSE PUBLISHERS LTD of
Eardley House, 4 Uxbridge Street, London W8 7SY.
Trade paperback edition first published
in Great Britain and the USA 2020 by
SEVERN HOUSE PUBLISHERS LTD.

British Library Cataloguing in Publication Data
A CIP catalogue record for this title is available from the British Library.

ISBN-13: 978-0-7278-8969-0 (cased)
ISBN-13: 978-1-78029-641-8 (trade paper)
ISBN-13: 978-1-4483-0340-3 (e-book)

Typeset by Palimpsest Book Production Ltd.,
Falkirk, Stirlingshire, Scotland.

THE BELLS OF HELL

This book is dedicated to lost friends.

ACKNOWLEDGMENTS

I would like to thank Laura Bellizzi, Angela Beske, Nicholas Blake, Lawrence Block, Kimberley Cameron, Alan Freberg, Thomas Loock, Richard Lupoff, David Vartanoff, and especially Linda Robertson for their assistance in pulling this thing together.

Among the writers whose works have helped me recapture this period are Frederick Lewis Allen, John Roy Carlson, Winston Churchill, Father Charles Coughlin, Basil H. Liddell Hart, Adolf Hitler, Franklin and Eleanor Roosevelt, and Arthur Train, as well as magazines and newspapers of the era.

From quiet homes and first beginning, out to the undiscovered ends, there's nothing worth the wear of winning, but laughter and the love of friends. — Hilaire Belloc

War is a contagion, whether it be declared or undeclared. It can engulf states and peoples remote from the original scene of hostilities. We are determined to keep out of war, yet we cannot insure ourselves against the disastrous effects of war and the dangers of involvement. We are adopting such measures as will minimize our risk of involvement, but we cannot have complete protection in a world of disorder in which confidence and security have broken down. — Franklin D. Roosevelt, 5 October 1937, Chicago

Pacifism is cowardice. Only war brings to the highest tension the energies of man and imprints the sign of nobility on those who have the virtue to confront it. — Benito Mussolini, 1932

Demoralize the enemy from within by surprise, terror, sabotage, assassination. This is the war of the future. — Adolf Hitler

The Bells of Hell go ting-a-ling-a-ling
For you but not for me:
For me the angels sing-a-ling-a-ling,
They've got the goods for me.

Oh! Death, where is thy sting-a-ling-a-ling?
Oh! Grave, thy victory?
The Bells of Hell go ting-a-ling-a-ling
For you but not for me.
  – British airman's song dating from WWI

ONE

Tuesday, March 1, 1938

Faust: How comes it then that thou art out of hell?
Meph: Why this is hell, nor am I out of it . . .
        – *Christopher Marlowe,* Doctor Faustus

On the thirty-fourth minute of the seventh hour of his last day on earth, Johann August Steuber stood up in his tiny cabin on C deck of the SS *Osthafen*, braced himself by the door against any last-minute whimsical dips or jounces of the ship, and quickly and methodically went through the pockets of his brown tweed suit and the compartments in his leather briefcase to make sure that he was taking everything that should be taken and carrying nothing that should not be carried. His *Reisepass* in the name of Herr Otto Lehman, 22b Hauptbahnstrasse, Nürnberg: *Ja.* His papers identifying Herr Lehman as an exporter of German mechanical toys: *Ja.* His guidebook to New York City with the rice-paper list of contacts pasted behind the picture of the Statue of Liberty: *Ja.* His letter of introduction to Frau Bittleman, the landlady of the boarding house on 92nd Street in Manhattan who was hopefully expecting him: *Ja.*

He located some bits and scraps of detritus: an overlooked theater-ticket stub tucked in a jacket pocket, a Berlin U-Bahn 2. *Klasse* ticket crunched into a small ball in the inner pocket of his vest, and, *Gott behüte!*, a short note from his butcher beginning *Lieber Herr Steuber* in a small outer flap of his briefcase. He put the room's metal ashtray on the washstand, dropped the material in, and set it afire with a paper match from a packet from the Adlon Hotel in Berlin. After a second's thought he added the matchbook to the blaze. When had Otto Lehman been in Berlin? Small details prevented large problems. He spent a long moment in contemplation of a half-empty pack of Juno Cigarettes he pulled from the jacket's outer pocket. He had bought them at the Adlon just before he left. But, he decided, a pack of cigarettes is a pack of cigarettes. The government tax stamp on the bottom with its little red swastika held no indication of where in the Third Reich the pack had been purchased. He shoved the pack back into his pocket.

Three hours earlier, at 4:30 in the morning, the *Osthafen* had docked at Pier 5 at the foot of Joralemon Street, Brooklyn, New York City, the United States of America, its sixteen-day crossing remarkable only in that the ship's ventilation system had only broken down once, and the engines not at all. Most of the passengers who had stayed awake to see the aging liner sidle past the Statue of Liberty shortly before midnight slept through the humming and throbbing, as two tugs pushed the *Osthafen* into the slip with a minimum of noise and thrashing about.

Disembarking began shortly after eight a.m., the customs officials taking their positions in the forward lounge and commencing their rummaging about in the passengers' luggage, asking searching questions, and examining passports. It was ten thirty by the time Steuber, his Otto Lehman passport stamped, stepped onto the gangway and headed toward dry land.

His two steamer trunks awaited him, intermingled with the others on the oversized luggage wagon; a porter awaited him with a hand cart to take him and his luggage through to the cab stand; and two large men in brown double-breasted suits, brown fedoras, and well-polished brown shoes awaited him by the exit doors.

One of the men stepped forward, blocking Steuber. 'Otto Lehman?'

'Yes?' Steuber took a step back. 'I am Otto Lehman. Who are you and what do you want?' He told himself there was no reason for alarm, but he could feel the muscles of the back of his neck tighten.

The man pulled a leather card case from his pocket and flipped it open. It held a gold badge pinned to the top and a government identity card underneath. He held it up about four inches from Steuber's nose. 'Federal Bureau of Investigation,' he said. 'I am Agent Parker and this is Agent Swallow. You are the man calling himself Otto Lehman?'

'Calling himself? What do you mean?' Steuber attempted to look indignant. 'I am Otto Lehman. Here—' He fumbled in his jacket pocket and pulled out a bundle of papers. 'My passport, my identity card, a letter of introduction to our New York office – I export toys, the finest German mechanical toys. I am here to demonstrate our new product line.'

He knew he was beginning to babble but he couldn't help himself. He had taken no more than ten steps off the ship and here, badge to nose, was the *verdammte* FBI. They were not supposed to be so good, so efficient, so all-knowing, this joke of a J. Edgar Hoover and his 'G-Men'. He closed his eyes and gathered himself and then opened them and smiled. Perhaps it was nothing, but if he didn't act normal it would certainly become something. In his homeland the Gestapo would already be frog-marching him down the street merely because he blinked twice.

Agent Parker took the papers from Steuber's unsteady fingers and pushed them down into his jacket pocket. 'We will give these our complete attention,' he said. 'You will come with us.'

'What? Why?' Steuber briefly contemplated running blindly off in some random direction, but caught himself in time.

'There is some question about your identity,' Parker said. 'It could be, could it not, that you are in actuality one Johann August Steuber, a member of the German Communist Party and an agent of the Comintern?'

'What?' Steuber managed to look horrified. He was, as it happened, horrified. 'How could anyone think that? Where did you hear this? How . . .'

'Come along, *bitte*, Herr Steuber,' Agent Swallow said, taking him by the arm, 'our car is over here.' He waved at the porter with the trunks to follow them, and they went.

Twelve minutes and fourteen seconds later a gray Chevrolet coupe pulled into an OFFICIAL PARKING ONLY space on the pier and two men in brown double-breasted suits, brown fedoras, and well-polished brown shoes emerged from the car. They walked rapidly past the thin stream of passengers still emerging from the ship or dawdling about their luggage and went up to the steward at the bottom of the gangplank. One of them pulled out a card case and flipped it open in front of the steward's nose. 'Special Agent Trower, FBI,' he said. 'Has a passenger calling himself Otto Lehman disembarked yet?'

'Lehman . . . Lehman . . .' The steward flipped through his

check-off list. '*Ja.* Herr Lehman has departed the ship. He had with him two steamer trunks.'

'How long ago?'

'Maybe fifteen, twenty minutes.'

'Did you see where he went?' the special agent asked.

'*Nein.* I do not myself even know which one he is.'

One of the porters, a thin, scrawny man with a nose that preceded his face by several moments, paused. 'Lehman? With the two trunks. Sure. Two guys picked him up. I had to put one of his trunks in the back seat with him and it was a tight fit, I'll tell you.'

'What two guys?' Special Agent Trower asked.

'I dunno, just two guys. They was dressed a lot like you, come to think of it.'

TWO

Oh, for a muse of fire that would ascend
The brightest heaven of invention!
           – *William Shakespeare,* Henry V

Lord Geoffrey Saboy, Cultural Attaché to the British Embassy in Washington DC, strode into the parlor of his Georgetown residence and struck what he fondly believed was a dramatic pose, with one foot on the seat of an upholstered chair he particularly disliked. But the house had come furnished, and there it was. '"It is a far, far better thing that I do, than I have ever done,"' he announced. '"It is a far, far better place that I go to than I have ever known." So have cook hold up dinner for me, I'll probably be a bit late.'

Lady Patricia stretched panther-like on the red chaise longue and smiled up at her husband. 'Good afternoon,' she said. 'And where have you been?'

'Out and about,' Geoffrey told her.

'And, no doubt, doing this and that?'

'Exactly!' He blew a kiss in her direction. 'How clever you are!'

'And now you're going out again?'

'In a few minutes. Sir Ronald calleth. And when the ambassador calleth, I goeth.'

'What is it this time?'

Geoffrey shrugged. 'He consults me on things about which I have scant knowledge, and I assure him that I will get up to speed – he is fond of the phrase "up to speed" – on said topic. And then quite usually he never asks me about them again.' He removed his foot from the chair and patted the cushion back into shape. 'Yesterday it was Spain.'

'Ahh?'

'Yes. Sir Ronald wants to know everything there is to know about Generalissimo Francisco Franco. His Majesty's government have, in their infinite wisdom, seen fit to recognize the Franco government although the war in Spain is still going on and the matter is far from settled.'

Patricia swiveled her body around, planted her feet on the floor, and sat up. 'I don't like Franco,' she said. 'He shoots people.'

'It seems to be a Fascist habit,' Geoffrey told her.

'Why on earth would our government do that?' she asked. 'Recognize Franco, I mean.'

Geoffrey came over and sat next to her. 'Because, O fairest of the fair, the PM is set on keeping the peace with Italy and Germany, and Franco is their man. Which is why Mr Eden, who doesn't trust the Nazis, just resigned as Foreign Minister and Lord Halifax has been called in to replace him. Halifax positively swoons into his porridge when he thinks on how delightful Hitler and Göring are. Or so I've been told.'

'What does Winston say?'

'Your friend Mr Churchill says preparing for war would give us the best chance of keeping the peace. As he has been saying for the past three years.'

'They should listen to him,' she said.

'Curious,' Geoffrey said.

'What?'

'It just occurred to me. Franco likes to call himself "El Caudillo", which translates to "the leader".'

'Yes?'

'Mussolini likes to be called "Il Duce" – the leader. Herr Hitler goes for "Der Führer". Do we see a pattern?'

'It must be their innate shyness.'

'Yes – that must be it.'

Patricia stood and adjusted the neckline of her lacy cream-colored peignoir. 'I also must prepare for the outer world,' she said. 'I have an assignation.'

'Surely not in the middle of the afternoon?'

She laughed. 'Not that sort – at least I don't think so. I have met this charming Italian Embassy person, and I have decided to cultivate him.'

'Ah!' Geoffrey said. 'Is that what they're calling it now?'

'Shame on you,' she told him. 'I don't make jocular remarks about your, ah, extramarital activities, now do I?'

'Perhaps because I don't parade them up and down in front of you and discuss their good and bad qualities.'

'I never!' she protested.

'You often,' he told her. 'But that's all right. I am here to take care of you at such times as you need taken care of,' he added, looking down musingly at the woman he had married. 'And you perform the same service for me. And, what is beyond all understanding, we are actually fond of each other.'

'There is to be a do at the Italian Embassy in a few weeks,' she told him. 'We should attend.'

'If it's to be a dinner party we should certainly go,' he agreed. 'Best food on Embassy Row. Is it to be a dinner party?'

'I don't know yet.'

'Well, in any case it will give us a chance to snub the German Ambassador. Herr Dieckhoff needs a good snubbing.'

'We certainly seem to be fulfilling that ancient Chinese curse,' Patricia commented.

'How's that?'

'"May you live," it goes, "in interesting times."'

THREE

Hell hath no limits, nor is circumscribed
In one self place, for where we are is hell,
And where hell is must we ever be.
　　　　　　　– *Christopher Marlowe*, Doctor Faustus

The red-brick building, which had been a warehouse for the DozeWell Mattress company, took up most of the block at the corner of Water and Gold, a few blocks from the Brooklyn end of the Brooklyn Bridge. One room occupied most of the ground floor and, with its high ceilings, much of the second. There was an attempt at a third floor perched on the west corner of the building, clearly an afterthought and about the size of three hotdog stands. The ground-floor room was large in all directions and damp and cold. It was not so much furnished as filled with discards: there were two discarded desks, four file cabinets half full of long-discarded papers, a pile of pallets, three rolled-up rugs, a smattering of discarded office chairs, and one discarded thirty-four-year-old human being named Andrew Blake.

Andrew had taken residence about six months ago, he wasn't sure. Time does odd things when you're out of work, out of friends, and no longer have any family to speak of. When he had first found the place he had moved his two beat-up suitcases, his piece of well-splattered painters' canvas that served as a mattress, and the red couch cushion that was his pillow into the manager's office, up a flight of stairs that hugged the north wall, presumably so the boss could oversee the helots working below. It even had its own small bathroom, with a white porcelain sink still with running water, which he scrubbed clean. He had also scrubbed out the medicine cabinet above the sink and arrayed within it his safety razor, soap, shaving brush, toothbrush, and tooth powder. But when his left leg twisted out from under him during an accidental encounter with a patch of slick ice, the resulting sprain made it painful to climb stairs; so he moved himself and his belongings to a small area behind a false wall he had discovered in the far corner, erected during Prohibition to conceal cases of whisky – the real stuff just off the boat – from casual view. This cut his stair-climbing to his once-a-day ablutions, and this is what saved his life.

He had consumed two not too rotten apples and half a head of cauliflower that he had scrounged from one of the waste bins behind the produce market on Bridge Street and was dozing fitfully on his canvas that Tuesday afternoon when the two men cracked the padlock on the Gold Street side door and pushed their way in. It was a little after two by the Ingersoll pocket watch that was one of the few possessions he refused to part with. The sky was slate gray, the streets still damp from the recent rain, and the produce markets had already closed for the day. Whatever the entrance of these men portended, Blake realized, it was nothing that would be good for Andrew Blake. He shrank back into his hiding place and lay down on his stomach to peer through a small rip at the bottom of the canvas false wall. A small rip? Surely it was the size of a hippopotamus and they couldn't avoid seeing him. He worked at stifling his sudden almost overwhelming desire to cough.

The men did a quick look around the large room, one of them speaking in staccato monosyllables like 'Here,' and 'That will do,' and 'Not yet,' and the other not speaking at all. The non-speaking man took a wooden chair from a corner of the room and moved it to the middle. The speaker stared at it critically and moved it six inches to his right and two inches forward. Then he stepped back from it, walked around it once, and nodded his approval.

It was perhaps five minutes before the door pushed open again and three men came in, two of them urging the third one forward between them. He seemed apathetic and uninterested in his surroundings, and kept his eyes down, staring at the floor.

His visitors, Blake noted, all wore suits. Three brown double-breasted serge, the fourth, the reluctant man, tweed and even more double-breasted. The fifth, the speaker, was a blond man with a square face, a short beard clipped straight across at the bottom, and eyes that somehow seemed too close together. His suit was a really dark blue or black, with a small collar and a long row of buttons down the front which were all, as far as Blake could tell, buttoned. The two who had been urging the man between them went out again and returned in less than a minute, lugging a pair of large steamer trunks behind them, which they dumped near the door. Then they took the reluctant man by both arms and steered him to the center of the room by the chair.

As they approached the chair the man being pushed suddenly lifted his head and looked around and, with a spasm of activity, made a violent attempt to twist away from his captors. For a second he broke free, but then the others grabbed him and propelled him further into the room. 'What is this place?' he cried. 'Where have you taken me?'

'Remain calm, Herr Steuber,' the man in the probably black suit said. 'You have nothing to fear. We merely want some information from you.'

'Information? What sort of information?' He twisted to look at the man in black. 'I know nothing. I sell toys, only. My name, it is Lehman. Otto Lehman.'

The man in black sighed. 'We have so far to go,' he said, 'and so little time.' He turned to one of the men in brown. 'Check out the building. Make sure we're alone.' The man nodded and trotted off.

The man in black turned the captive around by the shoulders and casually punched him in the stomach. He grunted and doubled over, and the man pushed him down into the chair. From where Blake lay, his cheek pressed against the cold cement of the floor, peering through the slit in the canvas, he could see that the man's hands were handcuffed behind him, and he couldn't be sure but he thought the man had begun to cry. His captors began fastening his arms to the back of the chair with some sort of twine. It seemed to Blake as though they had some experience in tying people to chairs.

There are some people, Blake found himself thinking, *who are worse off than I am.* The thought did not cheer him greatly. He couldn't take his eyes off the other man, the one who was methodically searching through the large room, looking under desks and kicking at the piles of pallets. Once he passed right by the concealed space and, if he had touched the wall, he would have known it was canvas. But he went on by.

'We are alone,' the man finally announced to his companions.

'And upstairs?' the man in black asked, gesturing toward the staircase with an upraised chin.

'Upstairs?' the searcher looked around. 'Ah, yes.' He started toward it.

Blake's breath caught in his throat. *The bathroom!* he thought. *That goddamn bathroom! What did I leave in the bathroom?* The man climbed to the upstairs landing and disappeared into the office.

After a minute the man reappeared at the head of the stairs waving a toothbrush. *Blake's* toothbrush. Blake held his breath and shrank back from his spy hole. 'I found this, Herr Weiss,' the man called down. 'In the washroom. It did not have dust on it.'

'There's a washroom up there?'

'Yes, sir. A small office with a washroom behind.'

'Is there anything in it beyond the toothbrush?'

'No, but the washbowl was free of dust, as was the toilet.'

'Ah!'

Blake breathed a sigh of relief. The essentially uncurious searcher had not looked in the medicine cabinet, which would have certainly occasioned a more thorough search.

Steuber twisted around in the chair and peered up at his captor. 'Herr Weiss? Herr Weiss? They said they were taking me to see Agent Reno! Where is Reno?'

The man who shrugged. 'What is in a name?' he asked. 'Call me what you like, it is of no consequence.' He turned to the man upstairs. 'You are an idiot,' he told him. 'Try to remember my name from one moment to the next.'

'Try using the same name from one week to the next,' the man replied, with a sharp shake of his head as though he were trying to clear it of settling flies.

'We will speak of this later. Whoever cleansed the washbasin may return. Ascertain which door is being used – clearly not the one we entered, that hadn't been opened for some time – and watch it.'

'Very well,' the man said, and started down the stairs.

Weiss turned back to his captive. 'Now,' he said. 'Back to those *verdammte* questions.'

'*Sie sind Deutsch!*' Steuber said, his voice high-pitched and strained. 'You are not FBI, you are Gestapo!'

Weiss smiled. It was not a pretty smile. 'Gestapo? *Nein*,' he said. 'The Gestapo – they have rules. Rules, rules, rules. We have only results.'

The interrogation lasted for three hours and was, for the most part, conducted in what Blake assumed was German. Blake retreated from the slit in the wall early, unable to watch without throwing up, which would assuredly have given him away. But it was not much easier to listen. The questions were barked, the answers were mumbled, and in between were the screams, horrible high-pitched screams, and the sobbing, and the pleading. And then, for a while, there were only the screams. And then the screams ceased. After a minute there was scrabbling and thumping and a murmured conversation in German. And then more thumping and the sound of opening and closing doors. And then there was nothing.

For a long time after the men left Blake remained as he was. Then he rose and knelt cautiously, weakly, supporting himself by clinging to the wood framing of the false wall. Then he threw up. After a time he pulled himself to his feet and came out into the room. Then he threw up again. The two steamer trunks were gone, but the man was still there. He tried looking at the man – the object; the body – on the chair. It was now naked, he saw, and he wondered when that had happened. But after a few seconds his eyes turned away of their own accord and he decided that that was a good thing. He could not stay in this place any longer.

He stuffed his few belongings into his suitcases and decided not to go upstairs to retrieve whatever was up there. Hoisting the suitcases, he edged around the room, staying as far away from the chair and its burden as he could manage. He left the building by a door on the far side of the room, a full block away from where the men had entered. Coming out on Water Street, he turned left and walked six blocks to the Taberna Lisboa, the bar where he bought an occasional pack of cigarettes when he had a dime that was otherwise unoccupied and had an occasional glass of beer when it seemed more important than buying food.

He went in and put his suitcases down beside the door. 'I must use your phone,' he told Benedito, the bartender.

'It is at the back,' Benedito said. He held out his hand. 'A nickel.'

'It's to call the police. It's an emergency'

'A nickel,' Benedito said.

'You call,' Blake said. 'Spring 7-1313. The police.'

'A nickel,' Benedito said.

Blake sighed and fished into his pocket for one of his precious nickels. 'Here,' he said, handing it over. Then he went back to the phone.

FOUR

Others find peace of mind in pretending,
Couldn't you?
Couldn't I?
Couldn't we?

      – *Oscar Hammerstein,* Showboat

Patricia fought like a cat, twisting and kicking and clawing, doing her best to dig her long red fingernails into his chest. Marcello worked with grim determination to hold her down on the bed, pinning her slender body between his legs, but she kept squirming and wriggling and bucking up under him until they were both panting with the exertion. Finally he succeeded in getting both of her arms over her head and holding them by their slender wrists in his left hand. With his right hand he worked at the buttons on her silk blouse, and slid the hand under her slip, cupping and squeezing her breasts, first one and then the other, and tweaking the hard nipples through her lace brassiere. He worked his fingers under the brassiere . . .

Suddenly she stopped fighting and lay back, motionless under him. 'Ah!' she cried. 'Wait a minute! Stop! Let go!'

'What?' Marcello Bruzzi paused, looking down at the blue eyes that were glaring up at him.

'Let go,' she said, 'for a minute.'

He relaxed his grip and she twisted free of him and sat up.

'And why, *cara mia*? What is the matter?'

'You're going to rip the bra.'

'Yes, perhaps, and so? I will buy you another one just as fine. Finer!'

'Yes, but I need this one,' she told him. 'I left the house wearing this one and it is wearing this one that I must return.'

She stood up, feeling the thick carpet under her bare feet, stepped out of her skirt, and unbuttoned and slid out of her blouse. Unhooking the bra, she shrugged and slid it off from under her silk slip, dropping it daintily on the bureau beside the bed.

'Ah, you women,' said Marcello, who had sat up in the bed and was watching this operation with interest, 'how you manage to learn these *intricato* – these involved maneuvers to take your clothes off . . .'

'It is because of men like you, my dear Marcello,' she said with a twisted little smile, 'that women practice such things.' She pulled the slip up to her knees, loosed the garter straps holding up her stockings and rolled them down, then stepped out of her frilly silk knickers, and tossed them and the stockings onto the bureau.

'Ah, *cucciola mia*,' Marcello moaned, 'the sight of those garments by themselves, just wantonly lying there waiting for your return, is enough to rise in me a sense of—'

'Yes,' she said. 'I can see what it rises in you.' With her palms she smoothed the slip against her belly and hips. 'I'll leave the slip on for now,' she said. 'I think the feel of silk under the hand is even more exciting than bare skin, don't you?'

'Ah!' said Marcello again as he thought this over, and then again, 'Ah!'

'Now,' she said, lying back against the bolster, 'where were we?'

'I forget,' he said. 'Perhaps we should begin again?'

They were lying on their backs staring at the ceiling some time later when the ornate gold-plated clock on the mantel chimed eleven times and tinged twice and hiccupped and was still.

Patricia rolled over and stared at the clock. 'The witching hour approaches,' she said, running her hand over his thigh. 'I must go before I turn into a pumpkin.'

He turned and raised his head, leaning his chin on his hands. 'What is this pumpkin?'

'*Zucca.*'

'Ah! A squash. That would be interesting. I have never, I think, made love to a squash. And why is it that you will turn into this squash?'

'Never mind. I'll take a shower now. Are you going to stay here?'

He considered. 'No, I think not. I must strive to arrive early at the embassy tomorrow morning. The ambassador, he is beginning to think that I may be dispensable.'

'You mean "indispensable"?'

'No, *cara mia*, dispensable. He is forming the opinion that he can, perhaps, do without my assistance. And that would create for me a catastrophe.'

She smiled and patted his face. 'But you *are* indispensable. Trust me. Perhaps I shall speak to your ambassador.'

Marcello pushed himself up and stared seriously at her. 'You would do such a thing. I know you. When you get an idea into your head . . .'

'But it is a good idea, is it not?'

He shook his head. 'No!' He shook it again. 'Positively not. Just think. The wife of the British Cultural Attaché, she is telling the Italian Ambassador that his military attaché he is indispensable. I shudder!' He shuddered.

She stuck her tongue out at him. 'Phooey on your mores and your customs and your stuffy Catholic Church.'

'And your Anglican Church, she is so much more tolerant of such things?'

'Phooey on that too. And phooey on sneaking up to hotel rooms or lying to room clerks – who know perfectly well what we're doing.'

'Ah!' Marcello said. 'But you must remember that they desire to be like the monkeys—'

She giggled. 'You mean, "monkey see, monkey do"?'

'No, *cara mia*, the other monkeys. The ones that see and hear not the evil.'

'And your friend who loaned us his apartment for tonight, is he also a monkey?' she asked.

'Not at all. He has been called back to Rome to consult with Il Duce. He is important. I must water his plants while he is gone. And in return . . .'

'And the military attaché is not important?'

He shrugged. 'We are not going to war with the United States sometime soon, I think.'

'And if you did?'

'I? Why should I do such a thing?'

'Italy, you silly *zucca*. If Il Duce were to declare war on America?'

'If such a ridiculous thing were to happen I should resign my commission, quit my post, and move to Brooklyn, New York, US of A.'

'Brooklyn?'

'And why not? There are more Italians living in Brooklyn, I am told, than in Napoli.'

'Surely not.'

He shrugged. 'In this, perhaps, I am mistaken. It is what I have heard, I have not myself counted the noses.'

Patricia pulled herself up and swung her legs over the side of the bed, her feet just touching the floor. She bounced on the mattress. Marcello enjoyed watching her bounce. 'You would not fight for your country?' she asked, letting the bouncing subside.

'You are thinking that I am the coward? Not so. I was awarded the Medaglia d'Argento al Valore Militare after the Great War. It is a very big deal medal, much like your British Military Cross.'

'Well!' she said, hunching toward him like a cat. 'That's exciting! What did you do?'

He shrugged. 'It is perhaps I should not have told you that,' he said. 'I was stupid. Also, I admit, brave. But mostly stupid.'

'But you won't fight the United States?'

'Ah!' he said. 'That depends. If the United States were to attack my beloved Italy, I would fight. But if Il Duce, in his arrogance and *egotismo . . . egotismo*?'

'Egotism,' she supplied.

'Yes, that. If he were to declare war on the United States, I would move to Brooklyn.'

She bent over to kiss him on the forehead and then walked across the deep carpet to the bathroom; he watched with renewed interest the way her thighs kissed briefly with each step. She turned to smile at him, as though she knew just what he had been thinking, before closing the bathroom door. Fifteen minutes later she opened the door and emerged in a puff of steam, one towel wrapped around the more interesting parts of her body while with another she was energetically pummeling her hair. 'Your turn,' she said, padding back to the bed.

He leaped to his feet and strode across the carpet, chest out, she noted with silent amusement, and stomach sucked in. After he had disappeared into the bathroom she quickly slid into her most intimate layers of clothing and then found her red handbag by the side of the bed and pulled out a gold lipstick case and matching compact.

The large dresser between the two windows on the far wall supported an oversized mirror. She danced over to it, turned on the table lamp, and began applying powder to various parts of her anatomy.

She paused when she heard the shower go on in the bathroom, took a deep breath, and set the compact carefully down on a bare spot on the dresser. Inserting the tip of a hairpin into a tiny hole next to the hinge on the compact, she pushed it in until she heard the merest suggestion of a click. Then, using both hands, she gave the base of the compact a little twist that split it in two. The bottom half held a shallow depression filled with a specially compounded dense wax smoothed to a perfectly flat surface. From the towel that enfolded her hair she removed a small, oddly shaped key on a thin gold chain. Holding her breath to add that extra bit of steadiness to her hand, she pressed the key firmly into the wax, first one side and then the other. She then carefully closed the hidden cavity in the compact and wiped any hint of wax off the key before going back to the bed and sliding the key in between the rumpled sheets. Pausing for a second to listen to the reassuring patter of the shower, she returned to her spot and stared at herself critically in the mirror before picking up the lipstick case.

It was two minutes later when Marcello burst suddenly back into the bedroom, dripping wet, the shower still going behind him. '*La mia chiave!*' he yelled. 'My key! Where is my key?'

She turned to look at him, lipstick poised in the air. 'Calm down,' she advised. 'What are you talking about? What key?'

'That key which I have around my neck.'

'You don't have a key around your neck,' she observed. 'Oh, wait – you mean that thing that was on the gold chain? That was a key?'

He lifted the blanket and shook two pillows out before throwing them on the floor, and then turned to glare at her. 'Yes, my little poppet, that was a key. What did you think it was?'

'I don't know. It didn't look much like a key. Some sort of talisman, perhaps. Something Italian.' She closed the lipstick and put it and the compact back in her purse.

'It is a key,' Marcello assured her. 'I have the care of it for my friend while he is in Rome, and if it is not found it is a problem *molto grave* for me. I will be – how you say? – dismembered.'

She looked startled. 'I don't *think* that's what we say,' she said. 'Unless your Fascist bosses are even more bloodthirsty than I imagined. So,' she looked around, 'what did you do with it?'

'Me?' He glared at her. 'I have done nothing with it. And yet it is missing.'

'Well!' She glared back. 'Don't look at me. It was around *your* neck. I remember because it kept hitting me in the nose when you, ah, moved.'

'Ah, yes. And just when, do you recall, did it stop this hitting you?'

'When you fell off me like a beached herring. You grunted something in, I suppose, Italian and rolled over.'

'And the key then came off my neck?'

'I don't know, but it stopped hitting my nose.'

'Then perhaps . . .' He stripped off the blanket and then the top sheet and something that flashed gold went with the sheet onto the floor. 'Aha!' he said, and pounced on it like a spaniel retrieving a tennis ball.

'Your key?' she asked sweetly.

FIVE

The City is of Night; perchance of Death
But certainly of Night . . .
       – *James Thomson,* The City of Dreadful Night

'**N**aked?'

'Naked. The guy was tied to a chair, beaten bloody, and stripped naked. Probably after he died – the naked part, that is.'

The 84th Precinct squad room had that faint smell of disinfectant, dried vomit, and stale cigarette smoke that haunts precinct houses, that seemed to have worked its way through the paint into the walls, never to leave until some distant time when the building was disassembled into its component parts. Detective First Grade Max Covitt imagined that he could also sense the cumulative man-years of fear and despair that had worked themselves as a sort of psychic burden into the fabric of the building. He didn't much believe in psychic burdens or psychic anything else, but nonetheless . . .

The three two-man teams of Brooklyn Homicide occupied five desks in a corner of the room next to the lieutenant's office. Detective Covitt's desk in the coveted spot by the window had been old when Teddy Roosevelt was Superintendent of Police forty years before and was still considered 'serviceable' by the department.

Covitt's swivel chair, almost as old as the desk, creaked in alarm as he leaned his two hundred pounds back and put his feet up on the pull-out stand that had once held a typewriter. 'My question for you is,' he said, looking up at the tall man in the dark brown fedora and light brown trench coat standing across the desk from him, 'what's Washington's interest in this here routine, if particularly nasty, killing? Not that I'm complaining, you understand, but the way I been told is that the FBI got no interest in local murders.'

'And, although you hate to mention it, no jurisdiction.'

'Yeah, well, and that.'

'Actually,' the man said, settling into the visitor's chair, 'I'm not FBI. And, technically, I'm not Washington. We have an office in the old Custom House in Manhattan.'

Covitt blew air from between his closed lips. 'The Lieutenant said you was FBI.'

'A misunderstanding.' The man took the leather folder holding his ID card out and passed it to Covitt. 'I'm with OSI, work out of the State Department.'

Covitt held the card in one hand and peered down at it while he scratched the bridge of his nose thoughtfully with the other. 'OSI?'

'That's right. The Office of Special Intelligence.'

'What's that?'

'Me, as it happens. And about six other guys right now. Although we hope to reach an even dozen agents by the end of the year.' He stuck out his hand. 'Jacob Welker,' he said. 'Special Agent, OSI.'

'Max Covitt,' Covitt said, taking the hand. 'Detective First, NYPD, Brooklyn Homicide. What makes you Special?'

'Excuse me?'

'As in "Special Agent"?'

Welker shrugged. 'I got no idea. Hoover started it. Haven't you noticed that all his agents are "special"?'

'Yeah. I wondered about that. Is why I'm asking you.'

'We're just copying Hoover.'

'Ah!'

'Why I'm here,' Welker said, 'is because your witness said the magic word.'

Covitt allowed himself to look puzzled. 'He didn't say much,' he said. 'Just how he saw four guys beating up on some other guy until they killed him. He spent most of the time hiding in the corner with his head down. Not that I wouldn't have done the same.'

'And then the attackers took away two steamer trunks and all the guy's clothing. Just your normal . . . what exactly?'

'Yeah, we wondered about that. They didn't want us to figure out who he was, maybe. If Blake wasn't hiding in the corner we might never figure it out. Even with what he saw, it's going to be tough. I figure knowing the murdered guy had two trunks may give us a shot. And, oh yeah, Blake says he thinks the guys were speaking German.'

'That's the magic word that got me over here,' Welker said. 'German. That and naked. What was the point of taking the guy's clothes off unless they were afraid we could learn something from them?'

'You mean, like where he was from?'

'Like that,' Welker agreed.

Covitt took his feet off the stand and planted them on the floor. 'You think they're German Germans? Like from Germany? I mean we got a lot of Germans living right here and they ain't all of them all the time peaceable.'

'True. But the steamer trunks kind of give you the idea that the vic was coming from somewhere. And the vic said, according to your guy, he thought the perps were Gestapo. We don't have a home-grown Gestapo over here. At least not in Brooklyn.'

'Maybe he was just being, you know, hyper-something. Maybe he didn't mean the real Gestapo.'

'Could be. But Hoover's boys lost a German yesterday. They were trying to pick him up off a ship that just came in from Hamburg, but another couple of guys got there first.'

'Ah,' Covitt said like it was all making sense now. 'A spy maybe?'

'Maybe. The Bureau got word that an agent was due to land, and they think this was him. They lost interest when he disappeared, figured his friends got to him first and they'd catch up to him further down the line. But then I heard about the corpse, and the magic word German, so I came to check it out.'

'A Nazi?'

'No. Hoover's not all that excited by Nazis. A Comintern agent.'

'A Commie?' Covitt shook his head. 'Who would'a thought? Hoover sure does hate Commies. But then how come he was German?'

'Well, they're not going to send a Russian. Not unless he's under deep cover. And to Stalin I guess these Germans are expendable. They're low-level nuisances while the real spying is done by professionals.'

'So he was nabbed by other Germans?'

'Looks like. The question is who and why. That's why I want to talk to your witness, and try to recover the steamer trunks and the vic's clothing.'

Covitt grunted. 'They're probably in the East River.'

'Maybe. Maybe not. If you throw the trunks into the river they're liable to bob up at an inconvenient time. Whereas if you distribute the clothing – we'll assume for now that they contained clothing and other personal crap – to, say, the Salvation Army, the Destitute Seamen's Home, and a couple of other worthy charities, they blend in and quickly disappear. The trunks themselves can likewise be disposed of thusly.'

'Or even dumped into the East River.'

'Or even,' Welker agreed.

Covitt stared at Welker for a moment and then sighed. 'Salvation Army, eh? It's an idea. I'll put a man on it. What do you think, German labels in the clothes, dropped off in the past two or three days, um, maybe a nice German leather dopp kit. Anything else?'

Welker shrugged. 'The clothing neatly folded and creased, as though they had just come out of a trunk after a long sea voyage, maybe. And, come to think of it, the labels are probably ripped out. Makes the stuff harder to identify, just in case.'

Covitt nodded, thought for a moment, and then called across the room: 'Weintz, I got something for you!'

A large man with a receding hairline and a protruding belly shambled over to the desk. 'I hope it'll wait till after lunch,' he said. 'I just sent down for a pastrami and mashed.'

'Mashed?'

'Yeah. I got a thing for Bernstein's mashed. They do 'em with little bits of fried onion.'

'Yeah? Well, enjoy. And after I want you should wander around to the thrift stores and second-hand clothing joints and like that.'

'Yeah? For what?'

Covet waved a hand at Welker. 'You tell him,' he said.

Welker explained his idea to the big detective, who nodded, took a few notes, nodded again, and went back to his desk and his pastrami.

'Good man, Weintz,' Covet said.

'Now,' Welker said. 'You know how I can get in touch with what's-his-name – Blake?'

'We got 'im,' Covitt told him.

'You're holding him?' Welker asked, sounding surprised.

'No, no. But he didn't have no place to go. Wouldn't go back to that warehouse, and who could blame him? And he's got no money, and I figured we might want him again. So we sprung for a room. We put him up at the Elderts on Myrtle Avenue.'

'Can I go see him?'

'Sure. It's like five blocks from here. I'll walk you.'

SIX

Would you that spangle of Existence spend
About the Secret – Quick about it, Friend!
A Hair perhaps divides the False and True –
And upon what, prithee, may life depend?
                              – Edward Fitzgerald,
                    The Rubaiyat of Omar Khayyam

I f you had strolled down Greene Street just north of Canal in Manhattan in the late 1930s you might have noticed the little shop four doors in from the corner, but your passing glance would have shown that it held nothing of interest, and you would certainly have moved on. The small display window might have held your attention for a second. Artfully covered by a thin layer of dust, it held two nondescript brass clocks of uncertain vintage, one facing forward and the other canted sideways as though it were trying to see what was going on down the block. But they were not worthy of note, and so you probably would not have noted them. A small unpolished brass plate by the side of the door said *Isaac Luthier – By Appointment.* The door was always locked and ringing the bell would produce no result. Unless, that is, you knew just how it should be rung.

It was three in the afternoon on Friday when Patricia exited her cab at the corner of Canal and Sixth Avenue and walked the three blocks to Greene. She turned the corner and stood in a doorway for three minutes to make sure no one was following her before going on to Isaac Luthier's door. After one last look around she gave the ring: three, three, one, two, and waited to be inspected. There was no visible spy-hole or bit of two-way mirror or lens that she could find, and yet Luthier invariably began his usual greeting, 'Ah, Lady Patricia, how good of you to come,' before the door was open wide enough for him to see who it was.

Isaac Luthier, known as 'The Professor' to his associates, was a little man with thinning hair, a carefully trimmed goatee, prominent ears, and a notable nose. His glasses were large with thick lenses. When he worked at the neatly cluttered workbench that took up a corner of his shop he clipped a second pair of lenses over the glasses so he could peer down at his work surface and see every dust mite between each grain of wood, or so Patricia imagined as she watched him.

Luthier was a true artist at what he did, which was to facilitate the removal of objects and documents from their secure locations against the wishes of the owner or, occasionally, permit the inspection of said documents without the owner's knowledge. He could teach a client several methods of removing letters from envelopes and then reinserting them without disturbing the seal. He had a mastery of the opening and closing of safes without leaving a trace of the transaction. This also required, of course, a complete understanding of door and window locks, burglar alarms, and concealed security devices, as well as the inner workings of safe and vault combination locks and time locks, both electrical and mechanical. But how to tell whether the householder was away for the evening or had just stepped out to get a pack of cigarettes; whether it was better to put a few drops of the blue liquid in the whiskey or the milk to assure that the servant would sleep through the night; whether the doorman could be approached with a proposition that he could most assuredly never tell anyone he had accepted – it was his unerring nose for such details that made him the artist. To sit at his feet while he explained such things was to receive a master course in a truly arcane craft.

'I need a key made,' Patricia said, handing Luthier her gold compact. 'And I have to be on the train back to Washington tonight.'

He turned it over in his hands and held it up to the light. 'Nice,' he said. 'Turn of the century. Paris? Yes, I think Paris. Matais et Fils, perhaps. Certainly influenced by Lalique.'

'The secret compartment opens . . .' Patricia began.

'No – let me,' he said.

He turned it over and back several times, flipped open the lid and closed it again, and then peered down at the hinge. 'Aha!' Reaching behind him he took the smallest screwdriver Patricia had ever seen and pushed the tip cautiously into the tiny hole by the hinge. When he felt the slight click he removed the screwdriver, put the compact between his palms, and gently twisted. 'If you use too much pressure it binds, if I am not mistaken,' he said. 'Whether deliberately as a security precaution or by a chance of the design I do not know.'

The two halves separated and he laid them on the table in front of him.

'So,' he said, looking at the impression of a key, pressed front and back into the smooth wax surface. 'What sort of wax?'

'A mixture of sixty percent beeswax and forty percent paraffin, I believe,' Patricia told him.

'Good, good.' He adjusted the two lamps so the reflections off the surface would be just so, and peered closely at the impressions. 'Hm,' he said. He readjusted the lights. 'This was on a chain,' he said, 'I can see the impression.'

'It was,' she agreed. 'I removed it while the wearer was, er, otherwise occupied.'

He looked up at her. 'Clever,' he said.

'Misdirection,' she told him. 'I was a magician's assistant as a wee child. I picked up several useful skills.'

'Ah!' He peered back down at the impressions. 'A Rabson Two Thousand – wait – no, no . . .' He took out a pair of calipers and measured something on one of the impressions then checked them against a steel ruler. 'No, this key's from a Twenty-Oh-Seven, if I am not mistaken.' He turned the compact around, readjusted the lights, and peered down again. Then he went over to his desk and riffled through some mimeographed pages until he found the one he wanted. He ran his finger down a column of numbers. 'Yes,' he said, looking up. 'A Twenty-Oh-Seven. Interesting.'

'You can tell that just from looking at the key impressions?' she asked.

'Yes, with a little assistance. Yes, certainly.'

'What makes it interesting?'

'The Twenty-Oh-Seven is a small wall safe, but quite expensive. It is made to be secured in the wall with long tamper-proof bolts and, if one wishes, a poured concrete footing. You cannot expect to merely break it out of the wall and remove it to be opened at your leisure. And even should you succeed it would do you little good. The box is of special alloy steel and the locking mechanism itself is complex, involving both a key and a combination.'

'Oh dear,' she said.

'Also,' he indicated the wax impressions with a pencil point, 'do you see those little nibs along the side of the key?'

She leaned over. 'No,' she said.

He readjusted the light.

'Yes,' she said. 'Those tiny bumps? I see them now.'

'Bumps in the wax,' Isaac said, 'depressions in the key.'

'What does that mean?'

'This part of the key, the part that goes into the lock cylinder, is called the "blade".' He ran an illustrative pencil point along the length of the wax impression. 'There are usually one or two grooves that run the length of the blade, as you can see. The small depressions in the blade are called "nibs", and are a unique feature of Rabson locks. In this model there are usually three of them, two on one side and one on the other. The edge of the blade,' he traced along the side of the blade, 'is called the "bit" and the notches in it are called "bites" or, for some reason, "bittens". They are very precisely cut. In a Rabson, if they are off by some small fraction of a millimeter the key will not work. And the bites alone are not enough. The nibs must also be precisely in the right place. The key blank is a special design that can only be supplied by Rabson and is of a non-standard thickness. And they never sell the blank, only the finished key. The Two Thousand series are all protected in this fashion. If you need a duplicate you call them and tell them the serial number of the safe and give them the unique identifying word picked by you when you bought the safe. They send the new key to you by courier, and you must sign for it and show identification.'

'Oh dear.'

'Yes,' Isaac agreed. 'If you have that among your possessions which you would conceal or safeguard, I would recommend the Rabson.'

'Then you cannot open it? Then I gave my body for nothing?'

He looked up at her with a bemused expression. 'Gave your body?'

She smiled an unreadable smile. 'So to speak,' she said.

Isaac raised his eyebrows and lowered his head to look at her over his glasses, a gesture that gave him a distinct owl-like expression. After a moment he pushed the glasses up on his nose and returned his gaze to the compact. 'Your, ah, sacrifice, whatever it may have been, was not in vain,' he said. 'The wax impressions look very clear, and I should be able to duplicate the key.'

'Oh good,' she said.

'But you will not have it with you on your return trip this evening. It will take some time.'

'How long?'

'Well.' He considered. 'I have to ever so carefully make a mold from your impressions. Then I must find a suitable blank of a non-magnetic metal and do a bit of shaving and filing and punching and clipping and muttering in a foreign language under my breath. So it will be a few days before the key is ready.'

'What language?' she asked.

'How's that? Oh. Take your pick: French, German, Yiddish, Arabic, Russian, Lithuanian . . .'

'Really?'

'I do not jest about epithets, they are a serious matter and must be judiciously chosen. Most people have a limited and paltry selection, and their speech is the poorer for it.'

'No, I mean . . . Lithuanian?'

'Indeed. The native tongue of some three million people. A noble language from a country with a noble history. In the fourteenth century, under Grand Duke Vytautas the Great, the territory of Lithuania encompassed much of what is now European Russia.'

'Say something to me in Lithuanian.'

Isaac considered. '*Tewe musu kursey esi danguy. Szweskis wardas Tawo,*' he said after a moment.

'Really?' she said. 'And what does that mean?'

'I could not shock your shell-like ears and despoil your innocence with a direct translation,' Isaac told her. 'When will you need the key? Do you have someone who can manage the combination? Or would you wish me to do the, ah, job?'

'Yourself?' she asked, sounding a little surprised.

'Why not? Am I, perhaps, too old?'

'Of course not!' she declared. 'But too valuable perhaps. If you should get caught . . .'

He shrugged. 'It would not be the end of the world. I have a very good lawyer, and he has had little to do these past few years as I have never been arrested or even, I believe, suspected of a crime.'

'Still . . .'

'And I like to keep my hand in. One can't go around telling others how to do something if one won't do it himself. So say I.'

'It's in an embassy in Washington. The safe, I mean.'

'I suspected as much.'

'At least I believe it is.'

'You don't know where the safe is?'

'Well, the key is kept on a chain around the neck of an embassy official, so I assume the safe is in the embassy. I could be mistaken, but where else it might be I couldn't begin to guess.'

'Ah! Then let us hope you won't have to. Have you access to this embassy? As a legitimate visitor, I mean?'

'Certainly.'

'Then let us discuss where such a safe might be concealed and how to best go looking for it.'

'Let us do that.'

SEVEN

The very first essential for success
is a constant and regular employment of violence.
– Adolf Hitler

Major Sir Henry Cardine stared glumly around at his room. The Hotel Kaiserhof, he decided, was no longer what the Hotel Kaiserhof had once been. After six decades as Berlin's *crème de la crème* hotel, home from home of passing royalty, the cream was beginning ever so slightly to sour. His room might be that of the aging maiden aunt of a minor noble, with green flocked wallpaper that was shifting gradually toward brown and furnishings that Victoria would have found a bit stuffy. The hotel staff seemed to have calcified with age into attitudes of fawning obsequiousness or sneering snobbishness, depending on the guest's perceived social status. Next trip, Sir Henry decided, if there were a next trip, he would stay at the Adlon or the Esplanade.

To add to his current displeasure, the Kaiserhof seemed to be infested with Nazi functionaries. Well, it *was* right across from the old Reichskanzlei, and Field Marshal Göring *had* been married here two years ago, so its popularity with the Party faithful was probably understandable. But he felt a strong distaste for the toad-faced self-important little men who infested the lobby, *heil*-ing Hitler every time they paused for breath. And the earnest blond youths with their slicked-back hair and their air of self-confidence, as though they had done something clever by being born, running about on errands of the utmost importance and looking at one as though one were some sort of insect as they strutted past. *Need a good thrashing*, Sir Henry thought. And then, as the thought broadened in his mind, *Let's hope it doesn't come to that. Not again.*

Sir Henry stared absently out his fourth-floor window at the vague expanse of Wilhelmplatz below as he buttoned up his waistcoat and adjusted his cravat. It was mid-morning of a chilly overcast Tuesday in late March, and he could barely make out the massive Chancellery behind its tall gates on the far side of the Platz. All he could see through the mist were the rows of long red banners bearing the omnipresent black on white Hakenkreuze hanging every twenty feet or so from the surrounding buildings or from thirty-foot-tall flagpoles boxing the park. *The Nazi Party*, Sir Henry thought, *must provide employment for a legion of flag makers.*

A tall man in his mid-forties with graying hair, a pencil mustache, and the erect bearing of a career soldier, which indeed he had been until two years before, Sir Henry had returned to Berlin as a representative of Eclipse Records, whose managing director had decided that a good classical music portfolio might be obtained cheaply from Wannesfrei Grammophon or Herzo Records, both companies having Jewish owners or directors. Since the Nuremberg Race Laws of 1935 it was clear that being a Jew in Nazi Germany was not a long-term proposition. If Sir Henry could scoop up the contracts before the Nazis got around to scooping up the directors, this would be the bee's knees or the cat's whiskers, or some other expression of approval which was twenty years out of date by the time the managing director got around to using it.

Not that Sir Henry knew anything about classical music, or the recording industry, or negotiating contracts, but he had once been stationed in Berlin and he had Eton and Oxford and the Welsh Guards behind him, and if a man with that background couldn't do anything he put his hand to, then what was it bally well all about anyway? Or so thought the managing director, who was married to Sir Henry's sister.

Berlin had become a gray city. When last he was here – when was it, 1932? Six years ago? – the city had been infused with a desperate flamboyance. *Let us live for today*, was the motto. *Yesterday was shit and tomorrow – who knows what might happen tomorrow?*

Well, tomorrow had arrived, with its swastikas and Hitler Youth corps and the Brownshirts in their hobnail jackboots roaming the streets like packs of jackals, breaking store windows, overturning pushcarts and stalls, and beating up Jews and Communists and homosexuals and anyone who got in their way. When his business here was done he would be happy to get back to London.

Shrugging into his suit jacket and donning his light brown trench coat, he stared thoughtfully into space for a long minute before sliding his precisely furled umbrella through the straps of his briefcase, tucking the briefcase under his arm, settling his black bowler precisely on his head, leaving his room, and bypassing the lift to trot down the four flights of stairs to the lobby. The concierge gave a bow precisely calibrated to Sir Henry's perceived importance, and murmured, *Guten Morgen, Herr Major Cardine* as he passed. He nodded back, nodded at the doorman, gave a shake of his head to the cabman to show he didn't need a cab today, and crossed the street to enter the Platz.

Sir Henry was undecided. Should he head for the U-Bahn station on the far side of the park, or should he just walk the twenty or so blocks to his meeting? The U-Bahn would get him there quickly but he was in no particular hurry, would probably stop for coffee anyway. Perhaps . . .

As he passed the statue of Prince Leopold, a tall man leaning against the granite base of the statue called to him in English, 'Major Cardine! Over here, Major Cardine!' The voice was soft but carried a certain urgency to it.

Sir Henry turned. 'Yes?'

'Could you please step over here for the moment, if you would be so kind? I would speak with you.'

The man was well dressed, but not like a businessman. Like an artist perhaps, with a long jacket of the sort one pictures an artist wearing and a floppy hat, not exactly a beret but wider and floppier. Not a threatening look. Sir Henry walked toward him. 'Do I know you?'

'No, Herr Major, but we have friends in common.' The man moved over to one of the park benches and sat down. 'Join me over here if you would, so we can speak quietly. I have something of the utmost import that I would discuss with you.'

'Really?' Sir Henry suddenly thought he had guessed the man's game. He was going to ask him for money. 'The utmost importance, eh?' he asked, venturing a tight little smile.

'Even so,' the man assured him.

As Sir Henry approached the bench, a man in a light brown trench coat suddenly appeared from around the far side of the statue and started walking hurriedly across the Platz toward the Chancellery. For a second Sir Henry was startled, fearing, he didn't know what, some sort of trap? But the man in the trench coat showed no interest in him as he scurried past.

'Sit, sit,' the man said. 'I will be brief.'

Sir Henry sat on the corner of the bench and looked the man over. 'And just who are you?' he asked after a moment.

The man thought this over for a long minute. 'You may call me Felix,' he said finally.

'Felix,' Sir Henry said, setting his briefcase on his lap and folding his hands over it. 'And what is your story, Felix?'

'Yes,' Felix said, 'I suppose I do have what you might call a story. And assuredly you shall hear it.' He paused, perhaps gathering his thoughts.

'You speak English well,' Sir Henry said for lack of anything more interesting to say.

'Yes,' Felix nodded, obviously pleased at the observation. 'I attended Cambridge for two years. That was many years ago, before the World War. I was an exchange officer, you might say. Some of your junior officers went to the University of Munich, I believe.'

So Felix was military. Then he certainly wasn't trying to borrow money – not from an Englishman. What, then? 'I was in Heidelberg for almost a year,' Sir Henry said.

'Yes. So we understand.'

'We?'

Felix waved his hand. 'No matter. We keep dossiers on all British officers. It is just good practice. You do the same about ours, I'm sure.'

'Not that I know of.' Sir Henry felt unaccountably annoyed. He rose. 'I must go on. I have an engagement at the present time. If you wish to speak with me, I am staying at the . . .'

'Yes. The Kaiserhof. Yes. Which is why I awaited you here instead of elsewhere.' The man patted the seat. 'Please, sit. I promise to be reasonably brief.'

Sir Henry considered just walking away, but his curiosity overcame his ire. How did this man know his name, and who were 'we'? Presumably the German army. But if so, what was their interest in him? And why the secrecy?

'Did you know,' Felix interrupted his thoughts, 'that you're being followed?'

'Followed?'

'Yes. By the Gestapo.'

Sir Henry resisted the urge to look around. His overly logical mind clicked off objections. 'How could you know that?' he asked. 'And why haven't I seen them? And if they are following me, what's the point of all this foofaddle?' He paused and then added, 'And why on earth would they be following me? Surely they have better things to do; arresting Communists, beating up Jews, and suchlike.'

Felix smiled, evidently taking no offense at this description of his country's secret police. 'We like keeping track of foreigners in this New Germany,' he said. 'And besides, you're a special case, are you not?'

'What in the world,' asked Sir Henry, 'would make me a special case?'

'Well, you are Military Intelligence, *nicht wahr*?'

'I'm what?'

'Oh, come off it. After almost twenty years in the British army you suddenly and unaccountably retire and take a job beneath your social station, and one that just happens to take you to Berlin? I mean . . .'

'I see,' Sir Henry said. 'So you think—'

Felix shrugged. 'It was not a difficult conclusion.'

'But in this case utterly mistaken, I assure you,' Sir Henry said. 'Perhaps the social standing of a career army major is not as high in Britain as it might be over here,' he added with a wry smile. 'I am what you see. My mufti is genuine, I assure you.'

'Ah,' Felix said thoughtfully. 'But of course you would say that in any case.' He shrugged. 'Perhaps it will not matter.' He looked at his watch. 'We have at most half an hour, I think. I must not be seen talking with you, it would not be healthy.'

'Healthy for whom?' Sir Henry asked.

'For me certainly. Perhaps also for you.'

Sir Henry ventured a cautious look around. 'But . . . If the Gestapo are indeed watching . . .'

'They are, at the moment, distracted,' Felix told him. 'When you left the hotel and started across the park their man in the hotel alerted your watchers and they were waiting for you on the far side of the Platz by the Chancellory. They are in a green Opel Olympia.'

'But when I don't show up . . .'

'Ah, but you have already showed up, and they are at this moment following you. As you are on foot, they have one man half a block behind you and a second driving the car perhaps a block behind him. I know this because it is procedure.'

'Excuse me?'

'Of course you are puzzled. How, you ask, can you be walking down Wilhelmstrasse and at the same time be here speaking with me? The explanation is simple. There are at the moment two Major Cardines. One of them is here speaking with me, while the other is walking at a leisurely pace down the Strasse. When he reaches the Café Karpinski he will seat himself and order a *kaffe mit schlag*, with or without a pastry, and purchase a copy of the *Berliner Tageblatt*.'

'Really?' Sir Henry asked, and then it came to him. 'That man – the one who left as you spoke with me . . .'

'Indeed,' Felix agreed. 'Brown covert coat, black bowler hat, regimental tie, carrying a briefcase much like yours with an umbrella tightly furled and thrust between its straps. Your doppelgänger for certain. Although I believe his ears are larger than yours. Also the tie is of the wrong regiment, but the Gestapo will most assuredly not be aware of this.'

'You were prepared for this? To meet me like this?'

'It was not difficult. The most problem was the bowler – they are not so popular here.'

'You watched me, to learn my movements?'

'No, we are not the Gestapo. We merely sat in the hotel lobby to see how you dressed and, perhaps, managed to read an official report on how you spent your day.'

'Why?'

'To contrive this opportunity to speak with you unobserved.'

'What will they – the Gestapo – do when they discover the deception?'

'We must hope that they do not. But they are men of little imagination and they are seeing what they expect to see so there is little chance of that. So long as we have finished our business by the time your doppelgänger returns we will be safe.' He paused and then added, 'I believe.'

Sir Henry thought this over for a minute. 'It seems to me,' he said finally, 'that you are putting me in an uncomfortable position. If the Gestapo do tumble to your little ruse they will certainly assume that I was party to the deception. How could they not? Then I'll be lucky not to be escorted to the nearest border with an armed guard.'

'That is so,' Felix agreed, 'and probably after spending a few uncomfortable days in a small room at Prinz-Albrecht-Strasse 8 trying to explain why you arranged such a farce. They will assuredly call it a farce; everything they don't like or don't understand is, to them, a farce.' He shook his head. 'If it is any consolation I will, by that time, probably be dead. If they catch me.'

'Well, in that case,' Sir Henry said, 'we should get on with our business – whatever that is.'

'I agree,' Felix said. 'I have a proposition to put to you. A, ah, deal as you might say.'

'What sort of deal?'

'Well, here is the problem. I made the certainly not illogical assumption that you were British intelligence, but you say you are not. In which case you are, most probably, not in a position to make the sort of agreement that I require.' He looked sharply at Sir Henry and then away again. When Sir Henry did not respond he went on: 'So then what I must request of you is that you put me in touch with someone who is in such a position. You can do this, yes?'

'I can certainly speak with someone in Military Intelligence when I get back,' Sir Henry agreed. 'But what am I to tell them?'

'That is the question.' Felix stared intently at a nearby tree. 'Tell them,' he said, transferring the intent stare to Sir Henry, 'tell them that an officer in the Wehrmacht, presently serving as an adjunct to the intelligence section of the General Staff, offers to provide them with information of military value in return for a small service. Tell them that this must be accomplished soon, if possible within the month.'

A small service? Then it was money after all, Sir Henry thought. *A gambling debt? Paying off some woman?* 'How big a service?' he asked. 'They'll want to know. Say a few hundred pounds? And you think your information will be worth that size, ah, service?'

Felix stood up, his body rigid, his face white. His hand was raised as though he were going to slap Sir Henry. 'You think . . .' he said. 'You suggest . . .' Slowly he regained control of himself and sat back down. 'Perhaps, after all, this is a farce,' he said. He shook his head as though to chase away some unwelcome thoughts. 'This is not simple for me. I am, in effect, becoming a traitor to my country, and whether I do it for money or for some nobler motive is not of the moment, *nicht wahr*?' He took a deep breath. 'I believe the true traitors . . . no, I will not get into that now. I assure you I have no need for money.' Another deep breath, and then he smiled. 'Certainly not from the British Secret Service in any event.'

Sir Henry felt a flush wash across his face and wondered if the other could see it. He had jumped to a hasty conclusion and, with that, insulted a brother officer. A German officer, true, but still . . . 'That was unwarranted and I apologize,' he said. 'Truly I am sorry. I had no right . . .'

Felix waved it away. 'Understandable under the circumstances. No, it is not money; it is a different sort of service I require.'

'I'll do what I can. How are they to get in touch with you?'

'That is the problem, is it not? I had thought this meeting would suffice. But not so. If there is a god up there, he spends his time laughing when we humans make our plans.' He shrugged. 'That is what makes war so interesting. So many men armed thus and so against so many men armed thus and so, using these tactics in this terrain, with the weather just so, the results should be determined. But just at the last moment someone misreads a message, or a horse throws a shoe, or a gun fails to fire, and so history is changed.'

'So . . .?' Sir Henry asked.

Felix took a deep breath and slowly let it out. 'So, have them put an advertisement in the classified section of the *Times*. Something innocuous with the name Felix in it and a phone number. I will endeavor to call from a safe phone and we can plan.'

'The London *Times*?'

'Certainly. Why not?'

'And the phone number?'

'I shall assume it is a Berlin number unless the message says otherwise. And not from the embassy or the homes of any official, such calls are certainly overheard. Overseas calls also are likely not to be so private.'

'I shall pass that on,' Sir Henry said.

'And please, with some haste. This is important.'

'You have my word,' Sir Henry said.

'And, oh yes, give them this.' He took a small packet of papers from his jacket pocket, perhaps three or four sheets folded into thirds, and passed it to Sir Henry.

'What is this?' Sir Henry asked.

'Call it a proof of my good faith,' Felix told him. 'It is a brochure for the War Museum.'

'I don't . . .'

'If a hot iron is passed over the back of the sheets, something of greater interest will be revealed,' Felix explained.

'Oh.' Sir Henry said, holding the papers as though they might spontaneously combust.

Felix laughed. 'Now I believe that you are not an agent,' he said, rising to his feet. 'I will now leave. Wait here until you see yourself approaching, and then return to the hotel. Your doppelgänger will destroy his resemblance to you and then wander off in another direction. Good luck!'

'Yes,' Sir Henry said. And then, after a second, 'You also.'

EIGHT

It'd take a guy a lifetime to know Brooklyn t'roo an' t'roo.
An' even den, yuh wouldn't know it all.
       – *Thomas Wolfe,* Only the Dead Know Brooklyn

The Elderts Hotel was a five-story red-brick building on the corner of Myrtle and Spencer, with a neon sign that read DERT when the manager remembered to turn it on, and an adjoining stable for a horse and carriage that, according to local legend, had once been rented by Aaron Burr. These days the Elderts had few pretensions. The most that could be said for it was that it was clean, in a liberal interpretation of that word, and it wasn't a hot-sheet joint: there was no two-hour rate, you had to pay for the whole night. And an extra fifteen cents if you brought in a companion of either sex or anything in between, and an extra fifteen cents if you wanted one of the rooms with its own bathroom instead of down the hall. And you had to be out by noon or you paid for another day – no exceptions.

'They give a special discount if you're on the job,' Detective Covitt said. 'I guess they figure it don't hurt to have a cop or two on the premises.'

'A rough clientele?' Welker asked, looking around at the bare lobby as they went in. It had all the grace of a public men's room and smelled vaguely of stale fried food.

'Not so much. But, you know, it is Brooklyn. Like they say, if it can happen here, it will.'

The room clerk didn't look up from the copy of *Astounding Science-Fiction* he was reading as they passed him and headed up the stairs to the third floor. 'There's an elevator,' Covitt said, 'but it ain't worked since the Coolidge administration.'

There was a rustling noise from within room 314 as they knocked on the door, and an eye peered cautiously at them through the peephole; then the door opened and a disheveled man leaned forward at a precarious angle and frowned up at them. 'Yes?' he said. 'Detective?'

'Glad to catch you in, Mr Blake,' Covitt said. 'I wasn't sure you'd be here.'

'Where would I be?' Blake asked.

Covitt eyed him. 'You been drinking?' he asked.

'A little,' Blake said, waving a hand toward the bottle of Muscatel on the bureau. 'I don't drink much, never have. But I thought that a few glasses of this stuff might make the pictures go away.'

'The pictures?'

'In my head. The pictures in my head.'

'Oh,' Covitt said. 'I gotcha. What you saw back in that room.'

'Actually I didn't see much.' Blake backpedaled into the room and waved them past him. 'It's the pictures I imagined while I was hiding behind the partition. I had my eyes squeezed closed, but I could hear what they were doing and these pictures came – and now they keep coming back.'

'That doesn't sound like fun,' Covitt said.

'Trust me, it is not.' Blake pushed the door closed and turned to face them.

'This here's Special Agent Welker,' Covitt said, thrusting a thumb in Welker's direction. 'He has some questions for you.'

Blake looked Welker over. 'I don't know anything,' he said. 'At least not anything I haven't already told the detectives.'

'Probably so,' Welker agreed, 'but let's go over it again anyway.' He looked around the tiny room. There was not much to see: a battered bureau that had probably once been white across from a battered, unmade bed that probably once hadn't sagged in the middle, and a wooden chair that had never had any pretensions of any sort. 'Can't really talk in here,' he said. 'No place to sit. Is that diner on the corner any good?'

'The Olympia?' Covitt considered. 'It's OK.'

'Let's go over. I'll buy lunch.'

The room clerk looked up as they were leaving, but he didn't see anything as interesting as 'Duel in the Space Lanes', so he went back to his magazine.

It wasn't quite noon and the Olympia was almost empty when they went in; the lunch crowd, if there was to be one, hadn't begun yet. They settled into a corner booth, and the waitress appeared a few seconds later with three glasses of water and almanac-sized menus. 'Morning, gentlemen,' she said. 'Coffee?'

They thought that was a good idea.

'Back in a minute,' she said.

Blake studied the menu like he'd never seen one before. 'They've got steak,' he said wistfully.

'Along with everything else human beings have ever eaten,' Welker said, turning the pages of the menu. 'This thing is a catalog of food. Three different kinds of sausages.' He flipped a page. 'No – four.'

'They make good burgers and nice crisp, greasy fries,' Covitt told him. 'As for the rest, you're on your own.'

Blake looked at Welker hesitantly, 'Uh . . .'

'What is it?'

'Can I have the sirloin steak plate?' Blake asked.

'Whatever you like,' Welker told him. 'It's on Uncle Sam.'

The waitress returned with their coffees and they ordered. Covitt went with the burger and fries, Blake with the steak, medium with baked and veg, and Welker ordered silver dollar pancakes, which the waitress assured him referred to the size not the color. She thought the question was the funniest thing she'd ever heard and went away chortling.

Blake poured cream into his coffee, drank off about a third, and filled it with cream again. 'OK,' he said. 'What do you want to know?'

'What can you tell me?'

'Not much. Four guys beat up another guy and I listened to him screaming. A lot. And there wasn't a damn thing I could do about it.' He took a deep breath. 'Made me feel like a real hero, it did.'

'Well,' Covitt said, 'like you said, there wasn't nothing you could do about it.'

Welker asked, 'Did you get a good look at their faces?'

Blake considered. 'One guy. The one who did most of the talking. The others not so much. I kept my head down a lot.'

'But would you know him if you saw him again?'

'Yeah, I'm pretty sure. Besides, I'd know his voice anywhere. Kind of high-pitched. Mean. And a couple of the others, I might recognize their voices, but I don't promise.'

'Good. I mean that you'd recognize at least one of them again. Good.' Welker leaned back, tipping his chair onto two legs. 'Can you remember anything that he said?'

'It was in German.'

'Anything that wasn't?'

'Well, he told the other guy to search the place. Scared the crap out of me, that did. Didn't find me though. Found my toothbrush.'

'That's it? Nothing else in English?'

Blake stared through the window thoughtfully. 'Yeah,' he said. 'There was something. Names.'

The front legs of Welker's chair thumped to the floor. His face had the expression of a man who has just seen a rabbit jump out of the sugar bowl. 'What?' he asked too loudly. Then a second later, in a more normal voice, 'What did you say? Names? They told you their names?'

'Well, they weren't talking to me,' Blake said. 'The guy that was searching the place called the boss guy Herr, ah, Herr something.'

'Close your eyes,' Welker suggested. 'Picture it happening.'

Blake shook his head. 'I don't want to do that,' he said. 'I really don't.'

'You never said nothing about names when we talked to you,' Covitt said.

Blake's face was white and his eyes opened unnaturally wide. 'I didn't remember,' he told Covitt. 'I didn't want to remember. I still don't.'

'That's OK,' Welker said. 'Take it easy.'

'I'm going to throw up,' Blake said. He got up and staggered down the aisle toward the men's room.

'You think I should follow him?' Covitt asked Welker.

'No,' Welker said. 'Let him go by himself. He doesn't need us watching him barf. Let him keep some dignity.'

Five minutes later Blake returned to the table and stared down at the bowl of soup at his place. 'What's this?' he asked, prodding the edge of the bowl with his finger and looking disappointed.

'Chicken noodle,' Covitt told him. 'Comes with the dinner.'

'Oh,' Blake said. He sat down. 'So I still get the dinner?'

'A salad too,' Covitt said. 'Soup and a salad.'

'Oh,' Blake said. He put his spoon in the soup cautiously, as though he half thought the spoon would dissolve, and then he brought it to his lips. 'Not bad,' he said.

'You never had a dinner before?' Covitt asked him. 'Like with soup, salad, and the works?'

'I guess,' Blake said. 'It's been a while. We didn't eat out much.'

'Where you from?'

'Pennsylvania,' Blake told him. 'outside Philadelphia.'

'How long have you been here – in New York?' Welker asked.

'I don't know. About seven or eight months, I guess.'

'You don't know how long you've been here?' Covitt asked, sounding surprised.

Blake shrugged. 'The time, you know. It's hard to keep track of the time when there's nothing to separate it into, like, little pieces. It just kind of passes by.'

'What have you been doing?' Covitt asked.

'Well, I came here to take a job.'

'Doing what?'

'Typesetting – Linotype or by hand. I'm a Linotype operator. I can also do letterpress, my dad had a letterpress shop, but there ain't much call for that anymore.'

'Oh, a newspaperman.'

'Books, mostly,' Blake told him. 'I worked for Janifer, Harris, and Company in Philly. Books on agriculture, textbooks. Did high-school graduation books, but that fell off; the kids can't afford to buy them. Then Harris died and they closed the business.'

'Janifer retired?'

'He was already dead.'

'Ah!'

'So I met a guy at a convention and he offered me a position here in Brooklyn. A job shop on Myrtle Avenue. Their Linotype guy had palsy or some such so bad he couldn't type, and they needed a replacement. A union shop, and I'm union – or was, I haven't paid dues for a while. And I didn't have anybody at home when my mom died, with my sister married and moved to Cleveland, so I figured what the hell.'

The waitress came over with plates precariously balanced on her arms and set them down, and Blake paused to stare at his steak.

'So you came here and he reneged on the job?' Covitt suggested.

'So I got here and the job was gone. The shop was closed.'

'Oh,' Covitt said. 'Yeah, that's happening. Still.'

'Eat your steak,' Welker said.

For a while there was no conversation while they ate, then Welker pushed his plate back. 'These names you overheard,' he said, consulting a scrap of paper he'd pulled out of his pocket, 'was one of them Otto Lehman, do you remember?' He waved at the waitress and pointed to his coffee cup.

Blake screwed his face up in concentration. 'Yeah, I think so.' After a minute he nodded. 'Yeah. That was the guy in the chair – the guy they beat up. One of them called him that. No, I'm wrong – they called him something else but he insisted that was his name, Lehman. At first.' He stopped talking and stared down at the table, then repeated, 'At first.'

'So he called himself Otto Lehman, but they insisted he was really someone else?' Welker asked.

'Yeah, that's about right. Lehman, anyway, I don't know about the Otto. At first. Then he agreed with them. Everything they said, he agreed.'

The waitress appeared at the table with the coffee pot, refilled their cups, and set the check down. 'No rush,' she said. 'Whenever.'

Covitt waited until she walked away, and then asked, 'Who's Lehman?'

'He's the one Hoover's boys were trying to pick up at the docks,' Welker told him.

'The Commie?'

'Right. When they missed him, they thought a couple of his pals got to the ship first, and figured they could get at him later. But when I heard about this,' he waved his hand at Blake, 'I figured the dead guy was Lehman and whoever picked him up wasn't so much his pal after all.'

'So the guy was a Communist?' Blake asked, pouring an unseemly amount of sugar into his coffee and then busily stirring it while watching the others.

'That's what an informant told the FBI. A man who would call himself Lehman was coming over from Germany to coordinate or instruct or direct some Communist activity in the United States, or at least in New York. But just what he was supposed to be doing here, we don't know.'

'Whatever it was,' Covitt said, 'somebody didn't want him doing it.'

'There's that,' Welker agreed. He stared at Blake for a long moment, his lips going in and out as though he were chewing on a thought. Then: 'Blake, how'd you like a job?'

There was about a three-second pause before Blake responded, 'Sure, what you got in mind? I don't suppose I have to add "anything legal" since I'm talking to a cop.'

'Mostly legal, I guess,' Welker said. 'I was thinking of getting you a job working in a print shop.'

'No shit? Letterpress? Rotary? Gotta be a union shop.'

'I don't know from the technical stuff. It's a place in the city, down on Broome Street. They print a lot of newsletters and other stuff for the Bund. We have an in there, I think. I'll have to work out the details.' He paused and looked from Blake to Covitt and back. 'I don't know if it's union. Probably not. You see, the job will just be a cover. I mean, you'll have to work it, but what you'll really be doing is working for us, watching and learning.'

'Watching what? Learning what?'

'Watching, with any luck, our German friends, and learning what they're about.'

'Hey,' Blake said, pushing back from the table, 'I don't know. I don't want to have anything to do with those people. Besides, I don't know who they are or where they are. And I don't want to. Those guys don't – what's that phrase? – work and play well with others? They don't do that.'

'Yeah, maybe, but you know what they look like and they don't know what you look like,' Welker told him. 'Hell, they don't even know you exist.'

'And,' Blake said firmly, 'I'd just as soon keep it that way.'

'Look,' Welker said, 'if you spot one of them I don't want you to do anything about it. Nothing that could put you in any danger. As a matter of fact, nothing at all. Just tell me.'

Blake thought it over. 'I'm not sure I'd recognize any of them but the main guy,' he said. 'And the guy that searched the place and found my toothbrush. Well, I guess that's about half of them, isn't it? But what makes you think that one of them is going to walk into the print shop anyway?'

'Ah!' said Welker. 'That's the other part of the job. I want you to join the Bund.'

'The what?'

'The Amerikadeutscher Volksbund, here in the city.'

'Excuse me?'

'It's the German-American Bund.'

Blake looked at him. 'The German-American what?'

'Bund. It means like association, or group.'

'What do they do?'

'They hold rallies, they give out pamphlets, they get into fights, try to intimidate Jewish shopkeepers and anyone they think is a Communist – which includes Socialists, they can't seem to tell the difference. And like that. We think they're financed and controlled to some extent by the German government, but we can't prove it.'

'But I'm not German. My folks are Scots and, I think French, if you go back a bit.'

'That's OK. As long as you're not Jewish or Negro or any of the lesser races, you'll be OK. They like to think that everyone who's Caucasian is a German at heart.'

'The "lesser races"?'

'Indian, Mexican, Chinese, like that.'

Blake shook his head. 'Weird,' he said.

'What do you think about Jews?' Welker asked him.

Blake considered. 'I don't,' he said. 'except for my Uncle Max. I think about him.'

'You have a Jewish uncle?'

Blake nodded. 'He married my mother's sister Edith. Nice guy. Was a colonel in the war. Artillery, I think. Tells stories. Makes boats.'

Covitt looked up. 'Boats?'

'Yeah. Sailboats mostly. Models.' He held his hands about two feet apart. 'Like this. For kids. The Kleinshif Model Company, that's him.'

'His name is Kleinshif?'

'His name is Ardbaum. I don't know where he got Kleinshif.'

'It means little boat,' Welker said. 'In Yiddish.'

'Oh,' Blake said. He nodded. 'Makes sense.'

'I been to one of them Bund rallies,' Covitt said. 'On the job. In Madison Square Garden, it was. They had a big American flag and a big I don't know what flag, kind of looked like the Nazi swastika, but not quite. And a big banner, said America First. And a great big picture of George Washington and a picture of Hitler. And the guy that gave the speech went on about how they were all patriots, and how the Jews control all the banks, and he kept calling Roosevelt "President Rosenfeld", which he seemed to think was very clever.'

'I thought you said he was a Communist,' Blake said.

'The guy who was killed was a Communist,' Welker explained, 'but it figures that the guys who killed him were something else. Probably Nazis, is my guess. He thought they were Gestapo. Anyway, that's what I'm going to pay you to find out. If we get lucky.'

Covitt put his coffee down and leaned back in the chair. 'What you going to do if you find him?' he asked. 'You can't hold him for anything, you got no proof.'

'I can't hold him for anything anyway, even if I wanted to,' Welker told him. 'I'm not a cop.'

'So what you going to do?'

'Improvise,' Welker said.

NINE

Man is not what he thinks he is,
he is what he hides.

– André Malraux

'I have to go away,' Geoffrey announced, 'for a few weeks.'

'Hmmm?' Patricia asked.

They were in the living room of their Georgetown house,

Patricia perched on a corner of the couch, legs under her in that way women find comfortable and men can't manage, Geoffrey in his blue dressing gown standing on one leg like a stork, teacup in one hand and buttered scone in the other. It was an exercise he practiced regularly. Standing on one leg for extended periods of time improved the sense of balance and, Geoffrey claimed, developed character.

'To London,' Geoffrey explained, 'and thence, I believe, to Germany.'

'Ahh,' she said. 'One of your mysterious disappearances for the Foreign Office?'

'Possibly,' he said. 'Perhaps even more mysterious than usual.'

'Where in Germany?'

'Further deponent sayeth naught,' Geoffrey told her. 'Deponent, in this case Sir George, merely sayeth, "You speak German, don't you, old man?" When I replied in the affirmative, he sayeth further, "You were at Oxford with HRH, I believe?" It took me a second to realize he was speaking of the erstwhile Prince of Wales, whom we called, among other things, David. When I sorted it out, I admitted as much, and he sniffed and told me to pack for a brief trip back to Blighty. He said "Blighty", by the way, not I.'

'Why would he care that you went to Oxford with the Duke of Windsor?'

'He didn't say.'

'Were you close?'

'David and I? Fairly close, I suppose. Close enough to call him "David", which was his cognomen of choice among his circle. Most of the other chaps called him "your royal highness", or "Prince Edward", or, er, well, never mind that.' He reached over for the bell pull. Half a minute later Milton, the butler they had gleaned from the last Passport Control Officer, who had been suddenly called away, appeared in the door. 'Martinis, I think, please, Milton,' he said.

'Um,' Milton said, and retreated back into the pantry.

'Did you like him?' Patricia asked.

'The Duke? I did. He was not very full of himself, for all that he was at the time Prince of Wales.'

'Have you ever met his wife?'

'The infamous Wallis? Not I.'

'It is rather romantic, I think, giving up the throne and all.'

'Yes, many see it that way, apparently. Although you know he never wanted to be king.'

'Really?'

'Yes, rather. Had he his way he would have been the second son, or even the third.'

'A reverse on Mr Kipling: *The Man Who Would Not Be King*.'

'He is not temperamentally suited for it. The king is, in many ways, more confined than the worst of his subjects. Although he eats better.'

'And dresses better.'

'Yes, that.'

'And is confined in much larger and more elaborate quarters.'

'True.'

'And . . .'

'I grant you all the exceptions you can cite, and yet he is confined – in his choice of companions, in his travels, in his let us call it occupation, in his public utterances, in his avocations, particularly the illicit ones. You, for example, were you queen, would certainly have to give up your favorite, ah, hobby.'

She thought that over for a minute. 'I understand that Catherine the Great—'

'Yes, she did, or so I've read. But she lived in a day before radio, or even newspapers, when the public had no access to court gossip. And yet the stories got out.'

'Or we wouldn't know them.'

'Just so.'

Milton stalked silently back into the room with a pitcher of martinis and two iced glasses, which he set carefully on the end table.

'Thank you, Milton,' said Geoffrey. 'Is Garrett in his room?'

'I believe so, milord.'

'Would you ask him to come in here, please.'

'Um,' said Milton, as he retreated back through the pantry door.

Geoffrey poured and distributed the beverage. They each contemplated their glass as they sipped. 'Yes,' Geoffrey said after a minute, 'I thought so.'

'What?'

'It isn't the alcohol that matters, it's the ritual.'

'Sometimes,' Patricia said, 'it's the alcohol.'

Geoffrey stared into his glass for another minute, and then put it down. 'I must pack,' he said.

'When are you going?'

'Tomorrow.'

'That's awkward,' Patricia told him. 'The party at the Italian Embassy is the Saturday after next, and I probably shouldn't go without you. All that stuffy protocol stuff, you know. Like in the nursery rhyme, the husband takes the wife.'

Geoffrey turned to stare thoughtfully at his lovely wife. 'I am glad, you know,' he said.

'Really? What of?'

'That I took you. That I married you.'

'Well, I should think so. I'm the perfect – what is it? – beard. Who is going to believe that a man with as desirable a wife at home as you have is going to go chasing little boys?'

'Little boys? Now really!'

'You're right. I apologize. You definitely prefer young men. I think that somewhere in your heart – or perhaps another part of your anatomy – you've never left Oxford.'

'One never truly leaves Oxford,' Geoffrey said. 'One always carries pieces of it about with him, regardless of one's, ah, proclivities.'

'Well, you know,' she said, 'I'm ever so glad I took you. You have no idea how useful it is for a girl like me to have a jealous husband waiting at home.'

'I do my best,' he said. 'I practice glowering at the men I suspect you of having been with.' He took her hand. 'You know,' he said, 'in my way, I really do love you.'

'And I you,' she replied. She rose and kissed him gently on the cheek.

Geoffrey turned his gaze to the wall opposite. 'You're still determined to go ahead with your scheme?'

'Indeed. Of course, why not?'

'I don't like it,' he said. 'It's dangerous.'

'Pooh!' she said. 'A little flash, a bit of misdirection, and there you are. I used to do more daring things six days a week and lived to tell about it.'

'As assistant to the Great Mavini? Not a reasonable comparison.

This is actually physically dangerous, and besides, we have no idea whether it would turn out to be worthwhile.'

'The only way to find that out, my love, is to do it,' Patricia pointed out. 'It's not likely that the Italian Ambassador is going to post a notice, "The following most secret documents are in the safe in my study", is it?'

'Yes, but how likely is it that the Italian Ambassador will have any documents, most secret or otherwise, that would be worth the risk? Picture the headlines: "British Cultural Attaché Lord Geoffrey Saboy, Viscount McComb, Second Son of the Duke of Caneben, apprehended Rifling Safe of Italian Ambassador." It won't do, you know. They always pull out all one's titles when one has done something reprehensible. The pater would have a fit, and my brother—'

'I'll do the rifling, my dear,' she assured him.

'That's even worse, if that's possible,' Geoffrey pointed out. '"Wife of British Attaché", et cetera. And how do you know that the safe is even in the study?'

Patricia smiled sweetly up at her husband. 'This is one of those things that you really don't want to know.'

Geoffrey turned to stare down at her, his eyes half closed. 'I have found that it is precisely those things that one does not wish to know,' he told her, 'that one cannot do without knowing.'

'I shall write that down,' Patricia told him.

'Well?' he asked.

'Well, there I was in the embassy with Marcello at one in the morning – he was on night duty – and we had retired to the ambassador's study to engage in some, ah, healthy exercise . . .'

'Oh dear!' Geoffrey shifted his gaze from his wife to a painting across the room. It was of a waterfall. It had come with the house. He didn't like it.

Patricia smiled a wide and knowing smile. 'I knew I shouldn't put that image into your head, my dear. I do believe you're jealous. You'd like to have him for yourself.'

'Nonsense,' Geoffrey said firmly. 'He is pretty, but he's really not my type. But,' he added sternly, 'the image I have, the image I'd rather not have, is of you and Nero—'

'Marcello,' she interjected.

'Yes. Him. Of you and him *in flagranting* your *delictos* when the ambassador walks in. It would ruin Marcello, and it would ruin us. He would be sent back to Rome in disgrace, with his wife – I believe he's married?'

'Yes,' Patricia said.

'With his wife weeping and wailing. And I'd be the cuckolded husband. I'd have to disown you and go about showing my shock and outrage. Go about back in London, incidentally, as I'd certainly be recalled.'

'My,' Patricia said, 'you are fanciful. It's that wee bit of adventure, you know, that adds spice to the event.'

'You get the spice,' Geoffrey told her, 'all I'd get is the tummy ache.'

Garrett came in through the hall door. 'You wished to see me, my lord?'

Ex-Sergeant Randolph Garrett, a tall, broad-shouldered, self-contained Irishman with a malicious sense of whimsy, had been in Geoffrey's employ since shortly after the War. He occupied various positions in the Saboy household as the occasion demanded: valet, aide-de-camp, confidential agent, chauffeur, bodyguard. He was, as Patricia had put it to a friend, Geoffrey's man of hench.

'Yes,' Geoffrey told him. 'I'm going away for perhaps two weeks. London and thence, I believe, Germany.'

'Am I to accompany you?' Garrett asked.

'Not this time,' Geoffrey told him. 'I need you to stay here and look after things while I'm gone. There are a few, ah, professional matters that you'll need to stay on top of, or, possibly sharply to one side of. And it might be that you may have to, quietly and discreetly, bail her ladyship out of jail.'

'Of course, my lord.'

'Thank you,' Geoffrey said.

Garrett bowed slightly and retreated back through the door.

'Bail me out indeed!' Patricia said, her voice rich with feigned indignation.

'I'm surprised it hasn't come to that already,' Geoffrey told her. 'What with your nocturnal trysts.'

'Well, we didn't get caught, did we? And if we had done, the ambassador would, in all probability, express his shock and outrage, and then hush the thing up. Perhaps see to it that I'm no longer invited to embassy functions. Perhaps, indeed, send Marcello home, which would not please him. But then,' she added with a pixieish smile, 'perhaps he would think it had been worth it.'

'Then again,' Geoffrey said thoughtfully, 'the ambassador could have decided it was an attempt at espionage. Some sort of honey trap.'

'No!' Patricia said. 'I would never think of trying to blackmail poor Marcello. Anything I get from our, ah, association will be by theft and subterfuge, fair and square.'

'Very reassuring,' Geoffrey told her. 'Sex is your weapon of choice, but you never indulge in direct assault.'

'I leave direct assault to Marcello,' she said.

Geoffrey sighed. 'Well, you know what Kipling said.'

'Something about being a man, my son?'

'I was thinking of, "There are nine and sixty ways of constructing tribal lays, And every single one of them is right!"'

'Kipling?'

'Even so.'

She smiled. 'Who would have guessed?'

Geoffrey put his glass down and carefully folded himself into the straight-back chair opposite the couch. 'You have a crooked tooth,' he told her. 'Funny, I never noticed it before. I think it's a bicuspid. It's right next to the pointy one on the left, which I think is a cuspid.'

She got up and went over to the mirror on the wall next to the bedroom door. 'Your left or mine?' she asked. 'Top or bottom?'

'You mean you never noticed it either?' he asked. 'With all the time you spend staring at yourself in the mirror, I would have thought that surely . . . Your left, on the top.'

She contorted her mouth in an effort to get a better look at the tooth in question. 'I don't see it,' she said. 'I think you're having me on.'

'I would never,' he said.

She turned to look at him. 'England,' she said.

'Yes.'

'Germany,' she said.

'I believe so.'

'The Duke.'

He shrugged.

'Hmmm,' she said.

'This is, I believe, quite hush-hush,' he told her. 'They're sending a flying boat for me tomorrow morning. So don't go mentioning it to any of your women friends. And most especially not to any Italians you happen to be sleeping with.'

'Cross my heart,' she said, using her pinky to do just that. 'I'm a patriotic slut.'

TEN

America is permanently on the brink of revolution.
It will be a simple matter for me to produce
unrest and revolts in the United States . . .

– Adolf Hitler

G eorge Vanders was short and stout, with shoe-polish-black hair parted in the middle and slicked down on both sides of his pasty white face. He squinted up at Blake suspiciously from behind the counter. 'So where you from?'

'Pennsylvania. Philadelphia. Got here a few months ago to work at a print shop in Brooklyn, but it closed.'

'Yeah,' Vanders acknowledged. 'That's what Jersey said. There's a lot of that going around. You union?'

'Yeah.'

'Well I'm not. I pay thirty-five cents an hour, take it or leave it.'

Blake shrugged. 'I'll take it.'

Vanders thought this over. 'You a God-fearing Christian?' he demanded.

Blake took a step back. 'Of course,' he said. 'Who says I'm not?'

'You drink?'

'A couple of beers now and then,' Blake said.

'Dope?'

'Excuse me?'

'You a user? Reefers? Muggles? Mojo?'

'Do I take drugs? No.'

'I don't hold with that stuff. Clouds the mind, and if you haven't got a mind, what have you got?'

Blake leaned on the counter across from the little man. 'Look,' he said, 'you need a typesetter. I'm a typesetter, fifteen years' experience.'

'Fifteen years?'

'I started young. Do I have the job or not?'

Vanders considered. 'Jersey says you're OK,' he said. 'But I thought the last guy, Binchy, Bunchy, something like that, was OK too, but he turned out to be a boozer. You're not a boozer?'

'Swear to God, I'm not.'

'A lot of you guys turn out to be boozers. Maybe it's something in the ink. Well . . . tell you what . . .' He reached under the counter and produced a couple of pages of handwritten copy and passed it over to Blake. 'Can you read this?'

Blake looked at, and then turned on the desk lamp on the end of the counter and looked at it some more. Much of it was printed in large, irregular block letters 'Sort of,' he said.

'Go back to the box,' Vanders said, with a gesture toward the back of the shop. 'If you can set it – clean, mind you – in, let's say, twenty minutes the job's yours.'

'What are the specs?' Blake asked, ducking under the counter.

'Eight by ten, half-inch margin all around, ten-point Bodoni. Heads maybe eighteen point, bold if you think it works. Subheads whatever. You figure out the spacing and whatever else. It should scream out at the reader is what Gerard says, whatever that means.'

'Scream?'

'Like I said, you figure it out.'

Blake took a deep breath and stared at the copy. It was racist garbage. 'I'm on it,' he said.

Blake had spent two days preparing for this interview. He knew, as well as he could, what to say and what not to say. He knew the three big ideas that motivated the people he was going to meet: that Roosevelt was destroying America and maybe he was a Jew, that America First meant we had to stay out of Europe and let Germany march forward to its true destiny, and that It Was The Jews. Everything that was wrong with this country; the reason you couldn't get a job, the reason your sister's boyfriend was cheating on her, the reason the landlord was bugging you for three months' rent, the reason the Giants had lost the Series last year, it was the Unseen Hand of the Jews.

The All-American Printing Co., on Broome Street just off Elizabeth, a couple of blocks north of Manhattan's Chinatown, was what is known in the trade as a small jobs press. It had a treadle-operated letter press behind the counter and a small electric rotary press occupying the back room. It did mostly handbills, newsletters, and tickets, much of it propaganda for the German-American Bund and the American Nationalist Party. The handbill Blake had been given to set advertised a coming event, and was to be posted in store windows and passed out on street corners.

Sixteen minutes later he locked the form and ran off a test page on the letter press. He brought the page up to the front and handed it to Vanders. 'You ought to get a Linotype,' he said.

'Yeah, I ought,' Vanders agreed.

'It'll pay for itself. It's like ten – twenty – times faster than hand setting.'

'I'll tell the boss,' Vanders said.

'Who's the boss?' Blake asked.

'I am,' Vanders told him.

'Oh.'

'What d'ya think of it?' Vanders asked, waving the page up and down in front of him as though he were drying it off. 'What it says?'

Blake took the page back from him and read it, something you don't actually do when you're setting type.

M E E T I N G   M E E T I N G   M E E T I N G

AMERICAN NATIONALIST PARTY

FREE   FREE   FREE   FREE

INNISFAIL BALLROOM   200 East 56th St.

Tuesday, April 5, 1938 at 6 pm.

Open to all true patriotic Christian Americans.

Hear the Truth!!!

Come hear the message of Father Coughlin broadcast live from his studio in Michigan and listen to our own Frank Gerard and other speakers. Join with other God-fearing Christian Americans who think as you do. Hear what Henry Ford and Charles A. Lindbergh have to say about the Jews.

**Learn what we must do today to protect and defend
America and the White Race against job-stealing foreigners,
Communists and Jewish warmongers.**

**Learn why Henry Ford called the International Jew the
World's Foremost Problem. See how International Jewry
has been steadily undermining our country and gotten us
into every war from the Civil War to the World War. Hear
why the Jews want to get us involved in another European
War. Learn how the Jewish Cabal is aiding the Chinese in
their unprovoked attacks against the Japanese forces in
Manchukuo.**

**Are you willing to fight for your country? We will show
you how. We'll show you what must be done. We must
defend our borders. We must stop Roosevelt and his Jewish
bankers from getting us involved in another foreign war!
We must be ready!**

No Jews will be admitted

'Well?'

'I wouldn't go,' Blake said.

Vanders squinted and looked at him hard. This was not the right
answer. 'Whaddya mean, you wouldn't go?'

'It's telling me all kinds of stuff I already know, and promising
more of the same,' Blake told him. 'And even if I agree with it,
how many times do I have to hear it? It should talk about some
new stuff, so's I'd want to go and hear what it is.'

'Like what?'

Blake shrugged. 'I don't know. Maybe how Roosevelt is making
a secret deal with the Jewish bankers – better if you name one, say
Lowenstein – to sell Indiana to Canada.'

'Why Indiana?'

'Why not?'

'You got a thought.'

'And you should say "free beer" in the handout. That would get
people in.'

'Say, you know how much it costs just to rent the hall? We're having trouble making the nut as it is.'

'I didn't think of that. How do you pay for the hall?'

'We get some donations from the National org. Also we sell newspapers and magazines in the back of the room. Books too. *The Protocols of the Elders of Zion* and *The International Jew* are big sellers. Also the collected writings of Father Coughlin. We've got some copies of Lindbergh's *We* that usually sell pretty good, but we don't make so much off them 'cause we have to get them through a regular book distributor.'

'There's got to be some better way to come up with money,' Blake said.

'You think of one, I'll pass it on to Gerard,' Vanders said. 'You ever been to one of these meetings?'

Blake shook his head. 'They don't have nothing like that in Philadelphia.'

'Yeah? Well they will. We're going to be all over the country. This is a movement. Father Coughlin's big. Big.'

'Yeah,' Blake agreed. 'I've heard of him.'

'Course you have. We have him as a speaker whenever he's in New York. Come to this meeting, you'll see.'

'OK, I'll come,' Blake promised. 'Even if there's no free beer.'

'Free beer!' Vanders shook his head. 'Free beer!'

ELEVEN

Providence has ordained
that I should be the greatest liberator of humanity
– Adolf Hitler

HRH the Prince Edward, Duke of Windsor, quondam Edward VIII, by the Grace of God, King of Great Britain, Ireland, and of the British Dominions beyond the Seas, Defender of the Faith, Emperor of India – a heady mouthful to have given up when he abdicated to marry the woman he loved – was not happy. But then the happiness of an ex-king was not something that the

British Government fretted over. It had not been thought proper for him to live in England since he gave up the throne – no, that's not right, since he married the twice-divorced Wallis Simpson – so he married Wally in France and they had been living there in virtual exile for the past year.

And now here he was, leaving Wally in their villa in the Bois-de-Boulogne and sneaking across Europe in a private rail car for a clandestine rendezvous with the Chancellor of Germany at some bloody hunting lodge in the Black Forest. Secret meetings were not his thing. Still, he had allowed himself to be convinced. At the personal request of the Prime Minister. For the good of the realm. And perhaps it would improve his chances of being asked to return to England. That would please Wally, assuage her disappointment at marrying an ex-king instead of a king.

He was to pass on some advice to the Chancellor, a mere suggestion, on behalf of Mr Chamberlain and the British government. He was to convey to Herr Hitler that His Majesty's government felt that invading Austria would not be a good idea. Let the Austrians have a free and fair election, and if they vote for *Anschluss* – union with Germany – then so be it, Britain will draw the blinds over the Treaty of Saint Germain and the Versailles Treaty and France will almost certainly go along. If the vote goes against *Anschluss*, accept the opinion of the majority. Hitler's desire for a 'greater Germany' – a union of all German-speaking people – could be achieved by closer social and political ties, without actually merging the two countries. And His Majesty's government was willing to discuss the return of Germany's African colonies, lost after the Great War, except for South West Africa, which was now a part of South Africa. But perhaps a Portuguese colony or two could be thrown in. A carrot, HRH thought, but no perceptible stick.

Not that it would be of any use in the long – or if it came to that short – run, he thought. Hitler would do what he would do. But it would show those who needed to know that His Majesty's government had done their best. And it might give the Duke a bit more influence with H.M.'s Government when he pointed out the futility, the unwisdom – was that a word? – of arguing with Hitler over European affairs. After all, Germany was in the midst of Europe, Britain was safely isolated by twenty-one miles of water. And the fleet. What was it the First Lord of the Admiralty had told the peers when it looked as if Napoleon was preparing to invade a century ago? 'I do not say that they cannot come, my lords, I merely say that they cannot come by sea.'

Perhaps, after all, the trip would be of some use. It was true that Der Führer seemed to like him. Hadn't he tried to arrange a liaison between him and that German princess – what was her name? – while he was the unmarried Prince of Wales? Well, the Duke thought, he could but try.

He turned away from the observation window. 'You know,' he told the tall, slender man sitting across from him, 'just between us, I never wanted to be king at all.'

'So you have mentioned, your royal highness,' Lord Geoffrey replied.

'I couldn't tell Wally. She was so looking forward to being queen. But it wasn't to be.'

Geoffrey took a complex pipe tool from his jacket pocket, located the proper extension, and tamped down the new load of tobacco in his pipe. 'There is some advantage in being the second son,' he observed. 'The parents don't expect as much from one. Mine certainly didn't expect much from me. And now that Percy has produced a son and heir, I seem sufficiently insulated from the title.'

'They wouldn't let me near the front during the War, not when there was fighting going on,' said His Royal Highness petulantly. 'I mean, they gave me a uniform, kept me busy and all that, but kept me strictly away from the action. Supposing I was wounded or captured or killed, they said, it just wouldn't do.'

Geoffrey wondered who 'they' were, the King or the government. Or perhaps both. He decided not to ask. 'They had a point,' he said.

'What would it have mattered?' asked Windsor, not so much to Geoffrey as to the Universe at large. 'I have two brothers, I was expendable.'

The Duke fell silent, and Geoffrey pondered his part in the coming proceedings. While HRH and Der Führer were exchanging pleasantries and negotiating on the fate of Europe, Geoffrey was to locate a man he'd never met, in a place he didn't know, ascertain that the man was who he said he was, whoever that might be, arrange a clandestine meeting with the gentleman, find out what he wanted and what he had to offer for it, make sure that it wasn't a complex ruse of some sort, and negotiate whatever deal was to be had. All that while keeping HRH out of whatever trouble was to be had in the middle of the Black Forest.

'*And,*' he had asked, '*how am I to make sure that it isn't some sort of trick?*'

'*Use your best judgment.*'

Right. And just how . . .

'He's an artist, you know,' HRH said, interrupting Geoffrey's thoughts.

'Excuse me, your royal highness?'

'Stop calling me "highness", His Royal Highness said crossly. 'Call me David. When we're alone, of course.'

'Of course,' Geoffrey agreed. 'Sorry. What were you saying, David?'

'He's an artist, Herr Hitler. Did you know? Wanted to be a painter before the war.'

'I didn't know,' Geoffrey said.

'He was also something of a poet in his youth, apparently. One of his aides pressed a chapbook of his poetry on me when I met him last year.'

'Was any of it any good?' Geoffrey asked.

HRH shrugged. 'Couldn't tell you,' he said. 'German poetry always sounds to me as though someone was coughing at you in an aggressive manner. Have you ever read Shakespeare in German? "*Zu sein oder nicht zu sein, das ist die Frage!*" I mean, I ask you.'

'I always liked Rilke,' Geoffrey said.

'Now it's architecture,' HRH went on. 'He has great plans for the city of Berlin. I saw a model when we were here last year. Quite impressive.'

'I believe I saw a rendering of the plans in some popular magazine,' Geoffrey offered.

'Fellow named Speer or some such does the design for him, but Hitler knows what he wants and he means to have it.'

'That's sort of why we're here, isn't it?' Geoffrey asked. 'Because Herr Hitler knows what he wants and he means to have it.'

'How's that? Yes. Yes. I see what you mean.' HRH fell silent.

It was nine in the evening when they detrained at Karlsruhe, stepping out into a fine, chill mist that somehow seemed to cheer the Duke up. They were met by a discreet four-man guard detail, who discreetly marched to the door of the railcar, discreetly stood at attention, and discreetly gave the Nazi salute to greet the Duke's party. The other people getting off the train looked discreetly away; it seemed the wisest course in the New Germany. Besides, they couldn't make out enough details through the mist to have much of a story to tell.

A man in a gray overcoat came forward, clicked his heels, bowed, snapped back to attention, and introduced himself as Obersturm-bannführer Rabenvogel. 'Welcome to Deutschland, your royal highness,' he said in excellent English, 'In the name of Der Führer I greet you. I am to take you to the Schloss.' He led HRH, Lord Geoffrey, and His Royal Highness's manservant to the first two of the two Mercedes sedans that awaited them. The second, apparently, was for their guard detail. A small van then pulled up to accept their pile of luggage.

An hour and some minutes later the cars turned off the narrow dirt road they had been on for the last ten kilometers and drove between a matched pair of huge, hulking stone figures. 'The famed gryphons of Schloss Eichenholz,' Obersturmbannführer Rabenvogel told them. 'Perhaps eight hundreds of years old.'

'Impressive,' the Duke commented. 'They look almost new.'

'They were very weatherworn,' Rabenvogel, told him. 'But it was four years ago that they were recrafted and refaced, and now they once again look as new.'

'Ah!' said the Duke. 'The old is new again.'

They pulled up in front of a pair of massive doors of some very light wood that had grown gray over the centuries since it was hewn. A line of servants stretched out from the doors to greet them, the men in Lederhosen and the women in white aprons over gray smocks. Several SS officers were standing at ramrod attention to one side, and a covey of official greeters in mufti stood by the door. HRH emerged from the car, accepted the bowing of the assemblage and the handshakes of the greeters with the aplomb of a royal duke, and entered the Schloss, the rest of his entourage following behind.

The entrance hall was a vast rectangle, with a wide staircase on the left side at the far end. On the right were a series of heavy-looking oak doors, one triple-wide and the others normal size except for two that looked unusually narrow, or perhaps it was a trick of the perspective. High on the walls on both sides leading to the staircase were the heads of dead animals: stags with wide antlers, stags with short pointed antlers, wolves, wild boar, and what Geoffrey thought was an ibex, interspersed with banners bearing a variety of coats of arms. From the high ceiling, flanking the staircase, hung a pair of long red streamers with a large white swastika centered in each.

A man in a flawlessly pressed SS uniform covered with silver braid came scurrying into the entrance hall from one of the normal-size doors. 'My apologies, your royal highness,' he said, stopping in front of the Duke and giving the sort of forward nod that can pass as a bow if you're in uniform. 'I should have been outside to greet you. I was held up by a minor emergency among the staff. Obergruppenführer Rudolf Hess at your service, your royal highness. The Reichskanzler has been delayed by a previously scheduled meeting with the American aviator Charles Lindbergh and his wife. They are good friends of the Reich. He will be flying in first thing in the morning. There is a small airfield about two kilometers from here. Your rooms are ready. I assume you dined on the train, but if you would like a bite to eat before retiring, or perhaps a little schnapps?'

'A small glass of sherry, perhaps,' said the Duke. 'In my chambers. And then to bed. It is, what, a bit before eleven? A little early to retire, but it's been a long day.'

As they turned to head up the wide staircase a young man with the unmistakable look of a British civil servant from his just wide enough mustache to his impeccable gray suit and old school tie approached and bowed. 'Your royal highness, Lord Geoffrey,' he said. 'Neville Pekes of the Foreign Office at your service. I trust you had a safe and pleasant journey. I arrived last night. They sent me along from the Embassy in Berlin to, ah, offer any advice ah, should any questions arise, don't y'know.'

'I wondered,' HRH said.

'Your royal highness?'

'I wondered that the FO was sending me alone into the wilderness without someone holding my hand and providing, as it were, direction. They do not seem to be overly enamored of my judgment in Whitehall.'

'Oh no sir, ah, your royal highness,' Pekes said, looking honestly shocked. 'I am not instructed to direct your negotiations or interfere in any way, but only to give you such advice and explanations of the FO's current policies as you may request. As far as I have been informed, they have the utmost faith in you.'

'Well,' HRH said. 'Well. I am pleased to hear that. Pointless to send me over here and then tie my hands.'

'I assure your royal highness that as far as I'm concerned your hands are quite untied,' Pekes told him.

'Well, well. Very good then. Don't fancy I'll need you, but I appreciate the FO sending you along. Good night, Pekes, see you in the morning.'

'Good night, your royal highness.'

On the way up the wide staircase Geoffrey leaned over to HRH and murmured, 'A thought, David: Do not say anything to me or anyone in here that you wouldn't want your mother or Herr Hitler to hear. The walls are certainly impregnated with microphones.'

'Yes, yes,' said the Duke. 'Yes, of course.' And he looked thoughtful as he turned in to his room.

At about quarter past nine the next morning Geoffrey ambled downstairs to the breakfast room. HRH and Pekes were already there, the Duke sitting in royal solitude at one end of the long table and Pekes at the other end. The Duke's manservant, whose name, if Geoffrey remembered aright, was Anders, was presumably eating below stairs, or wherever the servants gathered in a German Schloss. There were no Germans in evidence except two servers who stood one on each side of the sideboard and made no attempt to serve. Geoffrey filled his plate with enough ham, eggs, sausage, and what turned out to be chicken livers to last until lunch, and then added a bit in case lunch should be delayed, and went to sit with HRH.

'How did you sleep, your royal highness?' he asked.

'The bed was too soft,' the Duke grumped, 'and there was no night light. I don't like sleeping in total darkness, I always feel as though someone's creeping up on me.'

'They wouldn't dare!' Geoffrey said.

'That's what I tell them,' the Duke said, with a small smile. 'But they creep up anyhow.'

'We'll get you a reading lamp for tonight,' Geoffrey told him.

'I don't like to read so much,' said HRH, 'but I do like a night light.'

*   *   *

Geoffrey was thoughtfully munching on the last bit of ham on his plate and wondering why ham from swine raised in the Black Forest was so much tastier than ham from swine raised in the Home Counties, and had progressed to musing on why calling the animals 'swine' rather than 'pigs' made it easier to contemplate slaughtering them for their hams, when a deep humming vibrated through the room, rapidly resolving into the sound of an airplane flying low overhead. Judging by the general excitement and the people they could see through the windows rushing about outside, it would seem that Der Führer had arrived. And indeed, some fifteen minutes later a black Mercedes pulled up and Adolf came striding through the front door, a short but commanding figure in the brown uniform of *Führer und Reichskanzler*, with a swastika armband. On his left breast pocket was the Iron Cross First Class he had been awarded as a corporal in the World War, above some SS badge Geoffrey couldn't identify. There was no further identification or insignia; Der Führer being Der Führer, none was needed. Six men came through the door behind Hitler, two in military uniform, two in SS black, and two in black leather greatcoats. Geoffrey looked them over thoughtfully. One of them, presumably, was the man he had come here to meet.

Several recognition signals had been proposed, including a hothouse flower *boutonnière*, but Lord Geoffrey absolutely refused to wear anything that would ruin the line of his bespoke gray suit. One does not wear a buttonhole except at an event, and meeting Adolf Hitler was not that sort of event. Finally an acceptable alternative had been found: Geoffrey would place a white handkerchief with a thin blue stitching around the edge in his breast pocket, folded so that it went straight across rather than in two peaks as was traditional. This was high fashion in bohemian circles this year, although the suit jackets of his bohemian friends were certainly not of merino wool, exquisitely tailored by a Savile Row clothier whose grandfather had suited their grandfathers. Noblesse, Geoffrey reflected, gets one a better-cut suit.

HRH, Pekes, Herr Hitler and his various aides closeted themselves in the ballroom almost immediately – the Chancellor could only spare one day for this meeting – and Geoffrey wandered about making himself as visible as possible to the uncloseted Germans without actually flapping his suit jacket at them. The ones he saw showed nothing more than a polite interest in his existence. After a while he went outside and wandered about the grounds, which stretched off into the distance until they merged with the surrounding trees. He got as far as the formal garden which went along one side of the house, separated by a thick hedge from the less formal gardens beyond, and found himself in a deep discussion with the head gardener about just how one managed a topiary giraffe. The talk was proving linguistically interesting because, although his German was excellent, it had not before ventured in the direction of horticulture. He wasn't even sure that he knew what the terms were in English.

One of the army officers who had arrived with Hitler strolled over to the far side of the garden. Casually he turned around to stare at something in the middle distance, possibly the cluster of fruit trees – apple, pear? – just coming into leaf on the other side of the bordering hedge. Geoffrey noted that the officer's hands were clasped behind his back, thumbs locked, with his two pinky fingers extended.

It took Geoffrey a moment to realize that this was the sign that he had been watching for. He had thought the extended pinky countersign would be done with the man's hands clasped in front, a 'this is the church and this is the steeple' sort of posture. Perhaps in an attitude of deep introspection. But here it was. Unless, of course, the man made a habit of standing like that and was not actually his contact. Men had ended up hanged by the neck as a result of such coincidences. Thus the necessary extra step of verbal confirmation. He thanked the gardener with a little bow and meandered toward the waiting Wehrmacht officer.

As he walked the well-graveled path, Geoffrey had a barely-suppressible impulse to begin the conversation with, 'Hello. I am a British spy. Perhaps you have some military secrets you'd like to sell?' but he restrained himself. Instead, when he reached the officer he peered over the hedge. 'Apple trees, I believe,' he said. 'Although it's hard to be sure until they more fully assume their foliage.'

The officer turned to look at him. 'Foliage?'

'Leaves and such,' Geoffrey explained.

'Ah. I wouldn't know. To me, I'm sorry to admit, a tree is a tree.'

'Your English is excellent,' Geoffrey said.

The officer nodded. 'I studied in your country for a while,' he said. 'And I admire your British authors. Jane Austen. Oscar Wilde.' There it was, confirmation. Geoffrey completed the ritual. 'I have always been fond of Heinrich Heine,' he said.

'Ah, so,' the officer said. 'He was, I believe, a Jew.'

'Really? I wouldn't know.'

The officer shrugged. 'No matter. Let us walk.'

They paced together in silence for a few minutes before the officer said, 'You are, I believe, Viscount Geoffrey Saboy?'

'We, ah, style it differently,' Geoffrey said. 'The title is Viscount McComb. The name is Lord Geoffrey Saboy. The "Lord" is because I am the younger son of a duke, as a viscount I would only rate a "sir". The traditions are very strict about such things. Ridiculous I know.'

'Not at all,' the officer told him. 'Or no more so than here. I, for example am Oberst Altgraf Wilhelm Sigismund Marie von und zu Schenkberg. There are a few other names I could attach, but I never do. What, precisely, I am to do with all these names I do not know. I doubt that they impress those who are not already impressed by my Prussian bearing and air of command.'

'How does one, ah, abbreviate that?' Geoffrey asked. 'How are you addressed?'

'Oberst Altgraf von Schenkberg if writing or being overly formal, as when General Keitel wishes to reprimand me. Usually Oberst Von Schenkberg or, for my good friends, Willy.'

They walked on.

'So,' Geoffrey said after a minute. 'It is a pleasure to meet you, Oberst Von Schenkberg. What am I doing here?'

Another minute of silence, and then Von Schenkberg asked, 'You are empowered to speak for your government?'

'For a small and relatively unimportant part of it,' Geoffrey said, 'and in this matter only.'

'But . . . if you agree to something, it will be carried out?'

Lord Geoffrey considered. 'It stands a good chance,' he said. 'I can guarantee that whatever we speak of will not go beyond those who need to know, and that your identity will be protected. But I'll have to hear what the *quo* is before I can assure you that my government can offer a *quid*. Or should that be the other way around?'

They stopped walking and Von Schenkberg looked casually

around. 'It is not suspicious in itself that we are talking,' he said. 'I am supposedly cultivating you and ascertaining your opinion of the new German Reich. But cultivation is a casual thing, and if we are seen to be too earnestly conversing it might cause one to wonder. And wonder is what we must avoid.'

'If you like,' Geoffrey offered, 'I can complain later to HRH about the damn Nazi trying to chat me up.'

'Yes,' Von Schenkberg said. 'You could do that. If you could manage it in his royal highness's bedroom it would be useful.'

Geoffrey raised an eyebrow. 'Ah!'

'Or the breakfast room. That would do.'

'Aha! My suspicions are correct.'

'Of course.'

They sat on a decoratively baroque wrought-iron bench facing a marble statue of a carefully draped woman carrying an ewer on her shoulder and looking pensively at a barn in the middle distance. 'What I offer you – your government – is information on the strategic thinking of the General Staff and the directives of the Supreme Leader.'

'The which?'

'Oh yes,' Von Schenkberg told him. 'Last month it was announced in an official broadcast – there was no discussion of this beforehand as far as I know – that all political, military, and economic authority is to be placed in the hands of the Supreme Leader. I have never heard Herr Hitler actually call himself that, but that's how the broadcast described him.'

'It certainly does simplify things, doesn't it?' Geoffrey asked. 'And "supreme leader" has a sort of ring to it. Who would want to argue with the Supreme Leader?'

'Not a good idea,' Von Schenkberg agreed. He took a small brush from his pocket and began dusting off his uniform. 'Permit me to say first, I don't want to suggest that I offer more than I can deliver. I am Intelligence Adjutant to the OKW, so I know many things, but much in this best of all possible lands of ours remains unpredictable, subject to instant change at the whim of Der Führer, and many high-level decisions do not leak down to a mere colonel. At least not until the operation is well underway.'

'OKW?' Geoffrey asked.

'Oberkommando der Wehrmacht,' von Schenkberg said. 'A

brand-new creation of our leader and those around him. It came into existence early last month to put all of the staffs of the various branches of the military under one leadership. You could think of it as a sort of general staff of general staffs.'

'Ah!' said Geoffrey. 'And you are an officer in this OKW?'

'If only it were that simple.' von Schenkberg said. 'I am the intelligence liaison between the OKH, or Oberkommando des Heeres, the regular army chiefs, and the OKW. Exactly what my function is, or will be, has yet to be determined. We are all on what you might call a shakedown cruise. Time will tell what sort of niche I can create for myself.'

'And you want to pass information on to us?'

'I do.'

'Why?'

'Well, there is something I require in return. But putting that aside, I believe that this, ah, regime, these people, are evil and can bring nothing but disaster to my homeland. I believe that this "Thousand Year Reich" will be lucky to last for ten years, and that every year it goes on will bring misery to tens of thousands of people. And anything I can do to shorten its existence is ultimately for the good of my country. Although I will admit many will not see it that way.'

Geoffrey leaned against the back of the bench and stared off at the mountains – well, tallish hills – in the distance, jutting up over the treetops like the bodies of sleeping giants; there a shoulder, over there a knee. This, he thought, was the test. Was Oberst Altgraf Wilhelm Sigismund Marie von und zu Schenkberg truly so disillusioned with the rulers of his beloved Germany that he would sell them out to the British Secret Service, or was this a ruse to set up a conduit for feeding disinformation to His Majesty's government? And how could he tell the difference? C would ask for his assessment. Nothing for it but to keep probing and look for inconsistencies. If this is a ruse, the story would be well rehearsed, but on the other hand, even if it was completely sincere, the Oberst would certainly have been giving a lot of thought over just what to say and how to say it. At any rate, Geoffrey thought, he'd listen and almost certainly accept the man's offer if it were not too unreasonable. After all, it would be someone else who had to determine whether Oberst von Schenkberg's information was true or false.

'So,' Geoffrey asked, 'what is it that you require in exchange for this cornucopia?'

'Nothing for myself. Hastening the demise of this *verdammte* regime will be sufficient. And besides, the odds of my living more than a year or two if I proceed with this, are, let us say, slight. The Gestapo is not bright, but it is thorough, and it suspects everyone.'

'So, then?'

'I would like you to get three people – a woman and two children – out of the country. Settle them, perhaps, in London. Or the United States of America perhaps.'

'Your wife?'

Von Schenkberg shook his head. 'Helena, the Altgräfin, should not – indeed cannot – be moved. She has, ah, an illness – a disease – and requires twenty-four-hour care. She never leaves her room, and attempting to move her from the chateau would be difficult and possibly fatal.'

'How awful,' Geoffrey said. 'What sort of disease?'

Von Schenkberg gave him a look of mingled anger and pain, or so Geoffrey saw it. 'I'm sorry to ask,' Geoffrey said, 'but my superiors will certainly ask me.'

'Yes, of course they will,' Von Schenkberg said. 'The illness is probably one called *encephalomyeliti disseminata*.'

'Probably?'

Von Schenkberg shrugged. 'The diagnosis varies from month to month, from doctor to doctor, but that seems to be the consensus at present.'

'Ah!' said Geoffrey.

'It is good that I am a wealthy man,' Von Schenkberg said. 'Were I not, Helena would certainly have died some years ago.'

There was a minute of silence, and then Von Schenkberg said, 'But enough of this, I am distressing you.'

'No,' Geoffrey said, 'not at all.'

'Well then, I am distressing me. No, the lady I am asking you to spirit out of Germany is Frau Madeleine Fauth. She is my mistress, and the two children are my own.'

'I see,' Geoffrey said.

'You are shocked?'

Geoffrey laughed. 'No, not at all. But I do wonder why you wish to deprive yourself of the lady's, ah, services.'

It was Von Schenkberg's turn to smile. 'You think, perhaps, that she has become inconvenient? That this is my way to rid myself of an embarrassment?'

'I actually had not thought of that, but now that you mention it . . .'

Von Schenkberg pulled out an oversized handkerchief and wiped his face. 'No,' he said. 'You see . . . It has become dangerous for her to stay here. Dangerous for her, and dangerous for me.'

Geoffrey raised an eyebrow.

'She is, you see, a Jewess.' He waited for Geoffrey to respond, and when Geoffrey said nothing he went on, 'It is increasingly difficult, and has become actually hazardous for Jews in the Third Reich. They are deprived of citizenship, of employment, of all civil rights. They are rounded up and placed in concentration camps merely for being Jewish. You did not know this? It is so. I love Frau Fauth deeply, but what of that? I can only protect her up to a point. Our relationship has been of necessity kept secret, and if it becomes known that she and I are – involved – then I can do nothing for either of us. A German officer does not socialize with a Jew, and he certainly does not take a Jewess as his mistress and have children with her. Add to it that I am an adulterer, and my career is over.'

'Then,' Geoffrey said, trying to think out the details of this, 'why don't you leave the country with Frau Fauth?'

Von Schenkberg shook his head. 'Would it were that simple. I cannot leave my wife, she would certainly die. And I love my wife very dearly. You think that strange?'

'I did not say so.'

'It was my wife who insisted that I get a, ah, companion when it became clear that we could no longer have relations. She did not want me going with random women and risking disease, or worse, scandal.'

'An unusual woman,' Geoffrey commented.

'Oh, yes.' Von Schenkberg breathed a very deep breath, and then another. 'Her only request was that she did not want to know who the woman was, and that it should not be one of our friends.'

'So you found Frau Fauth?'

'Yes. She was – is – a couturier with a studio in Berlin. Very fashionable clothes for very fashionable ladies. I met her at the opera, it is now eight years past. *Otello*. We fell to talking, and we arranged to see each other the next night. And by the end of that second night we were together.'

'And her husband?'

'A fiction. To her neighbors I am Herr Fauth, a traveling man who is only able to spend occasional days with her.' He smiled. 'This also could become troublesome; the Gestapo have developed a habit of stopping random people and asking to see their papers. I do have papers in the name of Fauth, for renting rooms and such, but they could not stand looking at by anyone who knows how to look at papers.'

Geoffrey nodded and thought for a moment. This, he decided, was real. 'When can Frau Fauth be ready to go?' he asked.

'Tomorrow,' Von Schenkberg told him. 'We have been preparing. But she has no passport, and her papers are marked "*Jude*", so she wouldn't get very far without many questions being asked.'

'We'll see what we can do,' Geoffrey said.

'I thought perhaps,' von Schenkberg said, 'that I could arrange to get her and the children to Spain on a Luftwaffe cargo flight. For money these things can be done. Then she would have to be taken across the Portuguese border and thence to Britain. Could this, perhaps, be arranged?'

'I think I can manage something better than that,' Geoffrey told him. 'Perhaps not tomorrow, but soon. Does she speak English?'

'Oh yes, and also French and Italian and Polish and Yiddish. All fluently. Or so she tells me, I am conversant only with French and English.'

'Can you get me a picture of her?'

'I have in my wallet . . .'

'A passport picture?'

'Oh. Yes. Certainly.'

'And the children?'

'Of course.'

'I will arrange to get her a UK passport, and she will leave here as a British tourist. If I remember correctly, mother and children can be on the same passport if the children are under sixteen.' He considered. 'I think "Mrs Mabel Bellant". It sounds too plain to be an alias. I had a governess named Mrs Bellant. And the children – of what sex are they?'

'One of each,' the Oberst said.

'Then Bruce and Gertrude, I think.'

'Gertrude is a very common name in Germany,' Von Schenkberg said. 'It sounds German to my ears.'

'So? All right then, Priscilla, called "Prissy". Bruce and Priscilla.'

'That will do. I can have the photo – a group photo yes? – by the end of the week.'

'Good. Someone will contact you, and we'll have her on a train within a few days of that. Perhaps traveling with a British consular official, if I can manage it.'

'You have my thanks,' Von Schenkberg said.

'I think you will earn their passage,' Geoffrey told him.

'Indeed,' Von Schenkberg said. He looked around. 'There is one other thing that I would request of you.'

'Ah?'

'And that is that as few people as possible know who I am. If it can be arranged, no one but you. Certainly no one but whomever you must turn my, ah, case over to, and I would greatly prefer it if you could keep it to yourself.'

'I understand.'

'There are people in your country – and in your government – who are perhaps too enamored of the National Socialist system to be trusted.'

'I'm afraid you're right.'

'Any agents of yours in Germany must not know even of my existence. Your MI6 obviously must know that you have a highly placed source here, but they should not be told who I am. My information must go through you.'

'I cannot keep coming back to Germany,' Geoffrey objected. 'It would be noticed.'

'We will arrange dead drops – I have three picked out already in Berlin – where your people can retrieve messages, but they must not know who left them. And the life span of these drops is, of necessity, limited. Also we will use post-forwarding services, perhaps classified ads in the London *Times*. I have set up an accommodation address in Berlin that cannot be traced back to me, but, again, I dare not use it too often. Perhaps a short-wave radio, if I can obtain one without attracting attention. The receiver is, of course, not a problem. But the transmitter – there is already a watch on purchasers of transmitters and *elektronenröhren* – the radio tubes needed to construct such an apparatus. If one can somehow be obtained the transmissions will have to be short and infrequent. Luckily the *Forschungsamt*, our radio location people, are not yet too efficient. Although I'm sure that will change.'

'I will adhere as closely to these suggestions as I can,' Geoffrey agreed. 'But I'm now stationed in the United States.'

'Even better!' Von Schenkberg said. 'I can get letters into the diplomatic bag to be mailed from our embassy in Washington. You can arrange an accommodation address?'

'I can. I will.'

'And we will set up a system of codewords to reassure each of us that the messages are truly coming from the other.'

'I'm pretty good at that sort of game,' Geoffrey told him.

'Good.'

'And perhaps I might be able to acquire a radio transmitter for you. I will look into it.'

'That would be useful.' The German officer turned to look Geoffrey in the eye. 'We must be careful and prudent or one of us will die sooner than necessary, and I fear that one will be me.'

'I will strive to assure that doesn't happen.'

Von Schenkberg reached into his pocket and pulled out a silver cigarette case and held it out for Geoffrey. 'Please,' he said. 'They are made specially for me of the same tobacco used by the Kaiser.'

'Ah!' Geoffrey said, taking one. 'Are you a secret monarchist?'

'No, no,' von Schenkberg assured him. 'We just both like the same tobacco.'

Geoffrey examined the engraved crest on the cover. 'Your coat of arms?' he asked.

'Indeed. Framed with a gryphon on the left and a unicorn on the right. Symbolizing, or so my father would have it, fidelity in war and peace. Or at times, truth and honor, or strength and nobility; it varied with the times. The shield with the four chevrons was awarded to my great-great- and so forth grandfather by Frederick the Second after the battle of Hohenfriedeberg or possibly the battle of Soor – they were only a few weeks apart. And our family motto, *honore supra omnes*, was chosen by the same relative at around the same time. They took great stock in such things.'

'And you don't?'

'Oh yes, I do. But I recognize how essentially silly they are.' He shrugged. 'Such are the contradictions of life.' He closed the case and thrust it back in his pocket. 'I have a few matters to impart to you before you leave,' he went on. 'The idiocy of Our Leader is about to begin, and I can give your government a few extra days to prepare a response. Not that there is anything useful they can do, I think.' He stood up. 'But I believe, perhaps, we have been long enough at this for now. Let us go our separate ways.'

Lord Geoffrey rose. 'Of course,' he said.

'We will continue this delightful conversation after dinner, *nicht wahr*? I will continue to convince you of the wonders of National Socialism, *nicht wahr*?'

'I can feel the urge to goose-step coming upon me,' Geoffrey said, 'but I will resist.'

TWELVE

[The Jews'] greatest danger to this country lies in their
large ownership and influence in our motion pictures,
our press, our radio, and our government.
– Charles A. Lindbergh

Frank Gerard, Gauleiter of New York, New Jersey, and Connecticut, and Senior Colonel in the German-American Bund for the Eastern United States north of Washington DC, was a short man with too much belly, prominent ears, and black hair parted in the middle, slicked back and pasted down on both sides. He was striding back and forth on the narrow dais in front of his audience of three hundred or so assembled members or potential members of the Bund, growling about the evils of Communism and Jewish bankers. It was a little after nine, the speeches had been going on for almost three hours, and the audience was getting impatient to hear from the Guest of Honor, Manny Dietz, who had just come back from having a discussion with Der Führer – Der real Führer Adolf himself in Germany, not one of your local führers. Dietz had just been spotted coming in through a side door when the fight broke out at the back of the rented ballroom.

Andrew Blake was at a table in the back hawking various anti-semitic and pro-Nazi books and pamphlets. It had been three weeks since he started his job at the print shop and he was, he thought, beginning to be accepted. No, better than accepted, he was becoming invisible, just the guy in back of the shop setting type and the guy at the back of the hall during meetings selling stuff and yelling, '*Yeah, right, you said it!*' at random moments during the harangue from whichever speaker and volunteering to clean up after the meeting.

A short, nondescript man in a gray overcoat and crushed gray fedora was standing in front of Blake's table looking over a copy of Father Caughlin's weekly newspaper *Social Justice*, a best-seller with this crowd, when, just as Gerard was winding down with: 'It is well known that all the major newspapers in New York are owned by Jews,' one of Gerard's black-shirted thugs came over and poked the man.

'You a Jew?' the Blackshirt asked.

'What?' The man looked up, startled.

'You heard me, Jew – what are you doing in here?'

'Excuse me,' the man said, flinching as the thug swished a clenched fist in front of his nose, 'but I'm not . . .'

From the dais Gerard stopped talking and stared out into the room. 'Look,' he cried suddenly, pointing toward the back, 'there's one of them now!'

Everyone turned to look.

The man, obviously confused, put down the newspaper and backed away from the table. 'Listen,' he said, 'I don't want any trouble. I'm a reporter from the *Weekly* . . .'

'*A snoop!*' the Blackshirt yelled. 'A kike snoop!'

The audience was starting to murmur and a few stood up to see what was happening, which caused yet others to join them in standing. The murmuring got louder.

The thug used both hands to push the reporter back, then took a step forward and shoved him again.

'Keep your hands off me,' the man shouted, knocking the offending arms aside. 'What the hell do you think—'

The thug shoved again, this time knocking the man into the edge of a table and upsetting a stack of Christian Front pamphlets. By now two other Blackshirts had joined in and they took turns pushing the man, who was starting to look thoroughly frightened, back and forth between them. Then one of them balled his fist and punched the man in the stomach and he grunted with the sudden pain and doubled over. Blake retreated to the far side of the table next to the wall and tried to decide whether he should just stay there quietly or dive under the table until the noise stopped. Once again he was watching someone get beat up and he could do nothing about it. First of all it would blow his cover and second, anyway, he was too scared to move.

Most of the audience stayed where they were, but some came out into the aisles and started stomping and yelling. What the words were Blake couldn't tell, but he imagined it must have been something like what the Romans yelled in the Colosseum when some early Christian was being fed to the lions. Blake closed his eyes. After a few minutes the yelling died down. Gerard had turned up the sound system and was barking soothing things into the microphone to the effect that they had to keep it quiet or they would not be able to rent the hall again. Blake opened his eyes. The reporter was lying on the floor, bloody and twisted. Two of the men were kicking him, but after a minute they stopped and picked him up and carried him out towards the stairs. Blake concentrated hard and succeeded in not throwing up.

It took about ten minutes for the excitement to calm down enough for the meeting to continue, but then Manny Dietz took the dais and told them about meeting Herr Hitler and how he could see New Hope for the World in Hitler's penetrating gaze and how the people of Germany idolized their Führer and about the New World Order that had come to Germany and would soon come to all Europe and, after that, who knows, and what it would mean.

The meeting finally broke up a little after eleven, but with putting the books and pamphlets back into the little cupboard and straightening the chairs and such, it was almost eleven thirty when Blake trotted down the two flights of wooden stairs and pushed through the door onto 56th Street. He decided to walk the mile and a half or so back to his furnished room on West 28th Street. There was a slight drizzle falling, but he had a raincoat and a hat and a bunch of stuff to think about.

He seemed to have struck just the right attitude toward the Bund and its enthusiasms. If he came on too strongly, too much the Roosevelt-hater and Jew-baiter, it could ring false. It would certainly sound false in his ears, and that somehow might show. But as just a working stiff who had never thought these things out before, and was slowly becoming convinced, he was winning the trust of Frank Gerard. A few days before, Gerard had spent most of an hour explaining to Blake how the Jewish bankers and newspaper owners and movie makers were controlling the country, and giving the good jobs to the spics and the niggers while Good Christian Americans couldn't feed their families.

The important thing, Gerard insisted, was not to let Roosevelt – who was secretly a Jew, real name Rosenfeld – get America involved in the affairs of Europe. It was time to let Germany take the lead in European affairs. As any honest analysis of history showed, the Aryan race was meant to lead, to perhaps control the destiny of the whole world. It was being held back by the mongrel races and by the Jews. Gerard got a fanatical gleam in his eye after talking about Aryan superiority for a few minutes, his face frozen into a grimace, and his voice too loud for the room. Blake had found that he could more easily tolerate his job if he pictured his associates as a pack of nasty children. But now, after watching that man get beat up, Blake wasn't sure that he could tolerate his job at all. He could see that these people needed watching, but he wasn't sure that he wanted to be the man to do it.

As he was crossing 38th Street Blake suddenly got the feeling he was being followed. He paused for a moment to stare in the window of a trimmings and buttons store while he sorted out where the feeling was coming from. Interesting buttons, who knew that . . . Footsteps. That was it. There were people coming and going, passing and falling behind, even at eleven thirty. This was, after all, New York. But one set of footsteps wasn't going faster or slower, it was keeping pace with him, moving when he moved, stopping when he stopped, perhaps half a block behind.

The drizzle was turning into a real rain now, and he pulled up his coat collar and started walking again, and again there were the footsteps following. The sound that he had barely been conscious of a few scant minutes ago: tap . . . tap . . . on the sidewalk behind

– never closer, never further – now filled his ears. It took a conscious effort not to turn around to see who it was, to walk back and challenge his stalker, or to just start running and see if his unseen follower kept up. But until he understood what was happening it would be better not to let on that he knew. So he walked and walked and thought it out. It couldn't be a mugging – you can't mug anyone from half a block behind. It must be one of his new friends. But why? Obviously to see where he was going. But where would he be going at quarter to midnight? Home? Did they want to see if he lived where he said he lived? Luckily he had moved into the boarding house, breakfast and dinner – no lunch – the day before he had applied for the job. Perhaps they thought it would be interesting to see if he didn't go home but went – where? To a police station? To a newspaper? What destination would most trouble them, and what would they do about it? Probably, he decided, something quick and drastic.

As he walked the footsteps kept pace, neither approaching nor retreating but staying about a half-block behind. He toyed with the idea of turning a corner and skulking until he could grab whoever it was, but a new thought surfaced: suppose it was one of the men from the warehouse? Suppose they had somehow figured out who he was? He involuntarily shuddered before reason gained control. How could they find him? Not only didn't they know who he was, they didn't even know he existed. *Yes, but what if . . .?*

He turned the corner on 28th Street and walked the half-block to his building and up the three steps to the front door. He passed through the outer door and into the vestibule and glanced down at the small table that held the mail for all the boarders. Nothing for him, but he expected nothing. He used his key and went through the inner door, and then flattened himself against the wall as it closed and turned out the hallway light. There was a thin glass panel to the side of the door and, with no light in the inner hallway, he could look through it and see without being seen.

The outer door pushed open about thirty seconds later, and a heavy-set man wearing an overcoat too warm for the weather and a newsboy hat too small for his head clomped in. He paused in the doorway looking around suspiciously, and Blake involuntarily ducked, even though he was sure the man couldn't see him through the glass.

The man turned to the little table and began rummaging through the mail, pausing to take out a small notebook and a stub of a pencil, and write, Blake guessed, the names of borders who had not yet picked up their mail. He was at this for about a minute when the street door opened and a woman, Mrs Gompher, second-floor front, if Blake remembered correctly, pushed her way in backwards, bumping through with her behind while furling the oversized umbrella she was carrying. She turned and saw the man.

He held up his hand just in time to cut off what would have been an impressive scream and a downward slash from a furled umbrella. 'Stop that!' he yelled. 'You crazy old biddy – what the goddam do you think you're doing?'

She paused in mid swing and glared at him. 'You don't live here!'

He stood up and put the notebook back in his pocket. 'Ah,' he said. 'I understand. I do apologize for having startled you, madam. I was visiting, ah, someone. I was just leaving.'

'Well,' Mrs Gompher said, pulling the umbrella back to her side, but still glaring suspiciously at him. 'Really. At this hour. Who were you visiting? It was that Willa What's-her-name wasn't it? I knew that girl . . .'

'I'd rather not say,' the man said. And then, as an afterthought, 'There are some things a gentleman does not talk about.'

'Humph!' she said, as he sidled past her.

Blake found that he was shaking. He took a deep breath and held it for a few seconds as he tiptoed to the staircase. After another deep breath – and another – he started to go upstairs before Mrs Gompher could open the inner door and find him standing there. God only knew what she'd think then.

'The voice,' Blake said. He was sitting across from Welker the next morning in a booth at the New Amsterdam Coffee Shop on 8th Avenue. 'I recognized the voice. As soon as he said one word I knew who he was. He was one of the men in the warehouse. Not the leader, one of the others.'

Welker shifter forward in his seat. 'You're sure?'

'Damn sure. I couldn't have told you that I would recognize his voice, but as soon as I heard it . . .'

Welker stared across at Blake with such intensity that after a few minutes Blake shifted uncomfortably and asked, 'What? What?'

'Oh, sorry,' Welker said, shaking his head slightly and blinking. 'I was just thinking.'

'Yeah?'

'This is great news.'

'Great for you, maybe, but I'm not going back.'

'Why not? Come on, he doesn't know who you are.'

'Yeah? Then why was he following me?'

'To find out where you live. To find out whom you associate with,' Welker said reasonably. 'Trust me, if he had any idea you were in that warehouse he wouldn't have bothered following you, he would have killed you before you got home.'

'Oh, great,' Blake said. 'That's very reassuring. Did I tell you they beat this guy up? Right in front of my table a bunch of Gerard's Blackshirts beat this guy up. They knocked him down and they kicked him and he was all bloody and he had to be carried out. And for nothing. They called him a Jew. Maybe he was and maybe he wasn't. But still they had no call to beat the crap out of him like that.'

'Yeah,' Welker said. 'They do that. On occasion. "The bleating of the kid excites the tiger."'

'How's that?'

'Kipling, but I think he probably got it from an earlier source. They beat on this guy to get the crowd riled up to make the evening more exciting, something they'd talk about.'

'Shit!' said Blake.

The waiter appeared in front of their table balancing plates of food precariously on his arms. 'Bacon and scrambled with home fries,' he said, sliding the plate in front of Blake. 'Buttered roll.' One step sideways. 'Poached with ham, home fries, whole wheat.' A step back. 'Ketchup and mustard on the table. You want anything else?'

'Like what?' Blake asked.

The waiter shrugged. 'Hot sauce, A1 sauce, mayonnaise, extra butter, a bowl of grits – we got grits.'

'Really?' Welker asked.

'Yeah. Not many joints in New York got grits, but we got grits.'

'Maybe next time,' Welker said.

'Yeah. I'll be back in a minute with refills on your coffee if you like. First one's on the house.' He retreated back to the counter.

'The question is,' Welker said, turning back to Blake, 'what do they have in mind?'

'What do you mean?'

'They may be grooming you for better things. They may be checking up on your background before they ask you to join the inner sanctum.'

'Which is what, exactly?'

Welker shook his head. 'I have no idea. We'll find out as we go along, I guess.'

'Easy for you to say,' Blake said. 'You want me to go back while you stay safe in – wherever it is you stay.'

'Many are called,' said Welker, 'but few are chosen.'

'What does that mean?'

'I have no idea. Besides, I'm going to some of these meetings myself now. Blending in. Observing. If you see me, you don't know me.'

'It's a deal,' Blake said.

THIRTEEN

It is demonstrable that things cannot be otherwise than they are; for as all things were created for an end, they must therefore have been created for the best end. Notice, for example, that the nose is shaped for spectacles, therefore we wear spectacles.

– *Voltaire,* Candide

'All in all, I was quite favorably impressed with Herr Hitler,' HRH said, sitting forward in his seat as the train car jounced over some connecting points, and staring contemplatively at the cigar he was seriously thinking of lighting.

'Were you?' Geoffrey asked.

'He's very, you know, forceful. Says what's on his mind.'

'Yes,' Geoffrey said, 'and why not? I imagine one gets in the habit of being forceful when no one dares disagree.'

'Um,' said the Duke. And then, after a moment: 'He recommended a play that just opened in London. He saw the German production and says it's quite funny. *Tovarich*. It's a farce about a pair of Russian *émigrés* in Paris.'

'I've seen it,' Geoffrey told him. 'It's very amusing.'

'He assured me that the author was not Jewish. That seemed important to him.'

'One wouldn't want to be caught enjoying something written by a Jew,' Geoffrey said, nodding. 'Not if one were Herr Hitler.'

HRH seemed deep in his own thoughts for a minute. 'He seems to like me,' he said finally.

'I should think so,' Geoffrey said. 'You're a likable enough chap, handsome as the devil, a boon companion, good conversationalist. You have the aura of royalty, and yet are approachable. And you're an intensely romantic figure – although I'd suppose that last doesn't influence Herr Hitler a whole lot.'

HRH leaned back and stared across the table at Geoffrey. 'A romantic figure? What the deuce do you mean?'

'Come on!' Geoffrey said. He stood up and fished around in his jacket pocket for his pipe. 'Surely you realize: the King of England who gave up his throne to marry the woman he loves? What on earth could be more romantic than that? Young girls must swoon at the story. I'll wager that in a few years someone will write an opera about it. With the names changed, of course.'

'Oh,' said HRH. 'That.'

'Yes, your royal highness,' Geoffrey said, 'that.'

The Duke was silent for a minute, staring out the window. There was no moon and only the slightest changes in shades of black showed through the window, but still he stared, shielding his face with his right hand to see beyond his own reflection in the glass. After a minute he lit his cigar and turned to Geoffrey. 'I may have actually made some headway in the matter of the plebiscite,' he said. 'Hitler agreed that it might be wise to let the voting go on, since the Austrian people will certainly choose to unite with Germany.'

'He's not so sure of it as all that,' Geoffrey told him.

'Excuse me?'

Geoffrey looked up at the ceiling of the car, noting how the electric lamps had been made to resemble gas lights. *Things are seldom*, he thought, *what they seem*. He took a deep breath. 'The code name is "Otto".'

'Code name for what?'

'The invasion of Austria,' he told HRH. 'It is to begin the day after tomorrow. Troops are already massing at the border. Hitler expects it to be a bloodless coup, just several divisions marching in to the cheers of friendly crowds. His agents are already assembling the friendly crowds. The Austrians living around the German border are mostly pro-German, but those further away not so much. He doesn't know what would happen if he actually let the people vote, and he doesn't want to take the chance of being rejected. It would be a lot harder to justify invading if the Austrian people had said they don't want him.'

HRH carefully balanced his cigar on the small ashtray to the right of his chair. 'Really?' he asked.

'Really,' Geoffrey affirmed. 'And I understand that the plans for the affair were drawn up by that over-polite gentleman in the over-starched SS uniform that was hovering around Der Führer the whole time.'

'Deputy Hess?'

'Him.'

'How on earth,' HRH asked, the astonishment showing in his voice, 'could you know all that?'

'Oh,' Geoffrey said, waving his hand vaguely about. 'I've had my ear to the grindstone. One hears things.'

'Damn!' the Duke said with feeling. 'Bloody hell! You're sure about this?'

'I'm reasonably sure that that's the intention as of yesterday. Hitler has changed his mind several times, apparently, but my informant thinks that this time he's going through with it.'

'He lied to me!' the Duke said, sounding indignant.

'I imagine he does a lot of that,' Geoffrey said.

There was a jerking and a hissing and Geoffrey was thrown against a partition, almost losing his balance, but he managed to push himself up without actually falling as the train slowly and agonizingly came to a screeching stop along a section of track that curved sharply to the left, the engine momentarily blanketing the cars behind with a thick cloud of white smoke. A line of military trucks had pulled up along a road paralleling the track, and within seconds searchlights mounted on the back of the trucks were bathing the train cars in light. Geoffrey and HRH watched through the window as a flock of troops in black SS uniforms jumped from the trucks and ran out to surround the train with machine pistols at ready. A few seconds later a bevy of officers, along with two men in black-leather greatcoats, exited a pair of staff cars and climbed aboard the train about two cars down from HRH's private car.

'What the devil?' HRH unlatched the window and pulled it up. 'What are you fellows doing out there?' he yelled. 'Why on earth did you stop the train?' Then, at the uncomprehending looks, he switched to German: '*Was werden Sie tun, meine Herren? Warum haben Sie den Zug angehalten?*'

The closest SS guard looked up at the window and shook his weapon. '*Schließen Sie das Fenster,*' he yelled. '*Bleiben im Zug! Das geht dich nichts an!*'

The Duke pulled his head in and turned to Geoffrey. 'None of my business, is it?' he groused. 'Doesn't he know who I am?'

'Hopefully,' Geoffrey said, 'he doesn't.'

'Oh,' said HRH. 'Right.' He closed the window and sat down.

The conductor came knocking into the car a minute later, looking extremely nervous, bowed twice, and stuttered, 'Your royal h-h-highness—' He started on a third bow, but Geoffrey interrupted.

'What is it, my man? What's the problem?'

The conductor straightened up, standing at a close approximation of attention. 'Your royal highness will excuse, I am sure, this unfortunate interlude,' he said. 'I have informed the *Oberst* of who you are and, with hope, they will not be incommoding you. We shall be recommencing our journey shortly.'

'What's the holdup? Geoffrey asked.

'The . . . Oh yes . . . They are searching for some people. They have information that . . . it seems that some people may have boarded the train without proper identification. Forged papers, perhaps. I am only guessing, you understand, I don't know.' He wrung his hands together and then became aware of what he was doing and dropped them to his sides, where his fingers twitched nervously. 'I really don't know. How could I know?'

'What an awful fuss for a couple of stowaways,' the Duke commented.

'Indeed,' Geoffrey agreed.

'I believe they are *Juden* – Jews,' the conductor explained. 'And it might be that they are trying to leave the Reich with some belongings that should have been confiscated.'

'Belongings?'

'Yes, your royal highness; perhaps money, perhaps jewelry. It is forbidden for the Jews to leave with such things.'

'They can't leave with their own belongings?'

'Such is what I believe,' the conductor said. 'Again I apologize for the inconvenience. We should recommence our journey shortly. I believe the steward has your dinner selections, yes? The stewardess is here to commence setting the table and arrange for the meal, which will be brought in promptly.' He made a gesturing motion behind him and a young woman in a version of the blue uniform of the railroad staff came in and curtsied to them.

'I shall set the table up here?' she asked in English.

'Yes, certainly,' said the Duke, and the stewardess began pulling table linens from the cupboard and set about clearing and setting the dining table.

The conductor shifted his gaze nervously between the woman and the Duke. 'All is good, yes? Now I shall return to my duties.' He bowed and retreated back to the luggage car, which was positioned between HRH's car and the main body of the train.

Less than a minute later he was back, barely ahead of a German officer, who strode through the connecting door, snapped to attention in front of HRH, and gave the Nazi salute, clicking his heels together smartly twice. 'You will forgive this intrusion, Excellency,' he said. 'But I must examine the whole train, you see. Is there anyone else in the car with you?'

HRH muttered an uncomplimentary epithet and then turned. 'Anders!'

His man appeared from somewhere to the rear of the car, immaculate in his morning suit. The only one who dressed better than a British gentleman, Geoffrey reflected, was his manservant. 'Your royal highness?'

'You have anyone hiding back there with you?' HRH asked.

'No, sir.' Anders replied, showing no surprise at the question. 'I am quite alone.'

The Duke turned to the officer. 'There you have it,' he said.

The officer clicked his heels together, wheeled, and marched back out of the car, followed by the conductor.

'Damn nuisance,' the Duke muttered, going back to the window. 'And there's something going on out there.'

Geoffrey peered out the window.

'Off to the right,' HRH said, pointing.

'Oh. Yes.'

At the car two ahead of theirs a cluster of troopers were clambering about the undercarriage, along with much shouting and waving of flashlights. A young boy, perhaps fourteen or fifteen, in a neat gray suit and a newsboy cap, was pushed through a door a few cars up, and he stumbled down the steps, righted himself, and stood there looking confused. Somebody barked an instruction at him and he looked around, even more confused. The instruction was repeated, and he nodded and sat down on the grass verge along the track, compliant but confused.

A few moments later the flashlights had all focused on the far end of the car, and a spotlight on one of the trucks swiveled, its beam flooding the area in a harsh white light. A little man in a dark-colored business suit, perhaps gray, perhaps blue, was pulled out from under the car by an SS officer. The silver piping on the officer's uniform gleamed in the spotlight, creating weird tracings as he moved. Geoffrey noticed that the little man's suit jacket had four buttons up the front, all neatly buttoned from the collar down. It is, he thought, the sort of thing you notice when you don't want to notice anything else. The little man tried to keep his hands in the air, but his progress was a constant stumble as the officer prodded him along with the Nazi version of what the British call a swagger stick, and his hands dropped to catch himself and then jerked back up at the officer's barked command.

Two troopers crawled under the car and extracted a large leather suitcase, its brass fittings gleaming in the glare of the spotlights. At the officer's command, they laid it on the ground and forced the lid open, snapping the lock with some small instrument that Geoffrey couldn't make out. The officer stared down at it for a moment and then reached in and began pulling out its contents, handful after handful. Clothing, framed pictures, toiletries, all were flung onto the ground. He continued until the suitcase was empty, and then he drew his SS officer's dagger and slashed at the lining. Whatever he expected to find wasn't there. He turned and gesticulated some undecipherable waving of the arms and yelled some threats Geoffrey couldn't make out at the man, who cowered away from the officer, hands clutched together over his head.

The officer stamped his foot – Geoffrey had never seen anyone actually stamp his foot before except in a stage production of *Macbeth*, and then he thought it was overacting. But the officer seemed to be working himself into a frenzy over what the poor man in front of him either had or didn't have. He unholstered his automatic pistol and waved it about, while continuing to yell commands at his prisoner. Then, perhaps realizing that this was accomplishing nothing, he paused, pointed the automatic at the man, and barked an order. The man backed up two steps. The officer repeated his order. The man knelt down and began taking off his clothes; unbuttoning the four buttons of his jacket and removing it, following with vest, tie, shirt, shoes, pants . . . As each item was removed the officer grabbed it and felt it, squeezing it all over as though he were wringing it out after a wash. He wrenched the heels off the shoes, and then threw heels and shoes aside in disgust. The man stopped at his underwear, but at a barked command from the officer pulled it off with the rest. He stood there clad only in his socks while the officer continued his examination of the clothes. Then, with an excess of poking and prodding with the officer's stick, he forced the man to turn around and bend over and hold his ankles.

'That's a bit much, don't you think?' said HRH, peering through a corner of the window.

'This whole episode is a bit much,' Geoffrey agreed from his corner. There was a hypnotic quality to the scene that stopped him from looking away, although he really didn't – really and truly did not – want to see what was happening. He noticed that the stewardess was no longer setting the table, but had dropped the tablecloth and a cluster of napkins and was staring out the window across from her, her hand to her mouth and her eyes fixed in horror. He thought of going to her, but realized that anything he might do to reassure her might have the opposite effect, so he stayed where he was.

The officer called one of his men over and gave him instructions accompanied by some odd gesticulations. The trooper considered the situation and then wrapped a handkerchief around his middle finger and thrust it up the prisoner's rectum, an action that pleased neither of them. After a few seconds the trooper withdrew the finger and carefully pulled the handkerchief off his finger and cast it on the ground by the side of the road. He shrugged and stepped aside.

The officer appeared deep in thought for some moments, and then he gesticulated some more and barked a few commands, and the little man began to put his clothes back on, underwear, pants, shirt . . . He attempted to fasten the heels back on the shoes with no success, but he put the shoes on anyway. The SS troops were returning to their trucks while this was going on, leaving only the officer and his prisoner standing by the side of the train. As the little man was doing the top button of his jacket the officer said something, but the man just stared at him blankly. The officer repeated whatever he had said, and gestured with his gun.

The man backed away several steps, still staring at the officer.

The officer gestured with both hands this time – a go away, get out of here gesture – and holstered his pistol.

The man took two tentative steps away, made a tentative gesture toward his suitcase and then just turned and started walking away slowly, and then more rapidly, to the right, away from the train and the trucks. After a few seconds he began running.

The officer drew his pistol. '*Halt!*' he yelled. '*Halt!*' And then he took careful aim and fired, once, twice, three times, at the running man. The man threw his arms in the air, and crumpled to the ground.

The officer holstered his gun and walked calmly to the staff car. The searchlights on the trucks blinked out.

The two Englishmen looked at each other. Neither of them spoke.

FOURTEEN

With pride we see that one man remains beyond all criticism, that is the Führer. This is because everyone feels and knows: he is always right, and he will always be right.
– Rudolf Hess, 1934

Lord Geoffrey and HRH stood, a motionless tableau of disbelief, and watched through the window as two troopers grabbed the fallen man by the arms, hauled him over to their truck, heaved him into the back, and climbed up after him. Two other troopers came for the frightened and bewildered boy they had pulled off the train, who was staring at the Nazi officer, his mouth open, his face frozen in shock. They yanked him to his feet and prodded him forward, pushing him onto another truck. At a barked command the other troopers stiffened to attention, did a sharp right turn, and fell out to climb aboard their trucks, which promptly coughed their engines into life and commenced pulling away. The officer stood for a minute, his hands on his hips, surveying the scene before kicking the broken suitcase twice and then clambering in to his staff car, which followed after the departing trucks.

'The new Germany,' Geoffrey said softly.

'Surely Herr Hitler—' the Duke began.

'Surely,' Geoffrey agreed, 'Herr Hitler.'

The young stewardess had folded to the floor of the car by the table and was sitting there, her hands covering her face, her body shaking with silent sobs. Geoffrey went over and squatted beside her. 'That was a horrible thing to watch,' he said. 'I'm sorry. Who is that man? How do you know him?'

She looked up at him between her fingers. 'What?' She said. 'How did you . . . What do you mean?'

'I'm a friend, if you'll let me,' he told her. 'Is he your husband?'

She took a deep breath and then another. 'My father,' she said. 'I am only sixteen.'

'What?' HRH stalked over and peered down at her. 'Look here . . . Only sixteen . . . And you're not . . . You don't . . .' He turned to Geoffrey. 'You mean she's not . . .'

Geoffrey looked up. 'That's right, your royal highness. She doesn't work for the railroad. She came in here to hide. The conductor, obviously, is in on it.'

'Ah!' said HRH. 'But that could have caused trouble – I mean, for us, couldn't it?'

'I doubt it, your royal highness,' Geoffrey told him. 'After all, you are a Royal Personage and a Friend of the Führer. The worst that would happen is that they would pull her out of here while we protested that she hadn't served us our dinner yet.'

HRH thought that over for a minute and then asked, 'How did you know? That this girl was not, ah, what she seemed, I mean?'

'Observation,' Geoffrey told him. 'It's a curse, I can't help it. I knew the moment she came into the car, but I wasn't going to say anything. And then . . . this.'

The trained jerked to a start and slowly began pulling away from the scene.

The girl lowered her hands and lifted her face and turned to examine HRH and then Geoffrey. 'Are you going to turn me over to the Gestapo?' she asked.

'Is that who they were?' Geoffrey asked. 'They're gone, so you're safe for the moment.'

'The special border police,' the girl explained. 'A branch of the Gestapo. And they've certainly left someone on the train to go through the cars, one by one, until they find me.'

'We'll think of something,' Geoffrey told her. 'This handsome gentleman,' he added waving a hand toward HRH, 'is a Very Important Personage, and quite brave if it comes to that. And between us I believe we're capable of bamboozling any number of border guards.'

'Just what was it that you observed about this young lady?' the Duke asked Geoffrey. 'Honestly, how did you know?'

'To start with,' Geoffrey told him, 'the Chemins de fer de l'Est does not employ lady stewards.'

'Ah?'

'And,' he added, waving a hand at the stewardess, 'the young lady's uniform is a creation. The jacket is several sizes too big for her, and the skirt is almost but not quite the right color blue.' He turned back to the girl. 'Just why were they so interested in your father? And why are they looking for you?'

'We are Jews,' she said. 'That is enough.'

Geoffrey took the girl's hand and raised her from the floor, resettling her in a nearby chair. She did not resist. Indeed, she did not seem to notice the change. 'I know things are bad for Jews in Germany right now,' he said, 'closing businesses, firing teachers, doctors, lawyers, setting up work camps. But just shooting someone?'

'They come to your house and give orders,' she said simply. 'Wear a *Magen David* on your coat. Take one suitcase of only clothing and leave; we are giving your flat to an Aryan family. We are giving your shop to a party member. If you resist you will be shot. If you don't resist, they will take all your belongings, valuable or not, and send you to a camp. Where you will be treated like excrement and worked to death. Or shot.'

'Just for being a Jew?' HRH asked.

She nodded. 'Or a Roma – a Gypsy – or a priest, or a Communist, or a Jehovah's Witness, I think they're called, or an Unfit Person. They also do not like black persons, but there are not so many of them here. But mostly if you're a Jew.'

'An unfit person?' asked Geoffrey.

She nodded. 'Feeble-minded, deformed from birth, incurably ill. I understand it's also used to eliminate the – what would you say? – politically undesirable.'

'Well!' said HRH.

'Who was that boy they took off the train with your father?' Geoffrey asked.

'I don't know him,' the girl said. Then her lips formed a thoughtful O, and her eyes got wide and she stifled a gasp or a sob. 'Poor boy,' she said. 'Poor boy. They think he's me.'

'Why would they . . .?'

'Because I was dressed like a boy when I got on the train. Then Anton told us that they were looking for a father and son, so I changed into my skirt and he loaned me a jacket and I came in here.'

'Anton?'

'The conductor.'

'Ah! How do you suppose they knew – to look for a boy, I mean?'

She took a white linen napkin from the table and dried her eyes. She waited a few seconds and then dried them again, and crumpled the napkin in her lap. 'Someone must have informed on us,' she told them. 'The Gestapo pays a reward for turning in hiding Jews or escaping Jews or, I suppose, any other sort of Jews.'

She turned to the table and put her head down. 'He was such a kind man, my father,' she said. 'A thoughtful man, an intelligent man. He read – everything. He talked about everything. He was wise. He was a conductor.'

'For the railroad?' HRH asked.

She raised her head. 'For the Munich Symphony Orchestra. The musicians loved him. This is a rare thing, for a conductor to be loved by his musicians. Respected, yes perhaps. But loved? I am given to understand that this is very rare. But they—' She put her head back down, cradling it in her arms, and said nothing. She did not even appear to be crying any longer.

Geoffrey and HRH hovered over her in silence.

'What am I to do?' she asked whatever gods there be, her head still buried in her arms. 'Where am I to go?' And then, a few seconds later she began softly sobbing.

HRH retreated a few steps and sat down on one of the overstuffed leather chairs that the railroad believed suitable for royalty. He had encountered crying women before, but not in similar circumstances, and couldn't think of anything to say.

'You have no one?' Geoffrey asked.

She raised her head and stared at – something. 'I have an uncle in the United States of America,' she said. 'In Brooklyn, New York. Flatbush? My father and he had an argument when he left four years ago. Uncle Moishe tried to talk my father into going with him. "There are symphony orchestras in America," he said. "Fine ones," but my father said no, we are Germans and we will stay. And so . . . But I'm sure my uncle would take me in.'

'Well then—'

'But I have no money and no papers. I was on my father's passport and he . . . he . . .' She finally broke down completely, cradled her head in her hands, and began sobbing uncontrollably.

HRH looked alarmed, but Geoffrey told him, 'Let her cry for now. It is what we would do in the same circumstances.' He smiled after a few seconds and added, 'If we weren't raised British.'

'Look here, girl,' HRH said after a minute. 'We can lend you – give you some money. Enough to get you to America.'

'You would do that? I cannot – I would not—'

'Of course you would,' Geoffrey told her. 'And you shall.'

'But I have no papers. If I am not caught at the border, I will be held in France in a camp or sent back. They do not welcome refugees in France. They have their own troubles.'

Geoffrey looked her over critically for a minute, and then asked, 'If you don't mind, what is your name?'

'Sophie,' she told him. 'Sophie Hertzel.'

'And a lovely name it is,' Geoffrey said. 'Well, Miss Hertzel, it would seem that you have come to the only railroad car in Europe that can help you with this, and I think we will. You'll do.'

'Do what?' she asked.

'Come to England with me,' he told her. 'And thence, probably to the United States of Brooklyn.'

'I will?'

'As my wife,' he explained. 'Patricia is on my passport, and we have diplomatic whosis and are here on a secret, sort of, diplomatic mission. The various governmental busybodies will not look at us closely, if at all. They didn't as we came in and they won't as we leave.'

'Oh,' she said.

'We will have to get you made up to look more like an elegant lady. My wife is an elegant lady. And perhaps add a few years to your apparent age. I fancy that Anton can help us with that. Procuring makeup and garments and the like from some of the other passengers.'

The Duke began pacing back and forth down the narrow aisle. 'I'm not sure I like this,' he said.

'You know nothing about it,' Geoffrey told him.

'I don't?'

'You don't.'

'Oh,' he said. 'All right then.'

FIFTEEN

Who is in charge of the clattering train?
The axles creak and the couplings strain,
and the pace is hot and the points are near,
and sleep hath deadened the driver's ear,
and the signals flash through the night in vain,
for death *is in charge of the clattering train*
          – Edwin J. Milliken, 'The Clattering Train'
          (as abbreviated by Winston Churchill)

'America first,' Gauleiter Gerard bellowed from the tiny stage, fist raised, the holy fire of his Mission burning in his eyes, 'America last, and America always!'

'America first, America last, and America always!' came back the ragged return echo from the six hundred or so people in the phalanx of chairs facing the speaker.

They were gathered in the large meeting room on the ground floor of the Hotel Vandamm on 85th and Third and had spent most of the past hour listening to the rebroadcast of a rousing radio program on 'Social Justice' from Father Coughlin, the 'Little Flower Radio Priest', transcribed from his Royal Oak, Michigan studio. As always Coughlin had not been shy in blaming the rise of Communism, the global economic crisis, and the loose morals of today's youth on 'Jewish bankers'.

A skinny man with oversized glasses came up to the edge of the small stage and signaled something to Gerard by balling his right hand into a fist and beating it with his left. Gerard nodded and turned to face his audience. 'And now the moment we've been waiting for,' he told them. 'I've just been informed that Bundesführer Kuhn has arrived and will be with us shortly.'

Blake, who was sitting as far back in the room as he could manage without being out the door, wondered idly why an organization whose motto was 'America First' would give its leader the title of *Bundesführer.* Or, for that matter, why Gerard was a *Gauleiter.* Weren't there enough American titles to go around?

After a couple of minutes of restless murmuring among the audience, Fritz Kuhn, a short, bowlegged man with a massive rump and a thick neck, appeared at the rear door in a brown stormtrooper's uniform with a black Sam Browne belt, unadorned with any insignia. He swaggered up the aisle flanked by four stormtrooper guards, and pushed himself up onto the stage. To Blake he looked like a parody cartoon of a fat Nazi, but the audience went wild, stomping and cheering as he reached for the microphone.

'Today I vas accosted by a Joo, right out on the street,' Kuhn began without preamble, his heavy German accent making the *America First* banner behind him look like a bad joke. 'But my boys knew what to do mit him! Und that they did! Dis Joo vill not be accosting nobody no more.'

The crowd cheered and stamped its collective feet. 'Send them back where they came from!' someone yelled. 'On a leaky boat!' added a high-pitched voice.

Kuhn looked around and nodded his satisfaction at the audience's reaction. 'We must reclaim our birthright,' he yelled down at them.

'Save America from the mongrel races.' He paused for thought. 'Our goal,' he went on, raising one bologna-like fist above his head and shaking it back and forth, 'is a free America – an America what stays on its own shores und takes care of its own people. Right here, right now. America – America First!'

The crowd went wild.

'De troubles in Europe, dey are for the Europeans und we . . .'

Blake felt a tap on his shoulder and turned to find that Special Agent Welker had slipped into the seat behind him. 'Leave unobtrusively a minute after I do,' Welker told him. 'I'll meet you on the corner.' Welker got up and walked out the door without looking behind him. It was one of the things Welker had taught him, Blake reflected. Never sneak, never hurry. If you sneak, you look like you're trying to hide something. If you hurry you may be headed somewhere interesting. If you just walk you look like you're going somewhere you're supposed to be going. Also never whisper. Whispers carry further than normal low speech. And they arouse the curiosity of anyone who overhears.

Blake waited a minute, and then pushed to his feet, just as Kuhn was starting to explain how Roosevelt was actually a Jew named Rosenfeld, and walked out, fighting the impulse to glance around and see if anyone was watching. In the hotel lobby he went over to the counter and spent a minute or two asking the room clerk questions about room rates while he casually watched the meeting-room door to see if anyone came out after him. No one did. He thanked the clerk and left the hotel, managing to not quite run to the corner. Welker was waiting, staring in a shop window, examining the fascinating display of cosmetic products inside.

Blake stopped next to Welker. 'This makes me nervous,' he said. 'What?'

'I don't know. Being seen with you, I guess. We shouldn't be seen together.'

Welker shrugged. 'I've been going to a bunch of these meetings. I'm going to be one of the boys pretty soon – I'm practicing my Nazi salute. And I've led Gerard into thinking that I was an ordnance expert during the War. He thought that was very interesting – very interesting. He's cultivating me. My name, if anyone should ask you, is Schnek. Harry Schnek. Besides, as the old joke says, everybody's got to be somewhere.'

Blake refrained from asking, 'What old joke?' and instead asked, 'Why are we here?'

'Everybody's got to be . . .' Welker began, and then, seeing the expression on Blake's face, went on, 'My car's around the corner. Come. Our presence is requested.' Welker led the way to where his four-year-old black Plymouth sedan was parked and unlocked the door.

Blake looked the car over. It was not what he thought a Special Agent would be driving. He was not impressed. 'I thought you'd have something, I don't know, swankier. Newer, at least,' he said.

Welker opened the passenger door. 'Sit,' he said, and then walked around to the driver's side and climbed in. 'Two things,' he told Blake as he stepped on the starter and worked the throttle until the car sputtered and coughed into life. 'One, in our line of work you don't want a car that stands out – that's too flashy or too new or too expensive. You want to be as unobtrusive as possible. You live longer that way. Two, Roosevelt hasn't seen fit to give us money for new cars, or for much of anything else for that matter. We are a shoestring operation. This is my own car, and it's the best I can afford.'

'Sorry,' Blake said. 'I assumed . . .'

'J. Edgar gets all the fancy stuff,' Welker said. 'They even get a clothing allowance for those brown suits they wear. We, not so much.'

Blake couldn't think of anything to say, so he said nothing until they pulled to a stop on 92nd Street just off Amsterdam Avenue. There were three police cars parked haphazardly further up the block and a cluster of policemen around one of the brownstones.

'What's this?' he asked.

'There has been an accidental death here,' Welker told him. 'Or possibly a murder. I side with those who favor murder. "Those" in this case being Detective Covitt. You remember Detective Covitt? A perceptive gentleman. He took one look at the crime scene and called me, and I went to fetch you. Exactly why I'm not sure yet. Come along.' He got out of the car, gently closed the door, and started down the street toward the cluster of cops by the brownstone. Blake obediently trotted behind.

Covitt came out the front door of the house and trotted down the steps as they approached. When he saw them he waved them over. 'Glad you could make it,' he said. 'Good to see you.'

'You too,' Welker said. 'What are you doing here? I thought you were in Brooklyn.'

'Yeah, well, Manhattan Homicide's got a triple murder down on Wall Street, stockbrokers or something. When important people get killed they get the call. When some poor schleb falls down a flight of stairs, we hop on the subway and cover. So we're covering. In this case it turns out to be a lucky coincidence.'

'What have you got?'

'Guy named, ah, Massen, Karl Massen. German. Came home drunk last night, sometime late, we're not sure just when. Apparently slipped and tumbled backwards down the stairs. Broke his neck. Mrs Bittleman, the landlady, found him at six thirty this morning when she got up to make breakfast for her guests – it's a boarding house.'

'And?'

'And if Manhattan Homicide got the call it would have gone in as an accident; after all Massen's just off the boat, no time to get anyone pissed off enough to kill him. But my man Weintz covered and he spotted something and called me, and here we are.'

'Karl Massen. Just off the boat? A German national?'

'Yup. Came in two days ago. A dye salesman, apparently.'

'Die? Like tool and die?'

'No, dye, like pretty colors for your girlfriend's dresses. He represents – represented, ah,' Covitt flipped open his notebook and turned it toward Welker and Blake, pointing to a carefully printed line: *Vogel und Söhne, Chemische und Farbstoff Grosshändler*, it read. 'I got it off his papers,' he told them. 'It means "Vogel and Son, Chemical and Dyestuff Wholesalers". He was here, as I understand it, to sell German dyes to American fabric makers.'

'Sons,' Welker corrected. 'Vogel and Sons. Plural. There are at least two of them.'

'Yeah?' Covitt said, scribbling a note in the book. 'Thanks, I guess.'

'Anything to help,' Welker said. 'And we are here because?'

'Come with me,' Covitt said, and headed back through the front door.

They followed him up two flights of stairs. Blake was glad to see that the body had been removed and there was nothing to note his passing but a substantial blot of blood at the foot of the staircase. He had seen enough dead bodies for a while.

There were seven doors on the third-floor landing, one unmarked and the others stenciled in faded gilt paint in the middle of each door at about eye height: 3A, 3B, 3C, 3D, 3E, and T. The door to 3B was open and a man in a rumpled gray suit was on his stomach on the floor inside, shining a flashlight under the bed. He pulled himself up as they arrived, and Welker recognized Detective Weintz.

'Nothing,' Weintz said, dusting himself off. '*Bupkis*. Whatever it is, it ain't here.'

'What are we looking for?' Welker asked.

'Something to connect him and that guy,' Weintz said, pointing to the door to apartment 3A, across the hall.

'Like what?'

Weintz shrugged. 'Whatever.'

'And why would we care? What would that mean, or establish, or whatever?'

Weintz looked at Covitt. 'You didn't tell him?'

'It was your find,' Covitt said. 'You won't get no department commendations or nothing, even if we end up making a case from it, so at least you should get the pleasure of telling him what you got.'

'Yeah, well . . .' He turned to Welker. 'I got a list of the people living here from the landlady first thing. Boarders and staff. You know, it's routine.'

'Right,' Welker agreed.

'Well, one of the names rang a bell, but I couldn't figure out what. So I came up to have a look at his room. Here, I still got the passkey.' He crossed the hall and unlocked the door, pushing it open. 'Take a look.'

They crowded into the doorway and peered into the room. Weintz reached in and turned the light switch.

Blake took an involuntary step into the room and felt his knees go weak. A buzzing noise from somewhere inside his head filled his ears. Slowly – it felt like it took forever – his legs gave way and he settled to the floor.

Welker and Covitt looked startled for a second, and then lifted him to his feet between them. 'What's the matter?' Covitt asked. 'You OK?'

'Here,' Welker said, 'Come sit down on the bed.'

'No, no,' Blake said, his voice louder than he intended. 'Into the hall. Please. Into the hall.'

They helped him into the hallway, and he leaned against the wall by the door.

'What happened?' Welker asked.

Blake took a deep breath, and then another. 'It's him!' he said finally.

'Him whom?'

'The dead guy. Lehman. It's him. It's his trunks. In there.'

Welker looked into the room and saw the pair of steamer trunks side by side under the window. 'Those trunks? You're sure?'

'I remember them. I'm sure 'cause of the labels and everything,' Blake told him. 'The big long rectangle and the little round red one. They're what I looked at when I looked through the crack. I didn't really want to look at – you know.'

'Yeah, I thought maybe,' Weintz said, nodding. 'It's been a couple of months, but I thought I remembered the name. I spent most of a week looking for those trunks. And here they are.'

'The question is,' Welker said, 'how did they get here?'

'I got a better question,' Covitt told him. 'How did the dead guy get here?'

'What?'

Covitt nodded at Weintz. 'You tell him.'

'Yeah,' Weintz said. He turned to Welker. 'The guy renting this room – his name is Otto Lehman, is what he told the landlady. And he's got the papers to prove it.'

'Oh,' Welker said. 'Oh. That's what you meant about the name. Son of a bitch!' He thought about it for a minute, and then asked, 'Have you seen him?'

'He ain't been home from work yet.'

'Good,' Welker said. 'Here's what we'll do.'

'Maybe he's run,' Covitt suggested. 'Taken a powder.'

'Um,' Welker said. 'Give me a minute.' He went into the room and prowled around for a while, and then came back out, closing the door carefully behind him. 'Nah,' he said. 'He'll be back.'

'How do you know?'

'Well, I can't swear to it, but I'll give you six to one odds. He left his toothbrush and his razor and fifteen bucks in cash in the top drawer. Nah. If he killed Massen, he'll figure we can't connect them.

And, as it happens, we can't. We can connect him to the other dead guy 'cause he took his name, but he doesn't know that.'

'We can't even say that Massen's death wasn't an accident,' Covitt said. 'Maybe he did take a header down the stairs.'

'What odds will you give me on that now?' Welker asked.

'Yeah,' Covitt said. 'Like you say. But we can't prove it. Unless the medical examiner can come up with something.'

'Let's go,' Blake suggested. 'Or at least let me go. Away from here. I don't want to be here when whoever this guy is gets back.'

'I want you to get a look at him,' Welker said. 'See if he was one of the guys in that warehouse.'

'I was afraid you were going to say that.' Blake shook his head, paused for a second, and then shook it again. 'I really don't want to. If I look at him, then he'll look at me. And I don't think that's a good idea.'

'He doesn't know who you are,' Welker reminded him.

'And I'd just as soon keep it that way.'

'Come on! He has no way of knowing, or even guessing, that you can ID him.'

'I don't think that matters to these guys. I think he'll say, "This guy is looking at me funny, I think I'll kill him." Except he'll say it in German.'

'We'll fix it so he doesn't know you're looking at him,' Covitt said. 'I'll be with you.'

Blake looked at him. 'You know,' he said. 'You're a cop. You carry a gun. You arrest people. Me, I'm a typesetter. I set type.'

'We'll set you up in a van across the street. You'll see him, he won't see you.'

'Yeah?' Blake thought it over for a second. 'I don't think so.'

'Why not?'

''Cause – supposing I identify him – then you'll arrest him. Then there'll be a trial and I'll have to testify. Then the guys you haven't caught will come after me.'

'I think,' Welker said, 'I can ease your mind on that point. There's no way Covitt can arrest him on your identification. I mean, technically he could, of course, but it would be futile and counter-productive. The smart thing to do would be to keep him under surveillance and see where he leads us. Like we're doing with the guy at the Bund.'

Now Covitt turned to look at him. 'What are you saying?' he asked. 'And just why is that?'

'Because we'd blow our hand and we could never get a conviction.'

'Come on – we'd have an eye-witness.'

'Not much of one.' Welker patted Blake on the shoulder. 'No offense.'

'I am not offended. Indeed not,' Blake said.

'Picture the cross-examination,' Welker told Covitt. '"Now, Mr Blake, you were hiding behind a screen, what, twenty feet – thirty feet – from the victim? And the lighting – I understand there were two light bulbs burning, is that right? Not very bright, were they? And the men, they were how far away from you? And your testimony is that you were so horrified at the scene that you really didn't look at it – just sort of glanced and then glanced away. And this while you were cowering behind the screen, afraid of making a sound, afraid of being seen yourself? Is that right?" And that's just off the top of my head. The defense attorney will have had time to refine his questions and get them just right.'

'They sounded pretty refined to me,' Blake said.

'And besides,' Welker went on, 'we don't want to get just one guy, we want to round up the whole group.'

'First you have to find out what the hell group it is,' Covitt said. 'And just what the hell they're up to.'

'You've got it,' Welker said. 'My point exactly. We need to figure out not just what they're doing but why they're doing it. And if it's worth murdering for, it's certainly something we want to stop.' He turned to Blake. 'What do you say? You'll be perfectly safe. And you won't have to testify.'

'You're sure?'

'Sure. If we can't get something on them better than your identification, there's no point in even arresting them. Like I said.'

Blake sighed. 'OK,' he said. 'Bring on your van.'

'Good,' Detective Covitt said. 'Good.'

SIXTEEN

Listen! No, listen carefully; I think I can hear something – Yes, there it was, quite clear. Don't you hear it? It is the tramp of armies crunching the gravel of parade-grounds, splashing through rain-soaked fields, the tramp of two million German soldiers and more than a million Italians – "going on maneuvers"

– Winston Churchill, radio broadcast to the US

'The President will see you now.'

Jacob Welker pushed himself to his feet and followed the secretary down the corridor and into the Oval Office.

Roosevelt gestured him into the chair beside the massive Hoover desk and waved the secretary out of the room.

Welker eased himself into the wicker-back chair. 'Good afternoon, Mr President.'

Roosevelt closed the stamp album he'd been perusing and looked up at Welker. 'One of the few things that relaxes me,' he said, 'and I have no time for it anymore.'

'You're a collector, sir?'

'In a small way. I try to give it a half-hour or so every evening. It clears my mind.' He put the album aside. 'I can give you about ten minutes,' he said. 'I have to meet with the Zog sisters at three.'

'The . . .?'

'The three sisters of King Zog of Albania. Princesses,' FDR looked down at a note on his desk, 'Myzejen, Ruhie, and Maxhide.'

'Maxhide?'

'That's what it says. And Myzejen and Ruhie. And, presumably, the Foreign Minister. For tea.'

'Tea?'

'You're unusually monosyllabic today,' Roosevelt commented. 'I trust you were sufficiently discreet in coming here.'

'I am in Washington to attend a reception for Count Ciano at the Italian Embassy this evening,' Welker told him. 'A few of my SIM buddies from the war are gathering for the event and they asked if I could make it. As it happens, I could.'

'The SIM?' Roosevelt asked. 'That's the Italian Secret Service?'

'Yes, sir.'

'And what is it that they think you do?'

'Last they heard I was still with the Continental. I shall not disabuse them of this notion.'

'Good, good,' Roosevelt said.

'Also there's a Brit that I served with who should be there. He's their cultural attaché over here, but I wouldn't be surprised if he was still in the Game. If so, I think we could be, ah, mutually beneficial.'

'The game? You mean spying?'

'Yes, sir. that's what we call it – "the Game". After all, espionage and counter-espionage are, in many respects, like a great game. Only the penalty for getting benched can be quite severe.'

'War itself,' Roosevelt said reflectively, 'can be looked at as a great game. One I fear we will be drawn into all too soon.'

Welker nodded. 'I'm afraid you're right,' he said.

'There is an old Chinese curse,' the President told him, 'that goes, "May you live in interesting times." And I'm afraid that we do.'

'And they look to be getting even more interesting,' Welker offered.

'The unemployment numbers are creeping back up,' Roosevelt said, leaning back and fixing a cigarette into a long ebony holder. 'Unless somebody does something, even the Democrats will start to turn against my New Deal before it's had a fair chance to work. And I'm the somebody.' He took a silver lighter from the desk and used it for its intended purpose.

'The people have faith in you, Mr President,' Welker said.

'For the moment,' said Roosevelt, putting down the lighter. 'Now to our particular problems of war and peace. First we talk money.' He pushed a scrap of paper across the desk. 'Here's your budget,' he said, 'for the year. The fiscal year, actually, which is even a bit longer.'

Welker looked down at the figure on the paper. 'Well,' he said. 'If this is my yearly pay, it is munificent. If it is the budget for the entire OSI, it's . . .'

'My discretionary funds,' the President interrupted him, 'are not very discretionary. It is an act of faith to even call them funds. If Eleanor ever finds out what budget I took this money from, I'll never hear the end of it.'

'Your wife, Mr President,' Welker said, 'is a remarkable woman.'

'So she is,' Roosevelt agreed. 'So, the OSI, is that what we're calling it?'

'Yes, sir. The Office of Special Intelligence.' He pulled out the leather folder and showed the President the ID card inside. 'Notice the State Department crest on the left. We're ostensibly an investigative arm of State.'

Roosevelt nodded. 'I'll tell Hull to put you on the list – whatever list is appropriate. Should have done that last month, in case anybody asked. You'll have to draw up a mission statement.'

'A mission statement?'

'For the file. What you intend to do. That is, what the Office of Special Whatsit intends to do, and what authority you exercise, and that sort of thing. And I'd just as soon it stayed as *sub rosa* as possible.'

'Yes, sir,' Welker said.

'And make up a new ID with a space for Hull to sign them, but don't go waving them about.'

'I don't expect that we'll need to show the ID very much, sir,' Welker said.

'A good thing,' Roosevelt said. He swiveled in his chair to stare out one of the tall windows behind his desk. 'The Republicans would have a field day if they thought I was setting up my own police force.'

'We don't have any police powers,' Welker reminded him. 'Can't arrest anyone or even detain them. We don't even have badges.'

'That wouldn't matter to the Republicans,' Roosevelt said. 'Lodge is looking for something to batter me with and this would do fine, real fine. Better than most. I can hear him now: "The President is setting up his own Gestapo. What does he want a police force for? No man is safe in his bed." And then J. Edgar would go to work on them.' FDR turned around again to look at Welker. 'You know Hoover's got dossiers on half the members of Congress. Probably a good bit more than half. Got one on me.'

Welker didn't need to look surprised. 'You're joking sir!'

'He hinted as much last time he was in here. A couple of pointed comments – which I won't repeat.'

Welker shook his head. 'You have to admit, the man has balls.'

'If I didn't need you for other things,' Roosevelt said, 'I'd be tempted to put you on him, see what's in his closet.'

'Yes, sir. And about those other things—'

'Ah yes.'

What was now christened the Office of Special Intelligence had begun some months before when Roosevelt became convinced by Frank Knox, his Secretary of the Navy, that Nazi infiltration of the United States could soon become a serious problem, and that Hoover and his FBI were not interested in doing anything much about it. J. Edgar was so firmly focused on 'The Communist Menace', when he wasn't going out and personally capturing big-name gangsters and bank robbers, that he had no men to spare for watching Nazis or Fascists or your more quotidian criminals.

'Someone,' Knox said, 'should be taking a close look at our home-grown Nazis and see what support they may be getting from the Master Race back in Germany. Remember in the last war the Kaiser's agents succeeded in blowing up a few things before we caught them. And they did that before we were officially at war.'

'I remember,' Roosevelt said. 'And I've listened to a couple of Hitler's speeches on the short wave. He's one scary son of a bitch. Who can we get?'

Knox had talked to his friend Bill Donovan, and Donovan came in to talk to Roosevelt and recommended Jacob Welker for the job. As a newly commissioned second lieutenant when the US entered the World War, Welker had gone to France with the 17th Balloon Company of the AEF, and had spent a few months in the wicker basket of an observation balloon before somehow finding himself seconded to the Army Intelligence Coordination Bureau, working with the British Secret Intelligence Service and the Italian Servizio Informazioni Militare, both organizations, he found, much more sophisticated and capable than anything the Americans had. At the Bureau he perfected the delicate art of passing action-able intelligence on to American field commanders along with carefully worded descriptions of just how the said commanders could best use the information. He soon developed the perhaps a bit unreasonable opinion that most senior officers seemed incapable of grasping anything more complex than 'You here – enemy there'.

When the war ended he came back to the States with a captain's bars, a disgust for the military, and no marketable skills. He got his bachelor's in Political Science from Columbia University, briefly contemplated becoming a lawyer, and then went to work as an operative for the Continental Detective Agency – Discreet Professional Service – Offices in All Major Cities and Overseas. He spent time in the Chicago, New York, San Francisco, and Berlin offices, with a three-month side trip to Istanbul and Cairo to help break up an art-smuggling ring. And then Donovan had called him, and now he was sitting opposite the President of the United States for the second time.

'I think we have made a start,' Welker said. 'Something is going on. We don't yet know exactly what it is, but we may have a handle on it. A tenuous handle perhaps, but still . . .'

'With the Nazis?'

'Yes, sir, with the Nazis.'

Roosevelt nodded and leaned back in his chair, looking interested.

'There was this murder in New York a few weeks ago,' Welker went on. 'A German national just off the boat was tortured and killed. It wasn't pretty.'

'Tortured? I'll be damned!' Roosevelt shook his head. 'Who was he?'

'He seems to have been a man the FBI were looking for, supposedly a Soviet agent sent to coordinate something-or-other with whoever, the details are not clear.'

'A Soviet agent? That's Hoover's specialty.'

'The Bureau lost track of him when he landed, and didn't connect the man they were looking for with the dead man, who was left naked and with nothing to identify him. But I saw a police report of the murder and followed up. It turns out that there was a witness. The victim was almost certainly killed by German, that is Nazi, agents. The question is, why?'

'Tortured!' Roosevelt slowly made a fist and held it in the air in front of him for a moment before lowering his closed hand gently to the table, a gesture that seemed to Welker to be barely controlled anger. 'This – this virus – is spreading. We must do what we can to pull it out at the root before it is established over here.'

'Yes, sir,' Welker said.

'Well,' the President said, 'get to it! Keep me informed. I have given instructions that any calls from you are to be put through. If I'm not here Miss LeHand, my private secretary, can be given any message. But if you have to give it to anyone else, be vague. At least until I set up an actual liaison for you here in the Executive Office.'

'Yes, sir,' Welker said. Roosevelt thrust out his hand and Welker shook it. 'Thank you, sir,' he said.

'No, thank you,' Roosevelt said. 'Hell of a time we've picked to be living through, isn't it?'

'Yes, sir,' Welker agreed. 'It sure is.'

SEVENTEEN

Some ladle out the blarney
In the mitt camp of a carney
And some lecture on the Cosmic Oversoul
But their names would be mud
Like a chump playing stud
If they lost that old ace in the hole
　　　– *William Lindsay Gresham,* 'Nightmare Alley'

The long-range Savola-Marchetti SM 75 carrying Count Ciano landed at Washington-Hoover Airport at 3:30 Friday afternoon, having completed the Rome to Washington flight in four days, nine hours; stopping briefly in Morocco, Dakar, Fortaleza, Caracas, and Havana, for a total distance of a little over 9,000 miles. After shaking hands with the pilot, the copilot, the navigator, and the radio man, Count Ciano and his assistant, the *bellissima* Arianna, climbed aboard the waiting Embassy Lancia and were driven into Washington.

Gian Galeazzo Ciano, conti di Cortellazzo e Buccari, Foreign Minister of Italy, son of WWI war hero Admiral Constanzo Ciano, son-in-law of Il Duce, Benito Mussolini; handsome, clever, *multo importante*, commander of La Disperata bomber squadron during the invasion of Ethiopia, trusted liaison between Mussolini and Hitler, holder of ten thousand secrets from two dozen capitals of Europe and Asia, was by his own estimation a charming man and a skilled negotiator. And it would require both charm and skill to accomplish his present goal.

The civil war in Spain looked to be winding down – of course Generalissimo Franco had been promising victory for the past year, but this time it looked like progress was actually being made. And it was essential that the United States be friendly to the new Fascist government when it was proclaimed. The US had not taken sides during the past three years of fighting. Neither Fascism nor Communism were particularly popular in the United States, and as long as the two were at loggerheads in the continuing war it was natural for the US to stay out. But the side that won would come into sharp focus, as questions of recognition and trade and business relationships slid into view.

So here he was; Count Ciano the negotiator, Count Ciano the charmer, ready to perform for assorted members of Congress and the President's staff. A meeting with President Roosevelt had not been yet arranged, but no doubt it would come to pass. But first, that very evening, a gala reception for the assorted diplomats on Embassy Row and many of those same Congressmen and officials. And before that a nap. He thought briefly of asking Arianna to share his bed, but decided he was too tired.

At six that evening the limousines began pulling up one by one in front of the Italian Embassy at 16th Street and Fuller, to disgorge their passengers and then float off to that secret land where limousine drivers go to smoke and drink strong coffee and eat Gruyère sandwiches on baguettes or liverwurst on rye, depending, and await the appointed hour of their return. It was quarter to seven when the Rolls carrying Lady Patricia Saboy pulled up and Garrett, Lord Geoffrey's aide, who was playing the role of chauffeur for the evening, lumbered around to open the passenger door for Lady Patricia and her escort.

'My uncle, Professor Isaac Luthier,' Patricia explained as she went along the reception line. 'My husband is not yet back from England.'

Isaac looked amazingly resplendent in white tie. The cut of his bespoke jacket and trousers had a vaguely un-British look to the discerning eye, but the drape and the stitching were those of a master tailor.

When some days before Patricia had expressed concern about Isaac's ability to, ah, 'belong', he had reassured her. 'All clothing is but a costume, designed to create an illusion,' he told her, 'and creating a believable illusion is my stock in trade, as it were. Besides, my father was a count, so dressing like a penguin is part of my heritage.'

'A count?' she had asked. 'Really?'

Isaac nodded. 'Count Feodor Petrov Androvitch Schenk Lubonowski. The fourth Count Lubonowski. I would have been the fifth.'

'But he was and you're not?'

Isaac shrugged. 'Sometime prior to the World War my father got into a dispute with the King over who could do what and with what and to whom. I believe it involved a *Coryphée* – a lead dancer of the *corps de ballet*. I was too young to understand or care much about the details. As a consequence of the contretemps, the King in a prolonged moment of pique – the process took something over four years – had my father stricken off the rolls. In the next edition of the *Almanach de Gotha* there was a white space where my father's name had been. And I believe, to emphasize his majesty's point, there was a black line through the white space. Our lands reverted to the crown and my father moved to Paris, taking with him most of the family and what little money he had salvaged. I spent six years at Taunton, an unusually sadistic British public school, where I learned maths, Latin, Rugby, how to speak proper English, and revenge. By the time I graduated Papa had gone through the remaining money, so I was left to live by my, fortunately considerable, wits. I was, for a brief while, the male ingenue in a theatre company in Poland, fencing master at an academy in Berlin, croupier at a *chemin de fer* table in Monte Carlo, a smuggler of antiquities from various Middle Eastern countries, and a gigolo on a transatlantic ocean liner.'

'A gigolo?' Patricia asked. 'You don't seem the, ah, physical type.'

Another shrug. 'I was young, I was not unattractive, I dressed well, I spoke well, and I was reasonably priced.'

'Really?' Patricia asked. 'Is all that true?'

'Perhaps,' Isaac said. 'Incidentally, I have been giving some thought to our evening's activities, and I have a plan. And a new camera I want to try out.'

'You're going to go to the reception with a camera? Patricia asked. 'People will talk. Or are you going to be taking pictures for the society page?'

'No one will know,' Isaac said, reaching into his pocket and pulling out a silver object about the size of a bundle of four cigarettes.

'That's a camera?' Patricia asked.

'And a very good one. It's a Minox, the latest in spy technology.'

'German?'

'Surprisingly it's Latvian. Perfect for photographing documents. See this chain on the end? That little bead gives you the exact distance to get a document in perfect focus. Uses special tiny rolls of film. All you need is a strong reading lamp to get quite readable pictures.'

'Well,' Patricia said. 'I'm pleased to be able to give you a chance to play with your new toy. The question is, how am I going to get you into the ambassador's office?'

'I have a plan,' he told her. 'Back when you were assisting The Great Mavini, did you do any mind-reading or mentalism?'

'No,' she said. 'Mostly birds and escapes, and showing off my body to an admiring crowd while Mavini did something clever.'

'Did you enjoy it?' he asked.

'I did. Max Mavini and his wife were both lovely people. And it is something of a rush to be applauded six days a week.' She looked at him. 'Does this help?'

'Your stage presence may. Also your practice with misdirection. Did you know you were a psychic?'

'A what?'

'Trust me,' he said. 'Madam Sosostris and you are as sisters. Or soon will be. I have a monograph by Phillip Gold, a noted practitioner of the arcane arts, on what we call "cold readings" for you to study, and a deck of tarot cards for you to practice with. It's a new deck, and the desired aura will surround you better if it looks to be a bit used. So throw the cards on the floor and walk on them a bit – but not in your heels. We want them dusty and used, not punctured.'

'It shall be as you say, O wise master,' Patricia said, bowing.

'Harrumph,' said Isaac.

At the end of the reception line stood Marcello with a tall, elegant woman whom he introduced as his wife. For some reason Patricia had pictured her as being short and dumpy, and it took a moment to fit this woman into her preconceived image. Her English was excellent – better than Marcello's. 'My dear, let me introduce you to Lady Patricia Saboy,' Marcello said. 'It is she that I've been telling you about. Lady Patricia, this is my wife, Livia.'

Livia took Patricia's hand and for a moment Patricia's mind went blank. *'The lady I've been telling you about?'* Why yes, I have been bonking your husband. He's quite good in bed, don't you agree? But her wits returned in time to hear Livia say, 'It's so nice of you to help Marcello with his English, he is so stubbornly resistant to learning a new language.'

'Ah,' Patricia said, 'if I spoke the language of Dante and Machiavelli, perhaps I would not see the importance of learning another.'

Livia smiled sweetly. 'And Boccaccio,' she said. 'Let us not forget Boccaccio.'

She knows, Patricia thought. 'But then we have Shakespeare,' she said, with a polite smile, 'and Dickens and Jane Austen.'

'Yes.' Livia's smile was, if anything, a bit larger than Patricia's. 'We have a lot to teach each other.'

'Come, dear,' Marcello said in a blandly innocent voice, taking Livia's arm. 'Let me introduce you to the French Ambassador.'

'Of course, *caro mio*,' Livia said, patting him on the hand and allowing him to lead her away. 'Your English is improving already.'

Isaac looked after the retreating couple. 'Something?'

'No, not really,' Patricia said.

'I think perhaps something,' Isaac said. 'No matter. Let us wander about meeting people so that I may become your bland and uninteresting uncle and fade into the overly polished woodwork.'

Patricia almost fell into an unladylike fit of giggling, but stopped herself in time. 'Bland and uninteresting, are you? And I am Marie of Rumania.'

'Could be,' Isaac agreed, lifting two glasses of prosecco from a passing tray. 'There is a resemblance.' He handed her a glass and lifted his in toast. 'Are you ready for the night's adventure?'

'Shouldn't we wait until people are more settled down?' she asked.

'We should commence setting the scene,' Isaac said, 'defining the terms, creating the fog of expectation.'

'Ah?'

'Never mind. Did you read the book I gave you?'

'Now's a fine time to ask,' she said, 'but as it happens, I did. I even practiced a bit with the cards.'

'Excellent. We will now establish your reputation as a psychic, and the assembled multitude will soon be lining up for a reading. Just tell them what they want to hear, and resist the temptation to tell them the truth. Remember the Sibyls' lament.'

'The Sibyls . . .?'

'The Sibyls were a group of women in ancient Greece who possessed the ability to foretell the future.'

'Yes,' Patricia said. 'I read about them.'

'Unfortunately they could only tell the truth about what they saw. The "Sibyls' Lament", by some unknown poet, goes something like:

"Our gift is to know what you do
Our fate is to speak what we hear
Our curse is to tell only true
Our portion is hatred and fear."'

'Poor women,' Patricia commented. 'They didn't use tarot decks back then, did they?'

'I believe they used pigeons.'

'Pigeons? What did they do with them?'

'I didn't ask.'

'And their, ah, clients didn't like what they heard?'

'Often,' Isaac said. 'There is a price for knowledge, on the other hand there is a far greater price for ignorance.'

'Why is philosophy always so dour?' Patricia asked. 'Whatever happened to "happily ever after"?'

'It burned up in the Reichstag fire,' said Isaac. 'Now, whom shall we importune first?'

Patricia settled in an easy chair with a coffee table between her and a chaise longue in a corner of the reception room. The sister of the Bulgarian consular officer, a slender woman of serious aspect in an ill-fitting beige dress with puffy sleeves, was the first to sit across from Patricia and her artistically tattered tarot deck. Her name was Magda, and she was delighted to learn that she would soon meet a tall man who would become important in her life. 'You see your card is Temperance,' Patricia told her, 'which shows that you are moderate and thoughtful in everything you do.'

'Perhaps too thoughtful,' Magda agreed seriously.

'And this card, one away from yours,' Patricia said, turning the card over, 'represents the man. Ah, the Seven of Cups. Good.'

'How good?'

'This indicates the man is reasonably wealthy, and since seven is an old number, it probably means inherited wealth.'

'I do not care about such things,' Magda said.

'Of course not,' Patricia agreed, 'but given the state of the world today, it may become important.'

'Yes,' Magda said thoughtfully, 'that is so.'

'And separating you,' Patricia turned over the cards separating them, 'well!'

A clot of diplomats passed, laughing uproariously at who knows what. Magda waited impatiently for them to recede far enough for conversation to resume, and said, 'Yes?'

'It's the Magician.'

'So something magical . . .'

'Actually no,' Patricia said. 'It signifies progress into the future.'

'Ah! So we will have a future. That's nice. And how long before I meet this man?'

Patricia took up the cards and shuffled the deck. 'Here, pull out one of the cards – any card.'

Magda closed her eyes and pulled a card from the offered deck.

'The Four of Pentacles,' Patricia said, turning the card over. 'You will meet the man, or perhaps realize how important he is if by chance you have met him already, in four—'

'Four?'

'Days, weeks, months, I cannot be sure. But certainly not years. So by summer at the latest.'

'Thank you,' Magda said. She stood. 'It was . . . interesting. I don't really believe any of this, you know.'

'Of course not,' Patricia agreed.

By the third reading – a young lady named Anna Metzl, who was a secretary at the Austrian Embassy – Patricia had a grasp on what she was doing and had to remind herself not to become over-confident. Although it seemed that if you told people good things about their future, they would figure out some way to believe them. Anna was most concerned about whether she would have a job next week, when the Nazis finished taking over the Austrian Foreign Service. In the course of the reading Patricia managed to slip Anna a card with her phone number. It might be useful to befriend a former secretary at the Austrian Embassy. And perhaps she wouldn't lose her job, which would make her even more useful.

As Anna got up Patricia saw a tall dark-haired man standing behind her, a plate of pâté, cheese, and thickly sliced bread in one hand and a glass of prosecco in the other, apparently waiting. Patricia gestured to the empty chair, but the man shook his head. 'Excuse me, but you are Lady Patricia Saboy?'

'That's right.' Now that she had a good look at him, Patricia decided that it would be quite nice were he to sit next to her. She repeated the gesture. 'Sit,' she said.

'I knew your husband in the war,' he said, this time accepting her offer and dropping into the empty chair. 'And I was in touch with him for some years after. I had hoped to see him here. That is, if he is Lord Geoffrey and not some other Saboy entirely. My name's Welker.' He put down the prosecco and extended his hand. 'Jacob Welker.'

'You're American?' she deduced, taking the hand, holding it for perhaps a bit longer than absolutely decorous, and then releasing it.

'Yes,' he said. 'I worked liaison with Lord Geoffrey's field intel-ligence outfit for a while. We both spent much of our time trying to convince our superior officers that everything they knew was wrong.'

She laughed. 'Did you succeed?'

He grinned. It was a grin that would serve usefully in a variety of circumstances. 'Almost never,' he told her.

'He doesn't talk about the war much,' she said.

'No.' The grin went away. 'Most of us don't.'

'Well,' she said. 'It's a pleasure to meet one of his companions. And what are you doing now, in the absence of war?'

'Until quite recently I was an operative for the Continental Detective Agency,' he told her.

'Ah,' she said. 'Do I detect a theme in your choice of professions?'

He laughed. 'Inadvertent,' he said.

'So. Has the man chosen the job or has the job chosen the man?'

'I think we hunted each other through a thicket of distractions. And I must congratulate you.'

'How pleasant. And what am I to be congratulated for?'

'You are the first person, I believe, who didn't immediately respond either "That must be very interesting," or "You must have some fascinating stories to tell," when I told them I was with the Continental.'

'Really?' she said. 'That must be very interesting. I'll bet you have some fascinating stories to tell.'

'Properly embellished,' he told her, 'they could hold your attention for minutes at a time.'

She smiled at him. 'You must visit us,' she said. 'I'm sure my husband would be pleased to be back in touch with you.' She riffled through the tarot deck until she found the Three of Cups and wrote on the face with her pencil. 'Here,' she said, handing it to him. 'Our address and phone number here in Washington. Actually Georgetown. Do call.'

'Won't someone miss the card from the deck?' he asked, taking it and sticking it in his pocket.

'Not likely,' she said. 'Besides, I would have no idea what to say if it turned up, so it's better for all if it doesn't.'

'Ah!' he said. He produced a card of his own from a vest pocket and passed it to her. 'Turnabout,' he said.

'New York?' she asked, reading it.

'I have to go back this evening,' he told her. 'But I'll be back in DC next week. Let's see if we can have dinner then. I'd like to chat with Lord Geoffrey about a few things of, ah, common interest.'

'The Office of Special Intelligence,' she read. 'What is that?'

'A boring government agency,' he told her. 'The name was picked to impress people I have to talk to.'

'I'm impressed, so it's working,' she said. She tucked the card into her cleavage, noting with pleasure how his eyes followed her hand. 'Well, I must get back to foretelling the future.'

'Are you good at it?' he asked.

'I'm not sure,' she told him. 'I predict that we shall meet again soon. What do you think?'

'I'd like that,' he said. With a quickly disappearing sad smile, he got up and walked toward the bar.

His place was quickly taken by a short lady with a thin face and a wonderfully pointed nose, who reminded Patricia of a sparrow as she perched precisely on the edge of the chair. 'My dear,' she said, 'it's so good of you to do this. Of course, most people here will think of it merely as entertainment, but we know better, don't we?'

Patricia looked inquiringly at her. 'A pleasure to meet you,' she said. 'I am Lady Patricia Saboy. And you are?'

'Oh, yes. Silly me. Monica Withers, but you must call me Birdie. Everyone does.'

'Birdie,' Patricia acknowledged.

'Do you get good results with the tarot?' Birdie asked.

'It depends,' Patricia said.

'Yes, of course. I've never had much luck with the tarot. I prefer the yarrow stalks.'

'The yarrow . . .'

'Yes. You know. The *I Ching*. I swear sometimes I think there's a little old Chinese man somehow on the other side of the book guiding the falling of the stalks, telling me what I have to know. I mean it's uncanny at times, positively uncanny. My husband actually consults it all the time for his work. It's uncanny, I swear.'

'Your husband?'

'Yes, you know, Sir Daniel.'

'Ah,' Patricia said, the light dawning. 'Sir Daniel Withers, the Australian—'

'Ambassador, yes that's him.' She pointed across the room. 'The one with the pint in his hand. I keep telling him, at these events, champagne or white wine or even a cocktail, but no – he will have his pint. Especially when he can get some beer that isn't American. You should hear him go on about American beer. "Call themselves a great country," he says, "and they can't even make a decent pint."'

'So, shall we do a reading?' Patricia asked.

'Oh no, no!' Birdie brushed aside the thought with a wide gesture. 'I just thought – you know, two souls beating as one and that sort of thing. There is so much more' – another wide gesture – 'out there than we are aware of without a little assist from the *Ching*, or the crystal, or, to be sure, the tarot; the little invisible hands that guide the fall of the cards or the yarrow stalks. Really, there is so much to know and so little time. And we are surrounded by un-believers. Surrounded.' She stood up. 'You must come over. We have a little society that meets every so often. Call me at the Embassy.'

'Yes,' Patricia agreed. 'I believe I shall.'

EIGHTEEN

With cat-like tread, upon our prey we steal
In silence dread, our cautious way we feel
No sound at all, we never speak a word
A fly's foot-fall would be distinctly heard
       – *Gilbert & Sullivan*, The Pirates of Penzance

By Patricia's fifth reading there was a small clutch of people around her little table waiting their turn to discover what the unseen spirit guiding the fall of pasteboard cards from a shuf-fled tarot deck could tell them about their futures. By now the party had gathered steam, the nine-piece orchestra was playing operatic favorites, the chatter was pitched above the music, and there was no way a quiet conversation could be held anywhere in that room. Patricia sought out some likely looking embassy official – not Marcello, who seemed to be avoiding her, but Signore Sabatini, a short, important-looking man who had a spade beard and wore across his jacket a red sash with several medals pinned to it. She explained the problem and asked for clearance to go upstairs and set up a table in the second-floor hallway. Sabatini laughed. 'Certainly. I will send someone to assist you in setting these things up. And you will read my wife's cards and tell her that she really must go visit her mother in Como, who misses her dreadfully, will you not?'

'Of course,' Patricia agreed.

'Come.'

Walking up the stairs with Signore Sabatini, the first break she had had from practicing her new avocation in over an hour, she realized that she was really enjoying herself. There was the challenge of interacting with her clients ('In the trade they're called "johns" or "marks" or "fish",' Isaac had told her, 'but not to their faces') and telling them what they wanted to hear – at first a generality that sounded ever so specific to the one hearing it: 'The cards say there is something troubling you, something of a very personal nature.' Who didn't have something of a personal nature troubling them? And then let the subject expound and expand, going where she will, and follow so closely as to seem to be leading. 'And here is the Knight of Staves, representing an important man. Notice the card is reversed, which means he is turned away from you. Any idea who that could be?' and pretty soon they were treading an unexpected byway, and the cards somehow came to mean what they had to mean. Patricia realized that one could actually do good with these readings, and that one had to be careful not to do harm.

They went upstairs and located a solid-looking folding table with a chess board incised in the top and two comparatively lightweight chairs with leather seats and backs. Sabatini helped Patricia set them up in the hallway at the head of the stair right across, as it happened, from the ambassador's office, the left wall of which contained a Rabson Twenty-Oh-Seven wall safe.

Uncle Isaac came up a minute later, bringing the next client, a slender young American in tails at least one size too big for him, who told Patricia that his friends Johnny and Swet had dared him to get the reading, and there was only one question he needed answered.

'We can do that,' she assured him. 'And what's your name?'

'Oh,' he said. 'I'm Izzy. Izzy Haist. My friends call me Izzy Ridiculous. Except some call me Izzy Wizzy, and they've made up a rather rude limerick about it.'

'Really?' she asked. 'Let's hear it.'

'Oh, I couldn't possibly,' he said. She thought he blushed, but the lighting in the hall wasn't strong enough to be sure.

'Well, all right then,' she said, 'but I'm very disappointed. I've always wanted to hear a dirty limerick.' She shuffled the tarot deck one, two, three times. 'You sound American,' she told him. 'Are you with the government?'

He thought that over for a minute and then leaned forward. 'Can you keep a secret?'

'Oooh,' she said, leaning in until their heads almost touched across the table. 'A secret! I love secrets. I'll do my best.'

'We don't belong,' he said in an intense but slightly squeaky undertone.

I've often had that feeling, she thought. She said, 'I see. In what sense?'

'We, my friends and I, are party crashers,' he told her.

'Really?' she asked, actually surprised, remembering the three guards at the door. 'How ever did you manage that?'

'We came in with the caterers. I took a case of champagne off the truck and brought it in, and Swet had a long roll of, I guess, pâté.'

'And Johnny?'

'He started talking to one of the waitresses and walked right in with her. He's good at talking to girls.'

'Very resourceful,' Patricia told him. 'I commend you and your friends.' She leaned back and shrugged her shoulders to relieve the muscles tensing up below her neck, then gave the deck one last shuffle and handed it to him. 'Here, cut the cards.'

He did so adroitly, cutting the deck in half and then sliding some from the middle to the top, and then cutting it in half again. He had learned to play poker, she surmised, with some people who had concerns about the forthrightness of their opponents.

She took back the deck. 'What is your question?' she asked.

'Oh no,' he said. This time she was sure he blushed. 'I mean, it's, ah, private. Very private.'

'All right,' she said, dealing five cards down in a row on the table. 'Not a problem. We'll let the tarot decide.' She glanced up at Isaac, who was standing behind Izzy Wizzy's chair. 'Close your eyes,' she told Izzy, 'and concentrate on your question.'

Izzy scrunched his eyes closed. Isaac sidled over to the right and turned to the door to the ambassador's office. He took a couple of slim, simple-looking instruments from his pocket and went to work on the lock.

'Try to picture your question as concretely as you can – concentrate on the image,' Patricia said, talking to keep Izzy concentrating on something other than any noises he might hear from behind him. 'If there's a person involved in your question, see her standing in front of you.' Patricia thought the 'her' was a safe guess.

Isaac had the door open and slipped through it, closing it silently behind him.

'Now,' she said, making it up as she went along, 'with your question firmly in mind, reach out and touch one of the cards.'

'Can I open my eyes?' he asked.

'If you wish.'

He opened his eyes and scrutinized the five cards as though one of them held the door to his future happiness. Finally he put his forefinger on the second card from the left. Patricia dealt another five cards face down on that one, carefully lining them up, and then paused for a moment to figure out what she was going to do next.

Izzy looked expectant, like a dog who just knew that there was a treat in your hand and you'd open it any second now. 'What now?' he asked.

Patricia turned the small stack of cards over. 'Let's see,' she said.

The newly revealed card was the Hanged Man.

'Oh gosh!' Izzy said.

'It doesn't mean what you probably think it does,' she told him, heading off his reaction. 'It is usually a very favorable card to get.'

'The Hanged Man?'

'Notice he's hanging by his foot. He's waiting around for something interesting to happen. If it's something good – wonderful! If it's something bad, well, this gives us warning so we can avoid it.'

'I see,' Izzy said. 'Well, which is it? What is he waiting for?'

Come on, Patricia thought, *I can't do this all by myself, give me a hint.* 'Let's look at the card covering it,' she said, turning the next card over. It was the Four of Wands. *Oh great,* she thought. *What can we get from that?* She took a stab. 'Wands are associated with emotions or feelings,' she told him. 'And since it's the four, a fairly low card, the emotions are not yet very strong.'

'But they could grow – the emotions, I mean?' Izzy asked seriously.

Aha! 'Let's see,' she said, turning over the card underneath. 'It was the Sorceress.' Oh yes,' she said, 'things are looking up!'

Footsteps and loud voices on the staircase. Two men and a woman, speaking Italian. She turned in her chair as they rounded the corner and saw Count Ciano and Marcello, and a very beautiful young woman dressed to emphasize that she was a very beautiful young woman, who was holding hands with Count Ciano as they climbed. Marcello had a key in his hands. It was, could there be any doubt, the key to the ambassador's office.

Patricia got up and walked around the table, giving the door to the ambassador's office two quick taps with the heel of her shoe as she passed. 'Let's see what the cards look like from your side,' she said. Izzy nodded, not seeming to notice how inane that sounded. 'It matters, you know,' she told him, leaning over his shoulder, 'whether the card is right-side up or upside down.'

'I didn't know that,' said Izzy.

'Oh yes,' Patricia told him.

She straightened up as the newcomers reached her. 'Count Ciano and Signore Bruzzi,' she said with a bright smile, 'and I don't know this lady.'

'Ah, Lady Patricia,' Ciano said. 'Let me introduce my secretary, Miss Arianna Amati.'

'Ah,' said Patricia. 'How do you do?'

Miss Amati nodded. '*Buonasera*,' she said. '*Piacere di conoscerla*.'

'Would any of you like your cards read?' Patricia asked the group. 'Past, present, future; all mysteries revealed.'

'Perhaps it would be wise were I not to reveal too many of my mysteries,' Ciano said. 'And,' he added with a sideways glance at Marcello, 'perhaps of yours also.'

And they say women gossip, she thought. 'As you say,' she said. 'Ah, Count, may I ask you a political question?'

'So, the lady is interested in politics?' Ciano asked with a broad smile. 'Such women are dangerous, just ask the Borgias. What is your question?'

'There is discussion at the embassy – my embassy – as to whether Hitler will be content with Austria, or is going to make further demands and perhaps invade other countries. Do you . . . What do you think?'

'Well, let me ask you – what do *you* think?' Ciano asked. 'Reflect – two years ago Hitler retook the Rhineland with no opposition, and this week he gained all of Austria, with damn little opposition. If you were Hitler, would you stop there?'

'Well . . .' Patricia thought. 'The Rhineland had been German before the war, and Austria is mostly a German-speaking country, so . . .'

'Yes, along with Serbian and Hungarian and Croatian and, I

believe, Turkish, as well as a few others. How do you suppose Europe would have reacted if Turkey had invaded East Austria to defend its co-linguists – if that's the word?'

'Close enough,' Patricia told him.

'Do you know,' Ciano said, lowering his voice as though imparting a great secret, 'that when the German Army marched into the Rhineland two years ago their guns were not loaded?'

'Really?' It sounded like the start of a joke, but Patricia couldn't imagine what the punchline would be.

Count Ciano nodded. 'The troops were under orders to retreat at the slightest sign of resistance. Der Führer was that unsure of himself.'

'Remarkable!' Patricia said. She had asked the question to stall for more time, but perhaps she had learned something useful. 'How can you know that?' she asked.

'I heard it from *l'imbianchino* himself.'

Marcello chuckled.

'*L* . . .?' Patricia asked.

'It means in English,' Marcello told her, 'the housepainter.'

'It is what Il Duce calls Der Führer – in private of course,' the Count said.

'So Mussolini dislikes Hitler?' Patricia asked innocently.

'Dislike? No – too strong a word. Il Duce has little, ah, respect for him. He is essentially a silly little man. But,' he held up a finger, 'silly little men in search of respect have caused great upheavals in the world before this. Think of Genghis Kahn. Think of Napoleon.' He turned as they heard two more men tromping up the stairs. 'Ah! Here they are. How timely,' he murmured, greeting the new arrivals with a precise wave of his hand.

In the lead was a short man in the overly starched uniform of a member of the SS, Hitler's own personal army, laced with an abundance of silver piping and adorned with several decorations that Patricia didn't recognize. She allowed herself to imagine him explaining the decorations to her.

'*This one,*' he would say, touching it fondly, '*was awarded for my conspicuous gallantry in throwing bricks through the window of a Jewish butcher shop. And this was presented to me by Der Führer himself on the occasion of my kicking a Communist while he was down.*'

Two steps behind him was a very blond man with a puffy face and a spade-like beard clipped straight across two inches below the chin. His dress suit seemed a trifle too small for him and his collar was clearly a bit too tight for his neck. There was one decoration pinned to the wide collar of his jacket. *It must be*, Patricia decided after examining his face and finding no humanity in it, *for extreme cruelty toward old women and defenseless children.*

'Ah, Oberführer Spaetz,' Count Ciano called, 'good to see you. Glad you could make it. And this must be – is it – Herr Weiss?'

'*Ja,*' the man in the dress suit agreed, clicking his heels and bowing from the waist. 'It is an honor, Count. An honor.'

'A pleasure,' Count Ciano agreed, 'And may I present,' he patted Patricia on the back, 'Lady Patricia Saboy, wife of the British Cultural Attaché and, if I may say so, a friend of Italy.' He turned to Marcello, 'I may say that, may I not?'

'Of course, *Signore,*' Marcello said, a faint pink tinge rising around his ears.

You bastard, Patricia thought, not sure whether she was addressing it to Marcello or Ciano. Maybe both. 'Who could not be a friend to Italy?' she asked. 'It is so full of the most wonderful ruins.' She smiled sweetly and walked around the table back to her seat.

'Yes, well – come, we have business.' With that Count Ciano turned toward the closed office door. 'Marcello, if you please.'

She held her breath as Marcello opened the door and turned on the light. But there was no sudden gasp or scream or thunderous demand for an explanation as the group entered the office and closed the door behind them. Patricia returned to her seat. 'Onward!' she said.

It was three years, or three weeks, or perhaps only twenty minutes, later when the office door re-opened and Count Ciano and his extended entourage emerged. They turned the light off, closed the door, and clattered back downstairs. Patricia was at that moment reading the tarot for Madam de Poul, a stout mature lady who was inclined to argue with the cards as they were turned over. Patricia found this a bit annoying, but at the same time it gave her a lot of information to work with as she threaded the path toward Madam's destiny.

About five minutes later, as Madam was insisting that she had no intention of taking any sort of trip in the near future no matter what the Tower in juxtaposition to the Six of Cups said, Patricia saw a small sliver of white paper emerge from under the office door. Patricia finished with the disputative lady as quickly as decently possible and then gave a double rap on the office door as Madam disappeared down the stairs.

The door opened, Isaac twisted out and closed it behind him. 'Well!' he said.

'I am not destined to die of a heart attack,' Patricia told him, 'because if I were, I would have done when they opened that door.'

'Thanks to your timely warning,' Isaac told her, 'I had just time to close the safe and secrete myself in an inconspicuous but highly uncomfortable hidey-hole. I had moved the desk lamp to a better position for my needs and had no time to put it back, but luckily it was not noticed.'

'Where in earth did you find to hide in that room?' Patricia asked, remembering the sparseness of it. Little more than a desk, two chairs, and a leather couch. An, as she remembered, overly slippery leather couch.

'The bathroom—' Isaac began.

'The bathroom? There's no place to hide in the bathroom.'

'The bathroom has a tub and a shower curtain,' Isaac reminded her.

'You pulled the curtain?'

'I didn't dare, it might have made someone suspicious enough to check,' he said. 'So I closed it ever so slightly and leaned against the wall, twisting my torso so as to keep it concealed. Someone did come in while I was there to, ah, tinkle, but he didn't look behind the curtain.'

'Did you have a chance to get into the safe? Was there anything in it?'

Isaac laughed. 'Yes to both. Also I overheard something, I think, quite possibly worthwhile.'

'I will burn an incense stick to Tyche when I get home,' Patricia said. 'Cardamom, I think.'

'Tyche? Ah, yes, the Greek goddess of fortune. You know the legend is that you can pray to Tyche and she may well grant your prayers, but she decides whether the fortune she grants is good or bad. It is a chancy thing, dealing with the gods.'

'Speaking of fortunes,' Patricia said, nodding toward the woman who had just come up the stairs, 'I believe my next client approaches.'

'We'll talk after,' Isaac said.

'Why don't you go downstairs and call for the car?' Patricia asked him. 'After this lady I shall feel fatigued and will say good night to Count Ciano and we can leave.'

'Excellent idea,' Isaac agreed.

NINETEEN

Let the ruling classes tremble at a Communist revolution.
The proletarians have nothing to lose but their chains.
They have a world to win.
Workingmen of all countries, unite!

– Karl Marx

Detective Second Harry Weintz was working at not becoming bored with his assignment – trailing the ersatz Otto Lehman. When you're bored you make mistakes, and Weintz hated making mistakes. Andy Blake had peered at the guy three times from the truck window and was pretty sure that this Otto was not one of the killers of the real Otto. Still, he must be somebody, he must be connected to the killers somehow, he must have some good reason for assuming the dead man's identity, and he must be doing something he shouldn't, or why bother? But a good tail job is a real pain in the ass; boring as hell ninety-five percent of the time, with brief moments of drama or comedy depending on how you look at it, as you dodge aside or look innocently into the window of a foundation-garments store or hunt frantically for a cab to follow the one your subject just grabbed. All the while carrying a change of hats, a reversible overcoat, and a false beard, which he had never actually used but you never know, in the continuous effort not to be noticed.

The subject, whom Weintz decided to call 'Otto' for want of a better choice, went through an elaborate procedure whenever he left the house: going maybe ten, twenty yards in one direction, stopping to tie his shoe, looking carefully around to see if anyone was interested in his movements, and then doubling back in the other direction confident that he was free of pursuers. To Weintz, who watched these maneuvers from the other side of the street and about half a block down, they seemed a sort of ritualistic dance to appease the gods of – of what? Of prudence? Of safety? Of secrecy? As Otto went on his way Weintz would casually begin his own ritual of following while staying out of sight.

The daily trips were of little note: to the grocery store on the next block, to the movies where he sat alone, to a nearby barbershop to get a haircut. Once he took the IRT to an optician on 14th to get fitted for a pair of glasses, once he went to buy a pair of shoes at Wiggins on Columbus and 84th Street. He ate regularly at the Schrafft's restaurant in the Hotel Dumont building on 79th off Broadway. It was on the subject's fourth visit to the Schrafft's that Weintz decided he wasn't so bored after all.

The Schrafft's had two entrances, one on the street and another in the hotel lobby. Otto as usual went in the street entrance and took a seat toward the back. Weintz went around to the lobby, with the idea of entering Schrafft's through the inside to be less notice-able. He paused next to a sad-looking palm tree to give Otto a chance to settle in, and was about to meander over to the restaurant when Otto emerged through the inside door and crossed the lobby, heading for a side corridor.

Ha!

Through the corridor and into an entrance to a service area and past two rooms and then down a flight of stairs, with Weintz hanging so far behind that he was afraid he was going to lose him. But Otto, protected by his ritual, clearly had no idea he was being followed. He headed for a room about halfway down the next corridor and paused to greet a short man in a long overcoat who stood in front of the open door smoking a cigarette. They both gave a sort of closed-fisted salute, and Otto went on into the room.

Weintz, not sure if he had been seen, pulled back behind the corridor door and waited for a minute before he peered around it again. The man in the overcoat was gone, and a short, skinny man wearing a chauffeur's cap was just going in the door.

There must be a meeting of some sort going on in that room, and at least one more way to get down to it. Weintz could either pull back to the hotel lobby and wait or find someplace where he could watch who came in and went out of that room. If it wasn't important that Otto not know he was under observation, Weintz could merely barge into the room and go, 'Here now, what's all this then?' like the Scotland Yard boys did in all those British movies. But maybe there was a decent hiding place somewhere along the corridor.

There was no one in the corridor now, it was as good a time as any. He went through the door and started down, trying the handles of the doors he passed. The third one turned just as he heard some voices and a door at the other end started to open. He swung his door open, stepped into the room, and closed the door quickly and silently behind him. The room was dark, but he decided not to look for a light switch. Dark was his friend. He leaned against the door, trying to hear if there were voices outside.

A flashlight clicked on from a few feet away, its beam aimed at his face. 'Son of a bitch!' a voice said in a whisper. 'I thought it was you!'

'What? Who?' Weintz could make out that there was a person, probably a man, holding the light but couldn't tell who it was. He flattened himself against the door and reached slowly behind his back for his service revolver.

'Weintzy, what the hell are you doing here?' the voice asked.

'Who the hell are you?' Weintz demanded – a not unreasonable question considering the circumstances.

The flashlight flicked up to show the man's face, then he turned it off. 'It's me,' the voice said.

'Conley?'

'Right! Got it in one.' Special Agent Alfred Conley of the FBI turned the flashlight on again, aiming it at the floor. 'And again – what the hell are you doing here?'

'Following a guy,' Weintz said. 'And you? You living here now?'

Conley chuckled. 'Stakeout,' he said. He turned the light over toward the corner of the room where a man wearing a pair of head-phones was sitting in front of a black box, fiddling with some knobs, and studiously ignoring both Conley and Weintz. On a table by his side were a large thermos, a stack of cardboard cups, a couple of bags of chips, and the remains of a couple of deli sandwiches. Someone, Weintz noticed, had not eaten his pickle. There was what Weintz thought was a pee bottle carefully capped on the floor next to the table.

'Dictaphone,' Conley explained. 'We got a couple of mikes planted in the room across the way. Which is where your guy went, right?'

'Right,' Weintz agreed. 'I'll tell you my tale if you tell me yours.'

Conley laughed again. 'You're a funny man,' he said.

What was funny about that? Weintz wondered. But he said nothing.

'Commies,' Conley told him.

'Communists?'

'Yeah. They meet across there once or twice a week, and we listen. We don't learn much 'cause they use code names and such, but every bit helps fill out the big picture. Now, your turn.'

Weintz wondered how much to tell Conley. Were we holding anything back? He decided that the stuff about the naked dead guy, and that this guy was probably a ringer, would keep, but he could open the bag on the rest. So: 'The guy I'm following, his name, as far as we know, is Otto Lehman. Lives in a boarding house on 92nd Street, where he may or may not have pushed another guy down a flight of stairs. My boss wants to know if and why.'

'Lehman?'

'Yeah.'

'Wait a minute. Wasn't that the name of – sure!' Conley clicked on a little lamp sitting on the corner of the table. 'This guy a German? Like fresh off the boat?'

'We think maybe,' Weintz told him.

'That's the guy we missed when he got off the boat a few weeks back. Our agents got there a few minutes after someone else whisked him away.'

'Sounds right,' Weintz said.

'We figured he'd turn up. He's supposed to be some sort of bigwig Commie. We'll have to go over what he says in there – see if he seems to be sort of leading the discussion.'

'You figure we can get a transcription of the cylinders?' Weintz asked.

'Probably,' Conley told him. 'I don't see why not. Have your boss ask my boss.'

'Yeah,' Weintz said. 'I'll do that.'

TWENTY

The soundest strategy in war is to postpone operations
until the moral disintegration of the enemy
renders the delivery of the mortal blow both possible and easy.
– Vladimir Lenin

Gauleiter Gerard was sitting at a small table in the speakers' area behind the stage in the Hotel Vandamm meeting room, staring into a mirror and powdering his face when Welker knocked on the door and came in. 'You wanted t' see me?'

Gerard swung around. 'Schnek? Yes. Come in and sit. I must finish making myself presentable for my public so we will talk while I continue, if you don't mind.'

'Course not,' Welker agreed. 'You do what you gotta do.'

'I have these pock marks of the face,' Gerard explained. 'The spotlight makes them look truly bad, so I cover them. The appearance must not distract from the message.'

'Very true,' Welker agreed.

'I am given to understand that you are an expert with explosives. Is that right?'

Welker shrugged. 'An expert? I don't know. I had some experience in the army during the War. Land mines and booby traps mostly.'

'You planted them?'

'I taught others how t' find and deactivate 'em.'

'But you could, if required, create one?'

'Oh sure. Much easier t' create a booby trap than t' disarm one. Much.'

'Ah!' said Gauleiter Gerard. 'And you could teach someone else how to do this?' Welker decided that he shouldn't appear too willing or too eager to create bombs. 'Say,' he said. 'Just what do you have in mind?' A question that he very much did want the answer to. 'I don't want any part in blowing up, you know, buildings or whatever, or doing anything t' harm the U S of A. I'm a patriotic American.'

'Of course you are. We all are.' Gerard finished his powdering and swiveled around in his chair to face Welker. 'There are certain places, certain events, that we would like to on occasion disrupt, if you see what I mean. Communist meetings, Jewish organizations . . . Did you know that there's a YMHA? That's H as for Hebrew!' Gerard managed to sound outraged. 'Young Men's *Hebrew* Association.'

'You want t' blow them up?'

'Well, we're not ready for that kind of stuff yet. But maybe blow out a couple of windows – something like that.'

'Well, I guess,' Welker said.

'So you think you could teach a couple of our guys kind of basic bomb-making?'

'It ain't going to be that easy,' Welker told him. 'Getting the stuff, for instance. There ain't that many excuses for going around buying high explosives. Which makes it easier for the G-men t' trace it back to you. I think blowing something up that ain't supposed t' be blown up is a Federal offense, so Hoover will come after you. I don't want Hoover coming after me.'

'I get that,' Gerard said.

'Course you could make it yourself. Nitro ain't that hard to make.'

'Well then . . .'

'But it ain't what you might call forgiving. You make a mistake and you ain't around anymore. And a lot of what was around you ain't around neither.' Welker was beginning to regret that he had picked this uncouth dialect for Harry Schnek, but now he was stuck with it.

'But you could make it?'

'Not me. I could maybe show someone how, and then they're on their own and I'm nowheres near what they're doing. I ain't kidding, that stuff is dangerous. TNT, dynamite, blasting powder, much better to handle. Still not what I'd call safe, but not like nitro.'

'We'll have to look around, see what we can get,' Gerard said, pushing himself to his feet, rocking the table and bouncing up little puffs of powder like a row of tiny dust devils. 'Got to go and arouse my people,' he said. 'We'll talk about this. Glad to have you in my corner.'

'Yeah,' Welker said.

TWENTY-ONE

'If seven maids with seven mops
Swept it for half a year,
Do you suppose,' the Walrus said,
'That they could get it clear?'
'I doubt it,' said the Carpenter,
And shed a bitter tear.

— *Lewis Carroll*

Geoffrey called her when his plane landed in New York. 'I'll be home tomorrow,' he said. 'Not sure what time.' The next morning he called back to add: 'I'll be bringing a surprise.'

'What sort of surprise?'

'Well, she's about five foot three, slender, young – quite young – attractive, in a coltish sort of way, and Jewish.'

'What?'

He laughed. 'I'll explain when I see you. Cheerio!' and he hung up.

It was three that afternoon when Milton went to answer the door and returned to announce, 'It's the master back, m'lady. And a young person.' He did not sound surprised. Geoffrey and Patricia had, late one night after a martini or two, spent an idle half-hour speculating on what it would take to surprise Milton.

Patricia was standing, a Scotch and soda in each hand, as Geoffrey strode into the living room, with a teenage girl a couple of cautious steps behind. Patricia handed Geoffrey one of the glasses and then turned to survey the girl. 'Well!' she said. 'Very pretty, but not at all your usual type.'

Geoffrey raised an eyebrow, something he practiced in front of a mirror and was quite good at. 'Tastes change,' he said. 'People mature.'

'My darling,' she said, carefully touching the edge of his glass with her own, 'I would hate to think of you ever maturing. So, how long have you been escorting this young lady, and how and where did you acquire her?'

'He didn't,' the girl began, looking startled. 'That is we didn't . . . I mean . . .'

Patricia took the girl's hand. 'I'm sorry, my dear,' she said. 'I didn't mean to upset you. Of course he didn't. But there must be a story behind why he brought you here, and I'm dying to hear it. Would you like something to drink? Not a Scotch, I think. Tea?' She pulled the bell pull for Milton, and then turned back. 'What is your name? And how do you come to be clinging – metaphorically – to my husband's bespoke coat tails?'

'Sophie, Lady Patricia,' the girl said. 'Sophie Hertzel. And your husband, I believe, saved my life.'

'Ah!' Patricia smiled at her husband. 'I'm not surprised. He has a knack for doing that sort of thing. Come, sit down, you must tell me the whole story.'

Sophie went and perched on the edge of the couch seat and stared across the room.

Milton appeared in the doorway.

'A tea service for the young lady, I think, Milton,' Patricia told him. 'And have we any cake?'

'I'll see, m'lady,' Milton said, and backed away.

'Now,' Patricia said, turning back to Sophie.

Sophie seemed disinclined to discuss the recent past, so Geoffrey took over the job, not dwelling unnecessarily on the painful parts. 'And so,' he concluded, 'we spent the morning in a hunt for Miss Hertzel's Uncle Moishe, who does not seem to be listed in the Brooklyn phone book. There is one Moses Hertzel, but according to his wife, whom we spoke to at length, he is from somewhere in Russia and he has no brothers, only a sister, she should rot in Hell.'

'No uncle?'

'Not yet, we'll keep looking.'

'Then she has no place to go?'

'At present, no place,' Geoffrey agreed.

'Then she shall stay with us until a relative can be produced.' Patricia turned to Sophie. 'Have you any clothes? No, of course you don't.'

'I do have a few things,' Sophie said. 'Besides what I'm wearing I have the boys' clothes I wore on the train and a change of underwear and a comb and brush.'

'We shall go clothes shopping tomorrow,' Patricia told her. 'And other things. A girl must have a variety of other things.'

'But I can't—'

'Of course you can. And school – you'll have to go to school. Your English is excellent, by the way.'

'Thank you. We lived in London for some years when I was a child. My father taught at the Royal Academy: piano and conducting. My mother played the violin.'

Patricia turned to her husband. 'Where can we send her to school? We'll need transcripts from her last school or something, won't we?'

'She has no papers of any kind,' Geoffrey said, 'and I don't see how we can get them. Not the real ones, anyway. But papers can be supplied. I'll get on it.'

'I haven't been to the *Gymnasium* – high school – for the last two years,' Sophie said. 'Jewish students were eliminated from the schools. I have been taught at home. So there are no papers to get.'

'Well,' Patricia said. 'A minor problem to surmount.' She reached over to the bell pull, and then sat on the couch and made patting motion on the cushion next to her. 'Here,' she said to Sophie. 'Come sit with me and we will tell each other our girlish secrets. Well, some of them anyway. And Geoffrey will – oh, that reminds me!' She twisted her head around to see where her husband had moved to. 'We're to have a visitor perhaps early next week. An old friend. He says he is, anyway.'

'Has he a name?'

'Welker.'

'Welker?'

'Think back to the War. American. Tall, good-looking, brown hair, little mustache. I don't know if he had it then, of course. Says you and he used to spend your time telling nasty stories about your superior officers.'

'Oh, that Welker. Captain Jacob. Joseph? Jacob. What's he doing here?'

'Don't you like him?'

'As a matter of fact I hold him in high regard. One of the few men I've ever met who's as intelligent as I am, give or take.'

'Really!' Patricia said. 'As intelligent as you, indeed! What happened to the customary public-school reticence and self-deprecation?'

'In warfare stupidity kills,' Geoffrey told her. 'And there was far too much of it about. It almost seemed a requisite for staff rank.'

Milton appeared in the doorway, a silver serving platter balanced in one hand.

'Ah, Milton,' Patricia said. 'Would you please tell Annie to make up the spare room? This young lady will be staying with us for a while.'

'Yes, milady,' he said. 'I have brought tea and a cheese sandwich for the young lady. Mrs Werther insisted on making a sandwich. And a slice of pound cake.' He set the platter down in front of Sophie and fussed with it for a few seconds, then stood up. 'And there is a letter.' He held out a white envelope.

'The post at this time of day?' Patricia asked.

'It was hand delivered,' Milton explained. 'From the Embassy. For His Lordship.'

'Ah!' Geoffrey exclaimed, taking the envelope. 'I wonder which of my recent sins is catching up with me?'

'Surely not,' Patricia said. 'You're still nimble enough to outrun your sins.'

'This month I am especially avoiding sins that begin with the letter "B",' he told her, 'including but not limited to Blasphemy, Back-Biting, Babbling, Bitterness, Bastardy, and Drinking Blood.'

'Babbling?' Patricia asked.

'Even so. In Paul's first epistle to Timothy he tells him, "Keep that which is committed to thy trust, avoiding profane and vain babblings."'

'Why,' Patricia asked, 'do you memorize things like that?'

'They sort of stick in my mind,' he told her. 'I mean, why on earth do I remember:

"The llama is a wooly sort of fleecy hairy goat,

With an indolent expression and an undulating throat,

Like an unsuccessful literary man"?'

'And, mind you, I could go on. But I will spare you.'

'I would be ever so grateful,' Patricia told him. 'And I require no further information on the lion, the yak, or the spider either, thank you.'

Sophie looked from one to the other of her two benefactors. Staying with them, she decided, might be interesting.

Geoffrey smiled at Patricia, transferred the smile to Sophie, and then looked down at the envelope in his hand. 'Sent from the embassy in Berlin by diplomatic pouch, or so it claims,' he said. He took a silver penknife from his waistcoat pocket and carefully slit the envelope open and removed the contents. 'Aha! That was fast.'

'What is it?' Patricia asked.

Geoffrey spent another half-minute examining the two enclosures and then passed the first over to her.

'A picture,' she said, holding it this way and that as though seeing if anything would fall out of the two-dimensional surface and into the room. 'A lady and two children.'

'And a draft on a London bank for a thousand pounds,' he said, waving the other document in front of him. 'Made out to me, with a note saying "*Ich bezahl immer meine Schulden.*"'

'I always pay my debts,' Sophie translated.

'Yes.'

'And just why does this person, whoever he is, owe you a thousand pounds?' Patricia asked, raising an eyebrow.

'I suppose because mine is the only name he knows,' Geoffrey told her. 'I shall hand the draft over to SIS, and they can decide what to do with it.'

'Yes,' Patricia insisted, 'but what is it *for*?'

'A passport for the lady and her children,' Geoffrey told her, 'and escort service out of Germany.' He turned and bowed slightly to Sophie. 'Although she will not have the privilege of being accompanied by a royal duke.'

'He is a nice man,' Sophie said reflectively.

'Yes,' Geoffrey agreed. 'Yes he is. Essentially. And,' he reached over and patted Sophie on the shoulder, 'we'll have to also get you a passport, or some sort of documentation. I'll look into it.'

'Who are these people and why do they need a passport?' Patricia asked.

'No more questions for now, my love. All will be revealed in the fullness of time. Back these go on the next flight to London to get the passports made up and the plan in motion. Now, when is Herr Welker coming over? Is he joining us for dinner?'

'Not today, I think,' Patricia said. 'Sometime early next week. He is coming from New York. Perhaps we should dine at a restaurant. And – oh!' She turned to Sophie. 'You're Jewish?'

'Yes,' Sophie told her, sounding a bit apprehensive. Jewish had not been a good thing to be in her recent experience.

'What do you eat? Or rather, what don't you eat? Pork, I believe. And something about milk and meat . . .'

'Oh, that,' Sophie said. 'I . . . we didn't keep Kosher. I eat whatever, although I am not overly fond of pork or ham. We were not particularly religious.'

'Oh good,' Patricia said. 'It does simplify things. Not that we'd have any objection to your being as religious as you like, but now we don't have to learn all those rules, and get two sets of plates and such.'

'Yes,' Sophie said. 'Truthfully, it always struck me as being a bit silly.'

'Most religions have some things that seem a bit silly to outsiders,' Geoffrey said. 'Sometimes even to insiders.'

'We have a friend,' Patricia told Sophie, 'Avram ben Daveed, or so he calls himself these days. Teaches Middle Eastern Studies at Princeton University in, I believe, New Jersey. Whenever he comes to Washington these days he comes to dinner. He brings his own food. At first we were insulted, now we are quietly amused.'

'He once made chicken soup for us,' Geoffrey offered, 'with balls in it.'

'Matzoh balls,' Patricia expanded.

'Yes,' Geoffrey agreed. 'It was very good.'

'The secret was in the feet,' Patricia added, 'or so he told us.'

'The feet?' Sophie asked.

'Yes, the chicken feet. They must be in the soup while it's cooking. I insisted that they be taken out before serving, but by then they had done their job, apparently. It was, I agree, very tasty.'

Milton reappeared. 'The young lady's room is ready,' he announced.

'Good,' Patricia said. She turned to Sophie. 'Why don't you go to your room and settle in. Ask Milton or Annie for anything you need. The room has a connecting bathroom to the other guest room, which is vacant at the moment. I'll loan you some things for the evening, and we'll go shopping tomorrow.'

Sophie stood up. 'I am not . . . I don't know what to say,' she said.

'You needn't say anything,' Patricia told her. 'Go, get settled, have a nap. We'll see you at dinner.'

When Sophie had disappeared in the direction of her bedroom Patricia moved over to the couch and beckoned to her husband. 'Come,' she said, picking up a bowl that seemed to be full of white beads and setting it on her lap. 'You must tell me all about HRH and your adventure. I assume you had an adventure. I mean even before you acquired the lissome sixteen-year-old.'

'I shall relate all,' Geoffrey agreed, moving to sit on the couch across from her. 'But first, how was the embassy party? And, a separate question, is that,' he asked, pointing at the bowl in her lap, 'a bowl full of pearls?'

She nodded. 'This is the four-strand pearl necklace your mother gave me,' she told him. 'All unstrung.'

'I see that,' he said. 'Why?'

'Well, it's quite lovely and I've decided to start wearing it again, but I'm a bit nervous about it falling apart – it's probably fifty years old. So I've decided to clean the pearls and restring them. Which involved a week in a baking soda and vinegar bath to finally elimin-ate the memory of your mother's favorite perfume.'

'I wondered why you reminded me of Mother while you were wearing them. So it was more than just the pearls themselves.'

'It was the Chanel.'

'Yes. Now that you mention it. And now? You don't just thread them onto a string?'

'Ah, men,' she said. 'It is a delicate and time-consuming process. Each pearl must be knotted in place so if the string breaks you only loose one pearl. And the knots must be tiny, so that all you see are the pearls.' She demonstrated, sliding and knotting a pearl in place on the doubled silk thread, and then doing another.

'Very deft,' he said. 'Now you must tell me how you avoided going to prison. I suppose it's too much to hope that you decided not to burgle the ambassador's safe.'

Patricia grinned. 'We did it,' she told him. 'And we were wildly successful. Although there were a few scary moments. And truthfully I'm not sure just what it is we got. And,' she added, 'I've acquired a useful new skill.'

'Really?'

'Really. I can tell your fortune with a deck of cards.'

Ah!' Geoffrey said. 'I have an uncle who lost a fortune with a deck of cards, but I suppose that's not the same thing. But do go on.'

'You first. Tell me all.'

'Fair enough.' Geoffrey settled back and related the story of the past few days, emphasizing the scenery and the personalities of the people they had met. Patricia was especially interested in close descriptions of scenery and people. He found that he had difficulty in conveying his image of Herr Hitler. 'He's short,' Geoffrey began, 'and intense. He does not project a feeling of great intellect but one of great assurance. He walks as though,' he fished for an image, 'as though if he were to walk into the sea he would expect it to part around him. And those around him watch him as though they were waiting for him at any instant to turn water into wine. Although Herr Hitler, I am given to understand, is himself a teetotaler. Also a vegetarian.'

'Really? Does he smoke? Or screw? Or does he prefer men?'

'I understand, none of the above. And homosexuals are a dis-favored class in the New Germany. I have heard some disturbing rumors about a niece, I believe, who apparently committed suicide under strange circumstances. But to be fair rumors are . . . rumors. One cannot put credence in them.'

'So. Did you take to him?'

'Take to him? No. He frightens the bloody hell out of me. Although HRH seemed quite taken with him. But then I think Der Führer was quite impressed that he was in a private conver-sation with a member of the Royal Family. He was on his best behavior.'

'But he frightens you? Is it what he's doing with Germany? Or the way he's treating the Jews and Communists?'

'Yes, all of that of course. But more. He personally frightens me. He leaves me with the feeling that if I were standing between Herr Hitler and the door he would walk right through me, were it not easier to go around.'

'Well!' she said.

'Enough of that,' he said. 'Now your turn. Tell me all about how you didn't get arrested for safecracking.'

Patricia smiled and leaned back in her corner of the couch. She related her foray into l'Ambasciata d'Italia with Uncle Isaac and a deck of tarot cards, and had Geoffrey chuckling three times and only looking panic-stricken once, which she thought was about right. He was professionally interested in her description of Count Ciano and the two visiting Germans, and nicely restrained his curiosity about Isaac's foray into the ambassador's office until she reached the end of her story. 'And,' she said with a dramatic flourish, 'and . . .' she reached into her oversized Briani alligator purse with the gold fittings and fished around. 'Shit!'

'What?' Geoffrey asked, looking startled. It had been a heartfelt *Shit!*

'I thought they were – oh, I remember.' She got up and left the room, coming back a minute later with a manila envelope in her hand. 'I put them in my stocking drawer for safekeeping.'

'What exactly?'

She handed him the envelope. 'I'm not sure. Isaac says they're pads – well, pictures of pads. He has this camera, a Minox I think, kind of looks like a pocket cigarette lighter, all the rage with German spies, and he took pictures of pages of this pad he found in the safe. He says you'll know what they are. He says they'll either be of great value to you or of no use whatsoever, and he can't tell which, but he rather hopes the former. He had to develop them himself because nobody knows how to do it in this country; the camera apparently isn't for sale over here yet. And besides who could you ask to print pictures of secret Italian documents?'

Geoffrey took the packet of photographs out of the envelope and riffled through them. There were thirty-two three-by-four-inch surprisingly clear prints, most of them showing pages of typewritten letters arranged in lines and columns, eight apparently random five-letter groups forming a line, and lines all the way down the page. The first one he looked at began like this:

21 2367

WEEDK GROBD QORPN YTMQZ PUMJK TDWWP ATNHD AHASW

DQTHY AJTKO HQHOM GEULL WOEBT SOVTL DLEFE PBGIT

And so on down the page.

He stared at them blankly for a while and then comprehension came. 'Son of a bitch!'

'To which particular dog are you referring?' Patricia asked.

'What we have here,' Geoffrey told her, 'is a rum-ti-tum. Haven't seen one since the War.'

'A rum . . .?'

'It's what we called them. The proper name is, I believe, a one-time pad. They came into use late in the War for encrypting messages at brigade level and above. Ours didn't look exactly like this – the layout was different – but I'll wager that's what it is.'

Patricia took one of the photos and held it up to the light. 'So this is a secret message?'

'Not exactly, my love. This is the watchamacallit – the code that lets a message become secret.'

'Oh,' she said. 'Of course.'

'Actually,' he said, 'the idea is very simple. You take your message and write it over the letters on the pad – one letter of your message on top of each printed letter. Then you add the two letters together to come up with your code letter.'

'Oh,' she said. 'Of course. You add two letters together.'

'Look,' he explained. 'You give each letter a number value. A is one, B is two, C is three, and so on. Then you add together the message letter and the code letter – as numbers, if you see what I mean, and use the resulting number, ah, letter as your encrypted value. To decrypt it you do the reverse. If the number is larger than twenty-six, you subtract twenty-six and use the result. It's very time-consuming but your secret messages stay secret. Provided you rip that sheet off the pad and never use it again.'

'Twenty-six?'

'That's how many letters there are in our alphabet.'

'Of course. So, will these be useful?'

'Actually yes, I think. Traffic to the embassies, if it isn't in the diplomatic pouches, is sent by radio, which is unreliable and may be intercepted, or by regular overseas cable, and then delivered by your faithful Western Union delivery boy. And why not? If it's encoded by one-time pad, it's unbreakable.'

'Unless you have a copy of the pad,' Patricia offered.

'Unless,' Geoffrey agreed. 'We'll need to turn them over to our American friends, if we have any. They will be ever so grateful.'

'There's more,' she told him, looking smug. 'Uncle Isaac overheard part of the conversation between Count Ciano and the two Germans.'

'Really? And?'

'There is something big getting set to happen in New York,

apparently. Sometime soon. Something of great value to the Reich, which should please the Italians. Something that will displease the Communists.'

'Why the Communists?'

'He didn't say.'

'What sort of thing?'

'Isaac didn't hear. Apparently the German, whichever one was talking, was vague about it.'

'New York?'

'New York.'

'We should tell someone.'

'Yes, but what?'

Geoffrey shrugged. 'I don't exactly know,' he said.

TWENTY-TWO

> *All the world's a stage,*
> *and all the men and women merely players:*
> *they have their exits and their entrances;*
> *and one man in his time plays many parts . . .*
> — *William Shakespeare*

Major Sir Henry Cardine did not expect to be back in Berlin so soon. Indeed, he had no plans to be back in Berlin ever again. But a mortal's fate is oft thrust unwitting into the hands of the gods. The gods in this case being the wallahs at MI6 who spoke to him of Duty and Country and managed to work in references to Nelson and Wellington and, somehow, Robert Browning and Tennyson, until he would have proudly marched into the Valley of Death. Or even Berlin.

So here he was: black bowler hat, regimental tie, briefcase, furled umbrella, and a growing sense of unease. Since he'd landed at Tempelhof Airport he'd had the feeling that he was being followed, but he imagined that all foreigners in Berlin these days felt they were being followed. And probably a lot of Berliners. His handlers in London had said he should not make any attempts to find out if it were so but to behave naturally, whatever that might be under the circumstances. Which made him feel like a goldfish trying not to see if anyone was peering into the bowl. But his was not to reason why, his was but to . . . he decided not to finish that quote even in his head.

He checked in to the Kaiserhof, where he was given a room on a lower floor overlooking the loading dock, thus showing the management's appraisal of his current status. After an overnight stay and a brief meeting with the departing manager of Wannesfrei Grammophon, which served to explain his presence to any unseen watchers, he was scheduled to meet his newly created sister Mabel Bellant and her two children Bruce and Priscilla in the Kaiserhof lobby at two. They would be accompanied by the man he knew as Felix. He had a brief message for Felix. And then he would give Mabel her passport, and escort her and her progeny out of the country as rapidly as possible while avoiding the appearance of haste. They had – what was the word the MI6 bloke was so fond of . . . notionally? That was it – notionally been in Switzerland until a few days ago when she had decided to visit Berlin and travel home with her brother. The passport had all the required visas and border stamps to support the story.

He re-entered the hotel at quarter to two and repaired to a corner table in the bar to indulge in a fortifying Scotch and water – no ice, thank you – before the gathering up of his new clan. He was on his second Scotch half an hour later, at quarter past two, when Felix slid onto the chair across the table and nodded. 'Hello again,' he said.

'Hello,' Sir Henry said. 'Good to see you.'

'So,' Felix said, 'you are not of the Military Intelligence? And I almost believed you.'

'I was, ah, recruited for this one task,' Sir Henry told him. 'Because we knew each other. Believe me, this is not my chosen profession.'

Felix nodded his understanding. 'All the sneaking around and lying,' he said, 'seems rather ungentlemanly, eh?'

Sir Henry allowed himself a slight smile. 'Rather unsporting,' he agreed. 'But necessities of war and all that.'

'We are sometimes not given the choice,' said Felix. 'Now, to the present business.'

'I am ready,' Sir Henry said, reaching into his jacket pocket for his notional sister's new passport.

'There's a problem,' Felix said.

Of course, Sir Henry thought, *there's a problem. What would life be if there wasn't a problem?* 'What sort of problem?'

'I should say rather, there's a delay. At least if we are fortunate that's all it is.'

'How long a delay?'

'Well,' Felix said, 'it's hard to say. Apparently the Gestapo came by to arrest Madeleine just as she was preparing to leave.' He waved at the waitress. '*Steinhäger, bitte.*'

Sir Henry frowned. 'Madeleine?'

'Oh yes, sorry,' Felix said. 'Your Mabel Bellant.'

'I see,' Sir Henry said. 'The Gestapo? So she's under arrest? That sounds as if it could engender rather a long delay.'

'It's actually a rather amusing story,' Felix said, 'which we may be able to laugh at in ten or twenty years. It seems that just as the Gestapo were ready to enter her studio a staff car pulled up in front – with a motorcycle escort no less. Reichsmarschall Hermann Göring emerged and strode through the door and up the stairs. He had dropped by on his way to someplace important to pick up a gown that Madeleine had been fitting for his wife. But the Gestapo agents, not knowing why the Reichsmarschall had come by, retreated in temporary confusion. The possibilities, you see, were, let us say, interesting. They fell back and set to watching the building while waiting for someone higher up to decide what to do.'

The waitress set a small glass in front of Felix and he stared down at it.

'How did you find out all this?'

'Madeleine's studio is on the first floor of a commercial building,' Felix explained. 'The proprietor of the cheese store on the ground floor, who is a friend, observed what was happening and ran upstairs to tell her, passing the Reichsmarschall, who was on his way back down. Madeleine grabbed her suitcase and hurried back downstairs with the cheese-store proprietor. She slid the suitcase under the counter, put on an apron, and began selling cheese. When the Gestapo entered the building twenty minutes later, they found a sign pinned to the studio door saying closed for the day, back tomorrow at ten.

They broke down the door anyway and tossed things about before they left. A couple of them are watching the building in case she returns while the others go to her apartment to pick her up, or so I would assume. They will be disappointed.'

'I still don't see—' Sir Henry began.

'How I know all this?' Felix picked up the glass of Steinhäger and downed it in one continuous gesture. It did not seem to have any effect on him. He gestured at the waitress and she brought him another. 'She called me,' he told Sir Henry. 'After the Gestapo men left she snuck back up to her studio and called me. She didn't want to use the cheese man's phone to keep him from being implicated in our problems.'

'But if they can trace her call back to you?'

'It is a phone that will be disconnected tomorrow in an apartment that I will never go back to.' He sighed. 'Oh, what a tangled web we weave . . .'

'Why, at this time—' Sir Henry started.

'Ah! You have touched the important question. Why indeed? There is a general and gradual roundup of Jews, but they don't usually send a contingent of Gestapo after one unimportant Jewess. I'm afraid it has to do with Herr Fauth.'

'Herr . . .?'

'Herr Fauth – the lady's husband. He is, of necessity, a somewhat shadowy figure.'

'Shadowy?'

'Yes. You see I am Herr Fauth, and since I can only occupy that, ah, personality part of the time, he is a vague and partial presence in Madeleine's life. Quite possibly the Gestapo have become curious about Herr Fauth and have decided to see what his response will be when they arrest his wife.'

'So what now?' Sir Henry asked.

'So I have to get her away from the cheese shop before six o'clock, which is when it closes. She cannot remain behind after the shop closes. Even the Gestapo are not that stupid. Luckily the children are already out of the house, and I have had them sent ahead to Tempelhof, so all we have to do is somehow get Madeleine out of the cheese shop before six.'

Sir Henry frowned. 'We?'

'If you have nothing better to do.'

'This is not the sort of thing I'm good at,' Sir Henry said.

'Few of us are,' said Felix. 'And there is no time for me to engage one of that few. I regret having to ask you to assist me in this, an action you are neither prepared nor equipped to do, but I have little choice.'

'Equipped?' Sir Henry asked.

'Mentally, I meant. If you are indeed not an agent of Military Intelligence then you have not received the training for such clandestine operations.'

'That is true,' Sir Henry admitted. 'I have not. I could not successfully disguise myself as, say, a German businessman well enough to fool a schoolchild.'

'Ah, but a German Army officer you could probably manage,' Felix said. 'Certainly well enough to fool a civilian.'

'Is that what you want?'

Felix patted the air with his hand. 'No, no,' he said. 'It was just a random thought. Army officers are one large fraternity the world over, although occasionally we have to fight each other.'

Two SS officers in their black and silver uniforms entered and strutted up to the bar. Sir Henry gestured toward them. 'What of those, ah, gentlemen?' he asked. 'Are they part of our fraternity?'

'I would say not,' Felix admitted, glancing at them, his face impassive.

'You don't think they would actually fight?'

'Oh, no,' Felix said. 'It's not that. They will most assuredly fight. Some of them, I understand, are fighting in Spain, and doing very well. Weasels, I understand, fight very well. But there is some essential level of humanity that the Schutzstaffel seem to have absented from their makeup.' Felix downed his second glass and stood up. 'Come,' he said. 'If you are willing to help me, come.'

Sir Henry found himself standing before he had actually decided what he was going to do. Then he mentally shrugged. *In for a penny* . . . 'What do you need me to do?' he asked.

The plan was alarmingly simple: lure the Gestapo watchers away and then pick up the lady and run – or preferably walk calmly – around the corner before they returned. A taxi would be waiting to take them to the airport, where if the gods had smiled upon them the lady's two children would be waiting. Felix was to do the luring whilst Sir Henry and his notional sister did the calm walking.

'And if we are stopped?' Sir Henry asked.

'Madeleine – Mabel – will have her passport, and you will be escorting your sister back home. If they press you, you will allow your annoyance to turn into indignation – you British are quite good at indignation. They are looking for a single Jewish woman, not a British lady traveling with her brother. And she does not look like what they believe a Jewess to look like. You should have no trouble blustering your way through.'

'What if . . .' Sir Henry paused. 'Oh, never mind. There are a thousand what if's and whichever one I attempt to plan for here will be the wrong one.'

'Much like a battle, yes?' Felix suggested.

Sir Henry nodded thoughtfully. 'Yes,' he agreed. 'Let us go.'

'I will go out first,' Felix told him.

'Yes,' Sir Henry agreed. Then he paused and took Felix's arm. 'Oh, wait one second. Before I forget, I have a message for you.'

'Yes?'

'From Lord Geoffrey. He is arranging to get you a radio transmitter. On the outside it will look like a – what do you call it? – a "people's receiver".'

'Yes, the ubiquitous *Volksempfänger.* The party is trying to get one into every German household so that all can listen to der Führer's words.'

'Yes – that. So it will be a bit less problematic should it be discovered.'

'A bit less,' Felix agreed.

'But it will actually be able to transmit and receive in the something-or-other band. I don't know the technical stuff, but all will be explained. And he suggested that you use a book code, so there's nothing incriminating to carry around.'

'Save the transmitter itself,' Felix agreed. 'And the book?'

'Lord Geoffrey suggests *Mein Kampf.*'

'Ha!' said Felix.

'Sort of on the principle of *The Purloined Letter*, don't you know.'

Felix nodded. 'Yes. Yes of course. Something so much in plain sight that it becomes invisible.'

'That's it,' Sir Henry said.

'All right,' Felix agreed. 'Then let's get on with it. I'll go now. You will wait for three minutes and then leave through the front door and turn right. There will be a taxicab waiting for you at the corner. The driver will have a green cap.'

Sir Henry grimaced. 'Are you trying to turn this into a spy melodrama?' he asked sourly. 'Why don't I just get the cab in front of the hotel?'

'Because the doorman whistles for a cab if you want one as you leave, and he may whistle for the wrong cab.'

'Ah,' Sir Henry said. 'Of course.'

A dusty black taxi awaited him at the corner, the driver immersed in the day's *Völkischer Beobachter*, which he tossed aside with a disgusted '*Scheissblatt*,' as Sir Henry climbed into the back seat. He gave a two-finger salute and, without a word, pulled away from the corner. After two left turns he pulled up and Felix stepped out of a doorway and got in. They sat there for three or four minutes until Felix was satisfied that no car had followed, then he tapped the cabbie on the shoulder and they started out careening across Berlin. They turned onto Friedrichstrasse and continued south until, after about ten minutes, they slowed and turned down a block-long street called Ulmgasse and parked a bit in from the corner.

'Now,' Felix said, opening the taxi door, 'begin the fun and games. We will stroll together around the corner to the cheese shop. I will enter with you and proceed by myself through the inner door to the stairway and thence up to Madeleine's studio. There I will turn on the lights and appear in the window, perhaps wearing a bonnet and shawl. The two watchers – we believe there are only two – should both scurry inside to capture me. I will be elusive, turning back into a respectable German gentleman, and pass them on the staircase. In the meantime you will gather up Madeleine, and, when you see two men in black-leather greatcoats enter the stairs, scurry around the corner to the taxi. What do you think? It has the virtue of simplicity, no?'

Sir Henry followed Felix out of the taxi. 'We can but try,' he said.

Felix turned and gave him a quizzical look, and then punched him lightly on the arm. 'Cheer up,' he said. 'The fate of civilization depends on what you do here today. Centuries from now your name will be either praised or cursed depending upon the outcome of this, ah, operation. So don't take it so seriously.'

'Well,' Sir Henry said, 'that's certainly reassuring. Let's go do this.'

'One second,' Felix said, 'I almost forgot.' He reached into the shoulder bag he was carrying and brought out a copy of the London *Times*. 'Stick this in your briefcase,' he said. 'It's a day old, so I suggest you start doing the crossword to explain why you're carrying it.'

'And why am I carrying it?'

'Pass it on to the people at MI6,' Felix told him. 'It contains the location of the three dead-letter boxes I will use until and unless I get the transmitter, and how to access them. Tell them, "cabbage".'

'Cabbage?'

'Cabbage. Red cabbage.'

Sir Henry shrugged. 'Red cabbage it is,' he said, unfastening the straps on his briefcase and thrusting the paper inside.

They walked around the corner, chatting about what Sir Henry could never remember; Felix the perfect Junker in his dark-brown double-breasted suit, gray hat, and distinctly military air, Sir Henry almost a caricature of an English gentleman with hat, tie, briefcase, furled umbrella, and look of unassailable dignity. Sir Henry had to resist the impulse to exaggerate every gesture for the benefit of the unseen observers presumably lurking somewhere about. When they reached the shop window of Käse Beske, about eighteen steps in from the corner, they paused to admire the three rows of cheeses on display. Then, after a brief discussion and much pointing at various cheeses, they pushed open the door and went in together.

Madeleine stood behind the high counter, a black-and-white-checked apron covering her from the neck down and a red-and-white kerchief wrapped somehow around her head concealing her hair and most of her forehead. Her eyes widened as they walked in, but she gave no further sign of knowing either of them. 'May I help you?' she asked in German.

'Time to commence practicing your English,' Felix said, leaning over the counter to give her a kiss. 'This gentleman is Sir Henry Cardine, a major in His Majesty's Army, recently retired, or so he claims. And you are his sister Mabel.'

'Of course I am,' she agreed. 'It is a true pleasure to meet you, brother Henry. I may call you Henry?'

'Either Henry or, ah, Pugs.'

'Pugs?'

'It was my nickname in school. It's what my, ah, other sister insists on calling me.'

'I think,' Madeleine said, 'I prefer Henry.'

'I also,' Sir Henry agreed.

'I must run upstairs,' Felix said. 'I have a little charade to perform to draw the watchers inside, at which you must scurry away from here and around the corner with your loving brother. Karl is waiting there to drive you to the airport.'

'But,' she began, 'the children?'

'Kohlmann picked them up. They should be at the airport waiting for you.'

'Thank God!'

'Passport!' Felix said.

'Ah, yes.' Sir Henry pulled it from his pocket and handed it to Madeleine as Felix headed for the door in the back.

'Be careful!' Madeleine called. Felix waved briefly in reply as he vanished through the door.

Madeleine opened the passport to the description page and held it up to the light. 'Mabel,' she said. 'Mabel Bellant. I must practice responding to "Mabel".' She stared critically at the picture, and then turned the passport sideways to see if that would improve the image. 'I am very, how you say, frowsy.'

'I would never say such a thing,' Sir Henry insisted. He looked around the shop. 'Is there no one else here?'

'Otto is in the back. He is the owner.'

'You must get ready to leave.'

She took off her apron and undid the kerchief, releasing and running her hands through her shoulder-length blonde hair. 'I will tell Otto,' she said. 'I must thank him.'

Sir Henry stood by the window and looked out, pursing his lips and doing his best to appear to be inspecting cheeses. It was perhaps two minutes before a man in a black-leather greatcoat appeared from a doorway across the street, looking up at a window above them. He stared at whatever was happening in that window for a minute and then gestured and a second man came from an alcove to join him. They strode across the street together and pushed through the outer door to the building.

Sir Henry waited a few moments to be sure they did not come out again, and then called to his new sister, who came hurriedly from the back room. 'It's time,' he said. 'We'd best go. You have a suitcase?'

She handed him a small wrapped package. 'A going-away gift from Otto,' she told him. 'A half-kilo of *Edelpilzkäse*.' Then went behind the counter and returned with a small valise. 'Onward,' she said, giving him an almost smile.

'That's all you're taking?'

'Three trunks holding everything I own have supposedly been shipped ahead to wherever-it-is,' she told him. 'If they haven't been confiscated by the Gestapo. Everything I used to own has been distributed amongst various charities.'

'Confiscated?' Sir Henry asked.

'Certainly if they had been sent with my name. Jews are not allowed to leave with any property – if they're allowed to leave at all. But Willy says they've been adequately disguised.'

'Willy?'

'Oh yes, that's right,' she said. She smiled. 'My husband Wilhelm Fauth. You know him as "Felix".'

'Well!' Sir Henry could think of nothing to say to this, so he picked up his new sister's valise and held out his arm. 'Let us go.'

'Indeed,' she said, slipping her arm in his. 'There is no longer anything for me here.' She took a deep breath. 'Except Willy, of course. Always excepting Willy. But he can take care of himself. Or so he says. And perhaps . . . perhaps.' Another deep breath and she was almost pulling him out the door. 'Let us go.'

They rounded the corner at a hasty walk and headed for the waiting cab. Karl was behind the wheel, reading yet another newspaper. Sir Henry couldn't make out which it was, but it had oversized headlines with the words *Der Führer* amongst them.

Just as they reached the cab they heard pounding footsteps behind them and a short, plump man in a black-leather greatcoat came skidding around the corner waving and gesticulating in their general direction. '*Halt!*' he yelled. '*Bleiben Sie sofort stehen!*'

They stopped and Sir Henry took his hand off the door handle of the cab and turning to face the chubby man.

'Gestapo,' Madeline said calmly. 'What could he possibly want with us?'

'It is a puzzle,' Sir Henry agreed, pleased to note that his nervous system was reacting calmly to this sudden threat. 'Yes, my man,' he called. 'What can I do for you?'

'Englander?' the man asked, coming to a stop in front of Sir Henry.

'Indeed,' Cardin replied calmly. 'And who are you, and by what right do you come running up after us? We paid for the cheese.'

'What?' the man paused for a moment adjusting his mind to replying in English. 'What is it you are speaking about?'

'The cheese. Isn't that why you're running after us? Did the storekeeper complain?'

The man shook his head violently as though trying to clear a gnat from his ear. 'I know nothing of that,' he said. 'I am a police officer. May I see your papers, please?'

'It is no wonder,' Sir Henry told him in the most arrogant voice he could manage, 'that fewer and fewer Englishmen are choosing to spend their holidays in Germany these days. Stopped on every street corner by officious idiots like yourself. If you're a policeman, where is your uniform?'

'You will show me your papers, please,' the man repeated, his face wooden. 'I am of the Gestapo. We do not wear uniforms.' He pulled an identity disk from his pocket and held it some inches from Sir Henry's nose. 'This is my identity. Now I would see yours.'

Sir Henry thought he could go two or three more rounds like this, but decided antagonizing the man further would be counterproductive. A bit of pushback to show one won't be easily pushed around but not enough to produce a violent reaction, that was the ticket. 'Of course,' he agreed, pulling his passport from the pocket of his jacket and handing it to the tubby gentleman of the Gestapo.

The man opened it and stared at the page for a moment before turning to Madeleine. 'And you, Fräulein?'

'My passport?' She opened her purse and fished around inside it. 'It's here somewhere. Ah yes – here it is.' She took it out with a slight flourish and handed it to the plump man. 'You'll have to excuse my brother,' she said. 'He's jealous because he didn't get to spend the last two weeks in Switzerland with us. I think your country is perfectly lovely.'

The man opened her passport and stared at it, rubbing his fingers over the photograph and the ink as though trying to see if they'd rub off. 'Frau Mabel Bellant?' he asked.

'That's right.'

'But this is not Herr Bellant?'

'That's right,' Sir Henry broke in. 'Mabel is my sister.'

The plump man stared speculatively at Frau Mabel Bellant. Then he took a small photograph from the flap pocket of his jacket and stared speculatively at it. Then he looked back at Frau Mabel. 'It could be that you are actually Frau Madeleine Fauth, could it not?'

'Who?' Madeleine asked, doing a good job of looking surprised.

'Come now,' the officer said, and he turned to look at Sir Henry. 'And perhaps it is that you are the mysterious Herr Fauth?'

'See here,' Sir Henry said, 'I've had about enough of this.' He took a step toward the man, who backed up and reached under his greatcoat. Sir Henry could see the bulge of a bulky pistol holster under his dark gray jacket. He chose to ignore it for the moment, but he moved no closer. 'I don't know what you think you're doing, or who you think I am, or for that matter who you think my sister, Mrs Bellant, is, but there's my passport with my photograph in it, and her passport with her photograph in it, and if that's not good enough for you I suggest you call the British Embassy. They know who I am.'

'Perhaps,' the plump man said. 'And perhaps I should take you both in for further interrogation. Your embassy can be contacted from Gestapo headquarters should that seem advisable.' He backed up two steps, taking a whistle from his pocket and raising it to his lips.

Karl swung himself from the driver's seat of the taxi behind the tubby Gestapo agent and in one continuous motion raised a rolled-up newspaper and smashed it across the back of the man's head. With the incongruous visual effect of a movie cartoon the newspaper did not crumple, and the man's head snapped backward, his eyes rolled back, he made a soft gargling sound and fell to the ground.

Madeleine made a soft squeaking sound and clapped her hands to her mouth, her eyes wide.

'Quick,' Karl said, stooping down to take the Gestapo agent by his shoulders, 'help me get him into the boot.'

'Is he dead?' Sir Henry asked. He crouched and grabbed the man by the feet.

'We have no time to find out,' Karl said. 'You must get to Tempelhof by six. I'll take care of him later.'

Between them they swung the man into the boot of the taxi and closed the lid. Sir Henry helped Madeleine into the back seat and climbed in after her.

Karl took several deep breaths and started the engine, then turned in his seat and smiled the ineffable smile of the taxi driver. 'Welcome to my taxicab, *mein herr und frau*,' he said. 'Where might I have the pleasure of taking you?'

'Tempelhof, driver,' Sir Henry said. 'With reasonable haste.' He paused, and then added, 'And thank you.'

'All part of the service,' Karl said. 'Anything for the *Oberst*.'

The car swung around the corner.

TWENTY-THREE

And oh, how sweet a thing to be
Safe on an island, not at sea!
(Though some one said, some months ago –
I heard him, and he seemed to know;
Was it the German Chancellor?
'There are no islands anymore.')

– Edna St Vincent Millay

Patricia leaned back and pushed the remains of her coddled eggs and particles of toast aside as Sophie appeared at the door of the breakfast room. 'Good morning,' she said, reaching for her coffee cup. 'Come and help yourself to food and sit down. There's all sorts of breakfast things on the sideboard. If you don't see something you like we'll ring for it. Pour yourself a glass of orange juice. Of course there's the matter of eggs – how do you like your eggs?'

'I think,' Sophie said, 'that a bowl of cereal would do me nicely, thank you.'

'Oatmeal? Or something cold and crunchy?'

'Oatmeal? I like the oatmeal, if it isn't all watery.'

Patricia waved a hand toward a double-hulled silver serving bowl on the sideboard. 'That contraption keeps it nice and warm,' she said. 'And it isn't a bit watery. Indeed, it tends to get lumpy after a while – but it's only been fifteen minutes or so, so it should be fine. How are you feeling this morning?'

'I did not sleep well. I think I had bad dreams, although I don't remember them. And I woke up several times and I was crying. And I don't remember why. I mean, I know what, that is, what I have to cry about. But I can never remember why I'm crying at that moment, and it feels as though it's something else entirely.'

Patricia sighed. 'Your recent past has been pretty awful, hasn't it? I'd say if you feel like crying then you should bally well cry. Not that I'm an expert on this sort of thing.'

'But that's the thing, you see,' Sophie said. 'It's not that I feel like crying – it's that I suddenly find that I am crying. It surprises me that I am crying.'

Patricia nodded. 'Your unconscious mind is going over things that your conscious mind would just as soon ignore, at least for the moment. Trust me, I know these things for I have read the writings of Dr Freud.'

'I know of him,' Sophie said.

'Yes, but not too much, I hope.' She took the girl's hand. 'As time passes you will . . . no, you won't forget, you won't ever forget – but the pain will ease.'

'I don't want to forget.'

'Of course not,' Patricia said, making a vague downward gesture. 'Sit. Eat your oatmeal. Drink your orange juice. Have a cup of coffee. Do you drink coffee?'

'Yes. Thank you.'

'I wasn't sure. You'll have to be sure to tell me what sixteen-year-olds aren't supposed to do, so I can tell you not to do it,' Patricia told her.

'All right,' Sophie agreed.

Patricia waited until Sophie was finishing her oatmeal before interrupting by holding something up in front of her. 'Pemmy was emptying out the pockets of the boy's jacket you were wearing when the fates brought you to us,' she said. 'To send it out for cleaning, you know. And she found this in the lining.' It was a stiff cardboard packet about two by three inches taped shut on all four sides. She handed it to Sophie.

Sophie took it gingerly, as though something might suddenly spring out and bite her thumb. 'What is it?'

'You don't know?'

'No. I've never seen it.'

'Perhaps your father . . . I didn't want to open it, it's yours after all.'

'Yes,' Sophie said. 'Perhaps my father . . .' She held the packet back out to Patricia. 'Please – you open it.'

'Are you sure?'

'I think so. Please.'

'All right.' Patricia took the packet and examined it. 'It's pretty well sealed and I don't want to . . . I think at the top, here.' she looked up. 'Do me a favor, child, and bring me my purse – it's on the edge of the couch.'

Sophie retrieved the small black clutch purse from the couch and moved around to the other side of the table and sat back down. Her eyes welled up with tears.

Patricia pulled a pair of small scissors out of the purse, but now she paused in her attempt to open the packet. 'What is it, Sophie; what's the matter?'

'It's – whatever this is – it's my poppa coming from the past, from last week, to speak to me for perhaps one last time. It's . . .'

'I understand,' Patricia said. 'He was pretty wonderful, your poppa?'

Sophie burst out crying. Patricia fished a handkerchief out of her purse and handed it across the table. 'Silly me,' she said. 'Of course he was. I actually saw him conduct once, I believe. Mahler's Fifth. In Vienna about three years ago.'

Sophie nodded and wiped her eyes. 'Yes, possibly. He was guest conductor for the Vienna Symphony for the first half of the thirty-five season. He loved Mahler.'

'I could make some trite comment about how good he was,' Patricia said, 'but I'm no judge. My father is a musician – amateur, I mean – piano, church organ, and for some reason viola. He used to tell me what to listen for, but I'm not sure I ever actually hear it. I like some music and I dislike other music, but I never know why. But I remember liking the Mahler.'

'It was the last Mahler performed in Vienna. His music was banned in Germany as "degenerate", and the ban soon spread to Austria.'

'Degenerate?'

'Mahler was a Jew.'

'Ah!'

'My poppa, he was very good, everyone said so. And these music people, they do not say kind things to you if you do not deserve them. Even then if you do, sometimes, they do not say kind things.'

There was a silence. Patricia stood up and refilled her coffee cup from a silver urn on the sideboard that bore the Saboy family crest. 'These people,' she said, turning back to Sophie, 'these Nazis – they have a lot to answer for.'

'Yes,' Sophie said, 'but why . . .'

'Why what?'

'Why are they getting away with what they do – arresting people: Jews, Communists, Socialists, Catholic priests, anyone they feel like it – and putting them in camps? No trials, no charges even, just a knock on the door in the middle of the night. Why are they able to do what they do? Why is no one stopping them?'

'That is a question,' Patricia agreed.

Geoffrey appeared in the doorway resplendent in a plum-colored dressing gown and a red fez with a tassel that hung over his right eye, and advanced into the room. 'Morning, my dears,' he said. 'I trust you've left me a kipper. I have my fancy set on a kipper.'

Patricia smiled. 'We have spared you a kipper,' she told him. 'Shall I order your eggs?'

'I have stopped at the kitchen and cook is, even now, boiling a brace of eggs for me,' Geoffrey told her. He poured a cup of coffee, decanted a measured amount of cream, and sat down.

'You are truly a sartorial delight this morning,' Patricia told him. 'The fez adds a certain *je ne sais* very much at all. That is, I hardly know . . .' She paused.

'Words fail you?' Geoffrey asked. 'How very rare. Anyhow, I have worn the headpiece in honor of our young guest, who is, I believe, of the Jewish persuasion. It is the closest thing I could find to a yarmulke.' He smiled at Sophie.

'We didn't,' Sophie began. 'I mean I don't . . .' She suddenly burst into tears.

'What?' Geoffrey looked startled. 'What did I do?'

Patricia reached over to pat Sophie on the shoulder. 'He didn't mean—'

'No, no,' Sophie said, dabbing at her eyes with the napkin. 'It's nice. It made me feel – I mean – thank you. It was sort of a joke, yes?'

'Yes,' Geoffrey admitted.

'But a nice joke. I thank you. You can take it off now.'

'I don't know,' Geoffrey said thoughtfully. 'I think it makes me look . . .'

'Take it off,' Patricia told him. 'We love you. We will not discuss how it makes you look.'

Geoffrey took the fez off and put it sadly aside as his eggs arrived. He slithered a kipper onto his plate and added a slice of toast, then sat down and set about the delicate business of decapitating the first soft-boiled egg.

'We have a small mystery here,' Patricia told him a few minutes later, as he was pouring his second cup of coffee.

'Ah!' he said, turning to look. 'What sort of mystery?'

Patricia held up the little cardboard packet. 'This was found in the lining of Sophie's jacket – the one she was wearing on the train. We were about to open it when we were distracted by the sight of that red growth on your head.'

Geoffrey grinned. 'Red growth indeed. No need to cast asparagus. Why, at Oxford every year we . . . Never mind about that now. As you don't know what's in the envelope, Sophie, it must have been put there by someone else. Presumably your father?'

'It must, I mean, I don't know,' Sophie said.

'Shall we find out?' Geoffrey asked.

'I don't want to open it,' Sophie said. 'I mean, I'd like her to do it for me,' she said, with a gesture toward Patricia.

'Of course,' Geoffrey agreed.

Patricia retrieved her scissors from a corner of the table and carefully eyed the packet. After a minute she worried a hole into one corner and then inserted one blade into the hole and slid the scissors across the top. 'Now,' she said, reaching two fingers inside and gingerly extracting a small white envelope, 'what have we here?' She tried the flap and found that it wasn't glued down.

'Curiouser and curiouser, said Alice,' Geoffrey said, leaning in closer. 'Tip out the contents. Here – wait a second.' He took a clean white napkin from the sideboard and spread it on the table. 'Onto this.'

Patricia turned the envelope over and shook it gently over the napkin. When nothing emerged she tried tapping it on the side, then the other side, then the bottom which was now the top. Finally six small objects fluttered out and fell onto the napkin, followed after a second by two more.

'Stamps,' Geoffrey said. 'What do you know!'

'Stamps?' Sophie echoed, sounding puzzled. 'Why would . . .'

'Let me see if that's the last of them,' Patricia said, peering into the interior of the small envelope. 'I think there's one more. No – two!' She stuck her pinky inside the envelope and wiggled it about, and several more small paper rectangles fell to the napkin. 'I think that's – no . . .' She carefully pried the packet apart, finding several more stamps hiding in the folds. 'I think that's – yes, that's it.'

'Sixteen stamps,' Geoffrey said, nudging them gently into a row. 'They all, ah, seem to be German, and they're all overprinted – what? – "K-i-a-" uh, "Kiautschou", whatever that might be, but they don't seem to be otherwise related.'

Sophie peered down at them. 'Related?'

'Yes. You know, part of the same series or theme or what have you.'

'They must be collectable,' Patricia said. 'And I think they must be quite valuable,'

Geoffrey looked up at her. 'My dear,' he said. 'I didn't know you knew anything about postage stamps.'

'Nor do I,' Patricia told him. 'But what other possible reason could Sophie's father have had in sewing them into the lining of her jacket? Didn't you tell me that when those horrible guards assaulted him they seemed to be looking for something?'

'Yes.' He turned to Sophie, who was staring at the stamps but perhaps seeing something else. 'These, my child, would seem to be your legacy.'

TWENTY-FOUR

Yesterday This Day's Madness did prepare;
To-morrow's Silence, Triumph, or Despair:
Drink! for you know not whence you came, nor why:
Drink! for you know not why you go, nor where.
                                        – Edward Fitzgerald,
                              The Rubaiyat of Omar Khayyam

'We have been watching you,' Gauleiter Frank Gerard told Andrew Blake, leaning over and putting his arm around his shoulder in a determinedly cheerful manner. 'We believe that you have a great potential and can be of greater use to the Cause.'

Watching me? The thought did not cheer Blake up. There was, to Blake's eyes, an undertone of menace in every gesture of Gerard's, no matter how bland the facade. 'Anything I can do,' Blake said. He did not mean it.

'We have devised for you a special task,' Gerard went on.

'What sort of task?' Blake asked, thinking *Why me?* so loudly that he was surprised Gerard couldn't hear it.

They were standing behind the front counter in George Vander's print shop. It was dusk and the daylight through the shop window was vague and uncertain, filtered through a gray and cloudy sky. The lights in the back of the shop were off, and a single bulb above the counter merely served to cast the rest of the shop into unfriendly shadows. Vanders, having been asked to leave them alone for a few minutes, had shrugged and gone out for coffee. That had been enough to raise Blake's panic level to the boil, and Gerard's attempt to achieve a friendly smile did not relieve the pressure.

'We have had our eye on you for a while,' Gerard told Blake, which did nothing to reassure him. Although the image of them – whoever they were – sharing one eye between them like those mythical Greek sisters would have amused him if he'd been able to find anything funny at that moment. 'You do not say much, but you do what is needed, and that is good.'

Now Blake was thoroughly puzzled and even more worried. What was it that he did? Put out chairs before the meetings? Sell magazines and books at the back of the hall? Get followed home by a man he'd rather never meet?

Gerard paused and was looking at him as though he expected a response. Blake managed a grunt of assent and a meaningful nod. 'I try my best,' he said.

'Yes,' Gerard agreed. 'And you do not make a fuss. You believe in the cause but you are not a shouter. I distrust shouters and fuss-makers.' He pushed himself to his feet. 'You are a follower, my dear Blake, and not a leader. And this is good. We have enough leaders, we need more dependable followers.'

'Well—' Blake began.

'And you do not live wildly or beyond your means, or draw attention to yourself,' Gerard went on. 'You do not go drinking or gambling or whoring in the evening like so many single men.'

So this, whatever it is, is why I've been being followed, Blake thought.

'And so we have an assignment for you. You can turn it down, of course . . .'

Blake was relieved to hear that.

'But we think you will find it interesting, certainly interesting. It will require self-control, and the ability to manage your feelings, but you can do that if needed, yes?'

We? Why do they, whoever they are, think that?

'I admit I am interested,' Blake said, wondering if the lie showed on his face. He wasn't interested, not at all. He didn't even want to hear about it. He wanted to go away somewhere. 'Tell me about it,' he said.

Gauleiter Gerard walked back to the letter press looking thoughtful, paused, then turned and walked back. 'Do not say anything until you have heard me out,' he said. 'This is, um, an unusual thing we ask of you.'

'OK,' Blake said. *Shit!* He thought.

'We want you to join the Communist Party,' Gerard told him. 'Go to meetings – Communist Party meetings. Get to know who is there.'

Blake stared at Gerard. He did not have to feign shocked surprise. If he had made a list of the ten – fifty – things Gerard might be going to say, this would not have been among them. Hell, make that a hundred. A thousand. 'You want . . .' The words stopped coming.

'I know,' Gerard said. 'They are scum – Jews, Negro-lovers, college professors. I don't know how much you know about them.'

'Not much, actually,' Blake told him. 'They march, hold rallies; a lot like us, actually that way. They're pacifists and they're for Negro rights, and a better deal for the working man, or so they say. But it's all propaganda. They get their orders from Moscow and their eventual aim is to subvert and destroy the American way of life.' He was quoting what he remembered of a Bund pamphlet he had printed a few days before.

Gerard bobbed his head back and forth in an exaggerated nod. 'That's right,' he said. 'So you can see . . .'

'What?' Blake asked, honestly puzzled, when Gerard paused. 'What can I see?'

'How can I put this? We must have eyes on them. We must know what they are doing, what they intend to do. You can keep your job at the print shop, and you will be paid something extra for this work.'

Blake pushed his chair back from the desk. 'You want me to be a spy?' He stood up and felt faint so he sat down again. 'I can't, I mean, I really can't.' Then the incongruity of his claiming to the Bund that he couldn't be a spy struck him and he almost giggled. What would Gerard have thought if he had giggled? Probably not the truth. But still . . .

'No, no, not a spy,' Gerard insisted. 'We have already some people inside their organization. But it is difficult for them to commune with us. We want you to go to meetings and whatever, sit quietly in the back and hear what there is to hear, learn what there is to learn, and not draw attention to yourself. That is all. Meet the members but do not, how to say, impose on them. We do not ask you to sneak into their headquarters or follow anyone about.'

'Then why . . .?'

'You will learn much just by being there. The size of the meetings, where they are held, who speaks, who comes. Who is important, who is not. Who the leaders are. You can gather up their printed material. Once in a while, in a manner to be determined, one of our people who is deeper into the party may pass you some information to be brought back to us. You will not know who this agent is, and the information will be in some innocent form that you can show to anyone interested.'

'How are you going to manage that?

'We're working that out. There are several possibilities.'

Welker was just leaving his office to take a cab to Penn Station and there board the evening train to DC when Andrew Blake got through to him on the phone. 'What am I to do?' Blake asked.

'What's the problem?'

'I've got to see you right away. I don't know what to do.'

'About what?'

'I don't understand what's happening, why they're doing this, and I don't know what I should do. We have to talk.'

'About? Never mind. Where are you?'

'I'm using the payphone across from the print shop.'

'Meet me at the Café Figaro on MacDougal Street. I'll be there in about fifteen minutes. Try not to be followed.'

The Figaro, a Greenwich Village coffee house catering to artists, writers, musicians, and those yearning to join their ranks, was not a place where they were liable to run into anyone who knew either of them. Welker got there first, and took a table toward the back where he was able to watch Blake as he came in. He had a good view of the street through the plate-glass windows, so he might be able to spot an incautious tail if Blake happened to be wearing one. A few minutes later Blake came in looking anxious, took a moment to spot Welker in the dim light, then with great restraint managed to not quite run over to the table and drop into the seat opposite.

'What am I to do?' Blake began with no preamble. He wasn't actually wringing his hands, but it seemed to Welker that in another few seconds he would begin.

Welker resisted the temptation to reach over and pat Blake on the back, and instead used his deepest and most soothing voice, the voice he had used when he had to tell senior commanders something they didn't want to hear. 'You are to calm down, take a few deep breaths,' he said, 'look up at the ceiling – for some reason that seems to relieve tension – and then tell me what the hell the problem is.'

Blake paused for three deep breaths, glanced up at the ceiling and back down, then put his hands flat down on the table. 'They want me to be a spy,' he said.

'A spy?'

'Well, they say it isn't that, but it is. Gerard – he's the *Gauleiter*, which is like the boss of this area – came to talk to me. He says they want me to spy on the Communists.'

'Yeah, I've met Gerard. But they *what*?'

'You see?' Blake said. 'It makes no sense – I mean why me? – so there must be something else to it. But what? And why me?'

'Yeah,' Welker said. 'Why you indeed? Let's think this out.'

'I know what I think. I think I want to go somewhere else. Back to Pennsylvania. Raise goats. Take up knitting.'

'You knit?'

Blake shrugged. 'I could learn.'

Welker thought for a second. Whatever it was had truly shaken Blake up. Knitting? 'Just what did Gerard say?' Welker asked.

Blake found that he remembered the conversation almost word for word, and he repeated it to Welker, with added gestures. 'And then he said I could start Saturday, there's going to be a big Communist Party meeting at the Finnish Sailors' Hall on 96th and Lex, and I should just go and see what it's like. He added a few words about Negros and Jews and fellow-travelers, whatever they are, and said he knew I wouldn't fall for any of their crap and I should come and tell him what I think on Monday. What am I going to think? How do I get out of this?' Blake clasped his hands together but managed to refrain from wringing them.

'Well, you know,' Welker said, 'it might be interesting to find out what their interest in the Commies is. I don't see any problem.'

'Well, I do,' Blake told him. 'I'll be lying to two groups of people at once, and they don't like people who lie to them.'

'But you don't actually have to lie – just sit and listen.'

'Easy for you to say.'

'But, you know – how much is he going to pay you for this?'

'An extra five bucks a week.'

'Ah. That could be a problem.'

'How?'

'You may have to turn that money over to us. You're not allowed to take money from a person or group you're surveilling. Your job is OK. I mean, that's a job. But this extra – I don't think you'll be allowed to keep it. But don't worry – since you'll be doing extra work for us, I'll raise your pay by five dollars to make up for it.'

'So,' Blake asked, 'I have to give you the five dollars, but you'll pay me five dollars more to make up for it? That doesn't make sense.'

'You've never worked for the government before, have you?' Welker asked.

TWENTY-FIVE

Buttercup:
Things are seldom what they seem,
Skim milk masquerades as cream;
Highlows pass as patent leathers;
Jackdaws strut in peacock's feathers.
Captain (puzzled):
Very true,
So they do.
  – *Gilbert & Sullivan,* HMS Pinafore

F our days later Blake came into the Figaro, looked around nervously until he spotted Welker at a table in the back, and headed over. 'I am not happy,' he said by way of greeting as he sat down. 'I am not happy and I am frightened and I'm thinking I should go.'

'Go where?' Welker asked, leaning forward and looking attentive, his arms on the table, his hands cradled around his cappuccino.

'Philadelphia, maybe.'

'Philadelphia?'

'Maybe Kansas City. Los Angeles. Hawaii. Hong Kong. Somewhere not here.'

It was Saturday afternoon and the Figaro was full of uptown types who wanted to see the artists and poets and bohemians, or who had acquired berets and torn sweaters so they could pretend, just for the afternoon, that they *were* the artists and poets and bohemians. Blake and Welker were sitting at a table near the back, next to the giant bell-shaped espresso machine, which looked to Blake like a Buck Rogers rocket ship and made alarming hissing noises. Blake kept glancing nervously over at it while they talked.

'Why?' Welker asked. 'I mean, why do you want to go away? What happened? You see someone? Something? Someone do something to scare you?'

'I am not a courageous man,' Blake said.

'I know and that's OK,' Welker told him. 'For a man who is not courageous you've been plenty brave enough so far.'

'That's because you keep telling me there's no danger. And I keep almost believing you. But not this time, I think.'

'So you did see something?'

'Not exactly.'

'OK, then what?'

Blake took a deep breath and looked away from the hissing espresso machine. 'It's like this,' he said. 'I was in the front room of the 12th Street office waiting for Gerard, and—'

'Wait a second – what 12th Street office?'

'You didn't know? Gerard has this two-room office on 12th off Sixth Avenue. Second floor. Says "Indirect Investments Inc." on the door. Whatever that is. Anyway, I was in the front room waiting for him 'cause he said he wanted to talk to me about the Communists and he came into the back room without going through the front – there's a door in the hall that goes right to the back room, only it's always kept locked. But this time he went in that way. And he had someone with him and he didn't know I was there in the front room 'cause I hadn't bothered turning the light on.'

'What other guy?'

'I don't know. I didn't know his voice.'

'So you just sat there?'

'I didn't want to interrupt him. I was early anyway.'

'OK. So . . .'

'So after a little talk about, you know, this and that, Gerard says to the other guy, who I don't know who he is, he says the fall Buddha is to go.'

'What's that?'

'I got no idea. Anyway the other guy says, "For sure?" and Gerard says yeah, he just got the phone call from Weiss and the Buddha is a go, whatever it is.'

'The "Buddha"? That's what he said?'

'That's what I heard.'

'In the fall?'

'I think so. I was listening through a door, so maybe not. But I think so. It ain't going to be fall for a while yet, so maybe it don't mean the season. Or maybe he said something different. But that's what I heard, I think.'

Welker waited patiently for maybe fifteen seconds and then said, 'That's it?'

'Yeah. 'Cause that's when I left.'

'You just walked out?'

'Yeah. Before they knew I was there. I almost panicked and just kept going, but that wouldn't have been smart. So I went downstairs and walked around the block a couple of times and then went back in, like it was the first time, you know?'

'What is there about the Buddha that scared you?'

'It's not Buddha, it's Weiss. He said a guy named Weiss called him.'

'So?'

'So when he said the name I remembered. Weiss. All at once I remembered. That was the name of the guy who was the leader of the . . . you know . . . who killed – who beat up . . .'

'Son of a bitch! Finally!' Welker slapped the edge of the table, and Blake jumped. 'Sorry,' Welker said.

'I'm glad you're happy,' Blake said. 'I'm scared. I scare easy.'

'Come on,' Welker said. 'Weiss, whoever he is, wasn't even there. Just a voice on the phone. Not even that, 'cause you didn't hear him. He could have been calling from Jersey City.'

'He could take the Hudson Tubes, be here in half an hour.'

'And again, he doesn't know who you are. Hell, he doesn't even know you exist.'

'And I intend to keep it that way.'

Welker sighed and finished his cappuccino. 'Well, you went back up to talk to Gerard, right?'

'Right.'

'So, what did you talk about?'

'Oh, yeah. Well first I gave him the cards which he asked me to print up.'

'The cards?'

'Yeah. Here, I brought you one.' Blake fished around in his jacket pocket and handed Welker a pasteboard card. 'I thought you'd want to see it, 'cause I think it's kind of strange.'

Welker took the card and examined it front and back. The back was blank. On the front:

W P A

Having paid his dues for the year 1938

- -

Is a member in good standing.

The Workers Party of America

New York City Chapter

no_____ _____Sec

'What's this?' Welker demanded. 'You made this up?'

'Yeah, you know, at the print shop. Gerard gave me the copy and asked me to print them up for him. I did about fifty. It's like a membership card for Communists. Which, like I say, is a bit weird, considering.'

'It is,' Welker agreed. 'Why would the head of the local Nazis be giving you a Commie membership card to be printed up?'

'I don't know,' Blake said seriously. 'I'm supposed to give them to Lehman at the next meeting.'

'Lehman? You mean the, ah, substitute Otto Lehman?'

'Yeah, he's one of the big shots at the meetings. Which is also pretty weird when you think about it. What do you think they'd do if they knew he was a phony?'

'Let us not find out,' Welker said. 'Not right now, anyhow.'

'And Gerard is upping the ante for me, like I was afraid he would. Now he wanted me to hang around after the meeting and find out where they live – to follow them home or something. Not the regular people, like in the audience, but the important ones, like on the stage. I told him I'd be real bad at that. Which I would.'

'What did he say?'

'He said that was OK, he had a better idea. He would have me point out the leaders to someone outside as we left, and this other guy would do the following. I said if he could work that out that would be OK. To tell the truth I was just anxious to get the hell out of there before Weiss came through the door.'

The waiter, who had been studiously ignoring them, as is the custom with the Figaro staff, chose now to come over and look expectantly at Blake. 'You want something?'

'Coffee,' Blake told him.

'Cappuccino? Latte? *Au lait*?' the waiter asked, pencil poised over his pad, which was merely a prop since he never actually wrote anything down.

'Just coffee,' Blake said. 'American coffee.'

'Maybe a sweet roll?'

'Just coffee.'

'Yeah, OK,' the waiter agreed. 'Just coffee.' And he went off toward the kitchen.

'Well,' Welker said after a minute, 'that tells us something. Not very useful probably, but reassuring.'

'How's that?' Blake asked.

'Your Nazi friends—'

'Not my friends!' Blake interrupted in a forceful undertone.

'Yeah, sorry. The German-American Bund members with whom I am cajoling you to associate. Better?'

'Yeah, well,' Blake said. 'What about them?'

'They probably don't have a plant in the FBI,' Welker said.

'How's that?'

'I'm just thinking out loud,' Welker said. 'I figure if they had someone in the Bureau, which I thought was possible 'cause Hoover don't give crap about Nazis, then they'd already have the addresses of every Commie in the country, along with their shoe sizes and where they get their hair cut. 'Cause he's sure got his nose in a twist about Commies.'

'His nose in a twist?'

'Yeah.' Welker nodded. 'My mother used to say that, which is where I got it. Come to think of it I have no idea where she picked it up. It means like—'

'I can see what it means, I just never heard it before.'

Welker drank the last of his cappuccino and waved at the waiter, who was just coming out of the kitchen, and pointed down at his empty cup. The waiter nodded.

'So the question is,' Welker went on, 'why do the little baby Führers in the Bund want to know where the Commies live? And what's with the membership cards? What do they have in mind?'

'The cards I don't know,' Blake told him. 'I asked but he just kind of smiled and said don't worry about it. And about finding where the Commies live, maybe Gerard and his buddies are just looking for more people to beat up.'

Welker shook his head. 'Any random passer-by on the street will do for that,' he told Blake. 'Just call him a Jew or a Commie and start swinging. Draw a crowd, excite the faithful. When I went to see him—'

'When you what?' Blake interrupted.

'Oh yeah,' Welker told him. 'A couple of days ago. Gerard thinks I'm a hotshot ex-Army ordnance expert, and he's all hot to recruit me. So far I've agreed that the Jews are taking our jobs and that we shouldn't fight another war in Europe and he's hinted that it would be nice if he had a source for explosives and someone who knows how to use them. I don't know what he has in mind, but I rather think it would be good idea if I find out.'

'You don't want me—'

'To do the finding out? No. I'm going to act all hard to get, and he's going to lure me in by telling me all about it. If you don't want to know something people go out of their way to tell you about it. That's rule seven of the detecting business. You go on with what you were doing, and don't worry about Weiss. I'll take care of Weiss.'

'What are you going to do?'

'I don't know yet. It probably won't actually be me, but one of my associates. And we'll work out the details when we find out just who he is.'

'I still want to go to Pittsburgh,' Blake said plaintively.'

'You don't know anyone in Pittsburgh,' Welker told him.

'I could make friends.'

'Stay,' Welker said. 'Make friends here.'

TWENTY-SIX

Everybody needs something to believe in . . .
I believe I'll have another drink.
                                        – *W. C. Fields*

R estaurant Dimanche on Georgetown's M Street was housed in a red-brick building that George Washington would have been surprised to learn he slept in. It was certainly old enough, built, according to the brass plaque, in 1763, but for a couple of decades after the War of American Independence it had been a very exclusive club staffed with high-yellow ladies of negotiable virtue. During the War of Northern Aggression, as the proprietor of the house called it after he fled to the temporary safety of Atlanta, Georgia, ownership somehow passed to the Breckhouse family, and by the 1890s Jeffrey Breckhouse the Third was telling Jeffrey Breckhouse the Fourth how General Washington had spent the night – heck, the week – with his great-great-grandpappy in this very house on his way to Philadelphia to accept the presidency.

The restaurant had occupied the building for the past decade under the supervision of chef Michel Martine; Martine had apprenticed under Escoffier, and had been lured to Georgetown from the Hôtel de Paris in Monte Carlo by Alice Roosevelt Longworth, who complained about the lack of decent French restaurants anywhere around the capital. There was no sign outside announcing the existence of the Dimanche; if you couldn't find it you obviously had no business being there, and in any case you were not welcome without a reservation. It was weathering the Depression effortlessly – there was always money to be found for wining and dining Congressmen and government functionaries.

It was just eight o'clock on a rainy Tuesday evening as Lord Geoffrey Saboy's Rolls Royce pulled up across from the door of Restaurant Dimanche. The rain had lessened to a light drizzle for the moment but the clouds glowering overhead in the gathering dusk threatened a more substantial wetting in the near future. Garrett, who was doing his chauffeur imitation again this evening, dashed around the car to open the passenger door for His Lordship and Lady Patricia and made a show of holding an oversize black umbrella over them as they exited and guiding them to the front door. 'You may disappear until ten thirty,' Geoffrey told him, 'then return and loiter around at some discreet distance and in the fullness of time I shall whistle for you.'

Straightening his chauffeur's cap, Garrett gave a quick semi-salute. '*Kiel vi deziras, mian sinjoron.*' Then furled the umbrella and marched back to the car.

'*Tre bona, dankon,*' Geoffrey called after him before turning to follow Patricia into the restaurant.

'What on earth was that?' Patricia asked.

'What?'

'That "bankum dankum" stuff?'

'Oh – Esperanto. We've been practicing it. It's due to become the universal language, you know.'

'Really?'

'Everyone says so.'

'No,' Patricia said, shaking her head firmly. 'No, they don't.'

'No?'

'Trust me.'

'But once it's adopted it will put an end to wars and everyone will be kind to their mothers.'

'Honestly . . .' Patricia said. Then she turned and smiled at the approaching head waiter. 'Good evening, Arnold.'

'Evening, Lady Patricia, your lordship. Your guest awaits you in the bar. Will you join him or shall I seat you now?'

'We'll take our table now, I think,' Geoffrey said. 'Bring our guest over once we're seated.'

Two minutes later Jacob Welker, a pâté-smeared cracker in one hand and the remains of a Scotch and water in the other, followed the head waiter over to their corner table. He set down the cracker as Geoffrey rose to greet him, and they silently shook hands, each soberly surveying the other. After a moment Welker said, 'You haven't changed. Good to see you again.'

'I rather think I have, you know,' Geoffrey said. 'Ever so slightly. As have you. But that's all right. We were . . . young. It's been too long.'

'Yes,' Welker agreed. 'Although it didn't seem so at the time. Being young, I mean.' Then he turned to Patricia and took her hand. 'It is, I can honestly say, a pleasure to see you again,' he said, raising the hand to his lips and miming a kiss.

'Well,' she said, 'how courtly. But you two, you haven't seen each other in – what? – ten or fifteen years? And you just shake hands, one – two? With a "hello – good to see you"? Isn't that carrying British reserve a bit too far? And one of you not even British?'

'Funny,' Welker said. 'I am truly glad to see Captain Lord Saboy – or is it Lord Captain Saboy? I can never remember, but a fuss was somehow not called for.'

'The occasion of our last association was not one that leads to boisterous reminiscences,' Geoffrey agreed. 'But it is good to see you again. And it isn't either of those horrible appellations. It would be either "Lord Geoffrey", or "Captain Saboy", or "Captain Lord Geoffrey Saboy". Or if it's a state occasion—'

'Spare us,' Patricia said.

'You're right, dear, of course.' He turned to Welker. 'Let us drop the ranks and titles,' he said. 'I'm done with ranks and have no need for titles.'

'Good idea,' Welker agreed.

Patricia noted the head waiter standing silently by the table holding the menus and ostentatiously not clearing his throat. 'Perhaps,' she suggested, 'we should consider the food?'

Taking his cue, the head waiter stepped forward and pulled out the chair for Welker before handing the menus around. 'Chef Martine has two specials this evening,' he announced. '*Ris de veau aux champignons* and *Osso bucco à la Milanese*. And he told me to mention to his lordship that he could do for him a lobster with drawn garlic butter if he desires. And also tonight we have the *pommes soufflée*.'

'Thank you, Arnold,' Geoffrey said.

Arnold bowed and retreated, and Geoffrey turned back to Welker. 'Patricia tells me you've become a private 'tec.'

'For a while,' Welker told him, 'but now I'm back in government service.'

'The old game?'

'You could say that. Which is what I want to talk to you about,' Welker said. 'But later.'

'Perhaps,' Geoffrey said carefully, 'there is something to discuss. But it will require a bit of, ah, discussion.'

'Go over that again,' said Welker.

'Later,' Geoffrey said.

The waiter came and spoke and asked and suggested and nodded agreement through the moments of dinner-ordering, and it was decided that Geoffrey would indeed have the lobster while Welker opted for the sweetbreads and Patricia chose the filet of sole meuniere. Then Geoffrey spent the next few minutes in a deep discussion with the sommelier over what wine went most pleasingly with the entrees. A white certainly, but which? A Sauvignon Blanc? Perhaps, but . . . Geoffrey ran his finger down the wine list and suddenly stabbed an entry. 'Aha!'

'Monsieur?'

'This is new.'

'The Bourgogne Aligoté? *Mais oui.* We now have two cases which came off the boat last week. The wine, it has a fruity—'

'I know what it tastes like,' Geoffrey told him. 'I spent three happy nights in, I think it was August of '17 in the wine cellar of a chateau outside Mezières avoiding a German artillery barrage and drinking Aligoté with the eighty-six-year-old count who owned the place. He refused to leave. He wanted to be there in case the Boche broke through the line so he could destroy every bottle in the place before they could get at it. We will have a bottle of that to celebrate. We will discuss the dessert wine later.'

'Very good,' the sommelier said, and retreated.

Patricia frowned at Geoffrey. 'You could have consulted our guest as to the wine choice,' she said.

Welker laughed. 'As I remember your husband,' he said, 'he does not consult, nor does he suggest, he asserts.'

Geoffrey looked hurt. 'As I am the host, I select,' he stated.

'Keeping in mind the delicate palate of my lovely wife and the fact that my guest's tastebuds were shot off during the Battle of the Somme.'

'What,' Patricia asked, 'are we celebrating?'

'I suppose the fact that I am here to drink the wine. And Jacob also. And the fact that you are with us, my dear. After all, think of all the other places you could be.'

Patricia put her hand over his. 'There is no other place,' she said.

'How long have you two been married?' Welker asked.

'Fifteen years, is it?' Geoffrey said.

'Fourteen,' Patricia corrected. 'It just seems like fifteen.'

Geoffrey smiled at her and then turned back to Welker. 'Would you believe,' he said, 'that when I met her she was on the stage?'

'The stage?'

'Not literally at the moment. I actually met her in a pub, but she was, at the time, working as a magician's assistant.'

Patricia nodded. 'The Great Mavini. He made me disappear, and had me tied up with ropes and otherwise abused me. It was great fun.'

Welker leaned back in his chair. 'I hardly know what to ask,' he said.

'I will explain,' Geoffrey said. 'I needed to show up at a family gathering with a woman – to avoid having a woman thrust upon me by various well-meaning relations. The woman that I usually used for such occasions, in exchange for my performing a like service for her, was otherwise occupied. So a friend suggested that I meet her friend, who she said was quite suitable. "What does she do?" I asked. "Never mind," my friend said, "just meet her." So I did.'

Patricia laughed. 'We met at a pub called the King's Ars,' she said.

'The King's . . .?'

'It was the King's *Arms*,' Geoffrey explained, 'but someone had obliterated the "M" the night before, and they hadn't had time to repair it yet.'

'Auspicious, I calls it,' Patricia said. 'So I was sitting in the lounge when this bloke walks in, stared down at me for a minute, and then says, "You'll do. 'Ow much?"'

Geoffrey laughed. 'I did no such thing,' he insisted.

'Then he sat down and asked me what I did,' she went on. 'I told him that I appeared in a music-hall act, and he turned green.'

'That is so,' Geoffrey agreed. 'Quite green.'

'Then I told him that I was an "Honourable", and he cheered up.'

'The Honourable Patricia Sutherland, younger daughter of Viscount Mowbrey,' Geoffrey expanded. 'When I introduced her to my family as such there was no problem. No one would ever think of asking an "Honourable" what she did for a living.'

'And his family liked me so much,' Patricia said, smiling a cat-like smile, 'that six months later we were married.'

The food appeared and was eaten and remarked on and the conversation ebbed and flowed with tales of war and intrigue. Welker told amusing stories about his years as a detective for the Continental, and Geoffrey related his recent train trip with the Duke of Windsor to visit Herr Hitler, and how they had acquired a sixteen-year-old girl on the way back. Patricia soon noted that Geoffrey was not reticent about alluding to his amorous proclivities or his and Patricia's 'arrangement' with Welker, which gave her an anxious moment until it was clear that Welker already knew of Geoffrey's proclivities and neither disapproved of nor shared them. In either case she would have felt constrained from pursuing the handsome American should the time and opportunity present itself.

It was during dessert that Chef Martine had arbitrarily chosen for them and sent over, wedges of New York cheesecake on a bed of *confiture de fraise*, drizzled with crème fraiche, along with a bottle of Tomàs Aguas Select 1903 Port, to firmly establish that there's no food that the French chefs can't make better, that Welker put his fork down and said, 'Shall we talk?'

Geoffrey took a sip of the port then put the glass down gently. 'You talk,' he said. 'We'll listen.'

'Fair enough.' He thought for a second. 'I head a small intelligence organization working nominally out of the State Department.'

'Nominally?'

'Well, actually we report directly to the President. When we have anything to report. And by "we", I mean the six of us. Plus, of course, our secretary makes seven. As I said, small organization. We plan to expand. By the end of the year there may be an even dozen of us, if I can find the right men and women.'

'What sort of intelligence are the seven of you interested in?'

Welker thought that over for a second. 'German, or I should say Nazi, doings in or around the United States.'

'What about the FBI?' Patricia asked. 'I thought they—'

'Hoover is not particularly interested in Nazis unless they wave swastikas in his face while singing the "Horst Wessel Lied". He's hot for Communists and fellow-travelers. And bank robbers. And getting his name in the papers. But Nazis not so much.'

'So you are taking over where Hoover chooses not to tread?' Geoffrey asked.

'Roosevelt and some of those close to him believe that Hitler is the bigger threat, at least for the moment, both in Europe and at home,' Welker told him. 'And he must make progress ever so slowly at letting the American people come to that conclusion on their own. If he comes out and says it, the Republicans will blast him for being an alarmist and trying to get us involved in a war. "America First" seems to mean "screw the rest of the world, we have these oceans between us and them". So while no one else is looking or giving a damn, we have to work at preventing the Nazis from getting too large a toehold over here. You may remember that back in 1916 German agents blew up a munitions depot in New York harbor without bothering to declare war.'

'Oh yes,' Geoffrey said. 'The, what was it? Black Tom explosion. We were grateful to the Germans for that at the time, since we were already in the thick of it, and it helped pull you in the direction of joining us in the fight.'

'And we have indications that they're getting ready to do something over here once again. But at the moment it's still just vague hints, and we have no idea what or when.'

'You'd think they'd be doing their best to keep the US out of it,' Geoffrey commented.

'You would think that,' Welker agreed.'

'Curiously,' Geoffrey said, 'on our recent visit to Schloss Eichenholz, Herr Hitler assured me, well actually the Duke, that he had no warlike intentions. That was, you understand, two days before his troops marched into Austria to enforce *Anschluss* and create a greater Germany.'

Welker took a sip of port. 'I'm shocked,' he said. 'Lying to a royal personage. Shocked.'

'Well, one thing – we now have a useful contact in Germany. A well-placed contact who, with a modicum of care, may prove very useful indeed. And a bit of his information may well pertain to the US. If so, I will pass it on to you, thus enhancing both of our reputations. Which reminds me, does "red cabbage" convey anything to you?'

'Commie sauerkraut?'

'Probably not. The contact gave our agent a newspaper and said don't lose it, and when asked why, he answered "red cabbage".'

Welker stared off at the swinging door to the kitchen. 'It rings a bell,' he said. He stared off some more. 'Ah, sure,' he said after a suspenseful minute. 'I remember. Secret ink. You write the message with a fine-tip brush so as to not leave any scratches on the paper, using a very dilute solution of lemon juice. When it dries it disappears. If the solution is dilute enough heating will not bring it out, but for some reason red-cabbage-soaked water will. I think you may have to boil the cabbage in the water first, but I'm not sure. It's fast, it's reasonably secure, and it doesn't leave any incriminating di-ethyl mercurate of mumbo-jumbo or whatever around.'

'Aha!' said Geoffrey. 'I will pass it on.'

'Glad to be of assistance.'

Geoffrey looked thoughtful for a moment, and then said, 'It occurs to me that there is something you could do for us, what with your friends in high places and the like.'

'And what would that be?'

'Sophie – our sixteen-year-old – has no papers and no way of getting any. Perhaps with your contacts in the State Department . . .'

'Why not?' Welker said. 'I'll see what can be done.'

'Speaking of which,' Patricia added, pulling a small envelope from her purse, 'do you know anyone who knows anything about stamps? Postage stamps?'

'You mean of the collectable sort?' Welker asked.

'Yes. That sort,' Patricia said. 'Sophie came with this packet of stamps tucked into the lining of her jacket. Presumably put there by her father, and presumably of some value. If this is so, she could have a little nest egg to put her through college or whatever.'

'And until then?' Welker asked.

'Well, we've sort of decided that unless her missing uncle shows up we'll keep her.'

'She will become our niece once or twice removed, or something of the sort,' Geoffrey amplified.

'From the Jewish branch of the family?'

'One never knows, does one?' Geoffrey said. 'I have a great-uncle or some such relative on my mother's side who has a decidedly Semitic cast to his features. One hesitates to ask, after all, not knowing what the askee would think of the question. I have never heard him express his opinion of the Hebrew race one way or the other, but then I don't believe the subject ever came up.'

'What does Sophie think of it?' Welker asked.

'We haven't had a chance to discuss it with her yet, we may have to give her up to the missing uncle. However, she'll need the papers in any case.'

'Of course,' Welker said. 'As to the stamps, I know just the man to ask.'

'Really?'

'Yes. FDR is a noted stamp collector. Let me take these and I'll wave them at him when I see him Thursday. Along with the lovely story that goes with them. If he doesn't take them for his own collection I'm sure he'll know someone who will. And at top price, whatever that turns out to be.'

'Better than I had hoped,' Patricia said, handing him the packet of stamps, 'but welcome just the same.'

'There is, as it happens, something that we can do for you,' Geoffrey said. 'That is if my assumptions are correct.'

'I am all, or at least largely, ears,' Welker said.

'Two assumptions,' Geoffrey said. 'The first is that the Italian Embassy receives at least part of its communications with Rome through the overseas cable.'

'I would also assume that,' Welker agreed. 'It's much more reliable than short wave, but the messages would be heavily encrypted 'cause they'd think that we just might have a man posted at the Western Union office to read their stuff as it came in.'

'And my other assumption is that you do intercept and keep copies of said communications.'

'Reasonable,' Welker agreed, 'after all, they might one day accidentally throw out their code book with the trash. I could certainly find out. Why?'

'They use a one-time pad,' Geoffrey told him.

'I won't ask how you know that. But communications by one-time pad are, as far as I know, unbreakable.'

'True,' Geoffrey acknowledged, 'but my clever wife has acquired pictures of about thirty as-yet unused pages of it.'

'Wow!' said Welker.

'That's what I thought,' Geoffrey agreed.

'Hmmm,' said Welker. 'I have to get back to New York tomorrow morning, but I know a guy who's in what's left of the Black Chamber – now it's the Signal Intelligence Service, very hush-hush. I'll bet he would very much like to see those pages.'

'If there's anything interesting,' Geoffrey said, 'we get to see it. Fair's fair.'

'I'll make sure they understand,' Welker told him. 'And I'll be back here Thursday and I'll call you after I see FDR. Back and forth twice in one week; I think I'm going to buy stock in the Pennsy Railroad.'

TWENTY-SEVEN

A word is dead
When it is said,
Some say.
I say it just
Begins to live
That day.

– Emily Dickinson

'*May I sit at your table*
Will you buy me a drink
Shall we become lovers
Tell me, what do you think?
We could make love tonight, just tonight
And tomorrow never has to come
Until it's here.'

The follow spot picked up highlights in the red dress clinging sinuously to Elyse's slender body, the band played with unaccustomed subtlety as she sang:

'What are a few marks
To a spender like you
Compared to my virtue
Don't laugh – my virtue.'
Elyse paused and looked out at her audience, which had grown quiet as she sang, her gaze picking out individual members, men, women, and each knew the words were for them. And she went on:
'You look to be lonely
God knows I'm lonely too
Shall we each warm the other
Until the night's through?
Shall we make love tonight, all the night,
And tomorrow never has to come
Until it's here . . .'
The song ended but the band went on for a few bars as though it was loath to stop playing. Elyse stood there motionless as the music died out and the follow spot gradually dimmed to black. It took several seconds for the audience to begin clapping, but then the applause grew as the spot cautiously brightened again to find her still standing as she had been. She waited until the applause died away and then inclined her head slightly toward the audience and walked slowly to the back of the small stage and through the curtain. The houselights went back up, the band went back to playing happy oompah tunes, and the patrons in Berlin's Kabarett der Flöhe (Cabaret of the Fleas) resumed eating, drinking, talking, laughing, and pretending – if just for the moment – that life was good.

Neville Pekes, in what he thought of as his German disguise – a mud-brown suit, yellow dress shirt, and wide red, pink, and tan blotchy tie that he thought made him look a bit older than his twenty-eight years and sufficiently drab to blend in to the background – sat nursing his beer at a tiny table on the left side of the room, the not-too-new very ordinary looking suitcase by his feet. His view of the stage was constantly interrupted by the swinging doors to the kitchen as the waiters moved to and fro. What, he wondered, was he doing here? He would be approached. All well and good. He would pass the suitcase on to whoever gave the countersign. He should not allow the suitcase to be opened before he passed it on. How was he to prevent it if the police suddenly demanded to see the contents? What should he do if they stopped him, run like hell?

Sir Roger, Undersecretary of Everything No One Else Wanted, either didn't know himself or wouldn't tell him. *All will be revealed.* Ha!

He didn't much like field work, preferring his mundane job at the embassy, filling out forms, correcting the grammar in other people's reports, and translating German documents. Amazing that over half of the Berlin Embassy staff were not fluent in German. Some spoke scarcely any at all. But it was his absolute fluency in German that had earned him the interesting visit to Schloss Eichenholz, where he actually spoke to both Herr Hitler and the Duke of Windsor. Something to tell his children, assuming it was no longer secret by then. Assuming he ever got married.

And now it had got him to the Kabarett, will he or nill he. And, truth be told, he nill. What if he muffed it? The Assistant Secretary would not quickly forgive and even more slowly forget. He would probably not forgive himself. He would spend the rest of his career doing, well, just what he was doing now. He stared into the beer.

He had just about finished his drink, and the waiter had preemptively set a second one alongside the first, when Elyse came out from the back in an ivory dressing gown with a fluffy red collar and began working her way around the tables. He tried looking away and feigning disinterest, when part of him was honestly very interested indeed. But the ploy didn't work. When she reached his table she sat down across from him and smiled a world-weary smile. He was annoyed to discover that he was very pleased that she had done so.

'Buy a girl a drink,' she said. It took a second to register that she had said it in English, which didn't make him feel any less uncomfortable.

'Um,' he said, looking in all direction but hers. This was deucedly awkward. If anyone saw him . . . If the Foreign Office . . . A girl like this . . . a singer in a cabaret . . . Reflecting that he was here incognito, that no one from the FO would come in, that if they did, they would avoid his eye as much as he avoided theirs, he took a deep breath. Then a new thought: he was here incognito to meet someone. If his contact saw him with this woman would he . . .

Elyse leaned forward. 'Kiss me!' she said.

'What?' He almost jumped.

'Good,' she said. 'Now I have your attention.

'I don't . . .'

She shook her head. 'The British government entrusts you with its sensitive assignments and sends you out – all by yourself? I don't believe it.'

He almost suppressed a rising tide of indignation. 'Now see here . . .'

'But you are kind of cute,' she said.

The waiter appeared again with a bottle of champagne and two stemmed glasses. He made a production out of opening it, allowing the cork to arch across the room, and poured.

'I didn't—' Neville began.

'Of course you did,' she told him. 'You bought me an eighty-mark bottle of champagne, and that's why I am sitting here talking to you. It is all so mundane. Were I to sit here talking to you without the eighty-mark-bottle inducement then it would become of interest to anyone watching. Why you? And we don't want it to become of interest, do we?'

His mind felt sluggish, but finally he thought it was catching up. 'You're . . .'

'Elyse,' she said. 'I sing. Sometimes I dance. I can be rented for an eighty-mark bottle of champagne for up to half an hour, perhaps several times until I have to do my next set. I will go on again right after the acrobats. You will like the acrobats.'

'I thought—'

'That I'd be a man in a trench coat with the collar turned up, a fedora pulled low over his eyes, smoking a cigarette and talking out of the side of his mouth like in the American cinema?'

'I suppose. Something like that.'

'Pince-nez,' she said.

'What?'

'Pince-nez?' This time it was a question.

'Oh.' It was the countersign he had been given. But now the response had gone completely out of his mind. 'Uh.' He stared at the wall opposite for inspiration.

'Don't tell me I've made a horrible mistake.'

'Ah, pickelhaube.'

'That's better. Now we're official.'

'I wonder who makes up these words,' Pekes said. 'I mean, one is supposed to use them in an innocuous sentence in case you're speaking to the wrong chap. Now I can imagine using pince-nez—'

'I used to wear pince-nez,' Elyse offered, 'but they pinched my nose?'

'Exactly,' Pekes agreed. 'But "pickelhaube"? "I used to wear a pickelhaube but it squeezed my head"?'

'Lean forward and put your hand over my arm,' she instructed. 'Ah . . .'

'Merely for the benefit of any watchers,' she assured him. 'You're getting your eighty marks' worth.'

'Speaking of which,' he said, 'I don't know whether I have eighty—'

'Don't worry,' she said. 'It's covered.'

'Um,' he said, and he put his hand over her arm.

'Is that the transmitter?' she asked indicating the suitcase.

'I, uh . . .'

'You don't know. Of course you don't know. Why would they tell you what you were carrying? It might make you nervous. More nervous.' Her hand covered his and she smiled up at him. 'Just forget it when you leave,' she told him 'It will be taken care of. And here,' she put a white envelope on the table, 'stick this in your pocket.'

'All right,' he said.

She raised her champagne glass. 'A toast!'

'To what?' he asked, clinking glasses with her.

'I don't know,' she said. 'Certainly not to the future. Perhaps to the distant future. "Till the war-drum throbb'd no longer, and the battle-flags were furl'd. In the Parliament of man, the Federation of the world."'

'Tennyson,' he said.

'There is something about your English poets,' she said. 'Rupert Brooke makes me cry. Kipling makes me laugh.'

'And Tennyson?'

'He makes me think.' She downed her glass of champagne and allowed him to fill it again. 'Do you like it?' she asked.

'What, the champagne?' He took a sip.

'It isn't, you know. It's *Sekt*. Even the label is an ersatz imitation. It's actually pretty good, but they can charge more for it if they call it French champagne. And so they do.'

'What am I to do with the envelope?'

She smiled. 'Are you so anxious to leave me, then?'

'No – no, it's not that . . .'

Now she laughed. 'You should stay a while,' she said. 'Seduced by my hypnotic charm. Leave sadly when I go back to change for my next set.' She leaned in toward him. 'You do realize,' she said softly into his ear, 'that this is serious. Perhaps deadly serious.'

'No, I . . .' He paused. What had he thought? He hadn't really. 'I wasn't told,' he said. 'Sir Roger told me to come to this cabaret this evening and a man would meet me and take the suitcase. He told me it was very hush-hush, and to wear a green tie. You,' he added, sounding aggrieved, 'are not a man.'

'Thank you for noticing,' she said. 'You are not wearing a green tie.'

'Well, I don't own a green tie, so I put that bit of green ribbon on my hat.'

'What hat?'

'Oh,' he said, suddenly realizing. 'I checked the hat.'

She shook her head. 'You do not take this very seriously.'

'Truthfully,' he agreed, 'I thought it was all a bit of tomfoolery. I'm still not sure that it isn't. Some sort of joke.'

'I assure you that it is not a joke,' she said. 'As I said, if any of the watchers think that you are anything other than a slightly drunken customer trying to get the girl singer to agree to go home with him after the show, and perhaps feel her legs a bit under the table—'

'I would never!' Pekes said indignantly.

'A shame,' she said. 'It would add that touch of verisimilitude to this otherwise bald and unconvincing narrative.'

'Watchers?' he asked.

'What?'

'Watchers. You said "watchers".'

'Most assuredly there are watchers. The Gestapo has men assigned to watch the personnel of all embassies, but especially I believe the British, French, and Polish. Also their men spend time in clubs such as this to see who is being indiscreet with whom, and if they'd be of any use to blackmail. That is why this charade.' She made a small gesture with her hand. 'When I leave you, on the way to my dressing room, I shall go over to that fat man with the overly blond mustache across the room. He has indicated an interest in my, ah, singing.'

'That was a very good song,' Neville said. 'Evocative. And the way you sang it . . .'

'There is an interest in sad songs in Berlin today,' she told him. 'But not too often, and they must be balanced by a sort of manic gaiety. Most people can feel that there is something in the air. They do not know what, and they do not wish to know.'

Pekes did not know how to respond to that, and so he said nothing.

'You will please do me a favor,' she said.

'What sort of favor?'

'When your superiors ask you to describe the man who took the suitcase and gave you the envelope you will tell them that he was a tall, well-dressed man with a scar on his cheek. Yes, I think a scar on his cheek would be a good touch. His left cheek. He spoke German with a Bavarian accent. It was dark inside the cabaret, so you could note nothing else of interest. Do not overcomplicate the description.'

'And why,' he asked, 'should I lie to my own people?'

'To keep me safe. Some of your people,' she told him, 'are known to be sympathetic to the current regime. Some of them think Herr Hitler has brought order to the chaos that was Weimar. And again some of them may be vulnerable to persuasion of various sorts.'

'What . . . Who?'

She shrugged. 'I do not know. But it is possible, is it not? It is better not to take the chance. And nothing is to be gained by describing the "man" who gave you the envelope. In it is a brochure for a spa in Bad Salzuflen, you should visit it, it is very healthful. If the brochure is treated with the proper chemicals, and I do not know what they are but presumably the man who is to receive the envelope does, a list of transmission times and other such information will appear, so we never have to meet again. Also a message, I believe.'

She stood up. 'Goodbye. You should have touched my thigh, it is a nice thigh.'

He blushed. He could feel the heat in his ears.

'Stay here for a while,' she said. 'Drink your *Sekt*. Look sad.'

'I am sad,' he said. 'I should have touched your thigh.'

She smiled. 'Goodbye,' she said. 'Take care.'

TWENTY-EIGHT

You can't make an omelet
without breaking a few eggs
— old English idiom

Blake was already at the Figaro, his hands wrapped around a coffee mug, a sour expression on his face, when Welker arrived. 'It's about time,' Blake groused. 'Where the hell were you yesterday?'

'In Washington,' Welker said, sitting down and waving at a waiter, who promptly ignored him, as is the way at the Figaro. 'What's so urgent?'

'I got news,' Blake told him. 'I don't know what it means, but I got news.'

'OK. What is it?' Welker waved at the waiter again, who grudgingly came over and took his order for a cappuccino. 'And a piece of pie,' Welker added. 'Apple pie.'

'No apple,' the waiter told him, looking infinitely sad at the bad news. 'We got peach, lemon meringue, blueberry, which I don't recommend 'cause the blueberries come out of a jar, and we got cheesecake.'

'OK. Give me a slice of cheesecake.'

'Come to think of it, we got an apple crisp. That's a lot like pie.'

'Cheesecake,' Welker decided.

The waiter nodded. 'You got it,' he said.

Welker turned back to Blake as the waiter left. 'What's the news?'

'Well, first, you know those cards – the Commie membership cards that Gerard had me print up? Lehman gave them out at the Commie meeting yesterday. Said everyone should carry one, at least when they come to meetings. Shows they paid their dues. And to identify themselves to other members. Just why or when you'd want to do that he didn't say. And they've all been numbered with one of those numbering stamps. But what's weird is the numbers weren't sequential. Like he'd follow a three with a nineteen and then back to, maybe, seven, and like that.'

'That is interesting,' Welker admitted. 'Why would he do that?'

'Yeah, why?'

'Maybe he wants it to appear that there are a lot more members than there are.'

'Yeah,' Blake agreed. 'And why would he want that? Especially 'cause Lehman ain't really Lehman, he's a Nazi in Lehman's clothing. So what do you suppose he's up to? What do you suppose it means?'

Welker shook his head. 'No idea,' he said.

'Well, I wouldn't of asked to meet you just for that. It's weird, but it would have waited. There's something else.'

'OK,' Welker said.

Blake leaned forward and lowered his voice. 'He's setting up an action group. That's what he calls it, an action group. He needs a dozen people who are willing to put their words into action. He says. I don't like it.'

Welker lowered his voice to match Blake's. 'What sort of action?'

'That he doesn't say. Or when – he doesn't say that either.'

'How is he picking this dozen members?'

'First you got to volunteer – and don't say what you're thinking, 'cause I won't.'

'I didn't say a word.'

'Yeah but were thinking it, or you were going to be thinking it.'

'Actually not,' Welker said. 'He knows who you are, doesn't he?'

'Yes, 'Blake said. 'He passes me messages to take back to the *Gauleiter*. Sneaks them in a pamphlet or a copy of the *Daily Worker* and hands it to me.'

'So if he wants real Commies for whatever this is, he wouldn't pick you anyhow.'

'Yeah, I guess that's right.'

'Cheesecake?'

Welker swiveled around. The waiter was standing behind him with a slice of cheesecake in a small plate balanced on his open palm. 'Sorry,' Welker said, shifting to one side slightly to give the waiter space to put the plate down.

'The chef took the liberty,' the waiter said, 'to cover it with a raspberry puree that he made himself this morning.' He said it with the mournful air of a man who knew that his customer's next words were going to be, 'I hate raspberries.'

'Why, that's very nice,' Welker said, resisting the urge to ask, 'You actually have a chef?'

'Um,' the waiter said, and moved away.

Blake waited until Welker had turned his attention back across the table and repeated, 'I don't like it.'

Welker considered. 'You know,' he said, 'I don't much like it either.'

'That cheesecake any good?' Blake asked.

'I don't know,' Welker said, 'I haven't tasted it yet.' He took a forkful and tasted it. 'Yeah,' he said. 'It's very good.'

Blake waved at the waiter and pointed at the cheesecake and made 'give me a piece too' motions with his hands. The waiter stared at him for a moment and then stalked over. 'You want something?'

'Cheesecake,' Blake said. 'Bring me a piece of cheesecake.'

The waiter sighed and moved away.

'The question is,' Welker said, 'what now?'

'Easy,' Blake said. 'What I should do now is move to Oklahoma.'

'I thought it was Philadelphia or Kansas City.'

'Maybe a little further away. Maybe Guam.'

'Guam?'

'It's an island.'

'I know it's an island.'

'Probably no Nazis on it. Or Commies. Probably just nice peaceful Guamites.'

TWENTY-NINE

There are more things in heaven and earth, Horatio,
Than are dreamt of in your philosophy.
                    – *William Shakespeare,* Hamlet

'It comes together,' Welker said, 'but it doesn't seem to go anywhere.'

'What do you have?' Geoffrey asked.

They were sitting on easy chairs in Geoffrey's living room across a glass-top coffee table from each other nursing drinks – Scotch and water, no ice, and Scotch on the rocks. The Scotch was Glenkinchie, a single malt not yet sold in the US that, as Geoffrey's father put it, 'Goes down singing hymns.' Garrett had brought out a plate of strange twisted pastries for them to sample that he had just created from a recipe with an unpronounceable name in a language that didn't seem to actually exist. But the twisties were hot and fluffy and tasted of cinnamon and vanilla. Patricia and Sophie were out shopping.

'You first,' Welker said. 'You called me.'

'So I did. I have word from our contact in the German, ah, government. There is an active clandestine operation against your country that is set to mature sometime in the immediate future.'

'Sabotage?'

'Our contact doesn't know exactly. Perhaps not sabotage in the classic sense, not destroying things, since its object, he believes, is to keep America neutral and blowing up anything would seem to work against that ideal.'

'We are neutral.'

'Not neutral enough, apparently. My good friend Felix says that *Fall Bude*, whatever that may be, has been activated and is in progress.'

'Felix?'

'His code name. His true identity is known only to, I believe, three people.'

'Wise,' Welker agreed. 'I have heard of this falling Buddha before, but with no context.'

'It's "*Fall Bude*",' Geoffrey explained, spelling it. 'It translates to Case or Operation Booth, or Stall or Kiosk or Shack or something like that. Felix says Hess and Schellenberg, the SD guy, are name-dropping it and looking smug, but he has no idea of the context except that it is happening here.'

'"Booth", like telephone booth?'

'Or voting booth. Or—'

'Shit!' said Welker.

'Really?'

'One of my people overheard the phrase. "*Fall Bude*". But, like I said, I heard it as Buddha, B-u-d-d-h-a, like the god, and Fall, like the season. I never got to "*Fall Bude*", which I should have. It is, after all, in German. I am officially an idiot.'

'That realization,' Geoffrey told him, 'is the first step on the road to knowledge.'

'Shut up,' Welker explained. 'Besides, knowing that it's a telephone booth he's talking about instead of an Indian god doesn't really get us any further.'

'Buddha is not a god, you know,' Geoffrey volunteered. 'Buddhism is the path to enlightenment and the Buddha was one who was on the path to becoming enlightened. A whole different thing.'

'Big help,' Welker said.

'There is no useless knowledge,' Geoffrey told him.

Welker raised his head to stare at the ceiling. 'Some knowledge,' he said, 'is more useless than others.'

'Aside from verification of the codeword *Fall Bude*, which perhaps does put us a bit further up the path to enlightenment, do you have anything to bring us forwarder?' Geoffrey asked.

Welker lowered his gaze and looked thoughtfully into his glass. 'Yes,' he said after a moment. 'The head – calls himself a *Gauleiter* – of the local bunch of goose-steppers that calls itself the German-American Bund, a fellow named Frank Gerard, is in on it. He's the one who was overheard using the term. And he was talking to someone named Weiss, who was probably involved in a murder a couple of months back. But we haven't located Weiss yet, and all we know about him is his name and that he's a nasty son of a bitch.'

'Well, that's something,' Geoffrey said.

'And, unfortunately, it probably does involve the use of explosives, whatever it is. Gauleiter Gerard was very interested to learn that Harry Schnek was an ordnance expert.'

'Who is Harry Schnek?'

'I am. I'm Harry Schnek when I'm talking to Gerard.'

'Ah!' Geoffrey said.

There was a bustling at the door and Patricia and Sophie appeared, shedding boxes and packages as they approached. 'We've been shopping,' Patricia announced.

'Of course you have,' Geoffrey said, getting up and giving her a hug. 'We've been talking.'

'And?' Patricia asked, then held up a hand. 'No, wait a minute until we disembowel ourselves of these packages.'

Sophie giggled.

'Was that not the right word? No matter. A word should mean what I want it to mean, or what's a heaven for? Sophie, this is Mr Welker. He is a friend.'

'Hello,' Sophie said.

Welker nodded and smiled. 'Hello, Sophie.'

'We will join the conversation in a minute,' Patricia said, 'but first, let's gather up these packages and get them into the bedroom.' The two shoppers gathered and hefted and departed through an inner door. When they re-emerged eight minutes later Sophie was carrying a large glass of milk and Patricia a highball glass full of some amber liquid and two ice cubes.

They settled onto the couch fronting the coffee table and Patricia carefully put her glass down. 'What,' she asked, indicating the plate of twisted pastry, 'are those?'

'Scatapaskootchie,' Geoffrey told her, 'I think. Something like that. Ask Garrett.'

'I don't think I will,' Patricia said. 'There'll be a twenty-minute explanation that I don't understand and I'll end up convinced that the pastries were discovered somewhere in the asteroid belt and brought overland from Samarkand on the backs of gnus. I'll just eat one.'

'Wise,' Geoffrey agreed.

'They're very good,' Sophie offered, waving hers in front of her and then taking another bite.

'Mr Welker has something for you, Sophie,' Geoffrey told her.

She turned to face Welker. 'Mr Welker?'

'Miss Hertzel.'

'Sophie. I'm just Sophie.'

'And you must call me Jake,' Welker said. He reached into the inner pocket of his jacket and withdrew a long envelope. 'This is for you.'

She took it cautiously. 'What . . .?'

'Open it.'

She carefully peeled the flap back and removed the two papers within. 'A check,' she said, holding it up. 'This is a check, yes? And a . . . a letter.'

'So I believe,' said Welker.

She held the check up and peered at it. 'Ohmygod!' she said, and slowly and carefully put the check down on the glass table top as though it might burst into flame at any second. 'Oh my *god*!'

'What is it?' Patricia asked, picking up the check and holding it up to the light. After a second she put it back down. 'Oh. My. God.' She turned to Welker. 'The stamps?'

'Yes,' Welker told her. 'Fair market value, apparently. Notice the signature.'

'Well?' Geoffrey asked as she held the check up again. 'Share the, apparently, good news. What is it?'

'Four thousand two hundred dollars,' Patricia said. 'It's a check for four thousand two hundred dollars. It's made out to me but it says "for Sophie Hertzel, whose father was a great man" on the bottom. And it's signed – I can't make it out.'

'Franklin Delano Roosevelt,' Welker translated.

'Oh, yes,' Patricia said. 'Oh.'

'Mister President Roosevelt himself?' Sophie asked, her hand covering her mouth. 'He purchased my father's stamps? Four thousand and two hundred dollars?'

'I told Mr Roosevelt about you and your recent, ah, life and who your father was. He said that he never had the pleasure of hearing the great Aaron Hertzel conduct in person, but his wife may have when she was in England. And he has the RCA Red Seal recordings of him conducting Milhaud in, I believe Paris. He is particularly fond of *Le Boeuf sur le Toit* and *La Création du Monde*. Or so he said.

'Then he took the stamps out of their little packet and looked them over and arranged them this way and then that way on his desk and said, "Hmmm." Then he pulled a magnifying glass – like Sherlock Holmes – out of a drawer and looked at them through that. Then he pulled out a loupe – one of those things like an upside-down egg cup with a lens that watchmakers use to peer into watches and, apparently, stamp collectors use to peer into stamps – and said "hmmm" again, and "interesting" and "It could be – yes, it could be!" and called for an aide to bring him a big fat book from another room and peered into that for a while. Then he closed the book and stared at the ceiling for a moment. Then he said, "German colonial overprints. Nice and clean. A hitherto unknown issue. And they won't make any more of them."'

'They won't?' Sophie asked.

'That's what he said,' Welker told her.

'Highly unlikely,' Geoffrey agreed. 'Germany lost its colonies after the World War.'

'Then the president made a phone call and talked for a few minutes using the mystical language of stamp collectors. Then he pulled out a checkbook and we decided that Sophie certainly didn't have a bank account and probably didn't have any documentation that a bank would accept to prove who she was. So he made the check out to Lady Patricia.'

'We shall put it in the bank right away,' Patricia said, patting Sophie on the knee. 'Open a savings account in your name.'

'I'm not used to, you know, dollars, but it seems like an awful lot of money,' Sophie said.

'It is,' Welker agreed. 'It's almost three years' salary for the average working man.'

Patricia smiled at him. 'Something over four years' salary for the average working woman,' she added.

'For sixteen little pieces of paper?' Sophie wondered. 'It seems strange.'

'The oddness of collectors is without limits,' Welker volunteered. 'There are those who collect cigar bands, baseball cards . . .' At Sophie's puzzled look he explained, 'Cards the size of playing cards with pictures of baseball players on them.'

'Oh,' she said, looking only slightly less puzzled.

'Some of our wealthier brethren collect art work—'

'Well,' Sophie said, 'that seems . . .'

'Automobiles,' Welker went on, 'articles of clothing, usually but not necessarily those worn by famous people . . .'

'Death masks,' Geoffrey offered. 'Which seems to me to be unusually grotesque.'

'Antique tools,' Welker added. 'I know a man who has over sixty screwdrivers.'

'Just screwdrivers?' Patricia asked.

'He concentrates on screwdrivers, but he has a few hammers and hatchets and a wrench or two. And icepicks. He'd actually like to make a collection of old wrenches, he told me once, but nobody seems willing to give them up.'

'I,' Geoffrey announced, 'collect oddities and quiddities.'

'We knew that, my dear,' Patricia told him.

Welker turned back to Sophie. 'Why don't you read the letter.'

'Oh yes,' Sophie said. She picked the letter up from the table and unfolded it. 'It has a . . . what do you say? A letterhead,' she said. 'It's from President – no, it says "Mrs Franklin Roosevelt". His wife?'

'Eleanor,' Patricia told her. 'Eleanor Roosevelt. Curiously that was also her name before she got married. She and the president are cousins, I believe.'

'Fifth cousins once removed,' Welker said. 'Whatever that means.'

'It's quite simple,' Geoffrey told him. 'You see—'

'Please,' Patricia said. 'Not now.' She turned to Sophie. 'The letter,' she said.

'Yes.' Sophie sat down and began silently reading.'

'You don't have to read it aloud if you don't want to,' Patricia said. 'If it's personal or anything.'

'Yes, please,' Sophie said. 'I do not read aloud very well. I will read it one time first and then I will tell it to you.'

'Of course,' Patricia agreed, looking embarrassed for the first time that that Geoffrey could remember in many years. 'And if it's personal, why then—'

'She is very nice,' Sophie said after a minute, 'this Mrs Roosevelt. Very good.'

'Yes,' Patricia said.

Welker nodded. 'She has that reputation,' he said. 'And, from what I've seen, she earns it daily.'

Sophie read silently for a few minutes, and then she looked up. 'She wants to meet me,' she said. 'She wants me to come to the White House, and I should call for an appointment because she isn't there all the time.'

'We'll have to get you a new dress,' Patricia said. 'A White House dress.'

'She says the indignities being per– perpetrated against my people are unspeakable and that what happened to my father was horrible. She says she saw him in London and he was a great conductor, especially of the later Romantic composers, and that she wants – no needs – to help me. That what she says, "wants – no needs".'

'That's nice,' Patricia said.

'It doesn't seem somehow fair,' Sophie said. 'I mean, there are so many in need, so many hurt by these – these – monsters. And I

am a lucky one. I have been rescued. My father . . . my father . . .'
She fell silent for a moment and then she went on. 'My father was
killed, but I survived, and now I am safe. And I am with friends.'

'Yes you are,' Geoffrey said.

'New friends. And I'm so lucky. But there are so many others
who are desperate—'

'You think she should help everyone in need?' Welker asked. 'So
does she, but obviously she can't. So she helps who she can.'

'Yes,' Sophie said. 'Of course.' She looked back down at the
letter. 'She is going to arrange a meeting for me with the head-
mistress of Briarleigh School to see what form I should be put
in,' she said, and looked up. 'This Mrs Roosevelt, she takes a lot
for granted.'

'Yes,' Welker agreed. 'She does.'

THIRTY

Beware of false prophets, which come to you in sheep's clothing,
but inwardly they are ravening wolves.
Ye shall know them by their fruits.
                        – Matthew 7:15–16, King James Bible

Since it first opened in 1906, the massive red-brick armory
which takes up most of the block on Lexington Avenue
between 25th and 26th streets has been known as 'the Armory',
although there are actually six others in Manhattan. It is home to
the 69th Infantry Regiment, the famed 'Fighting Irish', a moniker
they first earned during the Battle of Gettysburg in 1863. In
1913 the Armory was host to the International Exhibition of
Modern Art, which became known as the Armory Show, and
introduced cubism to America and America to Picasso, Cézanne,
Matisse, and Van Gogh.

This fine Saturday evening in June 1938 it was hosting the seven-
teenth annual fund-raiser for the Disabled Veterans of the World
War, and four hundred of New York's elite – well, three hundred
eighty-seven by actual count – were gathered around the thirty-five

tables in the Great Hall. The turnout included Governor Lehman, Senator Wagner, Mayor LaGuardia, three US representatives, and a swaggle of city councilmen, who were proud – proud – to be seen with the line of wheelchair-bound veterans eating at their own tables along the far wall.

Cab Calloway and his Orchestra played on the improvised bandstand, thus establishing the hip credentials of the gathering. Rosenbaum & Daughters Caterers were supplying food and waitstaff at a hefty discount, happy to support the worthy cause. The bill of fare included canapés and champagne cocktails before dinner, a crisp lettuce salad, roast chicken Provençal, pommes Anna, and early peas for the entree, with strawberry shortcake for dessert. The wines a sprightly Chablis and a more somber Pinot. The waitstaff unobtrusive and professional.

Among the twenty regular waiters lay a trio of wolves in waiters' clothing. Seventeen of the waiters were as they seemed but three – as it turned out later three of the regular waiters – had been paid $20 each to allow someone to take their place. Some sort of practical joke, they were given to understand.

The three practical jokers faded from view one at a time after the entrees were served. Their leader, a stocky man with close-cropped hair and a face like a bulldog, went first, pushing a service cart ahead of him, then half a minute later the second man, tall, thin, and bald as a bright pink cue ball, followed. The third, a short man wearing an oversized apron that gave the impression he was hiding behind it, came a half-minute after, following the others down a corridor lined with plaques, medals, aging photographs, and bits of obsolete military gear. The first was waiting by a door labeled 'Authorized Personnel Only'. 'For this one we supposedly have the key,' the leader said and, after fiddling with the lock for a few seconds, pushed it open. The three went through to what proved to be a staircase landing, pushing the cart in and closing the door behind them.

The stairs going up led to the offices of the Regimental Commander, the Procurement Officer, the Officer of the Mess, the Training Officer, the Band Director, and the Sergeant Major. The three jokesters went down. The door to the basement was solid wood, with a steel band around the edge, an oversized serious-looking lock, and a small thick glass window. A handprinted sign below the window read: *No Admission Without a Signed Order from the CO or the Watch Commander – No Exceptions.*

They gathered in front of the door peering through the window as though searching for a hidden truth. The room inside was dark and nothing could be seen through the window. 'Now comes the difficulty,' the leader said. 'For this door we have not the key. Parker?'

'Yes, Herr Weiss.' The short man stepped forward and examined the lock. 'Yale,' he said. 'Nothing to it.' He took out a leather drawstring pouch and selected one tool from what looked like a set of dental picks, along with a short, flat ribbon of steel bent into a zigzag, and set to work. The others were silent, unconsciously holding their breaths, as a minute passed, and then another, and then – with a muted click the lock turned and the door opened. He put the tools away. 'We're in,' he said, but the other two had already pushed the door open and gone inside.

After a brief search the light switch was found and a double row of ceiling lights worked at illuminating the large room. The ceilings were high and there were occasional small heavily barred windows high along the wall to the right of the door. A long row of swivel-stacked M1903 Springfield rifles ran alongside the wall. Tacked to the wall behind the rifles was a typewritten sign:

THERE ARE MANY OTHERS JUST LIKE IT BUT ONE
OF THESE RIFLES IS YOURS. TAKE YOUR RIFLE ONLY.
TAKE GOOD CARE OF IT – IT MAY SAVE YOUR LIFE

The room was filled with the necessities of a peacetime army: boxes and cartons of supplies stacked in orderly piles behind eight-foot partitions and crisscrossed by meticulously straight aisles which met at precise right angles. From where they stood they could see what was probably a completely disassembled field kitchen, a ten-foot cube of boxes of iron rations, and racks holding carefully maintained harnesses and saddles for pack horses.

'So, Schutzmann, what are we looking for?' Weiss asked.

The tall man thought for a moment. 'As I have said, it will be, almost certainly, in a strong wooden box about thirty centimeters by perhaps forty. Possibly banded with iron bands. There may, of course, be many such boxes; in which case they will either be widely separated or in some sort of strong room. My assumption would be the strong room. In addition to the danger posed by the explosive – which is actually very slight as gelignite does not explode unless set off by a detonator – there is the question of petty pilferage.'

'Who would steal explosives?' Parker asked.

Weiss looked at him. 'We,' he reminded him. 'We would steal explosives.'

'We must also see if we can locate the detonators,' Schutzmann said. 'We could, of course, make our own, but it will simplify things.'

'Yes,' Weiss agreed. 'And it will further reinforce the narrative.'

'How's that?' Parker asked.

'Never mind. Let's just find what we came for and get out before someone happens by.'

It took them about six minutes to locate the eight-by-ten-foot area in the far corner that was set apart by a partition of thick bars like a jail cell with a door secured by a heavy padlock. Through the bars they could see the stack of heavy wooden boxes, each stenciled on the side:

USA XP 1923 GELIGNITE PR 17
EXPLOSIVES ** EXPLOSIVES
HANDLE WITH EXTREME CARE
KEEP AWAY FROM HEAT

'Goddam!' said Weiss.

'Yes,' Schutzmann said. 'It is the proper way. They are being careful.'

'They could have put up a real wall,' Weiss commented, 'if they wanted to be careful.'

'If these boxes were to blow up,' Schutzmann said, 'a wall, however real, would not help'

'Let me at that padlock,' said Parker.

In less than a minute he had the door open and Schutzmann and Parker were hefting one of the boxes, which according to the notation on the lid held twelve pounds of gelignite in six two-pound sticks, and stepping off toward the exit. Weiss had located a small box of blasting caps and was a few steps behind.

'Herr Weiss,' Schutzmann called, 'would you close that door please. Then it may be some time before they notice the absence.'

'On the contrary,' Weiss said, 'we shall leave it open. That way they will discover it the sooner. And one necessary final touch . . .' He took an envelope from his pocket and, using his handkerchief so as not to touch it, removed a Workers Party of America membership card from it and allowed the card to flutter to the ground. 'Now,' he said, 'let us get these boxes into the service cart and us and it away from here.'

THIRTY-ONE

The sword above here smiteth not in haste
Nor tardily, howe'er it seem to him
Who fearing or desiring waits for it.
    – Dante Alighieri, The Divine Comedy

Milton came to the door of the morning room, where Lord Geoffrey was indulging in coffee and a selection of pastries from Kantor Bros. Jewish Deli on M Street. 'Major Martell, my lord,' he announced, and then disappeared behind the door as the major entered.

Coming to a halt and stiffening to attention just inside the door, the Major announced: 'Major Chaz Martell, US Army Signal Intelligence, your lordship.'

'Um?' Geoffrey asked, waving the major in.

'I hope I'm not interrupting you.'

'Not at all,' Geoffrey assured him. 'Come in, Major. Have a cup of coffee and a piece of honey cake or a rugelach or two. I think that's how to say it. We have acquired a Jewish, I guess, ward, and we're trying the foods of her clan. They do well in the pastry department.'

'No thank you, Lord Saboy, I mean, I have already eaten.'

'Then just coffee? And it's Lord Geoffrey, not Lord Saboy. British forms of address are a minefield for the unwary. I was just awaiting the events of the afternoon and here you are. Delighted. What can I do for you?'

'I'm with the Signal Intelligence Service detachment at Fort

Meade. We have a recent Italian Embassy intercept that I've been instructed to share with you. I understand it was you who acquired the copies of the one-time pads we're using.'

'My wife, actually,' Geoffrey said. 'Come and sit down. She'll be joining us in a minute.'

'Uh,' the Major said, looking uncomfortable. 'I was told to pass these on to you. Nothing was said about your wife. These are Top Secret, you understand.'

'So is my wife,' Geoffrey told him. 'She is,' he added, stretching a point, 'one of Britain's top counterespionage officers in the United States.'

'Oh,' Major Martell said. 'Really? I had no idea. They didn't say.'

'And a good thing too,' Geoffrey said. 'Besides, they almost certainly didn't know. She's very good at her job. I'm trusting you not to divulge this to anyone.'

Major Martell eased himself into one of the upholstered chairs. He had the uneasy feeling of one who has just had a secret thrust upon him that one would just as soon not know. 'Well . . .' he said. 'So the pads are useful?'

'They are,' Major Martell agreed. 'We do have a man at the Western Union office sending us copies of all the Italian Embassy traffic along with, ah, other material. I shouldn't . . .'

'Better not, I am easily shocked,' Geoffrey said. 'But about the Italian stuff?'

'Most of the messages are sent in the normal diplomatic code. For a while we could read everything – I understand we bought a copy of the code from a man in Geneva. Then about six months ago they changed the code. But apparently messages direct to the Ambassador from Count Ciano – he's the Foreign Minister . . .'

'Yes, he is,' Geoffrey agreed.

'Well, those are sent using this one-time pad. Presumably so that even if the diplomatic code has been breached the most-secret stuff will stay secret. But in this case . . .'

'Yes?' Geoffrey asked helpfully.

'We have the pad. At least for the next twenty or so messages.'

'Right. And what have you found?'

'Oddly this most-secret stuff seems mostly to be gossip. You know, who's doing what and with what and to whom, as the old limerick has it.'

At this point Patricia came through the inner door and smiled brightly at the two men. 'My lovely husband,' she said. 'And a handsome guest. A major.'

'Yes, ma'am,' Major Martell said, rising to his feet. 'Major Chaz Martell, United States Army Signal Intelligence.'

'Welcome, Major Martell,' Patricia said, advancing and offering her hand.

Martell shook her hand briefly and gingerly. 'Thank you, ma'am.'

'What wondrous things do you have to impart to us?' she asked, sitting on the edge of the sofa and looking intensely interested.

'Well, Special Agent Welker said that we should notify you if anything turned up regarding a Case or Operation Booth.'

'Yes?'

'Well, we've only gotten three intercepts so far that keyed to the one-time pads, but the third one had a mention, although we don't exactly understand it. *Cabina di caso*, that's what it is in Italian.'

'What does he say about it?' Geoffrey asked.

'Here,' Major Martell said, taking an envelope from an inner jacket pocket and passing it over. 'Here's a copy of the original with an English translation on the next page. You read it. I'll have to have it back when you're done.'

'Of course. Here, sit, sit. Have some coffee.'

Major Martell sat gingerly on the couch while Geoffrey took the two sheets of paper from the envelope and unfolded them. He held them side by side, stared at them for a minute, and went, 'Umm.'

'Geoffrey, you pig,' Patricia said. 'Don't hog it. What does it say?'

'Umm,' Geoffrey said. 'It is from Count Ciano himself to Ambassador Anducci. He thanks him for his recent hospitality and says he was Saturday at a big house party at Claretta's—'

'That would be Clara Petacci,' the major interrupted. 'She is known to be Mussolini's, ah, mistress.' He looked vaguely embarrassed at having said 'mistress'.

'Yes,' Geoffrey agreed. 'And then he says, um, um, ah – here. He says that his man in Berlin reports that Hess—'

'That would be Obergruppenführer Rudolf Hess, Lord Geoffrey,' Major Martell interrupted again. 'He—'

'Yes, I know,' Geoffrey told him. 'As it happens I met him a few weeks ago.'

'Oh.' Major Martell poured himself a cup of coffee and diluted it with four heaps of sugar and a healthy dollop of cream.

Geoffrey looked back down at the paper. 'That Hess told Renzetti—'

'That would be Giuseppi Renzetti, the Italian Ambassador to Germany,' Patricia informed him sweetly.'

'Really?'

'Was that a sarcastic "really"? Yes. I met his wife at that party at the Italian Embassy a few weeks ago. She was over here visiting relatives. She did not want her fortune told.'

'Ah!' Geoffrey said. 'At any rate, he told Renzetti,' he looked back down at the paper, 'that *Cabina di caso* – "Case Booth" – was underway. That it was under the control of Herr Weiss, whom he – that would be Renzetti – had met at the *divertimento* a few weeks back.'

'I believe I also met the gentleman in question,' Patricia said. 'Short, with a puffy face, a short blond beard clipped straight across at the bottom, and piggy eyes.'

'Interesting, possibly useful,' Geoffrey commented, and then turned back to the message: 'And that Germany and Italy would soon have nothing to fear from the United States for some time.'

'Nothing to fear?' Patricia

'So he said. And America's eyes would be directed toward the East.'

'Like China?' Patricia asked. 'Japan?'

'He doesn't say.'

'What else?'

'That Renzetti should appreciate the pun.'

'The pun?'

'Ah – *Gioco di parole* – that certainly translates to "pun".'

'What pun?'

'Probably on *Cabina di caso*, or more probably the original German, *Fall Bude.*'

'If you can parse a pun out of that,' Patricia told him, 'you're welcome to it.'

'Well, as my old friend Willy Ley is so fond of saying, "German humor is no laughing matter."'

'What else can we glean from the message?' Patricia asked.

'Um, where was I? Oh yes. Oh dear.'

'What?'

'He, that is Count Ciano, suggests, on the basis of what Renzetti was able to make out of what Hess said, that Anducci – well, let me read it to you: "We can be sure of nothing, but it is our strong suggestion, based on Renzetti's perception of what Hess said, or rather what he deliberately did not say, that it would be a good idea if you keep all Embassy staff away from New York City for the next two weeks and particularly avoid A17 . . ."'

Geoffrey looked over at Major Martell. 'Two weeks from when? When did you intercept this?'

'Two days ago, your, ah, lordship. Just decoded it this morning. Came right over.'

'Oh great. New York in two weeks. And A17. What the blazes is A17, do you suppose?'

'It's turned up in several of the other decrypts – not that precisely, but letter-number combinations like that,' Major Martell said. 'Professor Friedman – my boss – thinks it's a nomenclature code. Somewhere there's a list of things, all identified by a letter-number combination, so you never have to write the name of the thing, even in your encrypted messages.'

'What sorts of things?' Patricia asked.

'Anything important that you're liable to mention: bridges, tunnels, government buildings, even people.'

'So something's going to happen in New York sometime in the next two weeks,' Patricia said, 'but we don't know what or where except that we should avoid A17, whatever that is.'

'That would seem to be it,' Geoffrey agreed. 'And that this Herr Weiss is in charge of it. How good a look did you get at him?'

'I'd know him again at midnight in a dust storm,' Patricia told him. 'He exudes an evil miasma.'

'You exaggerate,' Geoffrey said.

'Let us hope so.'

Geoffrey turned to Major Martell. 'Who else are you showing this to?'

'Colonel Garsten of Military Intelligence back at Meade; our liaison at the FBI will get a copy; and Special Agent Welker, of course. And that's about it. Perhaps we should alert the New York City Police Department, but I'm not exactly sure what we can tell them. And we can't reveal the source of our information, so that's a problem.'

'We'll let that be Welker's problem,' Geoffrey said. 'He evidently has some connections in the NYC Police.'

'We'll get a copy of this to him in the morning,' Major Martell said. He finished his coffee and stood up. 'I should be going. If I could have the document back, please.'

'Of course,' Geoffrey said, handing it to him. 'Thank you for sharing it with us.'

'Yes, sir. Of course.' Visibly resisting the urge to salute, he did a neat about-face and left the room.

'Well,' Geoffrey said. 'What do you make of this?'

Patricia stood up. 'I think we should go there,' she said.

'Where, New York?'

'Yes.'

'What on earth good could we do there?'

'What good can we do here?' Patricia asked.

'Yes, well, there is that of course.'

'They say that if you stand at the intersection of Forty-Second Street and Broadway sooner or later you'll meet everyone you know.'

'They do?'

'Yes they do. I could stand on the corner there and watch for Herr Weiss. You could bring me coffee and donuts. We could take turns, except you don't know what Herr Weiss looks like.'

Geoffrey considered. 'Actually,' he said, 'it's possible that we could do some good. If we could make some sort of half-educated guess of where what's going on might be going on, where Weiss might actually show up, we could hide behind a convenient potted palm and look out for the blighter.'

'How would we do that?'

'I think we go to New York and sit down with Welker.'

'I could force myself to do that,' Patricia agreed. 'Under great coercion, of course.'

'I noticed that you were attracted to him,' Geoffrey commented, 'but do keep it in his pants until whatever this is is over. You can be quite a distraction, I believe.'

'I am innocent of intent,' she told him.

'Really?' he said. '"While I am I, and you are you,
So long as the world contains us both,
Me the loving and you the loth
While the one eludes, must the other pursue."'

She pursed her lips in silent thought for a minute, and then said, 'Ah! I get it.'

'Robert Browning,' Geoffrey told her. 'Wise man, Browning. He understood much that continues to befuddle the rest of us.'

'And then he wrote it down, to befuddle us even further,' Patricia offered.

'At times,' Geoffrey agreed.

THIRTY-TWO

There is a tide in the affairs of men,
which, taken at the flood, leads on to fortune;
omitted, all the voyage of their life
is bound in shallows and in miseries.
On such a full sea are we now afloat,
and we must take the current when it serves,
or lose our ventures.

– William Shakespeare

B lake was staring down at his clam chowder. 'They've taken a room at the Waldorf Astoria,' he said.

Welker pushed the plate holding the remains of his hamburger to the side and centered his cup of coffee on the table before him. He had arrived at the Figaro first, a little after noon, and was already eating when Blake arrived. But he had waited patiently for Blake to ask the waiter if they really had clam chowder like it said on the board, to order the clam chowder with a toasted bagel and cream cheese and a cup of coffee, and to stare morosely at the giant espresso machine until the food arrived.

'Who?' Welker asked. 'Who has?'

'Lehman, or whoever he really is, he and his "Action Group".'

'At the Waldorf?'

'I thought clam chowder was red.'

'This is New England clam chowder, it's white.'

'Oh.' Blake stuck a tentative spoon into the chowder, lifted it to his lips, and tasted. He thought about it for a minute. 'Not bad,' he said. 'Different. Creamy.'

'What sort of room?' Welker asked.

'You know, a room. Like a bedroom. A room.'

'Not a meeting room or a ballroom or a . . . whatever else they rent?'

'Nope. Just a bedroom.'

'Why?'

'He didn't tell me. I didn't ask and he didn't tell me.'

'What did he say?'

'Lehman? He had me go rent the room for them under the name of Booth and then bring him the key. Told me to pay for a week in advance. Told me to stay away from the hotel after that. So that's what I'm doing.'

'Booth?'

'Yeah, that's what he said. Isaac Booth. He thought that was funny for some reason. I paid cash for a week.'

'When was this?'

'Yesterday afternoon. Six dollars a day. Can you believe that?'

'Hey, there are people around for whom six dollars a day is piffle. But the question is, why did Lehman become one of them? Why does he need a room? And why at the Waldorf for six dollars a day?'

Blake finished his chowder and carefully set the bowl to the side. 'It's for the Action Group, he says.'

'That's my next question,' Welker added. 'What the hell is the "Action Group"?'

'I told you about it a couple of weeks ago.'

'Yeah. You told me they were setting one up, but you didn't tell me what it is.'

''Cause I don't know what it is. He asked for volunteers for this Action Group 'cause he says we're just about ready for some meaningful action.'

'What kind of action?'

'He didn't tell me and I didn't ask.'

'How many guys?'

'Four guys. Maybe five. He peeled it down from nine or ten. A couple of the ladies volunteered too, but he said maybe next time, so it's all guys. Four–five guys. Tough-looking guys. The kind of nut jobs who hope that "action" means a fight, you know what I mean?'

'Do they do anything? Are they going to do anything? Hold meetings? Run around a track? Study ancient Persian manuscripts? Anything? Besides, presumably, going to a hotel room at the Waldorf?'

'You tell me,' Blake said. 'What Lehman went on about, and he seemed pretty pleased with himself, was that the Action Group would go down in history as the leading edge – the, ah, "pin that pricked the bubble of capitalism".'

'The pin?'

'I know. It sounds like bullshit to me too. What he said was that they were going to indulge in a practical application of Marx's theory of dialectical materialism.'

'A practical application?'

'That's what he said. And power to the proletariat, which he says a lot. I'm not sure he really understands half of that Commie crap he says, and I'm damn sure most of the group doesn't understand it either. But it sounds – you know – strong. And then he said all would be explained, but only to the Group, 'cause it had to be kept secret for the time. But the world would know when the moment came. And then they went off by themselves. But first he took me aside and told me to rent the room at the Waldorf. Gave me a hundred dollars in cash. Just in case, he said. But I gotta return the extra.'

'Well, at least it's a sign he trusts you.'

'I'm not sure that I trust me with a hundred dollars in cash. And what's happening – it's getting weird. Here we got a real Nazi who's a phony Commie giving money to a phony Commie who's also a phony Nazi to rent a room for a bunch of Commie toughs who don't know he's a Nazi. It's like a Charlie Chan movie where nobody is what he seems to be. And somebody always gets killed along about this point in the movie, and I'd just as soon if it wasn't me.'

'Well, keep doing what you're doing and keep your head down, and if you hear anything else of interest call my office. Don't use the phone at work – find a payphone.'

'I always carry a couple of nickels with me just in case,' Blake told him.

'One last thing,' Welker said. 'What's the room number in the Waldorf?'

'Four sixteen,' Blake told him. 'It's on the fourth floor.'

'Thanks.'

'Be careful,' Blake said. 'Whatever you're going to do, be careful.'

'You too,' Welker said.

Blake smiled and then frowned. 'You'd better believe it,' he said.

Three hours later Welker was at his desk in his tiny office, one of the five rooms the OSI had managed to acquire on the sixth floor of the Alexander Hamilton US Custom House at 1 Bowling Green, a stone's throw from the southern tip of Manhattan Island. Four of the rooms formed an office suite and the fifth, down the hall, would be filled with filing cabinets as soon as the requisition went through, in which to keep their records as soon as they had any records. The OSI was not listed on the call board in the lobby, and the name on the outer door said STATISTICAL MANAGEMENT GROUP, so if one didn't know where one was going, one would have a hard time arriving.

He was staring out the window across Battery Park watching a ferry swinging around for its trip to Staten Island when Rebecca, his secretary – well, actually she was the group secretary and receptionist and would do the filing when they had anything to file – peered around the office door. 'A lord,' she said. 'A real British lord.'

He turned his gaze away from the harbor. 'How's that?'

'And a lady,' she added. 'A lord and a lady. You should tell me when you're expecting a lord and a lady.'

'Sorry, Becky,' he said. 'what are you talking about?'

'Saboy. Lord and Lady Saboy. That's them.'

'Ah. They're here?'

'How would I know about it if they weren't?' she asked. 'Since you didn't tell me they were coming. They said they were expected. They are expected, aren't they?'

'Lord and Lady Saboy?' he asked. 'They are sort of expected, but I didn't know when. Show them in.'

'How do I address them?' she asked. 'I mean, like, "your lord-ship" or what? I'll do that, but I'll be darned if I'll curtsey or anything. We fought a revolution so I wouldn't have to curtsey.'

'I will defend with my life your right not to curtsey,' he told her. 'Call him "Captain Saboy", he'll like that. And call the lady

"Lady Patricia" or "Ma'am", as you like. You'll like them – they're
nice people. They're hoity but they're not toity.'

'Excuse me?'

'Never mind,' he said. 'Just show them in.'

'Does your mind ever know what your mouth is saying?' she
asked, and then disappeared out the door.

Patricia came in two strides ahead of Geoffrey and folded herself
into the hard wooden chair in front of the desk, making the chair
look like its one purpose in life was to embrace this woman.
'Something is going to happen,' she said. 'Did you get the decrypt?
Is that the word – decrypt? It sounds right.'

Welker stood up. 'Welcome,' he said, 'yes I did,' and then sat back
down and stared at them for a long moment. 'As President Roosevelt
told me a few weeks ago,' he said, 'there's this old Chinese curse—'

'I imagine there is,' Geoffrey agreed, pulling a chair over from the
corner and settling into it.

'"May you live in interesting times,"' Welker explained. 'That's
the curse: "May you live in interesting times." We got it. And
I think they're about to become even more interesting.'

'We, my lovely wife and I, have come to the same conclusion.
And we came to offer our assistance,' Geoffrey told him. 'Our advice
and our assistance. Without which you clearly cannot proceed. Do
we have any idea in which direction we are to proceed?'

'I think,' Welker said soberly, 'I think we may.'

'Oh dear.'

'Things have been moving,' Welker told them. 'Coming together.'

'I thought perhaps,' Patricia said, 'if we are to believe the Italians,
something, apparently, is happening in New York sometime in the
next two weeks.'

'At,' Welker told her, 'the Waldorf Astoria. Probably. And probably
this very week.'

'Really?' Geoffrey asked. 'The Waldorf? How do you know that
and why the Waldorf?'

'Our friends have taken a room there.'

'*Ça marche*,' Patricia said. 'Now we have the probable where,
all we need is the possible what.'

Geoffrey looked at her. 'What?'

'I don't know,' she said. 'Perhaps someone is coming to visit.
Someone important, and they're putting him up at the Waldorf.'

'Someone whose identity they don't want anyone to know, since they're renting it under the name "Booth",' Welker offered.

'Booth?'

'That's right.'

'*Ça marche* indeed,' Patricia said.

Rebecca appeared at the door with a tray. 'I thought you might like some coffee,' she said, setting the tray down on a corner of the desk. 'And some pastries. And Ogden would like to speak to you for a second,' she added to Welker, gesturing behind her.

'Thanks, Becky,' Welker said. 'If you guys will excuse me for a moment.'

'We will partake of your largesse in your absence,' Geoffrey said.

Patricia shook her head. 'Now why can't I think of clever repartee like that?'

Welker was gone for about four minutes. He returned shaking his head. 'I don't like it,' he said.

'Neither do I,' Patricia agreed. 'What don't we like?'

'According to one of my men who has a contact in the Bureau, they are looking into the theft of a box of high explosives from an uptown armory.'

'The Bureau?' Geoffrey asked. 'That's the FBI?'

'Right. God forbid we should just share information, but it doesn't work that way. The theft happened the day before yesterday at a gala dinner. Apparently several men disguised as waiters came in and made off with the stuff.'

Geoffrey put down his coffee cup. 'That can't be good.'

'It isn't. Hoover sees Reds under every bed – has for years. So he's going hot and heavy after local Commies now, trying to locate one of the thieves who conveniently dropped his membership card at the scene.'

'Really? Dropped his card?'

'Right. That's all he dropped, just his membership card. Must of just somehow fluttered out of his wallet, I'd imagine.'

'That doesn't sound likely,' Patricia commented. 'Even Mr Hoover must see that.'

'It is a sometimes unfortunate trait of human nature,' said Geoffrey, raising one finger professorially, 'that one tends to accept more easily those things that reinforce what one already believes.'

Welker grinned. 'I find that easy to believe,' he said.

'So,' Patricia said, 'what are we to make of this, free of Mr Hoover's Red bias?'

'This gets a little complicated,' Welker said. 'We have a man . . .' And he went on to explain Andrew Blake's connection to the local Nazis and how it grew.

'That poor man,' said Patricia, shaking her head. 'He should get a medal.'

'And he never will,' Welker said. 'Not only that, the notion would terrify him. His greatest desire is not to be noticed.'

'Bravery,' Geoffrey said, 'does not consist of not being afraid. It consists of doing something despite the fact that you're terrified.'

'Who said that?' Welker asked.

'As far as I know,' Geoffrey told him, 'I did.'

'Very good,' said Welker.

Patricia smiled. 'For how many thousands of years,' she asked, 'have women listened to men brag about their bravery and how well they withstand pain without instantly thinking that no man has ever borne a child?'

Welker regarded her for a moment and said: 'Almost every woman is braver than almost any man for so many reasons, but is careful not to tell him.'

Her smile widened. 'I knew I liked you,' she said.

'My lovely wife is so brave it approaches the foolhardy at times,' Geoffrey said. 'So far she has managed to avoid any lasting injuries or periods of incarceration.'

Patricia wrinkled her nose at him and then turned back to Welker. 'So Herr Otto Lehman, who is a high thingamajig in the local Communist gathering, is not really Otto Lehman but a substitute provided by the Nazis.'

'Yes,' Welker agreed.

'And he has formed an "action group" of party members to do we know not what, but it's going to happen in the next week with the aid of someone coming to stay at the Waldorf.'

'Or it's going to happen at or around the Waldorf,' suggested Geoffrey. 'And it involves gelignite.'

'Which is not good,' Geoffrey said. 'So what do we do – inform them at the Waldorf? Search the place from top to bottom?'

'Did you know that the Waldorf has over a thousand rooms?'

Welker asked rhetorically. 'It would take a while and we're not sure what we're looking for. We'd have to go through all the luggage in all those rooms, check all the closets and—'

'All right,' Geoffrey said. 'So . . . what?'

'So I guess we go to the Waldorf and nose around to see what we can see. And there's a Brooklyn detective who also knows what the pseudo Otto Lehman looks like. I'll see if I can get him on some kind of temporary assignment to join us.'

THIRTY-THREE

One who deceives will always find
those who allow themselves to be deceived.
– Niccolo Machiavelli

The man who called himself Otto Lehman paced back and forth silently for a minute in front of his four picked men. All ardent Communists. That could be checked, and assuredly would be after today. Three of them ranged about the hotel room, on the bed, on the ridiculously overstuffed chair, on the carpeted floor, attentively looking up. What had brought them here? Ken; small, wiry, with fierce eyes, from a patrician Boston family. Perhaps he felt guilty about his family's wealth when so many around him were suffering. Patrick, short but solid with a gently broken nose and callused fists; first generation Irish-American and proud of it. Believed the rich should be taken down a peg or six. Moses, the Jew, did something in the Garment Workers' Union. Lehman had picked him partly for the very Jewish name. The Communists were to be blamed, but if one of them were also a Jew it could help spread the acid of discord. A Negro would have been a welcome addition, but even though the CPUSA talked a lot about the Brotherhood of All Men, there weren't any blacks in the local group.

And the fourth, Tom, of course Tom, leaning against the wall and staring solemnly at him. Tom the known agitator, Tom the trouble-maker. Hard to control even in his chosen group – Tom would be the convincer.

Lehman turned to face them. 'It is simple,' he said. 'We will go over it one more time and then one more time again to assure complete understanding, and then tonight we will start silently, carefully, knocking through the wall, creating the hole through to the platform. And then covering it up with a metal plate so it will not be accidentally discovered. It should take no more than a few hours. And then we will be ready. And then, sometime in the next day or two, three on the outside, he will arrive and we will strike. And we will go, disappear back into the crowded city, but they will know who did this and why. And the world will understand what we are capable of.'

Tom, big and slow-moving, who had a surprisingly fast brain under his bulk, stirred and cocked his head preparing to speak. He always did that bit of head motion, Lehman had noticed. It was as though his vocal cords would only operate at the one angle. 'Why?' he asked.

'Why what, Tom?'

'Why do we have to wait until the last minute to place the explosive?'

Because you are not actually to place the explosives, you have yet another function, is what Lehman thought, but not what he said. 'Because,' he said, 'they sweep the tracks and the station area just before the train is due. So our only window is after the final inspection and before the train arrives, a period of perhaps an hour – two at the outside.'

The others nodded, but Tom, his head still tilted, asked, 'Why do we not so disguise the bundle that it will not be noticed? Then we can plant it before. Then we would only need one person in hiding nearby to set it off.'

And the one person, Lehman thought, *would of course be me. And that wouldn't do. Not at all.*

'Because the Secret Service guards have done this before and they know what the area is supposed to look like, and we have not devised a suitable way to disguise the package,' Lehman told him. 'Not for certain. And we will assuredly only get one opportunity. And before you ask, we cannot place it further down on the tracks themselves because the car goes through a shunting yard and we have no way of knowing which tracks it will be on before it reaches track 61. And at any rate, the explosive going off beneath the car, which is certainly armored, would almost certainly fail to do sufficient damage.'

'I see,' said Tom, thinking it over.

'Our advantage,' Lehman went on, 'what makes this possible, is the unused platform by the elevator shaft that we have discovered. So we can enter after the area has been swept and place the charge atop the elevator.'

'And get out?' It was Tom.

'Of course, and get out.'

'Oh-kay,' Tom agreed. 'If that's the way it is.'

'Now we will run through the procedure so each knows what he is supposed to do. We will go through the wall just so, at just such a height, and we will do it silently so as not to attract attention. After that you will all stay in the suite to be ready. Food will be sent in. This evening our watcher in Washington will begin, ah, watching. As soon as we get his phone call we will go to the electric panel room and create the breach through to the elevator access platform where we will await the arrival of the special car. We will have perhaps two hours. Now, come with me and I will show you the procedure!'

THIRTY-FOUR

To some generations much is given.
Of other generations much is expected.
This generation of Americans
has a rendezvous with destiny.
               – Franklin D. Roosevelt

The Waldorf Astoria was the second hotel of that name. Built a bit uptown from the original, which had been deconstructed in 1929 to make way for the Empire State Building, it was designed to impress. Opened in October 1931, it was the largest and tallest hotel in the world, taking up the whole block on the East side of Park Avenue from 49th to 50th Streets. At the top were the Waldorf Towers, holding one hundred luxurious suites with their own street entrance, and at the bottom, under the second cellar, lurked track 61, a private siding of the New York Central Railroad that connected with both the Waldorf and the New York City subway system. The great and the near great, the famous and the wannabe famous made the Waldorf their home when in New York.

'I think it's the title that does it,' Patricia said. 'Senators poo, movie stars pah, seen them all. But a British Peer of the Realm, that's the real stuff.'

'You don't think I laid it on a bit thick?' Geoffrey asked.

'Not a bit!' Patricia told him, holding his arm as the manager, with one last bow, exited 301, their newly acquired suite, and closed the door behind him. 'How dare they question your identity!'

'Well. We did arrive without prior notice and without a retinue as befitting a – what did he say? – "peer of the realm". Which as it happens, I'm not, actually.'

'Your father is,' Patricia said.

'Yes, but "Second Son of a Peer of the Realm" rather sounds more like a Gilbert and Sullivan patter song rather than a title to impress, don't you know.'

'But when you produced your diplomatic passport and they saw "Lord Geoffrey Saboy, Viscount McComb", an accredited representative of His Majesty's Government, they became all over – something – something gelatinous,' Patricia said. 'Though I think what really did it was when you said that your man was going to arrive shortly with the luggage. Americans, even rich Americans, don't have a "man".' She went through into the bedroom and bounced tentatively up and down on the nearest bed. 'Soft,' she decided.

'But why would I claim to have a title if I did not? And, more to the point, why would they care? If we'd gone up to the desk and announced ourselves as Mr and Mrs Potifer Pinchpenny from Leeds we would have laid our money down, signed the ledger, received our key, and been off to our room without anyone asking to see some identification at all.'

'Unless they thought that perhaps we weren't actually married,' Patricia commented. 'They wouldn't want you taking some floozy up to the room. Bad for the image of the hotel.'

'You're not just any floozy,' Geoffrey told her, blowing her a kiss. He walked over to the window and looked out at the facade of Grand Central Station across the street. 'What shall we do first?' he asked. 'Bearing in mind that we're strictly interdicted from going upstairs to visit the fourth floor.'

'We could chat up one of the celebrities supposedly staying here,' Patricia suggested. 'Until Jacob has something specific for us.'

'Oh, it's "Jacob" already, is it?' Geoffrey asked with a mock frown. 'Do keep your mind on business until this affair is over.'

'Oh, I shall,' Patricia agreed. 'I have immense patience. As does Jacob, I might add.'

'You've already had occasion to, ah, discuss this with Welker?'

'We have exchanged knowing glances,' Patricia told him.

'Ah!' said Geoffrey. He turned away from the window. 'Which celebrities, exactly, did you have in mind?'

'Well, there's ex-President Hoover – he lives in a suite in the Tower. And then, according to the concierge who whispered it because, as he said, they like their anonymousness – although why whispering keeps them anonymous I don't know – we have Charlie Chaplin and Marlene Dietrich. Not together, he assured me. But the stories he could tell . . . Luckily you returned from your phone call before he had a chance to do so.'

'I met Mr Chaplin once,' Geoffrey commented. 'Extremely bright man.'

'So, shall we knock him up, as you're acquainted? As one Brit to another.'

'I don't think so. I doubt if he'd remember me. Besides, we may be needed at any time.'

'Not likely,' Patricia said. 'Jacob didn't want us coming here in the first place. I believe he's going to take all the fun for himself.'

'That would be most unkind,' Geoffrey said. 'I'm sure "Jacob" wouldn't do that.'

'You're amused,' Patricia said.

'I am. I was in a war with the man, shot and shell and all that, and I still call him "Welker", or even "Captain Welker". You've met him – what? – three times, and it's "Jacob".'

'You're stuffy,' she told him.

'So I am,' he agreed. 'It goes with being the second son of a peer of the realm.'

The room phone rang, and Geoffrey picked it up. 'Yes? This is Lord Geoffrey. Yes. Put him on.'

Patricia went in to explore the bathroom and Geoffrey was just hanging up when she returned. He grinned at her. 'We're going to get in on the action after all. We're to meet "Jacob" in Peacock Alley, in,' he glanced at his watch, 'ten minutes. We'll have lunch with him and discuss our course of action. So we don't actually have time to do anything first.'

Welker awaited them at a small table in the outer bar in Peacock Alley, one of the Waldorf's more casually elegant restaurants. He nodded as they walked in and waved them to seats. 'Sit down. The hotel's security man is going to join us shortly. See if we can figure out anything.'

As they sat down a short, rotund gentleman in a well-cut dark-blue suit strode toward them from the far corner of the bar, smiling as though he were greatly pleased to see Welker sitting there. *Surely not the security man*, Patricia thought, observing his well-shined black shoes under fawn-colored spats, large bright blue bow tie, and the bowler hat swinging jauntily from his left hand.

'Mr Welker,' the man said, extending a large hand as he reached them. 'Mr Welker sir. A pleasure to see you. A pleasure. It has surely been a while. Quite a while.'

Welker rose and took the man's hand. 'Baron. You're looking prosperous.'

'Indeed,' the Baron agreed. 'Life has its ups and downs. This is one of them.'

'Let me introduce,' Welker said, indicating his companions, 'Lord and Lady Saboy. And this gentleman is known to his friends as the Baron.'

'Any friend of Mr Welker's,' Geoffrey said, rising to his feet and extending his hand.

'Enchanted,' said Patricia, smiling up at him.

The Baron gave Geoffrey's hand a firm shake and bowed at Patricia. 'Lord and Lady,' he said. 'And the real quill – I can always tell. A pleasure, a distinct pleasure. Well, I must be moving on.' He paused to give Welker a quick pat on the shoulder. 'We must talk over old times,' he said. 'Perhaps we could both learn something.' And with that he headed for the door.

They turned to watch him leave. 'What a strange man,' Patricia said. 'He surely isn't one of our miscreants?'

'He is indeed a miscreant,' Welker said. 'I like that – "miscreant". But he's another sort. I became acquainted with him in my previous profession. He used to be involved in a big store operation up on, I think it was, 56th and Lexington. The stores themselves, of course, could spring up anywhere in town.'

'Like a department store?' Patricia asked.

Welker laughed. 'It's what they call a "term of art". The art in this case being crime, specifically confidence games. A "big store" is a room set up to emulate a particular business, say a stock broker's office, a gambling den, or a horserace betting parlor. They will lure in gullible people, known in the trade as "marks", or "pickles", usually out-of-towners, separate them from their money by one ruse or another, and them blow them off – another term of art. By the time the mark realizes he's been had and returns, with or without the police, the big store and all who were in it have completely disappeared.'

'The ways of separating a fool from his money . . .' Geoffrey began, then allowed the rest of the sentence to die away.

'Indeed,' Welker agreed.

The waiter, in the well-starched white shirt and black trousers of the Waldorf restaurant staff, approached and hovered.

Welker looked up. 'We shall order lunch in a few minutes when the rest of our party arrives,' he said. But while we wait, perhaps a small libation? Scotch and soda for me, I think. Glenlivet. And . . .'

'Cognac,' said Geoffrey. 'Ah – Rémy. Neat.'

The waiter looked expectantly at Patricia, who waved a finger. 'A martini, please. Any old gin, any old vermouth.'

'Very good, of course,' the waiter said. And, after a beat, 'Excuse me for asking but is the gentleman who just left a friend of yours?'

'An acquaintance merely,' Welker said. 'But why?'

'I have been instructed to inform customers who are approached by the gentleman that he is, ah, not what he seems.'

'Really?' Welker looked amused. 'How so?'

'We're not exactly sure, sir. But he does seem to befriend our more prosperous-looking guests. It may be completely harmless, but the maître d' thought it worth mentioning.'

'Thank you,' Welker said. 'As it happens, I've known the gentleman for some years.'

'I see. Then—'

'Then your maître d's warning is probably well placed.'

'I see, sir. Thank you, sir.' He went off.

The Waldorf's security manager, a thin, harassed-looking man in a gray double-breasted suit that somehow managed to look like a costume on him, joined them at the table a few minutes later. Welker introduced him as Mr Kearny.

'Glad to meet you,' Kearny said. 'Although I have the feeling that you're about to add to my daily chores.'

'A busy day, is it?' Welker asked.

'It is raining hectic around here today,' Kearny told them. 'What new anxieties are you going to add to my load?'

'It might be that you have some guests, in room 416 I think, who are plotting some sort of trouble. And it could be that they have an explosive device.'

'Shit!' the security manager said. 'What sort of device, and why do you think so?'

'It's complicated,' Welker said.

'So is my life these days,' Kearny told him. 'We're about to have a distinguished guest. I hope these two events are not related.'

'More distinguished than the guests you are already hosting?'

'The President is due in later this evening.'

There was a pause while Welker and his two companions thought that over. And then, '*Merde!*' said Geoffrey.

'Son of a . . . since when?' Welker asked.

'Since when what?'

'When did you know he was coming here?'

'Been scheduled for about a week now, I think. Not exactly a secret. He always stays here when he's in town. Stays at Hyde Park when he can but it's, what, eighty miles from the city. So for short trips he stays here. The Secret Service has already taken over the thirty-fifth floor, where the presidential suite is, and the basement area.'

'The basement?'

'Yeah. They search and secure the basement and the tracks coming in.'

'Excuse me,' Patricia asked, 'but what tracks?'

'We have a private siding of the New York Central under the hotel,' Kearny said, pointing down at the floor. 'About, ah, three floors down from here.'

'"The President . . .' Geoffrey began. 'Damn! The President! Of course!'

They turned to look at him.

'*Fall Bude*,' he said. 'Operation Booth. Booth.'

'Are you all right?' Patricia asked. 'You look pale.'

'Don't you see it?'

Kearny shook his head. 'What is . . .'

'That may be the name of the whatever-it-is that may be underway here,' Welker told him, 'and . . .' He paused. 'Shit,' he said softly.

'You see it?' Geoffrey asked.

'What?' asked Patricia. 'Why are we shitting this time?'

'Operation Booth,' Welker said slowly. 'As in John Wilkes Booth.'

'Yes, I think so,' Geoffrey said. 'Don't you?'

'But . . . it doesn't make sense, does it?'

'Why not?' Geoffrey demanded.

'Because . . .' He turned to Kearny. 'Have you got a room where we could talk this over, with a little privacy?'

'We can use my office,' Kearny told him. 'Unless you're excluding me from the talk. Then—'

'No,' Welker told him. 'Of course not. We need you. And maybe the head of the Secret Service detail – as soon as we figure out what's going on.'

'OK,' Kearny said.

'And, a thought, can you put an unobtrusive watch on room 416?'

'Is that the room they're in? I can stick a guy in the linen closet down the hall,' Kearny said. 'And I could have housekeeping send a girl in to make up the room, if it hasn't been made up yet, see if she sees anything.'

'Tell her to be careful,' Geoffrey said.

'Of course,' Kearny said. 'I know just the girl for the job. Let's order lunch and I'll have it brought to the office.'

THIRTY-FIVE

Yesterday This Day's Madness did prepare;
To-morrow's Silence, Triumph, or Despair:
Drink! for you know not whence you came, nor why:
Drink! for you know not why you go, nor where.
  – *Edward FitzGerald*, The Rubaiyat of Omar Khayyam

Weiss walked through the Waldorf lobby trying to look as though he were the sort of man who'd walk through the Waldorf lobby. But it felt uncomfortable. He was nervous. As himself – which he would be again in a few days – the Waldorf would feel like home. As would the Ritz or the Adlon, where perhaps he would stay next week when he reported back to Berlin. But the part he was playing, the man he had assumed the identity of, would not be here. Is that why he was so nervous?

Was it because there'd be no Jews in the Adlon? Everyone he passed here in the Waldorf looked like a Jew. A rich Jew. Or a policeman. A Jewish policeman. A rich Jewish policeman? Were there such things? And they were all staring at him, were they not.

Ridiculous!

Why was he so nervous? It would not do for him to be noticed, but there were perhaps thirty people in the lobby and he was just one of them. An unnoticeable one of them. He was never nervous. Other men, weaker men, were nervous, upset, frightened; and he often had made them so. He had beaten men to death with his bare hands. He had made men, powerful men, scream for mercy before they told him what he wished to know. Before he killed them.

It was perhaps that back in Berlin they were watching the unfolding of *Fall Bude* with lip-smacking interest and Weiss did not want to disappoint. He took the elevator to the fourth floor and knocked on the door of 416.

'What is it?' came Lehman's voice.

'There's a question about the bill, Mr Booth,' he yelled.

A little muttering inside, and then the door opened and Lehman came out, closing it carefully behind him. 'I've been waiting for you,' he said. 'Everything is in readiness.'

'Come away from the door,' Weiss said. 'Let us talk.'

They walked down to the far end of the hall and turned the corner, stopping by a window at the end of the hall.

'You have the stuff?' Lehman asked.

Weiss took a paper bag from under his coat and removed from it an apparently unopened bottle of Casner Reserve, an inexpensive, unassuming local brandy. 'Here.'

'This will do it?'

'Assuredly. More than a few sips and you'll be unconscious for an hour. Longer.'

'Good,' Lehman said. 'I have glasses in the room.'

'You're not going to give it to them in the room?' Weiss said, sounding horrified.

'No, no. I don't want to have to carry them, and besides someone might see us. I will take them down to the third floor by the emergency stairs and we will enter the space. There we will complete the hole through to the shaft, and then we will celebrate. Have no fear.'

'Do they all drink spirits?'

'Yes. I made certain of that before I selected them. As I said, have no fear.'

'I'm depending on you,' Weiss said.

'Yes. And I on you.'

'I will await events in the lobby.'

'I will have Mr Booth paged, and you will come up. Not to the room, but directly to the third-floor space.'

'I will do so.' Weiss lowered his voice to a whisper: '*Heil Hitler!*'

'*Heil Hitler!*' Lehman responded. 'Someday soon we will not have to whisper.'

THIRTY-SIX

*A man who carries a cat by the tail
learns something he can learn in no other way.*

– Mark Twain

Kearny's office, behind a door labeled EQUIPMENT down a short hall from the registration desk, contained two desks, five chairs, a well-worn brown leather couch, and its own bathroom. On two of the light blue walls hung five colored prints of fishermen casting their lines into various bodies of water. On the third was a sort of draped fish net. On the wall behind Kearny's desk– the slightly larger one on the left – was a large map of New York city, and a lacquered wooden plaque displaying a New York City detective's badge and four service ribbons. On the desk was a framed photograph of Kearny in waders and a wide hat proudly holding up a fish about the size of his arm along with several smaller photographs of an attractive woman and several assorted children.

'The "equipment" sign on the door,' Kearny offered before they had a chance to ask, 'is Mr Wexell the manager's idea. He thinks a sign that says "Security" might make people think that we need security, which might then make them feel insecure.'

'Plausible,' Welker said.

'Always thinking, he is,' Kearny said. 'We got here anything a guest might want, all in his own room: maids, barbers, manicurists, pedicurists, laundry, dry cleaning, typists, notaries, playpens, nannies, private nurses; heck, we've got a doctor on staff and a three-bed infirmary.'

'Sounds like you never have to leave.'

'We got a couple of guests in the Tower who, I swear, don't go out more than once a week, if that.' He sat down behind his desk and leaned back.

'How long were you on the job?' Welker asked, indicating the plaque behind the desk.

Kearny turned to look at it, and then turned back. 'Eight years,' he said.

'You got bored?' Welker asked. 'Not enough excitement for you?'

'I took a bullet,' Kearny told him.

'Oh, sorry.'

'Weird,' Kearny said. 'I came on this kid robbing a liquor store in Queens. Said something clever like, "Hold it right there – drop the gun!" and he turns around and shoots me. As I go down he starts screaming, drops the gun, and puts his hands up. Says he didn't mean to and oh God he's so sorry. But there I am shot. So now I'm out on disability and he's up in Sing Sing.'

'Where'd he get you?'

'In the right shoulder. I was in rehab for a year – got most of the motion back.' He flexed his shoulders, rotating his arms. 'But can't get my right arm over my head. So I had to give up fly fishing. Can't cast properly nohow. Can't get any range.'

'A shame,' Geoffrey said. 'So what are you doing instead?'

'I'm thinking of taking up taxidermy,' Kearny told him. 'Now,' he said, 'just what the, ah, heck is going on? Start at the beginning.'

Patricia and Geoffrey turned expectantly toward Welker, who took a deep breath. 'There's a couple of different pieces to the puzzle,' he said, 'but I think they've all pretty much come together.'

'You don't have to give me the whole history,' Kearny told him. 'Start at the beginning of where the hotel is concerned. Just where we come in and how we got there. Which, I guess, will be pretty much all of it. And what the hell we're going to do about it.'

'We think,' Welker said, 'that there is a – what the police would call an "incident" – in progress that involves a bunch of American Nazis, with some help from their overseas brothers. The operation is code-named "Bude", German for "Booth". It would seem to be a false-flag operation using a bunch of local Communists as some sort of dupes.'

'False flag?'

'Yeah. That's what we call one group pretending to be another.'

'I get it. So these Nazis are pretending to be Commies?'

'We think so. And they've got a bunch of actual Commies as cover.'

'And they're here in the hotel,' Geoffrey said, 'and your President is due sometime soon, and "Booth" is probably John Wilkes – that would be what they've been chuckling about in Berlin.'

'You think they're going to try to kill the President? But why? I don't see how having Garner in would do them any good. And why pretend to be Commies?'

'That is the question,' Geoffrey agreed.

There was a double knock on the door and it was pushed open and a man and woman entered, each bearing a large tray full of food: assorted ham and cheese and chicken salad sandwiches, French fries, a house salad, a jug of milk, and an urn of coffee. After a couple of minutes of distributing food and pouring drinks the servers left, closing the door behind them.

'I think,' Welker said, picking up the conversation, 'to clarify things for all of us, we should take it from the top, see what the puzzle looks like when we get all the pieces in. There are probably some missing yet, but I think we should see most of the picture. Lord Geoffrey here, who is something-or-other with British Intelligence, has a chunk of it.'

'What we have from a highly placed informant,' Geoffrey said, 'and from Lady Patricia's larcenous tendencies, is that there is an operation set to happen here in New York in the next couple of days.'

It took about fifteen minutes to go over what they knew and what they could surmise from that.

At the end of which Kearny shrugged. 'It looks like somebody is going to try something against the President,' he agreed. 'But I can't see how they hope to do it here. The Secret Service isn't going to let that happen. Not after Florida.'

'Florida?' Patricia asked.

'Yeah. Back in '33, right before he took office, a nut named Zinger – Zanger? something – took a few shots at Roosevelt in Miami. Hit Cernack – the Mayor of Chicago – and killed him. Since then the Secret Service has been fanatical about not letting anybody near the President who has no business being there. It's rough in the open – like when he's in a car. But a place like the Waldorf, they got it sewed up eight ways from Sunday. Nobody's getting anywhere near the President unless he belongs there.'

'But if they've succeeded in planting a bomb,' Welker said, 'then . . . maybe we should have the President go somewhere else until we get this taken care of.'

'What size bomb?' Kearny asked. 'What are we talking about?'

'I think they have about six sticks of gelignite,' Welker told him. 'It won't take down the building, but, if used properly, it could do a bit of damage to, say, one corner of one floor.'

'Shit!' Kearny said. 'I'll get the agent in charge up here, and I suppose we'll have to tell Wexell, but God knows what he'll do. Anywhere between ignoring it completely and evacuating the building, and I couldn't tell you which.' He reached for the phone on his desk.

Patricia stood up. 'I'm going upstairs to get a wrap,' she said. 'Be back in a minute.'

THIRTY-SEVEN

What it lies in our power to do,
it lies in our power not to do.

– Aristotle

Weiss entered the fire stairs on the ground floor past the bank of elevators and listened for a minute to make sure he wasn't sharing the stairs with anyone else. Not a sound. He started climbing up. The prospect of action had a curiously calming effect on him, and he found himself marching up the stairs and singing in a lusty undertone. '*Die Fahne hoch! Die Reihen fest geschlossen! SA marschiert mit ruhig festem Schritt.*' He stomped solidly on each step, swinging his arms to the beat of Horst Wessel's 'Lied'. By the time he reached the third floor his feet were tired, his shoulders were sore, but he felt renewed; *Fall Bude* was finally underway. Berlin would be pleased. By tomorrow Berlin would be very pleased. He stopped on the landing and – for a second – he thought he heard something. *Verdammt!* Suppose someone had entered the staircase while he was singing? He might have endangered the whole operation. There must be no suggestion, no hint, that anyone but those *verdammter* Communists were involved. But after a minute and no further sound he decided that everything was silent, secret, and safe.

Weiss cautiously pulled open the door. It was not supposed to open from the stairs side, but two hours before Lehman had thoughtfully broken off a toothpick in the latch so he could bring his crew through. They should all be unconscious now, having partaken of Lehman's schnapps, and Weiss must now aid in the setting of the scene. The hall was empty.

So no one was to see him enter from the staircase, that was good. Now he would hurry to the . . . a door was opening ahead of him. A woman was coming out. Too late to re-enter the staircase unobserved. He tipped his hat in a way that effectively concealed his face and passed her by. But there she was, reflected in the mirror by the elevators, three-quarters turned away from him. An attractive woman in a tan dress. If he were a woman he would probably have a better name for the color, but to him it was tan. Brown shoes, a dark brown purse, a white blouse with a wide collar, and an impressive string of pearls around her neck. Very attractive. And then she turned to face the elevator and she could see his face in the mirror. And she was staring curiously at him. He should have hurried along.

And he recognized her. Which meant that she surely recognized him.

He turned.

'Why, Herr Weiss isn't it?' she said smiling at him. 'We met at the embassy.'

'Yes,' he said. 'Madam, no – Lady Saboy? The mind-reader. I do remember.' He took two steps toward her, extending his hand and then, before she took it, he had grabbed her by the neck and pulled her toward him, his other hand over her mouth. 'This is most unfortunate,' he said.

She clutched at his hand, trying to pry him loose, but he twisted her around and propelled her forward. She kicked back and got him on the calf, which hurt and angered him.

Her hands stayed at her neck holding on to the pearl necklace. Did she think he was a thief? But she was no longer trying to pry his arm away. Instead she suddenly went completely limp, and almost fell through his grasp. He pulled her up, keeping one hand over her mouth. But curiously she did not seem to be fighting him any more. Had she perhaps fainted?

He half tugged and half carried her around the corner of the corridor until he reached the door that said ELECTRIC PANEL on a little brass plaque. It had been left unlocked. He pushed it open. Throwing the woman inside, he stepped in after her and slammed the door behind him.

The woman lay slumped where she had fallen and did not move. Was she knocked out? Was she shamming? It did not matter. He moved aside the sheet metal plate that concealed the carefully chipped-away hole in the wall and called, 'Lehman!'

A muffled sound from within the hole and then a scrabbling sound and then Lehman's head appeared. 'About time,' he said, peering up at Weiss. 'I was beginning to—'

'We have a problem,' Weiss interrupted.

'Ah?'

Weiss pulled Patricia's limp body up to the hole. 'Here, take her shoulders.'

'A woman?' Lehman asked. And then again, this time it was a screech: 'A woman!' He pulled himself further out of the hole. 'What in the name of god are you doing with a *gottverdammte* woman?'

'She knows me,' Weiss told him. 'She recognized me.'

'So?'

'She recognized me *here* – in the hallway.' He shook his head. 'It would blow the whole thing if it were known I was here now. Now.'

'Yes, of course. But what are we to do with her?'

'Take her down with the others.'

'Really? And you think the investigators will not question the presence of a random woman with our four Communist bombers?'

'She is not a random woman. She is Lady Patricia Saboy, wife of the British Cultural Attaché.'

Lehman's jaw dropped open. Then he gathered himself. 'Worse. Much worse. Why on earth would she be here?'

'Just what she *is* doing here,' Weiss said. 'It will appear that she stumbled across one of our Commie crew in the hall and recognized him, so they grabbed her and brought her down to the landing, where they tied her up. And when the device goes off, ah, accidentally, killing the four, it will also take her.' He nodded, mostly to himself. 'That's what it will look like, and therefore that's what it will be.'

'I don't know . . .' Lehman said.

'You don't have to,' Weiss told him. 'Help me get her through the hole and down into the space.'

THIRTY-EIGHT

For all we have and are,
For all our children's fate,
Stand up and take the war.
The Hun is at the gate!

– Rudyard Kipling

Special Agent Michael Reilly, in charge of the President's Secret
Service detail, slammed down the phone and grunted, a sound,
Welker thought, much like that of an angry bear. 'Morons!'
he growled.

'They won't do anything?' Kearny asked.

'They won't believe me,' Reilly said. '"How do we know you
are who you are? How do we know this isn't some sort of practical
joke?" I'll practical joke them!'

'Damn!' Welker said. 'Can't stop the train?'

'Couldn't anyway, according to this guy,' Reilly told him. 'The
President's private car is already in the switching . . . something
. . . and can't be reached until it gets to Track 61 – which is here.'

'What more can we do?' asked Kearny.

'I can't think of a thing. We have men on the platform, men in
the elevator – hell, even put a guy on top of the elevator.' He looked
at Welker. 'Anything we've missed?'

'Dropping something from a higher floor?' Welker suggested.

'There is no higher floor,' Kearny told them. 'The car elevator
goes from Track 61 up to the street level and that's it. Lets out right
in the garage. There aren't even any cables – the thing works on a
hydraulic lift from below.'

'So we can't find them?' Reilly said. 'And we don't know what
they're up to for sure except that they're probably trying to kill the
President. Ain't that a state of things?' He turned to Kearny. 'Any
movement around that hotel room?'

Kearny shook his head. 'Not since the last time you asked. And
nothing in the room but a hat, a man's undershirt, a tube of toothpaste

with most of it squeezed out, and a bunch of Commie pamphlets. We got it staked out. Anyone goes near it, you'll know.'

'Yeah,' Reilly said. He gulped at a cup of long-cold coffee. 'It's the waiting, you know. The not knowing what the hell they have in mind.'

Geoffrey stood up. 'If you'll excuse me,' he said, 'I'll go and see what's keeping my wife.'

The phone rang and Kearny picked it up. 'Yes? Who?' He put his hand over the mouthpiece and turned to Welker: 'Some guy named Blake wants to see you.'

'Ah!' Welker said. 'I wonder what . . . Bring him in.'

'OK,' Kearny said into the phone, 'send him along.'

'Wait for a minute,' Welker told Geoffrey, waving him back into his chair, 'let's hear what Blake has to say.'

Geoffrey sat back down. It was about twenty seconds later that Blake opened the door and started in. When he saw all the people he stopped and blinked. 'Um,' he said, 'Agent Welker, could I speak with you?'

'It's OK,' Welker told him. 'They're with me. You can talk.'

'If you say so,' Blake said, coming into the room. 'I called your office and they said you were here, so I came over. Although here is not my preferred place to be right now. Is the President coming here this evening? When is he due?'

'Say,' Kearny said, rising to his feet behind his desk. 'Who is this guy and what does he know?'

'Blake is an informant who has managed to work his way into the group that's probably responsible for this. He is a brave and resourceful young man.'

Blake took a deep breath and fell into a wooden chair by the door. 'I don't feel any of those things,' he said.

'Why did you call me?' Welker asked.

'Oh, yeah. Two things – there's a wooden box of, it says, gelignite, in Gerard's office, under his desk, with two sticks missing.'

'How do you know?'

'That's the other thing. I heard them talking. In that office.'

'That office?'

'Yeah, the one on twelfth. I went up to give Gerard the money from the book sale from last night's rally. He left before I could give it to him and I don't want them thinking I'm holding out money.

So I went up there. Only the door was locked. So I went around to the other door – the one that goes right into the inner office – and they was in there talking. So I listened.'

'You listened at the door?'

'Yeah. I put my ear up – you know – against the door. I could hear real good.'

Welker looked at him with something approaching amazement. 'Weren't you afraid they'd catch you?'

Blake thought about that for a moment. 'You know,' he said. 'I wasn't, not at all, right then. But after, what I thought about what I'd done, I started shaking all over. I had to sit down.'

'I believe it,' Welker said.

'Who's this Gerard?' Special Agent Reilly asked.

'He's head of the local German-American Bund,' Welker told him.

'Nazis? I thought these guys were Communists,' Reilly said.

'They are, the ones here, mostly. It's complicated,' Welker told him. He turned back to Blake. 'What did you hear?'

'They're here,' Blake said, 'Weiss and Lehman. They're doing whatever they're doing right now, and they're going to be on a ship for Hamburg tomorrow. And he told the other guy, whoever he was, not to worry because it was going to be a small explosion so the evidence wouldn't be destroyed.'

'The evidence of what?' Reilly demanded.

'He didn't say.'

Welker grimaced. 'And I'm sure he didn't say where the explosion was going to be.'

'Or when,' Geoffrey added. 'Although I imagine it's going to be any time now.' He looked at his watch. 'Speaking of which, I'm really wondering what's keeping Patricia. If you'll excuse me . . .' He stood up again and went to the door. 'Back in a flash!'

'So what now?' Kearny asked.

'If you have an idea, I'm listening,' Welker said.

THIRTY-NINE

Pass not beneath, O Caravan,
or pass not singing. Have you heard
that silence where the birds are dead
yet something pipeth like a bird?
                                    – James Elroy Flecker

The space was perhaps ten feet by six feet. The floor was rough concrete; uncarpeted, unboarded, untiled. It had been a work area, enclosed by happenstance when the car elevator shaft was inserted into the almost-finished Waldorf Astoria as an afterthought, to connect Track 61 through the hotel to the street above. Only a thin beaver-board partition separated it from the elevator shaft, as Lehman had verified with the small hole he had poked through the board.

Four men were tumbled about the floor of the room in unconscious abandon, and one woman, hands tied behind her, feet bound, was sitting propped up in the corner and held captive by a rope looped around her neck and fastened to a pipe jutting out of the wall. In the opposite corner up against the beaver board was a black-leather satchel about the size of the proverbial breadbox.

Two other men were making their final preparations for quitting the room and leaving the others to their fate, a fate they were in the last stages of preparing.

'It takes some fifteen minutes for the President's limousine to be driven onto the elevator and for him to get in it and be taken up,' Lehman told Weiss, 'so as we hear the train pull onto the siding we set the fuse for twelve minutes and we depart.'

'It seems a bit chancy,' Weiss said. 'Suppose it takes longer? We will have blown up an elevator to what end? Roosevelt will escape.'

'If you wish to stay around until the last possible second you have my permission,' Lehman told him. 'We will have, nonetheless, accomplished our mission whether Roosevelt lives or dies.'

There was a stirring from the corner, and the men looked over. The woman had sat up, as much as her bonds would allow. 'You're going to kill the President,' she said staring up at them, her voice strangely calm given the circumstances.

'Perhaps,' Weiss said, with what he probably thought was a smile. 'Yes, perhaps. We are setting off a bomb which, if the timing works just so, may well kill your President Rosenfeld. But,' he added, indicating the unconscious men on the floor, 'it will most assuredly kill these unfortunate gentlemen. And, I am afraid, you.'

'Why?' she demanded. 'What can you possibly gain?'

'We?' Weiss shook his head. 'We will gain nothing – not directly. But these men here will certainly gain a bit of notoriety. Yes, I think so.'

She leaned back and stared at them. 'I have no words.'

'Good,' Weiss said. 'Then—'

'I hear something,' Lehman interrupted. 'Yes! Listen!'

From below came the sound of distant thunder, punctuated by squeakings and squealings and clackings, and then a loud screech that went on for perhaps fifteen seconds.

'It's here,' Lehman said.

'It is,' Weiss agreed. 'And we should be gone. Set the clock.'

Patricia watched as Lehman pulled an alarm clock from the satchel and gingerly reclosed the satchel and placed the clock on top. Three wires went from the clock to the interior of the satchel. 'This bit requires care,' Lehman said. 'It is designed so that if the wires are pulled loose the device will go off anyway.'

'Take your time,' Weiss told him. 'Be precise. If you feel the urge to sneeze, tell me and I will go up the hole first.'

'Ha, ha,' Lehman laughed. With his finger he moved the minute hand around to quarter to twelve and then pulled a tab from somewhere inside the clock. It began ticking. The ticks seemed to Patricia to be the loudest things she had ever heard, and each seemed louder than the last.

'Let us get away from here,' Lehman said.

'Yes,' Weiss said. He took one long look around the tiny room, kicked the nearest sleeping man in the leg for no reason, then turned and gave Patricia a stiff bow. 'It is regrettable that our acquaintance has to end so abruptly,' he said. 'Such are the fortunes of war.'

'What war?' she asked, her voice surprisingly calm.

'Always, somewhere, there is a war, is there not?'

The two men retreated through the hole in the far wall and Patricia could hear them clambering up to the next floor.

FORTY

And all my days are trances,
And all my nightly dreams
Are where thy gray eye glances,
And where thy footstep gleams –
In what ethereal dances,
By what eternal streams.

– Edgar Allan Poe

Escape artists have devised many subtle ways to release themselves from the ties that bind, and Max Mavini was one of the best. He had taught Patricia ways to hold her hands while her wrists were being tied together which looked quite natural, but allowed her to loosen the ropes and, with a bit of wiggling and stretching, free herself. And it worked *almost* every time. For the times that it failed on stage there were outs, clever changes in the script that changed the focus of the trick.

But here there were no outs. It had to work. It had to . . .

Patricia had – what? – twelve minutes to free herself and get to that clock. How to disarm it? She had no idea. But first things first. *Max*, she thought. *It's up to you. What you taught me back then may now save the life of the President of the United States. And, perhaps almost as important, my own.*

First twist the hands this way – so far so good. Now loosen the . . . loosen the . . .

FORTY-ONE

There is a tide in the affairs of men,
which, taken at the flood, leads on to fortune;
omitted, all the voyage of their life
is bound in shallows and in miseries.
— William Shakespeare

'She's not in the room,' Geoffrey said. 'One of the elevator men remembers taking her up to the third floor, but none of them took her down again.'

'She could have come down the fire stairs,' Kearny suggested.

'Perhaps,' Geoffrey said doubtfully.

'I'll have her paged,' Kearny said.

'If you would,' Geoffrey agreed. 'Though if she has just stepped into one of the shops, she won't be pleased about hearing her name over the public address.'

The phone on Kearny's desk rang, and he picked it up and listened for a few seconds. 'Now?' he said. 'OK,' he said, 'will do.' He turned to the others. 'The President's car is in the siding,' he told them. 'They were starting to move the limo to the elevator, but they've decided to listen to us, just in case. Roosevelt is going to stay in the train car until this is sorted out. Whatever is going to happen is going to happen now, or it's not going to happen.'

'Convoluted, but I see what you mean,' Welker said.

'We should go down there,' Geoffrey said.

Welker frowned. 'What about Lady Patricia?'

'I have a feeling that we'll find her somewhere around. She has a frightful instinct for being where the action is.'

Kearny stood up. 'I don't see how our joining the guys at the dock can help. They have everything we could think of covered. On the other hand we're not doing much good up here. Let's go.'

'It couldn't hurt,' Geoffrey agreed.

'It could if that bomb goes off,' Welker said. 'But I'd rather take my chances with a bomb than have to explain why I wasn't there when it went off.'

Special Agent Reilly got up. 'Yeah,' he said. 'I wouldn't like having to explain it either. Not after Florida.'

They crowded through the office door, with Blake coming hesitantly behind. 'The car elevator comes up to the loading dock on the 49th Street side,' Kearny told them, pointing to a corridor across the wide lobby. 'Down that corridor.'

The men started across the lobby, and were about halfway there when Blake noticed a man coming toward them and, for a few seconds, tried not to stare. Then he grabbed Welker's arm. 'It's him,' Blake whispered in a soft squeak. 'Over there, to our right. He's coming toward us. Don't look.'

'What? Who?'

'What's his name – Weiss. The killer.'

Welker resisted the impulse to turn and look. 'You sure?'

'Sure I'm sure. It's him. What do we do?'

'Where is he?'

'To the right. He just came out of where I think we're headed for.'

Welker took Blake's arm and stopped him. 'Face me and start talking,' he said. 'And don't panic. Remember, he doesn't know what you look like.'

'What should we talk about?'

'It doesn't matter. Just look natural.'

'He's getting closer.'

'Fine,' Welker said. 'We'll let him pass, and then . . .'

Suddenly Blake turned and threw himself at the approaching man. 'You son of a bitch!' he yelled.

The man – Weiss – froze, then took a step back, not sure what was happening. Blake grabbed at his jacket, but was twisted around and fell past him. Weiss recovered quickly and took another step back, drawing an automatic pistol from under his jacket.

'What is this?' he barked. 'Who are you? What do you think you are doing? Stand back!'

Welker raised his hands in a placating gesture. 'Listen, mister,' he said, taking a step forward, 'I don't know what this is all about, or what you two are fighting about, but this is no place—'

'Back!' Weiss yelled, waving his gun in an arc from Welker to

Blake. 'Keep back. I don't know what kind of trick this is, but I will leave now.'

The others in Welker's group had stopped a few steps beyond the altercation and were paused, undecided as to just what was happening. Reilly already had his service Colt .45 drawn and was taking a two-handed stance, aiming it at Weiss. Kearny was working at getting his revolver out of the quick-draw holster under his jacket.

Blake pushed himself up, throwing himself at Weiss again, and connected this time, grappling with him and seemingly ignoring the gun, which Weiss was trying to twist around so he could shoot.

They went down, Weiss concentrating on trying to get his gun in position, and Blake doing his best to get his hands around Weiss's throat.

The gun went off, the noise like a sharp clap of thunder reverberating in the cavernous room. Blake made a sound like the hiss of air coming out of a tire and fell away from Weiss, clutching at his side.

Weiss rose to his knees, but before he could raise his arm for a second shot Welker stepped in and kicked savagely at the gun and the hand holding it. The gun skittered across the floor. Weiss tried to scramble away, but in a second Welker and Geoffrey had grabbed him and were pulling him up, and Reilly was advancing with a pair of handcuffs.

'What do you people think you are doing?' Weiss yelled, as his hands were roughly twisted behind his back and the cuffs were applied. 'This is outrageous! I have done nothing! I will have the police on you!'

'Who is this guy?' Kearny demanded.

'Probably the bomber,' Welker said. 'But for sure he's a Nazi and a murderer.' He knelt down next to Blake, who was doubled up on the floor, his face white, both hands clutching at his side, where a large red stain was spreading beneath his outstretched fingers. 'Let me look,' he said.

Welker pulled Blake's jacket aside and used his penknife to slit open the shirt and undershirt. He pulled a vast pocket handkerchief from his own jacket and gingerly wiped aside the blood.

'How bad . . .' Blake began, and then paused, gritting his teeth. He began again: 'How bad is it?'

'You are the luckiest sun of a bitch this side of Canarsie,' Welker told him. 'It looks like the bullet went in here, through the fleshy part of your side below your armpit, and then right out again about two inches further along.' He pushed experimentally at the wound making Blake wince and grit his teeth. 'As far as I can tell, it didn't even break a rib. Here, put your hand right here and press.' He stood up. 'I'll get something to wrap it with so you don't lose too much blood, and then we'll get you to the hospital.'

'It sure hurts like hell,' Blake said.

'I'm not surprised,' Welker said. 'But you're going to be fine.'

'Help me get him back into my office,' Kearny said. 'We'll put him on the couch and I'll call the house doctor.'

'Good idea,' Welker said. 'Then we still have a bomb to find.'

'We pulled the President's car back without unloading the limo,' Reilly told them, 'so it's somewhere a few hundred yards down the track until we tell them it's OK to come in. Now let's go find that damned bomb.'

'Amazing it hasn't gone off already,' Kearny said. 'You'd think . . .' He paused, trying to decide just what you'd think.

'I'm going to find my wife,' Geoffrey said. 'This is beginning to alarm me.'

'I'll come with you,' Welker told him.

FORTY-TWO

'The time has come,' the Walrus said,
'To talk of many things:
Of shoes – and ships – and sealing-wax –
Of cabbages – and kings –
And why the sea is boiling hot –
And whether pigs have wings.'
                                                    – Lewis Carroll

They took the elevator up to the third floor. 'First thing,' Geoffrey said, 'is to check out our room again. See if I missed anything. Then try to determine where she might have gone from there.'

'I have a thought,' Welker said. 'Let's take a look in the fire stairs.'

'Good idea,' Geoffrey said. 'She may still be in the staircase. She may have . . .' He stopped without finishing the thought, and then added, 'Let's go and look!'

They went down the corridor to the stairway door and pushed it open. 'Pat!' Geoffrey called. 'Patricia!' The sound echoed in the narrow space.

Welker peered over the railing to the landing below and looked up to the one above. 'No sign of disturbance,' he said. 'But then, what would I see?'

'I'll go and look in our room,' Geoffrey said. 'Don't get locked in there, it only opens from the stair side.'

Welker examined the lock. 'This one doesn't,' he said. 'See! Someone's jammed a bit of something in the latch.'

'Curious,' Geoffrey said. 'Why do you suppose . . .?' Something on the carpeted floor of the corridor a few feet away caught his eye and he moved over to it to take a closer look. 'I'll be . . .' he said, bending over to pick it up.

'What?'

'It's a pearl.'

'No kidding. Real?'

Lord Geoffrey peered at it and then rubbed it across an upper incisor. 'It feels rough to the tooth,' he said. 'That makes it real.'

'Clever,' Welker said. 'I'll remember that, should the question ever arise.'

'Well, here's your chance,' Blake told him, pointing to a spot further along the corridor.

Welker walked over and picked up a second pearl. He looked at it, then back at where Geoffrey had found the first one. Then he turned and looked further down the corridor. 'I see what may be a pattern,' he said, 'and there's yet another pearl.'

'Patricia has a pearl necklace,' Geoffrey said.

'I remember,' Welker said. 'Perhaps she has been waylaid and is laying down a trail of pearls instead of bread crumbs.'

'That's not funny,' Geoffrey told him.

'No, it's not.'

'Bread crumbs?'

'Hansel and Gretel. It's one of Grimms' fairy tales.'

'Oh yes. They lay out a trail of bread crumbs, but the birds come and eat the crumbs so they can't find their way home.'

'That's the one. And there's a wicked witch.'

'Well, let's follow the trail of pearls, if such there be, and see where the wicked witch has taken my wife.'

Four more pearls took them to the end of the corridor where it turned right, and another five down the right turn, and then the pearls stopped.

'One of these rooms?' Welker asked.

'Let us hope,' Geoffrey said, turning to the door that said ELEC-TRIC PANEL. 'Let's try this one.' He turned the knob and pushed, and it opened. The light, a bare bulb in the ceiling, was on. The room was small with one wall of panels and switches and meters and a large fuse box and little else, and nowhere to hide. 'I guess not,' he said.

'Wait a second,' Welker said. 'Look at the floor.'

'Where?' Geoffrey looked down. 'Dust,' he said.

'No,' Welker said. 'Well, yes, dust. But also . . .' He pointed.

'The white stuff?'

'The white stuff. It's plaster. And recent, otherwise it would have disappeared into the dust.'

'Ha!' said Geoffrey. Three more steps took him to the far end of the room, where he squatted down and examined the floor and the walls. 'Nothing seems disturbed on these two walls,' he said, 'and this metal panel . . .' He banged on it with his knuckles.

'*Helloooo!*'

'What was that?' Welker asked kneeling down next to Geoffrey.

'It's her,' Geoffrey said. 'It's Patricia!' He pounded on the panel. 'Hello!'

'*Down here!*'

'It is her,' Welker said.

'We're here!' Geoffrey yelled. 'Welker and I! We're coming for you!'

'*Thank God! I can't hold this thing much longer. I think my fingers are going numb.*'

'What?' Geoffrey called.

'*Just get down here!*'

Welker looked at Geoffrey. 'Down where?'

'Somewhere behind this thing,' Geoffrey said, grabbing with

the tips of his fingers for the edges of the metal panel. 'Can we move it?'

'You take that end,' Welker said.

'*Be careful,*' came Patricia's voice. '*But do hurry!*'

They each took a side, prying at it with their fingers until, all at once, the panel sprang loose, slipping from their grasp and clattering to the floor, revealing a roughly square cutout in the wall and a dark crawlspace beyond.

'*What happened? Are you OK?*'

Geoffrey peered into the space.

'We're fine,' he called. 'Where are you?'

'*Down here! There's a hole! Hurry!*'

'Let me,' Welker said, lifting himself up and, bending at the waist, pushing himself into the space. He started trying to wiggle forward on his belly with his feet still sticking out into the room.

Using his arms and his shoulder, Geoffrey pushed Welker further along until only his shoes were sticking out.

'I found it!' Welker called. 'There's a hole in the floor here . . .' And his shoes disappeared into the crawlspace.

Geoffrey pulled himself up and started crawling after Welker. He could see Welker directly in front of him, silhouetted in the light coming from a jagged round hole in the floor. Welker was working at twisting his body around so he could get his head away from the hole and his feet down into it. Geoffrey grabbed him by the jacket and pulled him around.

'Thanks,' Welker said. He pushed his feet down the hole and allowed the rest of his body to follow, until he slid through and landed with a satisfying *thunk* on the floor below.

Geoffrey swiveled his body around and scrunched over to the hole and then followed Welker through, landing easily on the bare concrete slab some seven feet below. The space was no bigger than a closet and had no visible access, but a square hole some three feet by three feet, which Welker was busy climbing through, had been cut in one wall.

'Thank God you're here,' Patricia called from the far side of the wall.

Geoffrey followed Welker through this next hole, beginning to feel as though he were engaged in a truly odd game of tag. The next room was an oversized closet in which he saw four men lying about the floor, unconscious or dead he couldn't tell. Patricia was there, crouching by a board partition of some sort, with both hands clutching the top of a black-leather satchel. There was a rope around her ankles and a loop of rope on the floor next to her.

She looked up at them with a peculiar intensity. 'Please be careful,' she said. 'This thing is a bomb. I've got it stopped, but I don't know how to disarm it and I don't dare let go.'

Welker and Geoffrey both stopped where they were, studies in frozen motion.

'What is it that you're holding?' Geoffrey asked.

'An alarm clock. One of those round ones with the two bells on top. The sort you'd buy at a shop for about ten shillings. The glass is off the face and I'm holding the second hand so it won't move.'

'Is that clock the trigger?'

'Is that what you call it? It's got wires attached running down into the satchel.'

'Ah!' Geoffrey said.

'It's got some sort of tamper thing, so if you pull the wires you'll set off the bomb. Or so the man – Weiss – said. He was here. He is the one who grabbed me and tied me up. Weiss. So I got loose, thanks to Professor Mavini, and I'm holding the clock so the hands won't move. If they move, I think, the bomb's going to go off.'

'Oh dear,' Geoffrey said. 'We'd better do something.'

'We've got Weiss,' Welker said. 'We could bring him down here, let him disarm the thing himself.'

Geoffrey thought about that for a second, and then shook his head. 'Perhaps not,' he said. 'He might have a death wish, fancy himself a hero or something. What do you know about bombs?'

'In theory, quite a bit,' Welker said. 'In practice – let me get a look at the thing.'

'Please, be careful,' Patricia said as Welker came over.

'Extra-special careful,' he assured her. He peered down into the satchel. 'I can't see down in there,' he said. 'I can see the clock, but I can't see past it. Can you move your hands?'

'No,' she told him. 'I daren't.'

'OK,' he said. 'We'll do it by touch.' He slid one hand in gingerly alongside Patricia's and felt around under the clock.

'Do you have any idea what you're doing?' Geoffrey asked him.

'Strangely enough,' Welker said, 'I think I do. This design for an infernal device seems like one that I showed these guys while I was being a bomb expert.' He closed his eyes to concentrate on his sense of touch. 'The idea was to be able to construct it from parts easily obtainable in any hardware store.'

'So you taught them how to make this thing?' Geoffrey asked, sounding aggrieved.

'Be grateful,' Welker told him. 'If they'd picked up a copy of the US Army's Field Demolitions Manual, they could have done some really nasty stuff.' After a pause he said, 'Ah!' And then he added, 'I think . . .' And then, after another pause, 'Yes! That's done it. You can let go.'

Patricia slowly opened her fingers from around the clock and pulled her hand away from the satchel.

Brrrrrring!!!

The three of them froze – waiting. But nothing happened.

'It seems that you've done it,' Geoffrey said.

Patricia fell sideways onto the floor, and found that she couldn't stop shaking. 'So close,' she said.

Welker knelt and wrapped his arms around her, pulling her up so she was sitting, a bit lopsided, next to him. 'It's all right,' he said. 'Congratulations, you have probably saved the life of the President of the United States.'

Geoffrey came and put his own arms around them both. He found that he was crying. 'Patricia,' he said. 'I don't know what I would have done if you . . .'

Patricia giggled and leaned against his warm shoulder in its wonderful, scratchy wool jacket. As if her senses were fine-tuned, she could smell the subtle scent of his favorite soap. And another scent: Welker's cologne? She could grow to like the scent of Welker's cologne. She reached up and hugged them both. 'Don't be silly,' she said. 'You couldn't have done anything. You would have been killed too.'

Welker stood up. 'I'd better go tell the others,' he said.

FORTY-THREE

Now this is not the end.
It is not even the beginning of the end.
But it is, perhaps, the end of the beginning.
— Winston Churchill

'President Roosevelt regrets,' Welker told them, 'that he cannot give you a medal. The official word will be that this never happened. But he has informed your Prime Minister that you, each and collectively, have performed a great and heroic service to the, ah, "cause of freedom", is I believe the way he worded it.'

'Perhaps Neville will see that we're on the next honors list,' Geoffrey said. He turned to Patricia. 'How would you like to be a Dame of the British Empire?'

Welker laughed. 'Is that a real thing?' he asked. 'It sounds somehow smutty.'

'We take our awards very seriously,' Geoffrey told him. 'Even the smutty-sounding ones.'

'I don't think I'd like being a "Dame",' Patricia decided. 'It seems all corset and button shoes-y.'

'You're not at all button shoes-y,' Geoffrey assured her.

'I should say not,' Welker agreed. 'You're a genuine hero!'

Patricia laughed. 'And so are you,' she told him. 'And so are we all.'

It was three days after the attempted bombing and they were meeting for lunch in the Sert Room in the Waldorf. Welker was having the lamb chops, Geoffrey, a crab omelet, and Patricia, as seemed appropriate, a Waldorf salad.

'How is that little fellow, ah, Blake?' Geoffrey asked.

'He is doing well,' Welker told him. 'It turns out a rib was cracked, but he should recover completely in a week or two. He isn't as little as he seems,' he added. 'There's just something about him.'

Geoffrey grinned. 'Little but vicious,' he said.

'Usually very meek,' Welker said. 'He just saw red or green or something when he got close to Weiss. He had watched Weiss perform a particularly nasty killing.'

'What about those men I was sharing the floor with in that room?' Patricia asked. 'Have they recovered?'

'Three have, and are in Federal custody. The fourth is still in the hospital and hasn't regained consciousness. He must have drunk more of whatever the stuff in that bottle was. Weiss and his partner certainly didn't mean to kill them; he was going to let the bomb do that.'

'Speaking of the partner,' Geoffrey said. 'Have you got him?'

'Lehman. Yes. Picked him up as he was boarding the *Rotterdam*. He started talking even before they got him off the boat. Insisted the idea was not to kill the President but to make it look like the Communists were trying to. Like that makes it OK. We're looking for Gerard, the local Bund leader, who apparently was also in on it. We haven't got him yet, but we will. By "we" I mean the FBI, who seem to be coming around to the notion that the Nazis may be almost as dangerous as the Commies.'

'Well, good,' Patricia said. 'I'm certainly glad that this is over.'

'Over?' Geoffrey shook his head. 'I have a feeling that it's just beginning.'

Declaration as to Content, Style, and Population

This is a work of fiction leavened with a smattering of truth set in a remarkable period of human history. The characters in here are my creations, no matter what names they bear, and it is not fair to their historical counterparts to take anything I have said about them as what they actually may have believed, thought, or said. In some cases I have alluded to what it is reported they said and reproduced what it is asserted they thought, but as I was not present and do not claim to be a mind-reader, I can only say that I write in good faith and have not deliberately attempted to misrepresent the actions or beliefs of any historical characters.

Many of the plans, schemes, or actions described here, including some of the more unbelievable ones, are based on events that actually happened at the time, although perhaps not precisely when or how they are portrayed.

The quoted lines beginning 'the Llama' in chapter twenty-one are from Hilaire Belloc's poem 'The Llama'.

The quoted lines beginning 'While I am I' in chapter thirty-one are from 'Life In A Love', a poem by Robert Browning.

Lightning Source UK Ltd.
Milton Keynes UK
UKHW030059250920
370471UK00004B/85